Praise for the works of

T0272913

After the Summer [Rain]

...is a heartwarming, slow-burn romance that features two awesome women who are learning what it really means to live and love fully. They're also learning to let go of their turbulent pasts so that it doesn't ruin their future happiness. Gerri Hill has never failed to give me endearing characters who are struggling with heartbreaking issues and beautiful descriptions of the landscapes that surround them.

- The Lesbian Review

Gerri Hill is simply one of the best romance writers in the genre. This is an archetypal Hill, slightly unusual characters in a slightly unusual setting. The slow-burn romance, however, is a classic, trying not to fall in love, but unable to fight the pull.

- Lesbian Reading Room

After the Summer Rain is a wonderfully heartfelt romance that avoids all the angsty drama-filled tropes you often find in romances.

- C-Spot Reviews

Moonlight Avenue

Moonlight Avenue by Gerri Hill is a riveting, literary tapestry of mystery, suspense, thriller and romance. It is also a story about forgiveness, moving on with your life and opening your heart to love despite how daunting it may seem at first.

- The Lesbian Review

...is an excellent mystery novel, sheer class. Gerri Hill's writing is flawless, her story compelling and much more than a notch above others writing in this genre.

-Kitty Kat's Book Review Blog

The Locket

This became a real page-turner as the tension racked up. I couldn't put it down. Hill has a knack for combining strong characters, vulnerable and complex, with a situation that allows them to grow, while keeping us on our toes as the mystery unfolds. Definitely one of my favorite Gerri Hill thrillers, highly recommended.

- Lesbian Reading Room

The Neighbor

It's funny... Normally in the books I read I get why the characters would fall in love. Now on paper (excuse the pun), Cassidy and Laura should not work... but let me tell you, that's the reason they do. I actually loved this book so hard. ...Yes it's a slow burn but so beautifully written and worth the wait in every way.

- Les Reveur

This is classic Gerri Hill at her very best, top of the pile of so many excellent books she has written, I genuinely loved this story and these two women. The growing friendship and hidden attraction between them is skillfully written and totally engaging....This was a joy to read.

- Lesbian Reading Room

I have always found Hill's writing to be intriguing and stimulating. Whether she's writing a mystery or a sweet romance, she allows the reader to discover something about themselves along with her characters. This story has all the fun antics you would expect for a quality, low-stress, romantic comedy. Hill is wonderful in giving us characters that are intriguing and delightful that you never want to put the book down until the end.

- The Lesbian Review

Gillette Park

Other Bella Books by Gerri Hill

About the Author

Gerri Hill has thirty-seven published works, including the 2017 GCLS winner *Paradox Valley*, 2014 GCLS winner *The Midnight Moon*, 2011, 2012 and 2013 winners *Devil's Rock, Hell's Highway* and *Snow Falls*, and the 2009 GCLS winner *Partners*, the last book in the popular Hunter Series, as well as the 2013 Lambda finalist *At Seventeen*.

Gerri lives in south-central Texas, only a few hours from the Gulf Coast, a place that has inspired many of her books. With her partner, Diane, they share their life with two Australian shepherds—Casey and Cooper—and a couple of furry felines.

For more, visit her website at gerrihill.com.

Bella Books, Inc.
P.O. Box 10543
Tallahassee, FL 32302

Printed in the United States of America on acid-free paper.

First Bella Books Edition 2020

Editor: Medora MacDougall
Cover Designer: Sandy Knowles

ISBN: 978-1-64247-133-5

Gillette Park

GERRI HILL

2020

CHAPTER ONE

Mason stared at the body, unblinking. How many did this make? She felt a tightness in her chest as she squatted down beside him. The only visible trauma was the bruising around his neck. She swallowed, then forced her gaze to his face, which was bathed in sunlight. It was smooth and unmarred, the light brown hair above it cut short and neat. She reached out and touched his cheek gently, feeling the coolness of his skin. His eyes were closed, thankfully. Behind those lids were greenish eyes. She knew that from the school picture they'd been given.

She moved away from him and leaned against a tree, taking several deep breaths. When was it going to end? She slid down the tree until she was sitting. She'd already called it in. The guys would be there soon. And it would start all over again.

She'd returned to her hometown five years ago—or was it six already? She'd left when she was eighteen, two weeks after graduation. She couldn't wait to get away. Get away from what, though? Her mother? That was a given. Get away from the darkness in this town? Maybe. Isn't that why most left?

But why come back? Her mother was still here. The darkness was still here. She looked at the body again. Yeah…the darkness was still here. She couldn't take it anymore. How many would have to die? When were they going to *do* something?

Her radio crackled and she recognized Dalton's voice. "Where the hell are you, Mason?" She leaned her head back against the tree as she fumbled for the radio.

Yeah...where the hell was she?

CHAPTER TWO

"Mason, I know we need to do something...but a psychic? Can't believe you—of all people—would jump on that bandwagon."

"We have to do something. Every year it's the same damn thing. We have to do something. What would it hurt?"

Her uncle turned from the window he'd been staring out of. "You let Agent Kemp fill your head with this psychic crap, Mason? We had a psychic out here one time, you know."

"I know. Back in 2004." She held her hand up. "And I know it didn't go over well. I remember."

"You were still in high school." He sat down behind his desk, motioning for her to sit as well. "When I ran for county sheriff, it was on the promise that I'd catch this bastard. It's been six years and we're no closer than we were when the murders started twenty-something years ago."

"Twenty-three," she said automatically, knowing he knew this as well as she did. Everyone in Gillette Park knew this. She'd been ten years old when the first murder happened. It was 1997. Susan Shackle. Susie was a classmate...a playmate. She went missing one day after school. It was late April. Spring was in the air. She remembered stopping with Jimmie Beckman at Boulder Creek. Rock Creek, the kids called it. They'd crawled under the old bridge to toss rocks into the water. The creek—and bridge—was almost halfway between the school and her house. The road got little traffic; there wasn't anything beyond the school back in those days. Nonetheless, the city had built a bike trail next to the road. It had been gravel back then. When she got older, she rode her bike to school. But that day—like most when the weather was nice—she walked with Jimmie, Susie, Becky Kuhn, Amber Wright, and Joey Case. They all lived in the same neighborhood and usually met up at the corner of Flagstaff and School Road each morning. Joey was the oldest—eleven at the time—and he fancied himself their caretaker, herding them along the path to school as if tending sheep.

That particular day in late April, only she and Jimmie had walked home together. The others had gone to the library in town. She didn't remember why…some art project or something. She did remember her mother fussing at her for getting dirty—and shaming her for not being a dainty girl like her older cousin Amanda. And she remembered the phone call; Mrs. Shackle calling to see if Susie might be over playing with her. Susie never made it home.

They found her body two days later, up in the forest beyond the city park. The killer had hidden her under the old board planks that were used to cross Boulder Creek in a narrow spot. She'd been strangled. They closed the school for a week, and when it reopened her mother took her each day and picked her up each afternoon. Because they never found Susie's killer. Young Susie Shackle was strangled to death and her body dumped out in the forest, hidden in the creek. What Mason didn't know then was that Susie had been sexually assaulted too. She heard her father—then a sheriff's deputy— and mother talking one night when they thought she'd gone upstairs to bed. That had been three or four months after the murder. At the time, she didn't know what sexually assaulted meant, but she was pretty sure it wasn't a good thing.

It was that very year, after the aspen leaves had turned golden, that her father left them. That thought came to her without much emotion. After all these years, that was simply a side note. Uncle Alan—now the county sheriff—had been her father figure growing up. He'd more than made up for her father's absence.

"And now you want to bring in a damn psychic? Do you even believe in that stuff?"

"I'm not sure." Then she shook her head. "Okay, no, I don't. But Kemp says she's legit. Says she's helped them before."

He nodded. "She works with the FBI sometimes, I hear. They're pushing her on us, that's for sure. They've got a stake in this too. They have to feel like they're wasting their time up here, searching for ghosts."

"What's your hesitation, Uncle Alan? Other than you don't believe in that stuff."

"I don't believe it, no. That's my main hesitation. That and I fear she's going to be a quack like the last one. That was what? Fifteen, sixteen years ago now? She was downright weird. I was just a deputy at the time and didn't have many dealings with her, but she was weird."

"I remember. I was a little scared of her myself."

He folded his hands, tapping his index fingers together. "Chief Danner is ready to go along with it too. Says he had some dream about it." He shook his head. "A dream, of all things." His index fingers continued to tap together. "I don't know. Hell, it's worth a try, I guess. Every year when we get the first call, it's like we stop breathing, knowing it's starting again. We go through the motions of trying to find them, knowing all along that we'll only find them when he's through with them."

"I know. It's like we could just skip over that part and head out to the park or search the forest until we find the body."

"Right. Like you said, every year it's the same damn thing. How long are the good citizens of Gillette Park going to be patient?"

"You worried about reelection next year?"

"Oh, hell, nobody wants my job. When Parker retired, they had to practically force me to run, if you remember."

"That's because no one wanted A.J. Sims as sheriff."

He met her gaze and smiled. "When I retire, it'll be your turn. You've got what it takes, Mason. Not Brady," he said, referring to his son. "Brady knows it too."

She returned his smile fondly, knowing he thought of her as his own flesh and blood. "We'll see. You're what? Fifty-four? Fifty-five? You got some good years left. I guess we've got plenty of time before we have to worry about that."

He leaned back in his chair. "This job will age you quick. Maybe we'll get lucky this year. Maybe this psychic woman will pan out and we can put this nightmare to bed."

"Does that mean you're going to put the call in? Tell the FBI to send her up here?"

"I'm not crazy about the idea, but, yeah, we got to try something. Maybe this is the year it ends."

Mason was on board with a psychic because—to her—it was a last resort and she felt like they were doing nothing more than treading water. Time to swim or sink. If they couldn't resolve this with a psychic, then she feared they would *never* catch the serial killer. But her uncle's optimism was forced, as was hers. The nightmare had been going on for too long. And really, to be honest, she didn't believe the whole psychic thing. Mumbo jumbo bullshit? Probably. Yeah, she'd been in high school when the city manager had brought in a psychic over the protests of both the police chief and Sheriff Parker. She remembered the woman—short, round, wearing scarves and beads. The only thing she accomplished was bringing in some publicity to the murders. Bad publicity. The police department, the sheriff's department, and the town as a whole came across looking like a bunch of bumbling buffoons who couldn't get out of their own way. Even having the FBI on the case didn't seem to matter.

It didn't matter who was on the case, really. Every year, like clockwork, the murders started in either late April or early May and ended in October. Every year. And every year…two, sometimes three kids would lose their lives. There were never fewer than two and in the twenty-three years since they'd begun, there'd been more than three on only two occasions, 2004—the year the psychic was hired—and 2012.

What caused him to kill more during those particular years was anyone's guess. Over the years, the FBI had brought in profilers, trying to get a read on the guy. On the years the FBI came around, that is. A murder in April or May and another one in October usually didn't garner much attention from them anymore, especially a dead-end case like this one.

And now, apparently, they were going to bring in another psychic. She sighed as she left his office. A psychic was on the way and Mason hoped she didn't bring the whole damn circus to town with her. A psychic? Was she really on board with it? Yeah. But she would definitely keep her distance, as would probably most everybody else in town.

Gillette Park was a small town in the Rocky Mountains. Their population had swelled from a manageable four or five thousand people to well over fifteen in the last decade. Those flocking to the area were mostly young retirees, still active enough to enjoy the mountains—hiking, biking, skiing, kayaking—or the techies, those who worked from home and could live anywhere they wanted. The old downtown area—Old Town—had been revitalized with the influx of newbies, and artists and hip coffee shops had followed. It was hardly the same sleepy town it had been when she was growing up. Different on the outside, certainly. One thing remained the same, however.

The murders. That never changed.

CHAPTER THREE

Her daughter was restless, therefore she was restless. Lucy finally went to her, stilling her hands as she was drawing frantically on a piece of paper.

"What is it?"

Her daughter, ten years old, looked at her with big hazel eyes. Eyes that were neither here nor there. Lucy knew that look well. It used to scare her. At first. When Faith had learned to talk, things she said sometimes scared her. And sometimes they still did.

"Someone is coming."

Lucy looked behind them to the lone door, the door that was triple-locked—from the outside. But Faith shook her head.

"Not there, Momma."

"Then where?"

"Someone is coming to help us."

Help them? No, she didn't think anyone could help them. She'd been locked up here since 2009. Who was going to help them? She moved away from her daughter, going to the crate and sitting down. Faith had picked up the pencil again and started drawing. Lucy looked around the little room that had become both jail cell and home. After Faith was born, they'd made the room a little more comfortable.

They'd brought in a twin bed, a tiny table. As Faith grew, Stacy brought in toys and then books. Lucy had schooled her as best she could. She didn't know where they were, though. The damp, cold walls indicated it was someone's basement. From what little she'd learned from Stacy, they were still near Gillette Park.

Had her parents continued to look for her? Or had they resolved that she'd been killed? One more chalked up to the serial killer? Or maybe they thought she had run away? Did her mother cry for her at night?

It was the cat. Lucy loved cats. She'd been riding her bike on the trail beside School Road. It was one of those glorious spring days that hinted of summer. Two weeks until school let out. She remembered thinking she couldn't *wait* for summer to get there. Then she saw the cat. An orange tabby. It was on the trail and it stayed there right up until she rode upon it. Then, with a flick of its tail, it darted into the woods. She never once considered not going after it. She dropped her bike on the trail and followed. She heard the meow, saw a flash of tail behind a tree. Again, she followed, getting farther away from the trail and School Road. But the cat wasn't there. Nowhere. She turned in circles, looking for it. A bird landed on a tree branch beside her. A large blue bird. A Steller's jay. He cocked his head, looking right at her. She remembered jumping back when he squawked at her, as if protesting her very presence beside his tree.

She didn't remember much after that. She was grabbed from behind, a large hand covering her mouth before she could scream. As the jay continued to scold her, she was dragged deeper into the forest, the tall trees making dark shadows around her. She didn't remember much, no. She did remember thinking that she was going to be one of *them*. One of those poor kids who went missing each year. Missing? No. They were only missing for a little while. Her? For some reason, she'd been tossed into this cold, dirty basement instead.

She wasn't alone for long. Five or six days later—maybe a week—a boy came in. Barry Shepherd. She knew him from school, even though he rarely spoke to her. She was only a freshman and he and the other older boys hadn't bothered with her. Barry had been plenty scared. Then the man came. He was a big man, tall and muscular. A beard covered his face and he had a dirty cap on his head. The man made her take her clothes off. He made Barry take his pants off.

She closed her eyes as she remembered that day. And the next three days that followed. Then, on the fourth day, Barry didn't come. She never saw him again.

Stacy started coming after that. Stacy was about her age. Stacy brought food but didn't talk much at all. When Lucy realized she was pregnant, it was Stacy she turned to. And when it was time for her to give birth, Stacy was there with her—two young girls who didn't have a clue. Nature has a way, she supposed, because Faith came out just fine.

Stacy still didn't talk much, though. All these years—ten now—and she still didn't talk much. But she brought them things. Like a new calendar each year. Lucy—and now Faith—marked off the days, one by one. Faith didn't question why they were there. Much. She didn't know any different and Lucy had never found the words to tell her the truth. She didn't know what good it would do to tell her how she'd ended up in here. No sense in scaring her.

She felt tired, fatigued. She—and now Faith—were wasting away in this tiny dungeon with no end in sight. Getting weaker, physically. She could feel it. What if Stacy didn't come in one day? What if no one came to bring them food? There were others, she knew. She heard voices sometimes. Men's voices. And sometimes she heard Stacy scream. Sometimes Stacy had bruises. Sometimes Stacy had been crying.

"Don't worry, Momma. Someone's coming to help us."

She brought her attention back to her daughter, who was now sitting quietly at the table. Lucy got up and went to her, pausing to run her hand through Faith's soft curls—sandy-blond hair, much like Barry Shepherd's. Her gaze drifted to the paper and she nearly gasped. Faith had a gift. If they were out in the real world, Faith would be an artist. Her drawings were all based on her imagination, though. Faith had never been outside these four walls.

"It's a bird."

Lucy nodded. "Yes. How did you...where have you seen this? In one of the magazines?"

Faith stared at her, unblinking. "In your mind."

Lucy swallowed. Yes, Faith had a gift.

"What kind is it, Momma?"

"It's a Steller's jay." She reached out and ran a finger across the drawing. "That was the last thing I saw," she said quietly, almost to herself.

"After the cat?"

Lucy stared, her eyes wide. She'd never told Faith that story. She'd never told Faith how she'd come be here. Faith had never asked. She nodded slowly. "Yes. After the cat."

CHAPTER FOUR

"Everybody's pretty nice, in case you were wondering."

Grace glanced at Agent Kemp as he drove them through the Rocky Mountains. No, she hadn't been wondering. She hadn't given it much thought because, no, they weren't normally nice. What she had been wondering was why she'd agreed to this assignment. She'd first heard of the Gillette Park murders two years ago when she last worked with the FBI. One of the agents on the case had been in Gillette Park the year prior and was passing along little more than gossip at the time...most of which she dismissed as hearsay, even if her curiosity had been piqued. Didn't matter though. She'd told herself then that she wouldn't take any more cases. She'd told herself then that she'd concentrate on her book.

Roger Kellogg from the FBI had called her two weeks ago. She'd told him no, she wasn't interested. The next day, a file was delivered anyway. And a week after that, she'd called him back to accept the assignment. Now here she was, sitting beside Agent Kemp—the FBI agent who had worked the Gillette Park murders last year—on a one-way trip into the mountains, committed to staying through the summer...or until they kicked her out of town.

"Sheriff's office there has jurisdiction," he continued. "Technically."

That was because most of the bodies had been found outside the city limits in the forest. A handful had been found at the city park, if her memory was correct. She still found it hard to believe that in the last twenty-three years a serial killer had been preying on the young citizens of Gillette Park and no one had even come close to finding him. As far as she knew, there had never even been a person of interest.

She stared out the window, only absently noticing the trees speeding by as he drove. Trees and rocks and mountains—she'd seen little of it. As usual, she was lost inside her own head. It wasn't her habit to make idle chit-chat, but Agent Kemp was attempting to break the silence. She supposed she could use this time to garner some insight on the town.

"You spent last summer there?"

"Yeah. They had two bodies back-to-back. Both in May, about three weeks apart. Third body was in October, pretty much like always."

"In reading the file, I understand they've got surveillance cameras that would rival a major city yet there's never even been a glimpse of this guy."

"Yeah, he's like a ghost. The residents in town, they know what's going on. Come April, everyone gets a little on edge. By May, people are downright jittery. October comes, they finally breathe a sigh of relief."

"The sheriff's department, the police department—are they competent? I mean, out here in the middle of nowhere and all."

"Competent enough, yeah. They've got maybe twenty or so deputies and probably close to the same number of police officers."

"What is your take on the murders, Agent Kemp?"

He shrugged. "Maybe it's some mountain man who lives off the grid. There's a lot of them out there from what I understand."

"The FBI has sent…what? Three or four profilers over the years? I've read the file; they've been pretty generic. White male, twenty to forty, doesn't play well with others, outcast, and so on."

"Yeah. That's what you get when there's no evidence and never a sighting of the guy."

She turned in her seat to look at him. "Do you ever think it could be…something else?"

"Like what?"

"Something…supernatural?"

His eyes widened a bit, then he laughed nervously. "Now, doc, don't go spewing stuff like that. I told the sheriff you were legit. I told his niece you were legit. From what I know of her, she's not going to believe anything that's not—well, *explainable*. She's easy enough to get along with but she's got a little bit of an edge to her sometimes. Sheriff Cooper relies on her. She spent a number of years with LAPD. Taking a guess, she's going to be your point of contact. So don't go spouting *supernatural* crap, doc. Like I said, she's got an edge."

"Shouldn't matter. I've worked with the FBI enough to know about *edges*. I'm pretty sure I can handle her."

"Mason Cooper. She's a deputy. She usually gives the FBI hell, but we got along okay. There's an old dive of a bar where the locals hang out. Bucky's. I had to buy her many a beer to get her to loosen up. By the end of summer, we were buds."

"But?"

"But I didn't make any more headway on the case than anyone before me. There's nothing. Absolutely nothing. Some kid goes missing. Two, three days...sometimes a week later, a body is found. That's it."

"There's a pattern, Agent Kemp. There's always been a pattern to his kills."

"Sure. But Gillette Park is surrounded by forest. Got federal land, state land, some county-owned campgrounds, the city park, not to mention private land all interspersed around the town. There's been no pattern as to where he dumps the bodies. They've run every damn algorithm known to man and still can't come up with a pattern for that." He pointed up ahead to his left. "Got a great overlook here."

He surprised her by stopping. Surprised her even further when he got out. With a slight shrug, she did as well. She took a deep breath, finding the air fresh and sweet, the fragrant aroma of pine trees and other conifers wafting about. She cast her gaze out, finding a sprawling town down below, nestled in a bowl between the mountains. A three-sided bowl, she noted. The fourth side bled into a valley and even from up here, she could see that that was where the town was expanding to. She imagined at one time it was a quaint little mountain town. Unique. Now? No doubt chain restaurants and grocery stores had made their way up here. That's what happens with expansion. People are drawn to places like this, away from the hustle and bustle of a large city, only to miss the amenities. Soon, those amenities would follow them here and the small, quaint town they fell in love with would be ruined forever.

"You ever spent much time up in the mountains, doc?"

She shook her head as they got back in the vehicle. "I was born in Savannah. When I was nine, my mother married a navy man. Did a lot of traveling after that."

"Overseas?"

"Some, yes. Japan. Spent eight months in Africa. Bounced around the States some. Two years in Hawaii. That was my favorite," she said with a smile. "I was in high school." She didn't add that she cried her eyes out when they left. She hadn't wanted to leave the islands, no, but leaving her first love behind—Angelique—had been the hardest. "So no, I haven't spent much time inland. It's certainly beautiful up here."

"Hope you packed for winter then. Even in May, a late snowstorm can sneak up. And a jacket…gonna need a jacket at night."

"I did my research on the area, so yes, I think I packed appropriately." She'd shopped appropriately, in other words. Her normal wardrobe wasn't compatible with winter.

He pulled back onto the road and drove them down the mountain into Gillette Park. The road was lined with bright green aspens, their new spring leaves still shiny and vibrant. Spruce and fir trees dominated the landscape higher up. There was an occasional glimpse of a house on the hillside, and as they got closer into town, the forest gave way to buildings and streets, homes and businesses.

"You want to check in at the motel first or head straight to the sheriff's office?"

"We've been in the car for hours. I wouldn't mind taking a break before meeting everyone. Unless they're expecting us, that is."

"I'm supposed to call before we head over, that's all. We can get settled first." He glanced at her. "I said motel—and there are some newer ones over in the valley—but I booked us here in Old Town, same place I stayed last year. I booked you through October, like you requested. The Aspen Resort. And don't let the name fool you. It's comfortable and close to everything, but resort is a stretch."

The Aspen Resort was two blocks off the main drag…a collection of four buildings, each with four or five suites. Towering trees were intermingled throughout and she spotted three inviting benches in what looked to be a courtyard of sorts. There was a small swimming pool located next to the office, and large pots stuffed with colorful flowers were at every corner. Bright sunshine filled the air, but a cool breeze reminded her that it was early May in the mountains. When she'd left New Orleans, it had been quite balmy already. So much so that she'd been living in shorts for the last month. This would certainly be a change—the mountains. Most of her adult life, like her childhood, had been spent at sea level. She was out of breath just on the short walk to the office.

"Yeah…it'll take you a few days to get used to the altitude," Agent Kemp told her as he dutifully held the door open for her. "We're at eight thousand feet, at least."

Their check-in was uneventful, and fifteen minutes later, she pushed open the door to what would be her home for the summer. She didn't know if it was chance or bad luck that got her a room in the building nearest the office—and the pool. She imagined in the middle of summer, it would be filled with noisy kids. Agent Kemp was in the suite next to hers.

It was a large room with a king-sized bed, sofa and chair, tiny table, and a kitchenette complete with a two-burner hotplate, microwave, and small fridge. She placed her bags on the bed, then went to the window and flung open the curtains. Not the greatest of views, but it beat the apartment she'd just left. There was some green space and trees, and above the roof of the adjacent building, she had a glimpse of the side of the mountain.

Pretty, yes. The drive up had been beautiful, in fact. She could see why tourists flocked to the mountains, especially during the heat of summer. Her reason for being here had nothing to do with the weather, however. She needed the money this town was willing to pay her for her…her gifts. That wasn't the sole reason. She had four years of exhaustive research to go through. She had a book to write. She was planning to stay through October, whether she led them to the killer or not. Provided, of course, that they didn't run her out of town like they had the last psychic they'd hired.

The money and the time—no, those actually weren't the main reasons either. She'd tried to read through the file twice, and both times a giant claw had seemed to squeeze at her chest, choking her. She heard a voice, a young man's voice, telling her to stay away. It had frightened her at first; she couldn't seem to take a breath without pain. She'd had to close her eyes, to focus all her energy on her*self*, sucking in air, filling her lungs, letting it out again, over and over. By the time the pain left her, she'd collapsed in a heap of exhaustion, too weary to even make it to her bed. She'd been shocked to see that she'd lost almost an hour in her semiconscious state.

She'd waited two days before she tackled the file again. When she felt the unease start, she closed her eyes and concentrated on her breathing, keeping the worst of it at bay. She did that five or six times to get through the entire file. When she'd closed it, her mind saturated with the gruesome details of the murders, she'd again felt the weight on her chest, felt the air being sucked out of her.

She wasn't surprised by it that time; she knew what to do. A mere twenty-two minutes later she'd been pacing in her living room, the file now opened to a page from 2009. A school photo of a fourteen-year-old girl—Lucy Hines—stared back at her. Lucy Hines went missing like all the others, but Lucy—like most of the others—was never found. Grace didn't remember opening the file, didn't remember flipping to that particular page, but surely she had. She heard a voice in her mind then, a voice that she was certain was not Lucy Hines. It was a girl's childlike voice that beckoned her to come to Gillette Park. Begged her to come. She remembered the young man's voice telling her to stay away, but this child's voice was so compelling, she'd called Roger Kellogg back right then, saying she'd take the case.

She brought a hand to her chest now and rubbed lightly between her breasts. Yes, there was something evil in this town…something that lived in the shadows…just out of sight. She could feel it. Something was here, yes, but she wasn't sure if that frightened her or not. She hadn't been frightened by things she saw and heard, not since she was a kid.

That was the real reason she'd taken this case. Whatever lived in the shadows and preyed on this town wasn't going to go away on its own. She would have to find it, expose it. She may even have to go inside where it lived.

And hope she came back out again. Alive.

CHAPTER FIVE

"Keep an open mind, everyone."

Mason smiled at her uncle, wondering if he was taking his own words to heart. "My mind is as open as anybody's here," she said, eliciting a "Yeah, right" from Brady. But it was. She was going to give the psychic a chance, despite the grumblings of everyone else. Dalton in particular. He thought it was a "waste of time" and "goddamn desperate" and he told that to anyone who would listen.

Desperate? Perhaps. A waste of time? Well, they had nothing else to spend their time on. She looked around, nodding at her two closest friends—Brady and Dalton. Brady was her older cousin by a year, but they were close enough to be siblings. She and Dalton had gone through school together.

She looked past them to the others. The police chief had brought two of his officers along...Jenkins and Sheffield. She got along fine with Jenkins, but Sheffield had an attitude. He'd been a cop in Phoenix and thought he was better than everyone else, especially the lowly sheriff's department. Truth was, compared to most there, he *was* better. Her time spent in Los Angeles trumped his Phoenix, however. For the most part, he left her alone.

"And try to play nice," her uncle added. "Who knows? This might pan out."

Dalton snorted. "A damn psychic?" He shook his head. "This is a waste of time and money. I keep picturing some gypsy woman with a crystal ball."

Mason nodded. "Me too. I keep picturing that crazy woman who was here back when we were in high school."

"Yeah. She came up to the school to go through Deb Meckel's locker. Remember?"

Mason's smile faded as did Dalton's. Deb Meckel was a year behind them in school. She'd gone missing while walking home from band practice. She played the clarinet and the police had found it beside the sidewalk on School Road. Odd, because it wasn't in its case. According to her friends, she'd been carrying her case—with the clarinet inside—but she'd forgotten something at school and had gone back. A book for homework or something—Mason couldn't remember. The clarinet case was never found. Two days later, Deb's body was found clear on the other side of town, up near the trailhead by Gillette Creek. 2004. They had five murders that year. Deb was the second one.

A quick knock on the conference room's door—actually, the door of the breakroom that doubled as a conference room—and Sandy, the longtime receptionist and sometimes dispatcher, stuck her head in.

"FBI is here," she said in a loud whisper. "Agent Kemp and some woman."

Uncle Alan nodded. "Send him on back, Sandy."

As far as FBI agents went, Scott Kemp was okay. Friendly, amicable, without the arrogance and haughtiness that followed most agents. That was a plus, considering he'd spent the better part of six months with them last year. From what her uncle had said, he was assigned to them again this year, but he probably wouldn't stay for the duration, only long enough to get the psychic up and running.

When Kemp walked into the room, Mason nearly dropped the cup of coffee she'd been holding. The woman following him was *so* not a short, round gypsy with a scarf and beads.

"Hello again, everyone," Scott said, holding out his hand to shake first her uncle's, then Chief Danner's hand. He looked in her direction and smiled. "Mason. I guess you owe me a beer."

She smiled at that. Her parting shot last year was that she'd buy him a beer if he was unlucky enough to get assigned to their case again. The agents who filtered through town rarely made repeat appearances.

Scott stepped to the side, motioning to the woman behind him. "This is Dr. Jennings. She's the…well, the woman…the—"

"The psychic we hired?" her uncle asked, saving Scott from saying the word he was apparently stumbling over. He stood up and reached across the table, offering his hand to the woman. Mason was surprised at how amiable he was being, considering he hadn't wanted to hire her in the first place. "Dr. Jennings, welcome to Gillette Park. I'm Sheriff Cooper."

"Thank you."

"This is Chief Danner," he introduced, motioning to his left. He turned toward them. "Deputies Cooper, Cooper, and Wilcox," he continued, making them sound more like a law firm than sheriff's deputies. "Down there are Officers Jenkins and Sheffield."

Mason held her hand out, making brief eye contact as a firm hand took hers. Dr. Jennings was a little taller than average…five-seven, maybe even five-eight. Her light brown hair hinted at blond and her blue eyes were nearly cobalt. Her eyebrows were darker than her hair and one disappeared into bangs that swept from left to right. She noted all of that in the few seconds she was allotted as Dr. Jennings moved down the line, shaking everyone's hand.

"Nice to meet you all." Dr. Jennings settled into a chair almost directly across from Mason. "Who is in charge of the investigation?"

"In charge? It's a group effort," her uncle said as he sat back down. "Jurisdiction is based on where the body is found. In all these years, we've never stumbled upon the…well, the murder scene."

"I've read through the file, Sheriff. The closest thing to a pattern is who his victims are. The youngest was eight, the oldest was nineteen. I'm asking the obvious, of course, but all of the teachers, janitors—custodians—they've all been thoroughly investigated?"

"We have investigated pretty much everyone in the whole damn town by now, Dr. Jennings." He spread his hands out. "Hiring a…a psychic is sort of a last crazy resort. No offense, of course."

"None taken."

"We've tried this before. Way back in—"

"Two thousand and four," she supplied for him. "I understand it didn't go the way you had planned."

"I was a deputy in the department back then, but no, it was pretty much a fiasco. I think the woman thought she was on some kind of a reality TV show or something. Had the whole town up in arms by the time she left."

"From what I gathered from the file—and the FBI's briefing—she was run out of town." Dr. Jennings smiled. "I hope I don't meet with the same fate."

"Guess it depends if you plan to do a public séance at the park and call up Susie Shackle from the dead or not."

Dr. Jennings nodded. "She was the first girl murdered." Then she smiled again. "Speaking to the dead can be very beneficial."

"Susie Shackle's mother wasn't too impressed," her uncle said dryly. "This psychic woman was a quack all the way around."

"I'm sorry you feel that way."

"Look, I'm not even going to pretend that I know what your game is. Like I said, we're desperate and the FBI had some good things to say about you."

"There's no game, Sheriff Cooper. There are several different methods I can use to try to help you, but it's no game. I take my work seriously. I hope you will as well."

"I appreciate that. We just don't want to be taken for a fool again…you know, you take our money and run all the way to the bank. I mean, I know what we're paying you is nonrefundable, but we'd like some guarantee that—"

"There are no guarantees in my line of work, Sheriff Cooper. I told the FBI to make that very clear to you. The methods that I employ don't always work." She leaned her elbows on the table. "That being said—the vibes that I'm getting—I feel like I will have some success here. Perhaps. It won't be without a fight, however."

Mason frowned. What the hell did that mean?

"A fight?" Chief Danner asked the question Mason had not.

"My fight, not yours," she clarified.

Mason shifted uneasily. And what the hell did *that* mean?

"I would like a tour of the area," the psychic continued. "You had three murders last year. If I could see the sites where they were found, that would be helpful. That's where I'd like to start. I'd like to visit the sites of past years too. Can you have someone assist me?"

"You don't want to start with Donnie Redman? He was found just two weeks ago. He—"

"I'd like to start with last year," she said firmly.

"Okay. Your call, of course." He looked down the table, his gaze landing on hers. "Mason, why don't you do the honors."

She nodded, dreading it even though she had expected it. "Of course."

"I'd like to get an early start in the morning." Dr. Jennings looked her way for the first time. "I'll need coffee."

Mason nodded. "I normally stop by Dottie's each morning."

Dr. Jennings stood and pushed her chair away. "Good." She met her gaze and held it, long enough to make Mason feel uncomfortable. "A muffin and coffee would be a nice start to the morning." She turned. "Agent Kemp? Anything else?"

"I'm good if you are."

She nodded at him, then turned her attention back to the others at the table. "Nice to meet you all. I don't imagine there will be a need for these group sessions. I prefer to work a little more informally, and…well, off the radar." She smiled again—a forced smile—and Mason found herself staring, not sure what to make of this attractive woman who was a little on the odd side. "I hope you're comfortable with that."

"I'm not comfortable giving you free rein to our town, no. I'll assign Deputy Cooper—Mason—to be your escort while you're here. After what happened the last time, I'd prefer that you not do anything on your own. Mason will accompany you. It'll make it easier on you that way too. It's not like we've advertised your presence. In fact, no one knows except the people in this room."

"Very well." The psychic turned to her once again. "I like to start early. Seven? You'll pick me up? We're at the Aspen Resort. I trust you can find me."

Mason nodded. "I will."

They walked out, then Scott stuck his head back inside. "Mason, I'll take you up on that beer tonight. Bucky's?"

She nodded. "See you there." As soon as the door closed, she stood up. "So that was a little creepy, don't you think?"

"How so?"

"How the hell did she know that I have a muffin and coffee every morning?"

Brady laughed. "Duh, Mason! Because she's psychic!"

"I don't think I'm going to like her being here," Dalton offered. "Because, yeah, that kind of stuff creeps me out."

Brady nudged her hip as she stood beside him. "Psychic or not… she sure is cute. Didn't see a ring on her finger either. If you don't want to be her escort, Mason, I'll volunteer my services."

"Cute or not, she's still a weirdo," Dalton said.

"How about we keep all of this strictly business, huh?" Uncle Alan stood up too. "I'm not sure what to make of her myself. I was expecting someone older, that's for sure."

"I only hope it doesn't end up like the last time," Chief Danner added. "When word gets around town that we've hired her, people are going to be watching her every move."

"Maybe she knows that. Maybe that's why she likes to work 'off the radar' as she called it. She's done this before. I'm sure she's used to being scrutinized."

Uncle Alan pointed his finger at her. "You keep an eye on her, Mason. We don't need any crazy happenings going on. If she even breathes the word 'séance' you shut her down. As for the rest of you, there's no need to go broadcast that she's here. I'd like to keep it quiet for as long as we can."

CHAPTER SIX

Grace sat at the small table, her chin resting in her palm as she watched the minutes tick toward seven. To say she'd had a restless night was an understatement. Her dreams had been vivid...real. Like watching a movie in fast-forward, she'd been taken through the history of Gillette Park in lightning speed. She'd seen it all clearly when she'd first opened her eyes—still trembling from fear—but now, two hours later, the images had all but faded. One that stuck with her, for some reason, was a man. Don or John Cooper. He was in bed with a younger woman. A redhead. There was a loud banging on the door, disrupting the couple. In the background, a dark-haired child was crying.

She jumped when there was a knock on her own door. She stood up and, before opening it, took a more cautious approach.

"Who is it?"

"It's just me, doc."

She opened the door, finding Scott Kemp covering his mouth with a yawn. She nodded a greeting at him. "Good morning, Agent Kemp."

"Morning, doc. I know Mason is supposed to pick you up any minute. I'm going to do a grocery store run. You need anything? I don't know about you, but I like to have coffee pretty much as soon as my feet hit the floor."

"Yes, that would be wonderful. Come in." She went to the oil cloth shoulder bag she always carried and opened it, reaching into one of the side pockets for some cash. "That's very thoughtful of you, Agent Kemp. Something strong, please. A dark roast. Some sugar packets too, if you don't mind." She handed him the money. "I'll need to pick up a few things myself, once I get settled. I don't plan to eat out at every meal."

"I trust you got dinner last night."

"Yes. You were right. Pizza is the only thing that gets delivered in this town. What about you?"

"I hit up Mason for a beer over at Bucky's. They've got a pretty decent menu. Bar food, but good enough. Walking distance too."

"I'll keep that in mind." Another knock at her door signaled Deputy Cooper, no doubt. "My ride, I imagine."

"Sure you don't want me tagging along?" he asked.

"I work better alone, but thank you for the offer." She paused. "Did she question you last night?"

He laughed. "Pretty much, yeah, but I don't know a whole lot about you, so I wasn't much help. It was the muffin and coffee thing that got to her though."

She shrugged. She'd had an image of Deputy Cooper sitting at a booth—a corner booth—sipping coffee and eating a muffin.

"Blueberry is her favorite. Lay that on her if you want to totally freak her out."

She was smiling as she opened the door, finding Deputy Cooper leaning against the jamb, one hand casually resting on the butt of her gun. She was dressed the same as yesterday: beige sheriff's department shirt, jeans and boots, a belt—a Sam Browne duty belt she believed they called them—with holster and gun, a small flashlight, handcuffs and a canister…pepper spray, perhaps. Her hair was dark, nearly black, and as she met her gaze, she knew that Mason Cooper was the young girl in her dream who had been crying. The man had been her father.

"Good morning, Deputy Cooper."

"Dr. Jennings." Mason's gaze moved past her. "Scott."

It was only then that Grace realized how it must look. Here it was, not even seven in the morning, and Agent Kemp was in her room looking like he'd just woken up. He must have thought the same thing as he hurried over, holding up his hand with the cash in it.

"Making a run for coffee and supplies," he explained quickly. "If anything comes up today, I want to be kept in the loop. Got to justify my presence here, you know."

Deputy Cooper nodded. "You got it." She raised an eyebrow at her. "Ready?"

Grace went back to get her bag, then opened it, double-checking to make sure she'd put her notepad in—which she had. She put her hand inside, feeling blindly for another pocket, finding the digital recorder. She didn't often use it, but sometimes it was helpful. With a nod, she slung the bag across her neck and shoulder and followed Deputy Cooper outside.

The ride over to Dottie's was made in complete silence and Grace took that opportunity to study Mason Cooper. Early- to mid-thirties, perhaps. There were the tiniest of laugh lines around her eyes. Her hair was shorter in the front than the back—it looked thick, parted just off center with a few strands hiding her forehead. She seemed sure, confident. Most likely confident in that she didn't—and wouldn't— believe anything Grace said. She seemed detached this morning. Or perhaps she was just being guarded.

"You're not crazy about my being here."

It was more of a statement than a question. She knew the answer. Deputy Cooper glanced at her quickly, then turned her attention back to the road. They were riding in a truck, a Ford F-150 that had been customized for the sheriff's department. A wire mesh screen separated the front seat from the back, and her knee was butted against the barrel of a shotgun that was in some sort of a holding rack. The radio looked like an old-fashioned kind, complete with a long, curly cord. Of course, maybe that's how police radios still were. She didn't recall ever sitting in a police cruiser before.

They pulled to the right, angle parking along the street a few spaces down from Dottie's Café. There appeared to be a small breakfast crowd already.

"I don't have a problem with your being here," Deputy Cooper finally said. "Actually, I was on board with the hire. How much of this psychic stuff I believe, though, is still up for debate."

"Is it up for debate? Or have you already made up your mind?"

"Nothing else is working." She killed the engine. "We needed to do something, Dr. Jennings, even if it's something as drastic—and crazy—as this."

She was out and had the door slammed before Grace could even open hers. So Mason Cooper was on board, yet she wasn't a fan. That wasn't shocking. Believers were few and far between, that's for sure. Until they saw it for themselves, that is. The energy in this town was very high. She had no doubt that the deputy would experience *something* before too long.

Deputy Cooper held the door of the café open for her and Grace walked inside, only paying cursory attention to the other customers there, their conversations drifting to the background as quickly as the sound of the bell had when Mason opened the door. She glanced around, seeing several empty booths. She studied them for a second, then moved with confidence to the last one, against the far wall. She turned to Cooper.

"This is your booth, isn't it? I think you normally sit on this side," she said, pointing to the wall seat. She sat down opposite, noticing that the only reaction the deputy gave was a slight twitch of her right eyebrow.

A waitress hurried over. "Good morning, Mason."

"Good morning, Helen."

Two cups were placed in front of them, and the waitress expertly filled each cup within an inch of the top.

"Who's your friend?" she asked bluntly.

Grace and Mason looked at each other, both with questions in their eyes. That was something they should have squared away first. From what Sheriff Cooper had said yesterday, they weren't ready to let the townspeople know they'd hired a psychic.

"She's…she's a—"

"I'm a writer." That wasn't a lie, was it? "You have quite a history here."

The woman's easy smile changed into a frown. "History? That's a nice way of saying it, I guess. We've had people come before to write about us. Had someone come all the way from New York City one time. Nothing ever comes of it. Does it, Mason?"

"I'm just showing her around, Helen. As a courtesy."

Helen nodded, dismissing her words. "You want your usual, I suppose. What about you, ma'am?"

"Grace, please. And I guess I'll have a blueberry muffin too."

As soon as Helen walked away, Mason Cooper leaned closer, tapping her finger on the table. "Okay, Dr. Jennings…what game are you playing here?"

"What's that?" she asked, hoping she managed to keep her expression neutral.

"This," Mason said, motioning between them. "This thing you're doing. Like knowing which booth I sit in—that I normally order a blueberry muffin." She leaned back again. "I don't think I want you inside my damn head!" she said as loudly as she could while still maintaining a whisper.

At that, Grace smiled. "In your head? You said earlier you didn't think you believed in this psychic stuff."

"Yeah. And I don't. So who told you? Everyone knows this is where I sit. Who told you? Who told you I get the blueberry muffin most mornings?"

"You should relax, Deputy Cooper. Maybe it was a lucky guess." She smiled broadly. "I have more important things to do than to get in your damn head," she said, repeating Mason's words to her.

The waitress—Helen—came back with two plates, each containing an absolutely huge blueberry muffin. Helen must have seen her expression because she laughed.

"Yeah...ain't no little city-sized muffin. That thing will last you 'til lunch."

"Thanks, Helen," Mason said, already picking up hers and taking a bite.

"I'll be around with more coffee in a bit. Put this on your tab?"

"Oh, no," Grace said. "I—"

"Yeah, on my tab. Thanks."

"That's not necessary, Deputy Cooper," she protested.

"It's Mason, and a few bucks won't break me." She motioned to the muffin. "Try it already."

Grace eyed the fork that was placed beside the muffin. Mason was using her fingers, not the fork. Truth was, she wasn't really crazy about muffins. She wasn't really crazy about sweet stuff for breakfast. All it did for her was kill the taste of the coffee.

So why did you order it?

Yeah, only to agitate Mason Cooper, really. It was those adamant nonbelievers that she had the most fun with. She sighed and picked up the muffin, noting that Mason was already halfway through hers.

She took a bite. It was warm and soft and creamy, the blueberries mingled with...chocolate? *Oh my.* She closed her eyes as she chewed, savoring the rich taste. It was a gooey goodness and she nearly moaned. Okay, not nearly. She *did* moan.

"All prepared not to like it, huh?"

Grace put the muffin down, licking the corner of her mouth with her tongue. "I'm more of a savory breakfast eater, not sweet."

"But? The chocolate pushed you over the edge?"

"The edge?" She eyed the muffin again, seeing the melted chocolate oozing down the side. She could practically taste the rich sweetness in her mouth. "Yeah. Helen likes to say it's orgasmic. I don't know about that, but it's pretty damn good."

This time, Grace used her fork, and this time, she was prepared for the chocolate. She hoped her face was less orgasmic than the first time. Which was funny, wasn't it? The last time she'd had a true, curl-your-toes orgasm, she'd been seventeen years old. That alone was depressing enough to make her put the muffin back down.

"So, you read the file? We had two kids go missing in May last year. They were found on completely opposite sides of town. The third one—in October—was found in the park, beneath the swings. She was nine."

Grace nodded. "I've read the file. It's rather lengthy. The park has surveillance cameras, right?"

"Yes. In every damn corner. It was a stormy night, early snowfall. There are security lights around the park too. Had a bunch of them go out that night. All we have on camera is a bunch of shadows."

She nodded. "The lights worked again the next night."

Mason seemed surprised that she knew that. "Yeah, they did. We figure he used a spotlight or a laser or something to trip the sensors."

"No...I don't think that was it," she said quietly, searching for the image, but it danced just out of reach. "It was something else." Mason was staring at her, and she offered a quick smile. "Sorry. If he used a spotlight or even a laser, another camera would have picked that up, don't you think?"

"Scott and I must have looked at the feed a thousand times. There are ten cameras in the park. We've got every angle covered. None of the feeds picked up a thing. Nothing. Not even a rabbit hopping by or the deer herd moving through. Nothing."

Because the animals would have known, she thought. They would have sensed...something. Something evil. *Something*...in the shadows. It moved like a cat...quick. It—

"Dr. Jennings?"

She blinked at the sound of her name, focusing on Mason Cooper again. "Grace. My name is Grace."

"Are you okay?"

"Yes, fine. I had an image of something...but...well, it's gone now."

"Yeah, okay. Look, you're not just doing this to spook me, right?"

"Spook you? How can you be spooked by something you don't believe in?"

Mason sipped from her coffee, nodding. "Right."

Grace smiled. "I'm a quack, remember?"

Mason flashed a smile too. "You said you weren't."

"No, I never said that." She pushed the muffin away and picked up her coffee instead. "In 2004, there were five murders. Why do you think so many?"

"Who knows?"

"There was another year…2011, maybe? There were also five."

"It was 2012."

"Right. Was there anything odd that year?"

"Odd?"

"In 2004, you had a psychic here. What happened in 2012?"

Mason shook her head. "I don't think anything. I wasn't actually here then."

"Oh? I was under the impression that this was your home."

"Yeah…I was born and raised here. Moved away when I was eighteen. Came back five years ago."

Grace studied her, not wanting to intrude into her personal realm, but— "The sheriff, he's not your father." Of course, she already knew that. Agent Kemp had said he was her uncle.

"No."

Mason's answer was short, clipped. Grace sat her coffee cup down, then folded her hands together. "Your father isn't in the picture any longer." She tilted her head. "Your mother—" She stopped. It wasn't any of her business and it certainly didn't pertain to the case, but she could see it plain as day.

"My mother what?"

Grace met her gaze. "I'm not an imposter."

"My mother what?"

"Your mother drinks a lot to ease her loneliness. Now she's sick. That's why you came back." She tilted her head. "No. That's the *excuse* you used to come back."

Mason continued to stare at her, never blinking. "You could have found that out by doing a little research. It's no secret."

"But I didn't." She slid her coffee cup next to her uneaten muffin. "We should go." She paused. "I apologize. I shouldn't have intruded into your private affairs."

Mason leaned forward, her voice low. "Look, what are you doing?"

"Excuse me?"

"Are you like…inside my head? Reading my thoughts? Reading my mind?"

Grace smiled, fairly sure it was a smug smile even though she tried not to let it be. "You don't believe in that, Deputy Cooper. Remember?" She smiled wider. "A mind reader?" She gave a quick laugh. "Now who does that?"

"So now you're just toying with me."

Grace sighed. "I'm not a mind reader." That wasn't entirely true, but it certainly wasn't her specialty. Truth was, she hated poking around in people's thoughts. She slid out of the booth. "Can we go, please? I'd like to get started."

Mason offered a sigh too, then nodded. Grace walked ahead of her, conscious of curious eyes on her.

CHAPTER SEVEN

Mason kept her gaze firmly on the road, her mind reeling. Yeah, the woman could have found out those things...it's town gossip. But she'd only been in town a day. Less than a day. Even Scott didn't know about her mother's...problem.

"I apologize."

Mason held her hand up. "Stop saying that."

"You're not speaking to me."

"How did you know about my mother?" She heard Dr. Jennings—Grace—let out a heavy sigh.

"I...I see...*things*. Images."

"That's your game? You *see* things?"

"Again...not a game, Deputy Cooper."

"Whatever."

"If it makes you feel better, I didn't know your muffin of choice was blueberry. Agent Kemp told me that."

Mason blew out her breath. "Figures." She glanced at her quickly. "Tell me how this works."

"What do you mean?"

"I mean, I take you to the sites where we found the bodies. Then what?"

"Then I…I wait and listen."

"Listen?"

Again, another sigh. "What is it you're asking?"

"I just want to know what the hell to expect, that's all."

"You are welcome to wait in the truck. In fact, that might be best."

Mason wanted to agree with that. She didn't want to be around if she was going to be calling up spirits or whatever the hell she did. She shook her head and gave a quick eye roll. No. She did *not* believe in that crap. She didn't really know what she'd been expecting from the psychic. Well, for one, she hadn't expected her to be this young, this normal…this attractive. She'd been expecting the crazy gypsy lady from her childhood. She was prepared for that. She wasn't prepared for Dr. Grace Jennings. She certainly wasn't prepared to be this up close and personal to a damn psychic.

She turned onto School Road, noting how developed it was now. "I used to take this to school each day," she said, pointing to the bike trail. "We lived a couple of blocks up. There used to be nothing out here but the school. When the town expanded, this was the only direction it could go."

"The park that you all refer to—it's part of the school?"

"It's a city park, but yeah, close enough to walk to from the school. Nice park now. Back when I was a kid, it wasn't much more than an old ball field and a playground. The rest was forest. It's fixed up now. More like a greenbelt in spots. There's a creek that flows through it. Boulder Creek. We used to call it Rock Creek when we were kids," she said, old memories causing a smile to form.

"So the park is still wooded?"

"In spots, yes. There are a couple of ballparks—baseball and soccer, a softball field, a playground, got a small skate park too. Picnic area. The creek is big enough to fish. This bike trail here goes past the school and into the park now. There are hiking trails in the park too that meet up with some established trails in the forest. Oh, and a fenced dog park was added a few years ago."

"How large is the park? Acreage, I mean."

"I don't know for sure. Over a hundred, I'd guess."

"Yet you have cameras at all points?"

"Well, obviously not at *all* points, no. The ballparks, the playground, the skate area, the picnic tables…all that is covered. Got cameras on parts of the hiking trail. The back side is pretty much in the dark. Most of the hiking trails are in undeveloped forest, other than the hike-and-bike trail which winds through the park and fields."

"Where do most of the children go missing?"

"Different places. School...coming or going. The park too. Some simply vanish into thin air. One minute they're getting on the school bus, then next they're gone. One time, I think it was Amber Peterson, she disappeared while shopping with her mother at the grocery store. That was 2017."

"Surveillance camera showed what?"

"There's a blind spot in the cereal aisle...that's what it showed." She held a hand up. "And yes, an employee of the store would have known about the blind spot and we questioned every last one of them, including Mrs. Winkerman."

"And Mrs. Winkerman is who?"

"She's eighty-one and works in the bakery. Point is, Amber disappeared off camera and never showed up again." She slowed as she approached the park. The sign above the entrance was freshly painted: GILLETTE PARK CITY PARK.

"Original name."

Mason nodded. "Yeah, it is. Everyone calls it The Park, as if that's the formal name." She glanced at her. "Are you really writing a book?"

"I am. Or...I plan to. I've spent the last few years doing research."

"Research like you're doing here?" she guessed.

"Yes. It doesn't always involve murders, though, Mason. It's been two years since I last worked with the FBI on a case."

She pulled into the parking area near the playground. It was a cool, crisp morning with bright sunshine, yet the playground was empty. She turned her wrist, glancing at her watch. Quarter of eight. She supposed it was still a little early.

"I'll show you—"

"I'll find it," Grace said quickly. "If you could give me a few moments, please."

"I should probably come with you. You might have questions."

Grace smiled and got out. "I'll let you know if I do."

Mason watched her head toward the swings. She took her seat belt off and shifted in the seat, her gaze traveling past Grace's hooded sweatshirt and jeans to what looked like brand-new hiking boots. Truth was, Dr. Grace Jennings freaked her out a little bit. If you met her in passing, you'd say she was perfectly normal. As far as looks went, she was on the right side of attractive. She had a pleasant smile. Serious blue eyes, yes, but her smile could dim the intensity somewhat. She was...well, cute. Pretty. Not even close to fat but not so damn thin either. Normal. But then you talked to her for a few minutes and...

she *sees* things. Mason shook her head. That was simply too weird for her to comprehend.

There were three swing sets, each with four swings secured with chains. The wind was blowing from the west, causing the swings to sway gently. Grace Jennings walked slowly, pausing at the second set, but her attention was on the third. Mason's gaze went to the third swing of the third set. She could picture the body...nine-year-old Melissa Higgins. She'd been beneath the swing, facedown, her arms folded under her, her legs spread, one foot pointing in at an odd angle. She'd been missing three days. Like a lot of the others over the years, she never made it home from school.

The swing moved and Mason drew her brows together. Not the wind. All the others were still in their same, gentle motion. This one? It moved forward at first, then back...then it swung higher, as if someone...well, as if a ghost rider were taking it higher and higher, front to back, gaining height on each swing. She could feel her heart beating quickly, could sense her accelerated breath, knew her eyes were wide and staring. She had one hand on the door handle, but she didn't know why. Was she planning to dart out there?

Oh, hell no.

Dr. Jennings was moving closer to the swing now, arms hanging loose by her side. Her gaze seemed to follow the motion of the swing, back and forth, high in front of her, then back down and behind her. Mason's eyes widened and she gripped the door handle harder.

"Who the hell is she talking to?" she whispered. Her eyes widened even further when Grace held her arms out, palms raised, as if pleading with someone. "Oh, *man*," she groaned.

She opened the door, making herself get out. Her feet felt like they were stuck in cement as she walked toward Grace. Grace's gaze was fixed on the swing, but she could tell by the twitch of her head that she'd heard her approach. Mason stood still, watching as the swing slowed, then stopped altogether. After a few seconds, the swing did nothing more than sway gently in the breeze and Grace's shoulders relaxed as she let out a heavy breath.

A dozen questions formed, and Mason opened her mouth to ask them, then closed it just as quickly. She didn't really want to know the answers. Did she?

"She's gone."

Mason swallowed. "She...she who?"

Grace turned to her then, dismissing the question with a flick of her eyes. So, okay. She supposed it was a stupid question. She swallowed again.

"Okay, so you're saying that…that Melissa Higgins was…was—"

"Missy. Her friends called her Missy."

Mason held her gaze. "This is starting to freak me out."

"I told you to stay in the truck. In fact, I will insist on it next time."

With that, Grace Jennings headed in that direction, leaving Mason standing there—alone—by the swing that, just a few minutes ago, had been sent soaring high into the sky by…by a ghost rider. She turned and took off in a fast sprint toward her truck.

CHAPTER EIGHT

"Gillette Park. Why the name?"

"Park, not like the park we just came from. In the mountains, a high valley is referred to as a park. And Gillette was the name of a gold mine that put the town on the map way back when."

Grace turned in her seat, watching as Mason drove them across town to the area where the second body was found. She'd been rather quiet since they'd left the park. She knew Mason must have questions that were bursting to get out, yet she remained quiet, both hands gripping the steering wheel perhaps a bit too tightly.

"Ask."

Mason turned. "Ask what?" At the look Grace gave her, Mason smiled. "What? Stupid question?"

"Or…do you not want to know?"

"Is that a guess or are you reading me?"

"I told you, I don't read minds." Much, she added silently to herself.

"Okay…so you were…*talking* to her?"

"No. Well, I was talking, yes, but she wasn't really answering. She's afraid." She watched as Mason visibly swallowed.

"So…she was…on the swing?"

Grace smiled at that. Of course, that would be all that Mason would see...a swing flying wildly in the air without a rider.

"I'll need to come back. Alone. I think, if she trusts me, she'll come back. Perhaps talk."

Mason held up a hand. "How can you say something like that as if it's perfectly normal?" She hit the steering wheel. "Jesus! And you want to do it *alone*?"

"What? Are you going to protect me?"

"Oh. So now you're being funny?"

"What you don't understand is that this *is* normal for me. I see... *things*. I see images. I hear voices. I see...*people*. Dead people."

"Good god! This isn't helping!"

Grace nearly laughed at the look on Mason's face. "I was trying to put your mind at ease."

"Well, you're driving me crazy in the process. I mean, I saw the freakin' swing!"

"Yes. She was on the swing."

"Oh, man," Mason groaned. "Let's stop talking about it. My head's going to explode."

Where the town seemed to disappear into the mountainside, Mason took a small, dirt road that was cut into the forest. The road was so narrow, she wondered what they would do if they met another vehicle. No need to worry though. They crossed a creek or river or something on a one-lane bridge, then Mason turned into a clearing. There were two trucks parked there and she pulled beside them.

"That was Gillette Creek," Mason explained. "It flows through town in parts. This is a trailhead. The creek makes three waterfalls in its descent out of the mountains." She got out and Grace did the same. "Long hike, though, if you want to bag all three falls. The first one is only a little over a mile in. You're looking at eight miles to reach the third one."

Grace stared at her. "Are you saying that we're going for a hike?"

Mason shook her head. "Aaron Stills. Sixteen. His body was found about a hundred yards off the trail."

Grace held her hand up. "Walk me through this. Someone goes missing. If it's a child or a...a young person, you automatically assume the worst?"

"A town this size, people don't go missing. So, yeah. A parent calls in, we assume the worst. So does the parent."

She followed Mason as they headed down the trail. "But you don't just assume they're dead, right? I mean, you try to find them, you investigate the disappearance, right?"

Mason stopped and turned. "Of course. We check surveillance, interview who saw them last. It's by the book. There's never anything, though. Never."

"The murders started in—what? 1997?"

"Yes."

"You were how old?"

"Ten. Susie Shackle."

"Oh, yes. The one your psychic tried to talk to. Did you know her?"

"Susie? Yeah. She lived in the neighborhood. We walked to school together. Played together."

"When it happened, did you understand what *really* happened?"

"No. I only knew that everyone was scared. My mother. My…my father. He was a sheriff's deputy at the time."

Grace saw her shoulders stiffen at her words, but she gave no other indication that talking about her father distressed her. In reality, Grace knew that it did. She changed course with her questioning.

"Did you go into law enforcement because of him or your uncle?"

Mason turned around and glanced at her. "How do you know he's my uncle?"

Grace smiled. "Scott told me." She stopped. "And we're going to need to slow down. I came up here from sea level," she said between breaths.

Mason stopped and leaned against a tree. "From where?"

"New Orleans."

"Is that home?"

"Home?" She looked past Mason, only now seeing that they were on the edge of a rocky ridge, a view of a canyon—and the creek—spreading out beyond them. She looked above her head, the tall trees—pines and spruce and the like—reaching far into the blue sky. She was always so focused on what was in her mind, her head…what she was "seeing"…that she often lost sight of what was right in front of her. Beauty surrounded her and she hadn't even noticed. She looked back at Mason and shook her head. "No, not really. My mother…well, she was an unwed mother. When she married, it was to a navy guy, so we moved around a lot. I don't really have a home. We lived all over the place."

"Navy guy? Not a stepfather?"

Grace shrugged. "Oh, he was okay. But they then had three kids of their own, so…"

"So? So you became what? The forgotten one?"

"I was invisible, yes." She gave a quick smile. "Plus, I was a little different than other kids." Her smile disappeared, remembering the long talk they'd had. If she didn't quit making up stories about "seeing" and "hearing" things, they were going to take her to a doctor for "crazy" people.

"What?"

"Nothing. We should go," she said abruptly, walking past Mason on the trail.

Yes, she was invisible to her mother, certainly invisible to Rich. It followed that she became invisible to her stepbrothers and stepsister too. She was almost eleven when Todd had been born. Stevie followed eighteen months later, and when she was fourteen, Stephanie graced them with her presence. Stephanie was a beautiful child—charming and giggly. It didn't take long for the whole household to fall in love with her. By that time, Grace had already become the forgotten one and as Stephanie grew, she seemed to shrink.

She remembered being terrified of her so-called gifts and having no one to talk to. Her mother thought she'd lost her mind. Rich wanted to have her committed. She'd learned to keep everything inside, hidden away, so scared they were right, that she was crazy.

It was in Hawaii, when she met Angelique, that her world changed. She was fifteen, Angelique was seventeen. She had always been different, but different in more ways than being able to "see" and "hear" things. She knew at a very early age that she had no interest in boys. When she was young, she didn't know what label to put on it. As puberty stared her in the face, so did the truth. She wasn't really afraid of it—being gay. That part of her was of little concern. She'd gotten so adept at hiding her "gifts" from people, hiding being gay came easy. And hiding it was what she knew she had to do. Rich was born and raised in the deep South and "fags" had no place in this world, especially in the military. "God should strike them from this earth" was a favorite saying of his.

But Angelique...she was different too. Despite her beautiful name, Angelique was as tough as nails and could outperform any boy, whether it was on a surfboard or swimming in the ocean, playing volleyball on the beach or riding dirt bikes in the sand. Grace had been captivated the moment she laid eyes on her. Grace was a bumbling, fumbling fifteen-year-old kid and Angelique was a gorgeous dark-haired goddess. She fell in love hard...as hard as a fifteen-year-old can. Angelique rose out of the ocean, dripping wet, surfboard under one arm, the sun shining on her glistening skin...and Grace melted right there in the sand.

"We're coming upon it," Mason said from behind her, interrupting her thoughts.

Grace stopped, running her hands through her hair, shoving the old memories away. She needed to concentrate, to focus. She needed to be in the here and now, not on some faraway beach with her first—and only—love.

"Lead the way," she said, stepping aside to allow Mason to pass her.

The terrain sloped sharply downward as Mason got off the trail. Grace followed her, only to have her feet slip out from under her. She grabbed the rough bark of a tree as she hit the rocks.

Mason turned around and helped her up. "Turn sideways when you walk," she said.

Grace nodded, watching as Mason moved easily down the slope. She mimicked her walk, her feet turned, knees bent. She looked ahead of Mason, knowing where the spot was before she even stopped. In her mind, she saw the dark, discolored earth, an area the size of a small car. It seemed to be growing as they approached. It was a scene she'd seen played out before—at dump sites.

"Don't," she said, reaching out to Mason and grasping her arm. "You're...you're walking on it."

Mason stopped in her tracks. "Walking on...*it?*"

Grace tugged her back up the hill a few steps, her gaze still fixed on the spot. "Stay here."

"Okay. Yeah."

She took a wide berth, taking care not to touch the stained—tarnished—area. When she'd been in the park, there had been nothing like this. She'd simply been drawn to the swing—and the young child. She was getting no sense of a presence here. She looked up into the trees, listening, but there was no movement. It was as if the wind had died, the birds had fled.

"He wasn't killed here," she said, almost to herself. She turned to Mason. "How was he killed?"

"Stabbed. Twelve times."

Grace nodded. "The girl at the park was strangled. The third victim was also strangled?"

"Yes."

She nodded again. "So...he's not here." She spread her hands out. "I see...an area here...it's black, dark...discolored." She took a step forward. "It's shrinking now...fading as we talk." She looked up, seeing the breeze again rustling the trees, hearing birds chirping. "It's gone."

"Okay, all of that means what? Because I didn't see anything."

"This is where the body was." She pointed to the forest floor. "The area has been, I don't know, soiled," she said, hoping Mason understood what she was saying. "He wasn't here, though. There's no...no—" She struggled to find a word that would make sense to Mason without totally freaking her out. "Aura."

"Aura? You mean, like, a ghost?"

Grace smiled. "Do you believe in ghosts, Mason?"

Mason did not match her smile. "No. I do not. And when you leave here, I'd like to still have that mindset."

Grace walked over to her, studying her. She was definitely nervous. And of course, skeptical. "I don't like to use the word ghost. Too many Hollywood movies come to mind, both good and bad. Aura. An...an essence. A...a presence of something."

"Presence? Aura? Essence?" Mason gave her a smirk. "Spirit. Ghost."

She held her hands out. "Okay. Let's use spirit then."

Mason looked around them, turning a circle. "And I think this is the first time I've gotten spooked being out in the forest."

"There's nothing to be spooked about," she said. "Well, not at the moment."

Mason's eyes widened. "What the hell does that mean?"

Grace tilted her head. "Do you want me to be honest with you or—?"

"Yeah." Mason paused. "I think."

"Okay. I'm...well, some people might call me a medium. A psychic medium." She met Mason's gaze. "Do you know what that means?" She saw Mason swallow before answering.

"You...you talk to...to...the dead?"

"Not in the physical sense. Mental. Though there are those who talk and hear in the present realm."

"I saw you talking. At the swings."

She nodded. "I speak sometimes, yes, mostly for my benefit. It helps me concentrate to say the words out loud. What I mean is, if you were there with me, you wouldn't hear or see anything other than what I said. But I would hear. Mentally, but it would be as clear as if someone spoke the words out loud to me."

"A ghost? A dead person's...spirit? They talk to you?" Again, a skeptical look on Mason's face.

"Yes, they do. So when I said there was nothing to be spooked about...well, for one, there's nothing out here. Not right at the moment anyway. There was in the park. At some point, though, there could be something out here that isn't one of the kids who were killed. Do you understand?"

Mason took a step away from her. "You're freaking me out, I understand that." She looked around them again, glancing up into the trees. "It seems...really quiet all of a sudden. Like...*really* quiet." The words ended in a whisper, as if not to break the silence.

Grace looked up too, seeing the branches motionless, hearing the quiet—the birds had fled once more. "Yes," she whispered. "It's changed again." She looked down, watching as the forest floor transformed from the natural colors of fallen leaves and twigs and pinecones to the dark blackness that was spreading. They were standing in the middle of it now and it seemed to be climbing their legs. She looked around them, turning a slow circle. Someone was watching them. She took slow, even breaths, listening. She heard laughter among the trees—children's laughter. Then a dark voice, coming from beyond the laughter, behind it...inside it.

"*Go away.*"

It was spoken very quietly, almost subtly, like the wind whispering to her, only there was no wind. She stared into the branches, but she saw nothing.

"*Go away.*" Then a fit of giggles before more voices chimed in. "*Go away! Goawaygoawaygoawaygoawaygoawaygo...*"

A strong gust of wind hit her in the face, forceful enough to make her move. Mason, too, felt the impact, and she jumped back. Then all was still once again. She took a long, deep breath, then shook herself. The forest floor was as before—pine needles and twigs and scattered rocks. A cluster of birds, five or six of them, landed high in the trees above their heads, foraging along the pinecones for food, oblivious to them.

She turned to Mason, who was staring at her intently. She nodded. "Yes, I'm fine."

"I thought you didn't read minds."

"It didn't take a mind reader to find that question." She started walking back up the hill toward the trail. "I should be asking if *you're* okay."

"You went into like a little trance or something."

"Yes, that happens."

"Is that...normal?"

Grace smiled. "Normal?"

"Come on, Dr. Jennings, what the hell just happened?"

She stopped and turned. "We're back to Dr. Jennings? Okay... Deputy Cooper...something was watching us. Someone issued a warning. I heard laughter—children. Lots of them. Then a voice—a male voice—told me to go away. Then the children chimed in...go away, go away, go away." She shrugged, then walked on.

"Wait a minute." Mason grabbed her arm and spun her around. "A warning? What does that mean?"

Grace met her gaze. "It means that whoever your killer is, he is not acting alone."

Mason's hand dropped from her arm. "What the hell does that mean?"

CHAPTER NINE

"I don't know who the hell she is…or *what* she is," Mason said, downing the whiskey in her glass, "but she's freaking me out."

Scott nudged her arm. "Keep your voice down. I thought you didn't want the whole town to know who she was." Scott held two fingers up. "Two beers, Gary."

Mason spun around on the barstool, her back to the bar. Scott did the same. "Do you believe all the crap she says? I mean, do you believe all this stuff?"

Scott shrugged. "What do we know about it? If she said she heard it, then…"

"You should have seen the swing, man." Mason shook her head. "Then she goes into some trance out in the middle of the woods. I don't think I'm cut out for this."

"Who should Alan put on it? Brady? Hell, he'd piss his pants. Dalton? Dalton talks too much. It'd be all over town. Besides, to hear Alan tell it, Dalton is the most skeptical of all." He shook his head. "No one else in your department could handle this, Mason."

"What makes you think I can handle it? I don't believe in this shit to begin with. And it's freaking me out!"

"You can handle it because you have a different mindset, Mason." He reached behind them for the two mugs of beer and handed her one.

"You saw a lot a shit in LA that hardened you. I know all about being hardened. You see things differently then. These guys? This town, this is all they know. Other than the murders, this town is squeaky clean. No burglaries, no robberies…not so much as a jaywalker. Nothing."

"I know. It's like…because of the murders, everyone is on their best behavior. There are no drugs, no assaults, no rapes…hell, no trespassing."

"And for a town this size, that's weird as hell."

"Yeah, but what if—" She leaned closer. "What if she's right? What if there's really something out there?"

"Something? Yeah, you've got a goddamn serial killer out there. That's what you've got."

"Something more than that, Scott. Because she—"

"Come on, Mason." Kemp shook his head. "Whatever the doc is seeing, hearing…nobody else is. It's probably all in her head. All we want her to do is lead us to the killer."

"So you're saying all this psychic bullshit isn't real?"

"*She* believes it's real. That's all that matters."

Mason shook her head. "I saw the swing. I saw the freakin' swing, Scott."

"Could have been the wind."

"No. And out in the forest…she, like—I'm telling you—went into a trance or something. She was hardly breathing. I moved my hand in front of her face, her eyes, and she never even blinked." She took a big swallow of the beer. "Freaked me out."

"What did you tell your uncle?"

"Nothing. Told him I showed her around town, that's all." She smiled. "He'll think I've lost my mind if I tell him all this."

"Hey, he hired her. She's a psychic. Isn't this the kind of stuff he expected?"

"He didn't want to hire her. Everyone pushed. Hell, I agreed too. We had to do something, you know. But I think he thought she was going to walk around, do some chants or something, and tell us who the killer is. At least, that's what I was kinda hoping for."

"And she may. When she last worked with us, it was in South Carolina. Two kids—a boy and a girl—were abducted a week apart, both from prominent families. No ransom, no nothing. Brought her in about a week into the deal." He shook his head. "Now, mind you, this is all secondhand. I wasn't involved in the case."

"Okay. Go on."

"First day she's there, she says one of the kids is dead, the other is still alive. She goes into both houses, both bedrooms. Goes to where they were snatched, walks around a little, then says the boy is dead. Wrapped in newspaper. Parents, of course, freak out. Anyway, she comes up with all these clues as to where the girl is. She 'sees' an abandoned building. There's a view of a church from a second-floor window. Stuff like that." Scott grabbed a handful of peanuts from the bowl on the bar. "Took three days to find the place. They rescued the little girl. Got the bad guys too."

"And the boy?"

"Dead. Found the poor kid stuffed inside a trash can. And yeah, wrapped in newspaper just like she said."

"Damn."

"Yeah. Cool stuff, huh."

"Cool? The stuff of nightmares. How do you think she handles it?"

Scott nudged her arm. "I don't know. Why don't you ask her?"

He motioned with his head toward the door and Mason followed his gaze. Dr. Jennings was standing just inside the door, looking relaxed in her jeans and hiking boots—the same she'd had on earlier in the day—but a flannel shirt had replaced the long-sleeved cotton shirt and an insulated vest took the place of the hoodie. Like the boots, she assumed everything she wore was new. She didn't imagine she'd have need of these kinds of clothes in New Orleans. With a sigh, Mason waved her over.

"Hey, doc," Agent Kemp greeted. "Come for dinner?"

"I suppose I do need to eat, yes." Grace looked at her. "Do you have time for a chat?"

Mason stood, still holding her beer mug. "Sure. You want a beer?"

Grace shook her head. "I'm not really a beer drinker."

"Wine?"

Grace again shook her head. "Not while I'm working."

Mason cocked an eyebrow at her. "So you're working right now? Work chat then?"

Grace nodded, then glanced at Scott. "Agent Kemp, you should probably join us."

Now what? Mason wondered as she led them to an empty table. She was aware of a few curious glances. Most of them probably remembered Agent Kemp from last year—they'd spent enough time here at Bucky's. And by now, she assumed some knew that Grace Jennings was in town to write a book. Helen never failed to pass on news she heard at the café.

"I'm not sure how this is going to help or what I expect you to do about it," Grace started as soon as they sat down. "There was a soccer game…or match, I believe they're called. A boy will be reported missing very soon."

Mason leaned forward. "*What?*"

Grace met her gaze and gave a quick nod. "Yes. I was going over the file again…I saw the boy—he was carrying a soccer ball under his arm—and he got into a car."

Mason held up her hand. "Wait a minute, wait a minute. You 'saw' meaning what?"

"You know what I mean Deputy Cooper. Do I have to spell it out to you *every* time? I had a vision, okay?"

"He got into a car? Are you sure it wasn't his parents' car or whoever gave him a ride?" Scott shoved his beer mug out of the way. "Not that I'm questioning what you saw, but—"

"He was in distress," Grace said. "Scared."

"How old?" Mason asked, wondering if she really believed this so-called vision or not.

"Not terribly young. Twelve? Thirteen?"

Mason shoved her own beer away. Oh, hell. It wouldn't hurt to check it out. "There's a soccer league. They play at the park on weeknights." She stood. "Let's go out there. If it's fresh enough, maybe there's some evidence. Maybe someone saw something."

"Maybe your camera caught something," Grace suggested.

Mason motioned for her to get up. "Come on."

"Me?"

"Yeah, you. You can show me where it went down."

"But I don't know where. A vision is just that. I—"

"Come on," she said again. She wanted Grace Jennings along for two reasons. One, yes, in case she could pinpoint the spot. And two… if there was something out there, something *strange*, she'd just as soon not be alone. She turned to Scott. "I'll call Uncle Alan. He'll let Chief Danner know. You can help look through the surveillance feed."

"You sure you don't want me with you?"

"Technically, the police have jurisdiction at the park. Let's don't step on too many toes."

"Since when has that bothered you?"

CHAPTER TEN

Frankly, Grace was surprised at how quickly Mason acted. She didn't question her, she didn't demand a thirty-minute explanation, didn't require convincing. When they'd parted company that afternoon, Mason had been rather quiet. She'd been processing everything that had happened, no doubt. Processing and trying to decide if she—Grace—was crazy or not. And trying to decide how much—if anything—she believed.

"In reading through the file, the first killing is usually in early May, right?"

Mason nodded, never taking her gaze from the road. "Over the years, there have been a couple in late April, but for the most part, it usually starts in early May. This year, of course, we had the first one on April 28th."

"Do the police put out any warnings or anything? Signs? Ads in the paper or radio?"

Mason shook her head. "They used to. Back when I was in high school. It tended to make everyone a little anxious and jumping at shadows and spotting suspicious activity all over the damn place."

"So it's ignored?"

"Everybody already knows, doc," she said, using Agent Kemp's nickname for her. "People new to town learn about the murders pretty quickly. The old-timers? They don't need to be told it's May. Those with kids keep a tighter leash on them, that's all."

"And still, two or more end up dead."

"And the parents usually blame themselves."

The park was still lit up, the lights on the fields making it look nearly like daylight. There was a game being played on one of the fields, the other was empty. Small bleachers, only five rows high, were on three sides, obviously set up for when baseball was being played. For this soccer match, parents and supporters were sitting in lawn chairs along the sidelines.

Mason parked closest to the vacant field and turned off the engine. "You getting anything?"

"You mean like a bat signal or something?"

Mason smiled a bit sheepishly. "Sorry. I obviously don't know how this works."

"Let's walk."

She didn't really have anything to go on. Nothing concrete, at least. She'd been sitting in the chair, flipping through the file, rereading the old notes from the beginning, way back in 1997. The first thing she realized was that she wasn't having any difficulty making it through the file. There was no pressure on her chest, no anxiety, nothing choking her. She felt nothing whatsoever. Then she'd turned a page—she'd been on 2004—Deb Meckel—the year the psychic had been there—and the page had gone black. She'd stared at it, seeing a boy with a soccer ball. He'd been chewing gum and blowing a bubble. The image moved across the page, the boy sitting in the backseat of a car, staring out the window. There was crying. Then laughter. She knew the laughter hadn't come from him.

"It was a dark car," she said, surprising herself. She didn't recall getting a clear look at the car. "Four-door." She turned to Mason. "I know that doesn't help."

"Car? Not an SUV or truck?"

"No. Car. Like a sedan."

"Black?"

She shook her head. "I can't be sure. Dark...not light."

"Okay. So, let's walk around and...and, well, you let me know if..."

Grace looked at her thoughtfully. "Do you believe me?"

Mason frowned. "Should I not?"

"Most don't."

"Who? The FBI? Or...friends?"

"Friends? What's that?" The words were out before she could stop them. "I'm a freak, Deputy Cooper. My own family pretends I don't exist. Why would there be friends?"

She walked on, wishing she'd not divulged that. She saw Mason's expression change, saw a softening of her features. Saw questions in her eyes. There were no friends, no. Other freaks like her that she kept in touch with, she wouldn't call them friends. Most, she'd never even met in person.

None of that mattered now. She'd signed on to this case because she needed the money, because it would add to her research, and because it would offer her some solitude to begin writing, once the case was over. She was committed to staying through October, whether the case was solved or not. The last thing she wanted was to have someone in town—Mason Cooper, for instance—who felt sorry for her. Yeah, she was a freak. She'd known it for most of her life. At her age—thirty-four last month—she no longer concerned herself with friends or family or…or anyone else. She wanted to write a book. She didn't want to go back to teaching. And if the beginnings of this case were any indication, she was having second thoughts about assisting the FBI in the future. When the outcome was favorable, everyone did high-fives and got slaps on the back. When it wasn't favorable, they looked at her accusingly, as if she'd had something to do with it. As if she were to blame.

Now, for instance. The boy she'd seen in her vision—he would be dead by tomorrow. She wouldn't tell Mason that because it would make no difference. They wouldn't find him in time. Whether she told them or not, when they found the body—which she would most likely direct them to—they would look at her, wondering why she hadn't been able to stop it. They would look at her with blame in their eyes. She'd seen it all before, many times.

"Hey, doc…slow down, would you."

She stopped walking, knowing she was not accomplishing a thing with all these thoughts running through her mind. She took a deep breath and stared into the night sky, looking past the lights on the field, shutting out the noise as kids chased after a ball and parents clapped and cheered. She wondered how many parents were at the game because they wanted to be and how many were there because the calendar had flipped over to May and they'd already had one killing in town.

She felt Mason stand beside her, but she didn't look at her. She slowly closed her eyes, listening. She heard nothing. She moved on, going nearly to the end of the parking lot. She stopped again. Nothing. She turned to Mason then.

"I think it was down here...but, that's only my guess. I'm not... I'm not getting anything."

"Are you *sure* you saw something?"

"Yes, I'm sure. I was...I was going through the file. I was on 2004."

"The year the psychic was here."

"Yes." She frowned. Was it a coincidence that she'd seen the vision on that year? Or was there a reason?

"What?"

They were in the shadows, away from the lights. She couldn't read Mason's eyes. What did she tell her? Did she tell her there was something out here? Something evil? Would she believe her? When they were out in the woods earlier today, Mason hadn't wanted to talk about it. She didn't want to hear about the warning. Grace hadn't blamed her. It was a lot to take in.

"What happened out in the woods today...whatever's out here, it knows that I know." She saw Mason swallow nervously.

"It knows that you know *what*?" she asked quietly.

"Same as the psychic knew back in 2004." She reached out and grasped Mason's arm, squeezing it tightly. "There were five murders that year. The psychic knew."

"Grace, what the hell are you talking about?"

"Whoever is doing the killing, they're probably not doing it willfully. They may not even know they're doing it."

"You're making no goddamn sense," she said loudly.

"Yes, I am! You're not listening!"

"What I'm hearing is making me crazy! For god's sake—" Her cell phone rang and Mason pulled it out of the pocket of her jeans. "Yeah, Cooper," she answered. Her face hardened as their eyes met. "I'm out here now." She paused, Mason's gaze still holding tight to hers. "Copy that."

Grace didn't need to ask what news she'd received. "What's his name?"

Mason blew out a breath, then looked skyward. "Jason. Jason Gorman. He's twelve." She turned to her again. "Supposed to catch a ride home with the neighbor. Neighbor couldn't find him after the game, assumed he'd gone with someone else." Mason ran a hand through her hair. "Police are on the way to check it out. The park is their area, not ours, but you've got free rein...so..."

"And you're my...my handler?"

"Something like that, yeah. My lucky day."

Grace held her gaze for a second, seeing the wariness there. "I'll walk around some more, but I'm not getting anything. I don't think I will."

"Why is that? I mean, you knew what happened…with the kid. Why aren't you getting anything now?"

Mason's tone wasn't really accusing so Grace didn't take it that way. The question was more curiosity than anything, she supposed. At her hesitation, Mason spoke again.

"I realize how that sounded. I didn't mean—"

"I know. You're trying to understand how this works, even though you don't really *believe*. I know. Perhaps if we had some time, I could try to explain it to you in a way that would make sense. But then you would just freak out, so what's the point?" She held her hands out. "My guess is, he doesn't want me to know."

"You're not talking about the kid."

"No. Jason is still alive. When we find his body, maybe I'll—"

"That's right. They have to be dead first before they'll talk to you."

Mason turned away from her and Grace heard the disgust in her voice. She wished it didn't bother her. She'd heard it many times before—disgust. She clenched her fists without really knowing she was doing it, then walked farther away. She didn't expect to learn anything tonight. As she'd said, he didn't want her to know. Not yet. But she needed to put some space between them.

"I'm sorry."

Grace kept walking, away from the lights, away from Mason. It was times like this, when she got *feelings* like this, that she swore she would never do this again. She was used to it, yes, but that didn't make it hurt any less. She wasn't a robot. And like any normal person, her feelings could get hurt just as easily.

"Grace…I'm sorry."

She stopped walking but kept her back to Mason. "I know you don't understand. I wish I could snap my fingers and tell you everything you want to know and have you believe it. I wish I could lead you directly to the killer." She turned then. "It doesn't work that way, Mason. I'm a human being, flesh and blood. What I 'see' and 'hear'…they are images that come when they want, not when *I* want them to come." She walked closer to her. "Some people call what I have a gift." She squared her shoulders. "Well, it's not a goddamn gift. I'm a freak. I know that. You know that. So let's just work this out the best way we can. And whatever comments you have about me…well, it's probably best to continue talking to Agent Kemp about it…or keep them to yourself. We'll get along much better then."

She brushed past Mason, heading back to the truck. Even if there was something to be heard out here tonight, she was in no frame of mind to work it. By the time they got back to the truck, three police cars were pulling in, lights flashing. She glanced toward the soccer field where the action had come to a halt. Parents were standing, some gathering their children. They knew. She nodded. Yeah, they knew.

"I don't think you're a freak, Dr. Jennings."

Grace turned to her with a sigh. "Yes, you do, Deputy Cooper." She opened the passenger's door of the truck. "If you could take me back now, please."

CHAPTER ELEVEN

Mason tossed her keys on the small table by the door, then closed the door to the house she'd called home for the last five years. As an afterthought, she turned and locked it. She glanced around, wondering when it would start to feel like home. She didn't realize how little she'd brought back with her from LA until she'd unpacked. She'd had to scramble to stock her kitchen and, between Aunt Carol and the secondhand shop in town, she'd furnished the place. Maybe she should have bought new stuff, but her salary in Gillette Park didn't come close to matching what she'd been making in LA. She hadn't wanted to blow through her savings for new furniture.

She glanced at the TV, then picked up the remote. Her life in LA had been completely different from here—night and day. That wasn't only because of Shauna. Her life as a cop on the streets was never dull, never boring. Here? In Gillette Park? As Scott had reminded her, there was no crime in Gillette Park. No *normal* crime, that is.

Grace Jennings hadn't had to say the words. Mason could see it in her eyes. Jason Gorman would be dead by morning. Hell, he might already be dead. And there wasn't a damn thing they could do about it. The surveillance video showed a dark car parked in the very last spot. The license plate was conveniently caked in dirt, making it unreadable. The car pulled into the lot before the games even started. The driver never got out. The video showed the back door opening, showed Jason Gorman standing there with—as Grace had said—a soccer ball under his arm. And then Jason got into the back seat. The door closed. The car drove away.

It was as much evidence as they'd ever had, which wasn't much. The car was a Ford Taurus, dark gray, black or even blue. Older model, the guys guessed. 2010 or so. The police were checking vehicle registration, hoping to get a list of any matching cars in Gillette Park. Chief Danner had two of his guys looking at surveillance video around town, trying to spot the car. All patrol units, both police and sheriff, were on the lookout.

Grace Jennings only nodded when Mason had relayed that information to her on their drive back to the Aspen Resort. Apparently, Grace wasn't speaking to her. Could she blame her? She'd been rather rude to her.

She tossed the remote down without turning on the TV. She went into the kitchen and opened up the fridge. There was the leftover casserole that Aunt Carol had given her the other night. She was hungry, but not for that. She took out a bottle of water, but before opening it, she put it back inside and closed the door.

Did she think Grace was a freak?

Well…kinda, yeah. Okay. Yes, let's be honest. She did. A freak. Of course, she was only looking at it from her own perspective. Truth was, she was spooked by the whole thing. She imagined that most people who interacted with Grace in a situation like this probably felt the same way.

She opened a cabinet at the edge of the kitchen and pulled out a bottle of whiskey. Jack Daniels. She paused before pouring, thinking of her mother. Her mother's drink was vodka. At first, a splash in her orange juice. At breakfast. That's when Mason first knew that her mother had a drinking problem. Mason poured enough in her glass for a couple of swallows, then closed the bottle. The vodka in her mother's tonic turned into a little tonic in her vodka. Would she end up like that?

She picked up her glass. No. A few beers at Bucky's a handful of nights a week was the norm. Some nights, though…like now, she craved something a little more soothing. She took a sip, her thoughts drifting from her mother back to Grace.

What about family? Grace said that she was invisible. That her family pretended that she didn't exist. Why? Because she was a freak?

What was it that she had said? "Why would there be friends?"
Her family pretended that she didn't exist...therefore, *they* didn't exist. And apparently, friends didn't exist either. Because she was a freak. She leaned against the counter, staring at the far wall. Had she said something to reinforce that belief? Probably. She certainly hadn't said anything to dissuade it.

She set her glass down and went back out into the living room and grabbed her keys off the table. If she was going to salvage a working relationship with this woman, she owed her an apology, whether she thought she was a freak or not.

* * *

It was after ten and too late to be making a social call. She stood under one of the trees near the building where Grace's suite was. There didn't appear to be any lights on inside. She flipped the collar of her jacket up to ward off the cold breeze, then shoved her hands into her pockets, debating on whether or not to go up and knock. If Grace was already in bed, she wouldn't have to answer the door, she reasoned. She thought it best to talk tonight instead of waiting until morning.

She knocked twice, then twice more, waiting. She heard a quiet "Who is it?" from the other side of the door.

"It's me...Mason."

She heard the lock turn, then the door opened. Grace looked back at her, no evidence that she'd been in bed. In fact, she held a book in her hand. Grace didn't offer for her to come inside, she simply looked at her with raised eyebrows.

"Yeah...well, I...wanted to talk. If you've got a few minutes. I know it's late," she added. "I won't stay long."

Grace finally stepped back and opened the door fully. Mason went inside the dark room, lit only by a small lamp on the desk. The chair was pulled away. She supposed Grace had been sitting there reading.

"I need to apologize."

Grace met her gaze. "Need to? Want to? *Have* to?"

"All, I guess." She shoved her hands into her pockets in what she recognized was a nervous gesture. "You're right. I don't understand all of this—*any* of this. You have to admit, it's a little spooky. For anyone who is not you, I guess," she clarified.

"Spooky?" Grace moved into the room and motioned to a chair at the table. "Mason, this isn't like the movies where there are ghosts haunting houses and clanking chains and making scary noises. At least, not most of the time."

They both sat down at the table and whereas Mason crossed her arms across her chest—for security?—Grace folded her hands together on top of the table.

"I'll try to explain this in a way you understand. It's not like all day, every day, I have visions or I hear things or see things. It's not like that. Think of it as…as a drug dog, for instance. They're just a dog. But then the handler takes them out to sniff for drugs. Then they're working. When that's over, they go back to being a dog." She spread her hands. "I'm just a person. I eat and sleep and do all the normal things that you do. Except when I'm working. The difference is that I don't always get to determine when I'm working. Visions come when they come. I hear and see things at odd moments, I'll admit. I can't always—rarely can—control that. The times that I've assisted the FBI, it's never been like this. Two occasions, there were kidnappings. Another time, they had evidence of a murder, but they couldn't locate the body. I helped once when they had some hikers lost on the Appalachian Trail. Things like that. Any person with psychic gifts could have helped."

"Do they employ people like that often?"

"No. And when they do, it's kept very low-key. Like here, it's often used as a last resort."

"Why? If it's successful?"

"Because a psychic operates with little to no evidence. And it's not always successful. And if you are relying on a psychic to catch the bad guy, you stand to have the whole thing tossed out in court after a defense attorney labels the psychic as a fraud or a con artist and turns the trial into a circus. In the case of a kidnapping, you're trying to find someone, hopefully before they're killed. You're not worrying about evidence at that point."

"Isn't that what we're doing here?"

"In a sense, yes. Jason Gorman was kidnapped. What makes this different than most cases is that there is something out there… something evil."

"And this is where you start spooking me."

"I'm sorry. Trying to be honest with you is all."

Mason finally uncrossed her arms and rested them on the table. "Is it true what you said? Your family pretends that you don't exist?"

Grace drew her brows together. "I thought you wanted to talk about the case."

"No, I don't. It's late. I'd just as soon not talk about what evil lurks out here in Gillette Park." She tilted her head. "Unless that's too personal for you."

"Why did you leave here, Deputy Cooper?"

"Leave?"

"You left Gillette Park. Why?"

"Oh." She shrugged. "Left for college, then wanted to experience life in the city."

"A cop?"

Mason nodded, wondering if Grace knew that or if she were guessing. "Los Angeles. My father was a cop, my uncle is a cop, my cousin…kinda in the blood, I guess."

"Yet you came back."

Mason leaned back in her chair, wondering how Grace had flipped the conversation to her. "Your family pretends you don't exist?"

Grace smiled, acknowledging Mason's flip back to her. "They have their own family. I told you my mother married. They've got three kids. A family."

"I don't have to be a psychic to know you're leaving out an awful lot. They couldn't deal with your…your gift?"

"Oh, yes, my wonderful gift." Grace folded her hands again, her fingers twisting together. Mason watched them fold and unfold, the hands smooth, the fingers slim, nails neatly trimmed. "No, they couldn't deal. At first, they thought I was crazy." Then Grace laughed—a genuine laugh that brought a smile to Mason's face as well. "Of course, I thought I was crazy too." Her smile still lingered. "It scared the shit out of me." The smile disappeared. "They thought I should see a doctor. I heard them talking about me needing to be in an institution…about me being a threat to their kids."

"What happened? They kick you out or something?"

Grace shook her head. "I learned to…well, hide things from them. When I could. It was a big relief to everyone when it was time for me to move on to college. I was a smart, studious kid in high school and I received lots of scholarships. Rich—my mother's husband—was all too happy to pay whatever remaining expenses there were, just to keep me away from his kids."

"Do you see them?"

"No," she said without hesitation. "Like I said, they are their own family. I never really fit in."

"Your mother?"

Grace gave her a heavy shrug. "We talk on occasion. Once, maybe twice a year. They're in Florida—Jacksonville—which was where they were stationed when he retired from the navy." Grace tapped the table with an index finger. "Why did your father leave?"

Mason swallowed, wondering why—when she'd simply come by to apologize—their conversation was so personal. "He...he got tired of being married, I guess. He was a sheriff's deputy. It was the year the murders started. He left that fall. Packed a bag while I was at school and my mother was at work and just...disappeared. No note, nothing. Uncle Alan tracked him down about three weeks later. Found him in some motel up in Idaho. With a woman, much younger than him." She smiled then. "According to my mother, she was a red-headed floozy with huge tits." She shook her head. "She started drinking more and more after that and I started staying with Uncle Alan and Aunt Carol a lot. Their house became more of a home, really."

"You're an only child?"

"Yeah." She held her hand up. "And no, I don't see or talk to my father. I have no idea where he is nor do I care."

Grace smiled at her. "Now who's reading minds?"

Mason leaned back in her chair. "You don't have any friends?"

Grace sighed. "As you've indicated...I scare people. I'm weird."

"Yeah...you're a freak."

Their eyes held and Grace nodded. "I am. The key, though, is that I *know* I am. It makes a big difference to no longer deny it. People are mostly scared of me. Some are curious, but mostly scared. I don't imagine you'll be any different."

As they sat there in the shadows of a room lit only by a lamp, Mason saw with clarity that Grace so wanted to deny she was a freak... wanted it not to be true. And Mason guessed, if Grace were feeling particularly vulnerable or lonely, she may very well deny it. If only for a little while and if only to herself. That thought struck her as incredibly sad. Here she was, an attractive, normal-looking woman who harbored a secret she dared not tell for fear of being labeled a freak. A label she freely gave herself.

"I don't think you're a freak," she said softly.

There was a hint of a smile on Grace's mouth. "Yes, you do, Mason, but thank you for saying so. Besides, we're just getting started." Then the smile was gone. "I fear this case will be the thing nightmares are made of."

Mason met her gaze, looking into the blue depths, wondering what she was looking for. Some hope that there *wouldn't* be nightmares? Neither pulled away from the stare—Mason found she couldn't and Grace made no move to break the contact. She felt something pass between them, almost physical, yet not. She couldn't quite feel it, see it…understand it. Not quite. It was just under the surface, like a long-ago memory that was still out of reach. For a moment, she wondered if she should panic, if perhaps Grace had her spellbound or hypnotized.

Then Grace stood up, breaking the stare, breaking the connection. Mason wasn't even aware that she'd been holding her breath.

"It's late, Mason."

"Yes." She pushed the chair back, moving a step or two away from Grace. "I'll see you in the morning."

"Good night."

She paused at the door. "Good night, Grace. Lock up behind me."

CHAPTER TWELVE

Grace stood in Jason Gorman's bedroom, looking at a poster on his wall. It was of a soccer player, a young man in mid-swing, the ball already leaving his foot, its trajectory aimed with precision as it headed toward—and just out of reach of—the goalkeeper. She let it unfold, saw the ball whistle past the outstretched arms, heard the swoosh as it cut through the air. Score!

In the hallway, she could hear the mother asking questions, could hear Mason's gentle words. What was she telling her? Was she offering her hope when there was none?

She took a deep breath, then blew it out as she moved toward his bed. It was rumpled, as if hastily made up. The bedroom was neither tidy nor a mess…somewhere in between: discarded shoes on the floor, a pair of jeans slung across a chair, a backpack leaning against the wall. She bent down, picking up one of the shoes that was hiding under the edge of the bed.

As soon as she touched the shoe, she felt a jolt. She squeezed it tightly, her eyes open but unfocused, staring at the wall, staring at nothing. Beyond her vision she saw the woods, heard twigs snapping, heard heavy breathing. There was water…a creek. The moon was out—was it full? Was it the moon? No…it looked like the moon but… it was a soccer ball. There was a noise…an animal—

"Dr. Jennings?"

She jumped and the shoe fell from her hands. She blinked several times, finding Chief Danner watching her. She looked past him, seeing Mason still talking to the mother. Chief Danner bent down and picked up the fallen shoe. He was a middle-aged man, closer to sixty than fifty, she guessed. Trim, fit, as were most of the people she'd seen around town. From her time spent in the South, she was used to seeing overweight and even obese people—it was the norm. Not here. Everyone seemed active, healthy.

"Mason said to give you some time, Dr. Jennings, but time is what we don't have. Please tell me you know something."

She reached out and took the shoe that he held, but it was just a shoe again. She let a bit of her frustration show. She tossed the shoe back on the floor with its mate, perhaps more forcefully than she should have. "You've got to let me work, Chief. When I know something, then you'll know something. I can't be interrupted. Do you understand?"

He glanced over his shoulder at the mother. "We never know what to tell them. You never know how they're going to take it."

"I understand. I'm doing all I can."

"Of course. Sorry to have disturbed you." He turned to go, then stopped. "Please…if you could help in any way. We have the whole town on alert, looking for the boy."

She chewed on her lower lip, wondering how much Mason had shared with him. "The boy is dead," she said quietly. At his expression, she knew Mason had already warned him. "I'm trying to find something to lead us to his body. I'm sorry."

"How can you be sure?"

"I just am. I'm sorry," she said again.

After he left, she walked around the boy's room, picking up things randomly—a black Star Wars figure, an iPad, some sort of a robot, a couple of toy racecars, a Harry Potter book with a…a blue feather used as a bookmark. She flipped the book open, her gaze not on any words but on the feather. It seemed significant, for some reason. When nothing came to her, she closed the book and put it back where she'd found it. There was an unfinished jigsaw puzzle on a desk—a Star Wars theme. There was a baseball bat leaning against the wall.

"Hey."

She turned, finding Mason standing in the doorway. "I saw something with the shoe, but Chief Danner came in…"

"Yeah, sorry…I couldn't keep him out. He kinda outranks me."

"Patience isn't a virtue with the police—I've learned that." She moved closer to her, keeping her voice low. "Where's the mother?"

"Chief took her back to the kitchen."

"Do they have other children?"

"Yeah. Three. They're at their grandparents, I think."

Grace nodded. "He's by a creek. Last night. The moon was out." She looked skyward, as if she could see it. "It was about three-quarters of the way across the sky…full or nearly full." She looked at Mason. "I don't recall the moon phase last night."

"No? It was pretty. I remember looking at it when I drove over to see you."

"One of the downsides. I tend to be so focused on what I'm 'seeing'," she said, making quotes in the air, "that I lose sight of what's right in front of me. What's real." She glanced out the window. "It's beautiful here in Gillette Park, but I didn't even notice. On the drive up, I hardly gave the scenery a thought. Agent Kemp stopped at an overlook. It was only then that I saw how lovely it is up here."

"So you don't turn it on and off? You leave it on, hoping to see or hear something?"

"I guess."

"So your analogy of the drug dog doesn't hold true for you then."

"That was too simple of an analogy, I guess." She offered a weary smile. "I haven't found that on-off switch yet."

Mason nodded. "So he's by a creek?"

"There were thick woods, no clearings. I heard twigs breaking. Someone was carrying him. He sounded labored. And…his soccer ball. The ball will be with him."

"There are two creeks—Gillette Creek and Boulder Creek. They both flow through town at some point, then back out again. There's a river near town too. Goes through the valley, then cuts a deep canyon on the west side."

"This was in the forest, not town. Not steep like a canyon."

"We'll start where the creeks flow in and out of town and hike up from there. Come on. Let me call my uncle and get the search underway."

When they were back in the truck, Grace wanted to know more about how—and why—they conducted the searches.

"How long do you normally wait before you begin searching for a body?"

"Meaning when do we give up hope of finding them?"

"Yes. Actually, I find it quite incredible that people go about their daily lives here, knowing that each summer, someone will be killed. I mean, I can't really fathom it."

"What should they do? Pack up and leave?" Mason nodded. "Some do."

"There doesn't seem to be urgency."

"Keep in mind this has been going on for twenty-three years. It's a fact of life now."

"But you do get some media attention, right? Surely?"

"Sure. Depends on the news cycle. Every few years or so, we'll be featured. We were on *Dateline* one year. And *Unsolved Murders* too."

"Did you get screen time?"

"No, both of those happened while I was gone. But we do get some publicity. And as you know, the FBI pops in every so often. It's not like we're up here fighting this alone."

"Do people in town talk about it?"

"What do you mean?"

"Among themselves? I noticed in the café, with the waitress—Helen—when I told her I was a writer, she knew what I would be writing about, but she never mentioned the murders. She was a little abrupt, if I recall."

Mason was turning and Grace realized they were already at the park. From what she'd heard of Mason's one-sided conversation with her uncle, they were to start at Boulder Creek "by the footbridge" and another team—the police department—was starting at the creek in town, as it flowed past the school and into the park. Other teams were also hiking in both directions of Gillette Creek.

"Helen is one of the old-timers, born and raised here," Mason said. "Those of us who have been around since 1997 have been touched by the killings in some way or another. Family, friends…kids of friends. But no, I don't think people talk about it. Some things you don't have to talk about."

"It is what it is?"

"Exactly. Whoever the killer is…he's a part of this town, part of the history. Not a *good* part, but a part nonetheless." She killed the engine but didn't move to get out. "There's a game in town. It's all under cover, out of sight…but everyone knows it's there. Ronnie Miller's father started it back in 2002, I think it was. Ronnie's kept it up. You can place bets on the killings."

"Oh my god…you're kidding?"

"I wish I was. There are several different pots...date of first disappearance, date first body is found, how many killings there'll be, things like that. It's high dollar...hundred bucks a bet."

"How many people participate?"

"Mostly the old-timers. People new to town may not even know about it."

"So how many?"

"One of the pots last year was over ten grand. Total? I'd say four or five hundred people go out to the hardware store and place a bet or two. Some years, probably more."

"Why do you allow it?"

Mason shrugged. "Like I said, under the table, out of sight. Sheriff Parker—he was sheriff before my uncle—tried to put a stop to it one year, but it didn't matter." She opened her door and got out.

Grace looked at her across the hood of the truck. "The mother... she didn't seem exceptionally distraught. I thought that was odd."

Mason met her gaze but didn't say anything.

"It reminds me a little of *The Lottery*. They know it's going to happen to someone...they just don't know who."

Mason raised her eyebrows. "So they look the other way? Offer condolences with a sigh of relief that it wasn't their family that was hit this year? And if it is your family, you take it on the chin?"

"You would know that better than me."

They were parked near the soccer fields. There was still crime scene tape up by the last few parking spots. According to Mason, the car had simply disappeared, finding whatever blind spots there were in the surveillance cameras. They were able to track it for only three blocks from the park, heading north.

She walked to the tape, watching as the breeze ruffled it, making the lettering run together, making it hard to read. The park seemed empty, the playground deserted. It was a beautiful day, sunny and even warmer than yesterday, yet no one seemed to be out enjoying it.

"The trail starts over here," Mason said, heading past the yellow tape. "There's a footbridge that crosses the creek a little ways up. We'll follow the creek from there."

"Were we assigned this route because of its location?"

"I don't know. Usually when someone goes missing from the park, we find their body clear on the other side of town. But...you said a creek, so this is a creek."

"Are there others on the other side of town?"

"A few streams, that's all. Why? Could it have been that?"

Grace saw the trail they were heading to. It was larger than she thought, almost like the hike-and-bike trail that followed the road in. She thought back to the image she'd seen...heard. The water was loud, splashing over rocks at a brisk pace. Not something she would attribute to a small stream. "I don't think so," she finally said as she walked up beside Mason. "I didn't get a look at the water, I only heard it. It seemed larger." She spread her hands out. "Speaking of large..."

"The trail is like this around the fields, large and manicured. The real hiking trail will look like the one we were on yesterday."

They didn't speak as they walked. Their boots crunched on the pebbles, breaking the silence. She didn't know how Mason—or anyone else—normally handled the murders, emotionally, at least. Twenty-three years of them. How would anyone react? Business as usual?

"Mason, there weren't copies of the coroner's reports in the file that I have. Also, the FBI profilers didn't give you much. Is there a possibility that there are multiple killers? The cause of death is so different—strangulation, knife wounds, a drowning, blunt force trauma, and so on."

"Yeah, every possible way except gunshot. Profilers got nothing. White male, twenty to forty, a loner, possibly an outcast."

"Agent Kemp said you had what he called mountain men living around here...off the grid."

"Got a few, yeah. Living off the land, using solar power, that sort of thing. Got a few doomsday preppers too. Some of those folks can get pretty crazy, and they're stocked up on supplies and weapons, but for the most part, they're harmless. They live back in the hills and keep to themselves, come into town a few times a year."

"But they've been checked out?"

"Sure, but a lot of them weren't even here when the murders started."

"So could there be multiple killers?" she asked again.

"I guess. Or a copycat."

"Or two acting independently, neither knowing who the other is."

"Isn't that a little farfetched? I mean, we're up here in the mountains, far from any city. There just aren't that many people out here."

The trail came to a fork and as Mason had said, the trail that snaked off into the forest was smaller and not maintained like the one they'd been walking on. It was still wide enough to walk side-by-side and she put her hands into the pockets of her hooded sweatshirt to keep them from swinging and bumping into Mason's.

"Why did you come back to Gillette Park?"

Mason glanced at her. "I thought you already knew that answer."

"I think you used your mother as an excuse."

"Dr. Jennings? Psychology?"

Grace smiled. "Yes, actually."

"You practice?"

"No. I taught, but that wasn't my calling. I got little enjoyment from teaching." She shrugged, wondering if that was the first time she'd said that out loud to someone. She'd convinced herself she would love teaching. It was the opposite of love. She loathed it. "It did nothing more than pay the bills. I got out as soon as I could. I took a visiting professorship in New Orleans. Those always have an end date so I'm not locked in."

"When you consult with the FBI, they pay you a decent amount?"

"Yes."

"And the town is paying you, I know. Uncle Alan didn't say how much."

It wasn't a question and she didn't feel the need to tell her. "I live very simply. My salary from teaching went into savings. My salary from…well, from jobs such as this went to pay off student loans at first. I am currently debt-free and I have enough money in savings to get me through a few years."

"While you write?"

"Yes. So why did you come back?" she asked, changing the conversation back to Mason.

"You mean you don't know?"

Grace shook her head. "I told you, I'm not a mind reader."

"How did you know about my mother?"

"I…I had a dream about you."

Mason laughed. "So you're dreaming about me, huh? Should I be flattered?"

Grace blushed, which caused Mason to laugh again. "It was in the middle of nightmares…I don't think I'd be flattered."

"Why? Nightmares, I mean."

"So who is on whose couch right now? I thought I was asking the questions?"

They came to a small bridge—a footbridge—that crossed the creek. Mason stood in the middle, seeming to survey their position. The creek, while not exceptionally wide, was quite active—clear water flowing at a brisk pace over rocks and boulders. Grace leaned over the side of the handrail, staring into the water, imagining fish in the deeper holes.

The crystal clear water became dark, the deep hole black as night. She saw a face appear…that of a young girl, not Jason Gorman. She was smiling, her blond hair pulled to the sides in two pigtails. The girl lifted a hand, beckoning her? Or perhaps waving at her? Then the smile changed—the mouth opened and the loud scream that bubbled up from the creek turned into a shriek of terror and had Grace covering her ears. The water turned blood red when the girl's face disappeared, as if something—someone—were pulling her under.

"Grace?"

She knew Mason hadn't heard the screams, knew she couldn't see the blood in the water. She lowered her hands and took several deep breaths before she turned, meeting Mason's concerned eyes.

"Was there…was there another found here? At the creek? A girl?"

Mason frowned. "Why? What did you see?"

Grace swallowed. "A young girl was in the water…blond, pigtails, bow in her hair."

Mason's face turned white and she swallowed. "Susan…Susie Shackle was found here." Mason turned to look over the side. "They used to have planks across the creek, not a bridge. She was found lodged under the planks." She looked back up and Grace could tell her hands were shaking. "You…you think saw her?"

"Susie was the first one?"

Mason nodded. "A classmate…a playmate. When I was ten. We lived on the same block."

"She wasn't drowned, though."

"No. Sexually assaulted. Strangled."

Grace nodded. She had made a note to herself while reading the file that not all the girls had been sexually assaulted. That had made her consider the existence of a second killer.

"Back to my earlier question, could there be more than one killer? They're not all sexually assaulted. Of course, that in itself isn't defining. He's killed both boys and girls. I don't think the sexual part of it is what drives him. But why some and not all?"

Mason walked across the bridge to the other side. "You need to read the FBI profilers' reports. They make note of that, but I don't think they thought it was relevant."

"Of course it's relevant. There has to be a reason." She needed to go back and read the file again, this time making notes. Before, she was simply trying to get through it without…well, without having visions and without having her chest ripped open by whatever was attacking her.

"Do you have a guess?"

Grace shook her head. "I'm not a profiler. And I'm not a practicing psychiatrist."

"But you have a guess?"

"No. Truthfully, I haven't studied the file as much as I should have." She moved a little way from Mason, studying the ground and trees, hoping something would look familiar to her. "There's something I didn't tell you." She turned back to Mason. "When the FBI asked me to assist here, I told them I wasn't interested. They sent me the file anyway. The first time I was reading through it, something…something attacked me. I didn't know that's what it was at the time. My throat was closed, my chest was squeezed so tight, I thought I was having a heart attack. I had to…to remove myself from the present. It took almost an hour before the weight was lifted. And it was two days later before I attempted to read the file again. When I felt the attack coming, I closed the file and waited. It took—I don't know—five or six times to get through it just once. So I've read the file, but I haven't had a chance to *thoroughly* read it, to make notes."

"Something…attacked you? In New Orleans?" Mason's tone indicated that she didn't believe her.

Grace gave her a fake smile. "I know you don't understand, Deputy Cooper. Whatever…let's call it a force. Whatever force is out here, you can't see it or hear it or feel it…all you can see is a dead body. The result. Your killer is nothing more than a puppet, I think." She spread her hands out. "Which is why I say there could very well be more than one killer. And why they might not even know they are killing."

"Oh, come on, doc. This has been going on for twenty-three years. If they don't know they're killing…how can they leave no evidence? How can they hide their tracks? How can a car with muddy plates pick up a kid after a soccer game and no one see?"

"Because he doesn't want anyone to see."

They stared at each other and she could see the disbelief in Mason's eyes. It wasn't new to her; there was always disbelief. Until there wasn't.

Mason finally pulled her eyes away and motioned around them. "Any idea where to search? What side of the creek?"

"Are you asking for my opinion or if I have a notion?"

"Both. Whatever." Mason tossed up her hands. "Use your powers."

Grace stared at her for a moment, biting her tongue to keep her retort to herself. "Well, this side makes more sense, since it's farther away from the fields and parking lot. I'm not getting a feeling, though, so it's only a guess."

They walked silently among the trees, keeping the creek in sight. Nothing seemed disturbed to her.

"I'm thinking it's going to be Gillette Creek," Mason said, breaking the silence. "He was abducted here and taken away. I can't see the killer bringing him back here to dump the body."

"He obviously wouldn't drive his car into the lot. This would be quite a hike through the woods, wouldn't it?"

"Yeah. Over the years, though, bodies have been found miles away."

"Yet you've always found them?"

"There are two bodies that were never found. Both girls. They were a few years apart. One was in 2012, I think. The other, maybe 2009 or '10."

"Are you certain they're a part of this? Perhaps they ran away."

Mason shook her head. "No. Too young, I think. One was fourteen, the other thirteen. Good families, happy childhoods. Not runaways. There have been a handful that were found weeks later. One time—and this was while I was away—the kid went missing in April. They didn't find her until the next spring. Some cross-country skiers found her up here in the canyon." Mason waved ahead of them. "This canyon that the creek flows through, it's called Moose Gulch. We can only hike up a little over a mile before it gets really rocky and steep."

"What year was this?"

"I don't remember. We can find it in the file easy enough. She was seventeen. Pregnant."

"Okay, yes. I remember that one. It was really the only body that was badly mutilated."

"Yeah. Some from animals, but…"

"Yes." In other words, no sign of a baby. She pushed that thought aside, trying to think of something more appealing to talk about. "Are there moose here? The canyon—Moose Gulch."

Mason shook her head. "Don't think anyone has seen one in years. Not in my lifetime."

"You're what? You were ten when the first murder happened, so you're…thirty-three?"

"I am."

They walked on in silence, both glancing across the creek from time to time. The canyon was getting steeper, the boulders getting larger. She looked ahead, wondering how far they could go before they gave up.

"Do you search on horseback? Or with dogs?"

"Horseback and on foot. No dogs."

Before she could ask why they didn't use dogs, Mason's cell rang. She used the break to catch her breath and she sat down on a rock. Mason's side of the conversation was mumbled, muted, and she could only make out a word here or there. She could tell by her body language that they had found the boy. Mason pocketed her phone and turned around to face her.

"They found him. Gillette Creek. About a mile in."

She nodded, not knowing what to say.

"Knife this time," Mason continued. "Said he was bloody, head to toe." Mason met her gaze. "They found his soccer ball beside him. That's how they spotted him. The white ball."

Yes. Not a full moon...the soccer ball. Why would the killer bother with the ball? What did it mean? Or was it for her benefit?

"The kid we found a few weeks ago—Donnie Redman—had been strangled." She cleared her throat. "I found him." Mason turned her back to Grace and she could see that her eyes were closed. "He was the first one that I'd found."

"I see." She walked around to face Mason. "And it affected you differently?"

"It did. I don't know why. I've been to the other sites while the body was still there. This time, I was alone. I found him. And I sat with him and..." Her hands were balled into fists and Grace reached out to touch one of them.

"And?" she prompted.

"And I felt helpless and damn useless, that's what. What are we doing here? Kid goes missing. Kid gets murdered. We find kid. Rinse, repeat. Over and over."

"Mason, I'd like to tell you it'll be different this time. In fact, I will tell you that." Mason met her gaze. "It'll be different because I'm here. And if we were only dealing with a killer, I feel confident that I could lead you to him."

"But?"

"There's something else at play here. Even if you find the killer, I don't think it'll stop. He'll just use someone else. Which is why I think you may have multiple killers."

Mason's shoulders dropped. "I don't even know what to say to that."

"No. I don't expect you do. We'll learn more very soon, I think. You have to keep an open mind."

"Open mind? Doc, I'm trying to keep from *losing* my mind."

CHAPTER THIRTEEN

Mason sat at the bar, brooding—yes, she would admit that. She didn't hear the conversations around her, she didn't hear the country music coming out of the jukebox, and she'd missed Gary asking her if she wanted another beer. He brought a fresh one over, the mug frosty and cold. As he took the empty away, she stared at the glass, having no recollection of drinking it.

Scott Kemp had left town with barely a wave and a promise to be back "sometime next month" or sooner, if he got the order. Apparently, his assignment was to get Dr. Jennings up to speed and to only hang around if there was a snag. Guess the FBI didn't think the murder of a twelve-year-old boy was much of a problem. Two boys. Don't forget Donnie Redman. She closed her eyes for a moment, picturing him lying on the forest floor, his hair clean, soft. She knew it was soft because she'd touched it. She'd touched his cheek too. His skin was cold, but soft. A boy. An eleven-year-old boy, his life snatched away from him…for what? To satisfy some crazy with a need to kill? Or worse, if Grace is to be believed. It was the "or worse" part that had her reeling, wasn't it?

Didn't matter. Jason Gorman was number two. As usual, there was nothing. Nothing on video. Nothing where they found him. They even brought in Neal Addick—a hunting guide—to backtrack the route the killer would have used to bring in the body. He lost the trail after about a hundred yards. It was "like something snatched him up where he stood," he said. No more footprints. No broken twigs. No broken branches. No nothing. As usual.

When she'd relayed that information to Grace, she hadn't seemed surprised. Best she could tell, the good doctor was operating under the assumption that whoever was doing the killing was not working alone. And—best she could tell—Grace was also under the assumption that the *something* that was helping wasn't of this physical world. Yeah, that'd be the "or worse" part of this scenario.

She picked up the fresh beer and took a swallow. Yeah, that's what Grace thought. And that, of course, wasn't something she was prepared to deal with. She couldn't wrap her head around it. Couldn't—in all seriousness—even contemplate it. No cop in their right mind would even entertain the notion. Because it was crazy. Crazy talk.

Yet Grace believed it. Grace didn't think it was so crazy.

"She talks to dead people," she murmured as a reminder to herself. Yeah, Grace talked to the dead. Grace also saw little Susie Shackle in the creek, pigtails and all. Susie always wore pigtails. Always. And her mother always clipped a huge bow on the right pigtail. Susie had loved bows. Mason remembered the many times she'd left her house with a damn bow in her own hair, only to rip it off as soon as she was out of sight of the house—and her mother. Mason wondered how many she'd "lost" before her mother stopped putting them in her hair. She would often pass the offending bow off to Susie, who gladly took it from her. That particular day that she'd gone missing, Mason recalled it was a red bow Susie had been wearing. Well, she didn't know if she actually remembered that or if she *thought* she remembered it. It was in the file, what she was wearing, her last whereabouts…and the red bow. Grace had seen a bow. Was it red?

"Do you mind company?"

She didn't turn her head at the sound of Grace's voice. Somehow, she had been expecting her. "I guess that depends if you're looking for good company or not."

Grace sat on the barstool beside her. "Agent Kemp left the rental with me, but I don't know enough about town to get a decent dinner. He said the bar food here was pretty good."

"Gary will even tell you it's healthy, but don't believe him," she said when Gary materialized.

"Get you a beer, ma'am?"

Grace shook her head. "If you've got a good scotch…on the rocks," she said, surprising Mason.

Mason nudged her arm. "Does this mean you're not working?" She heard Grace sigh before answering.

"I'm tired. Not sleeping well."

"You mentioned you had nightmares. You have them often?"

Gary came back with her drink and placed the glass on a napkin, then quietly disappeared again. Grace picked up the glass and swirled the liquid around the ice cubes before taking a sip. She put the glass down again before turning to her.

"No, I don't have them often." She smiled—a quick, small smile— and Mason found herself returning it. She was pretty, attractive. It made her completely forget that Grace talked to the dead. "Some might say my everyday life is a nightmare, so how could I possibly have dreams that frighten me?"

"Do they? Frighten you, I mean."

Grace nodded. "These do, yes. I've been dreaming of the murders, of the town itself. Like a movie that's in fast-forward. As soon as I wake up, I remember it in vivid details. And yes, I'm scared. Shaking. But then it fades so quickly, I can only hold on to snippets here and there. In one scene, I'm locked in a box, in a dungeon or something. There is someone there with me, but then it all fades." She offered the same small smile again. "Then I can't remember *why* I was scared in the first place." She took another sip of her drink. "I dreamed of a young girl. She was knocking at a door. In the room was a man…with a younger woman, a redhead. The little girl was crying."

Mason stared at her, knowing—for some reason—that she wasn't talking about the murders any longer.

"The man in bed with the young woman…his name was Don or John." Grace looked at her apologetically. "Cooper. His last name was Cooper. You were the little girl."

Mason finally looked away from her stare. "Don. His name was Don. Only I was ten when he left…not really a little girl."

"No, you were much younger in my dream. Six, maybe."

She shrugged, feigning disinterest when in reality, she was beyond curious. "Never heard any rumors of him having an affair."

"Maybe the dream didn't mean anything. Perhaps it was symbolic only."

"Why would you have a dream of me?"

"I don't know. Why do I remember that one and not the others?" Grace looked over her shoulder at the gathering crowd in the bar. "Do they know why I'm here yet?"

"Probably not. Uncle Alan and Chief Danner are trying to keep a tight lid on it. Don't want people staring and pointing at the crazy psychic, you know." She tempered her words with a quick smile. "Maybe I should stay in my room and cook dinner instead of going out then. I hate to be stared at."

"Oh, they'll leave you alone. Like I said, people don't really talk about it. And a lot will be more scared of you than curious."

"The other psychic was run out of town."

Mason nodded. "In a way, yes. But she was over the top. Showed up all over town, at all hours, even at school during classes—she didn't care when." Mason frowned, a memory teasing her. She and the psychic—the gypsy—having a conversation. Had they ever spoken? No. She would have remembered that. She shook the memory away. "Of course, there was the séance. That was the kicker."

"I've been meaning to ask you about that." Grace shook her head when Gary came by, silently asking if she wanted another. Mason, too, shook her head. When Gary moved on, Grace continued. "Your uncle said the séance was to try to talk to Susie Shackle."

"Yeah."

"Do you know why? I mean, why Susie, in particular."

Mason shook her head. "I have no idea."

"Who would know?"

"Why does it matter?"

"I don't know, really. Susie was the first. Susie would know more than the others."

Mason had to squeeze her hand tightly around her beer mug to prevent herself from throwing her head back and screaming. She didn't know if she'd label Grace as crazy or not, but she was definitely bordering on creepy. "You talk about them as if they're still people."

"They still exist, yes," Grace said easily. "To me. And to your psychic who was here in 2004." Grace leaned closer to her. "This probably isn't the best place to be having a conversation like this."

"You got that right." She couldn't think of *anywhere* that would be a good place for this conversation. Anywhere or anytime. She finished off her beer, changing the subject. "What's on the agenda tomorrow?"

"What's on *your* agenda?"

Mason spread her hands. "I am to be at your disposal through your stay here or until I'm told otherwise."

"So you're out of the investigation?"

At that, Mason laughed. "Grace, there *is* no investigation."

"You have the body. Forensics—"

"Sure. And they might find an odd fiber or two, a smudge of something or other. Sometimes they do. One time, they found tobacco juice on the clothing, suggesting our killer either chewed or dipped, but there was no DNA. A few times, there have been fibers that didn't match the victim's clothing."

"So the police do nothing?"

"This is the first time we've had anything on video. I mean, the car. They'll continue going over video surveillance, hoping to get a glimpse of the car somewhere around town. Maybe going to the grocery store, the bank...somewhere." She motioned Gary over. "They'll talk to his friends some more, see if someone saw a stranger hanging around, things like that."

"You want another beer, Mason?"

"No. Dinner. What's good tonight?" she asked, knowing he'd say the bacon cheeseburger was exceptional this evening. She, in turn, would order the chicken.

"The bacon cheeseburger seems to be a big seller tonight," he said on cue.

"Guess I'll have the grilled chicken sandwich then. No fries." She turned to Grace. "What about you? Burger or something?"

"Grilled chicken sounds good. I will have fries though."

"Another drink?" he asked.

"No, thanks. I'll take my dinner to go, please."

"Me too," Mason said, ignoring Gary's startled expression as he walked away. She always ate dinner here. "You want to come to my place and talk in private?" The words were out before she fully comprehended their meaning. Did she really invite Grace—the crazy psychic—to her house? Grace hesitated a long moment before answering and Mason wondered what objections she had.

"Okay. Thank you."

Mason leaned closer. "That took a while. What's the issue?"

Grace shook her head. "No issue. I was weighing the sincerity of your offer. I haven't been invited to share dinner with anyone in... well, a very long time."

Mason nodded. "Fair enough." Grace didn't have to say the words. *A freak.* Damn...how hard it must have been growing up with that curse. Not just growing up. Apparently, it still followed her to this day. "To be honest, the offer came out before I really had a chance to contemplate it."

"Do you wish to rescind?"

How rude would it be to say yes? They saw enough of each other as it was. But no, she wouldn't withdraw the offer. She may be a little bit afraid of Dr. Grace Jennings, sure, but she wouldn't resort to blatant rudeness.

"No. Come over to the house."

CHAPTER FOURTEEN

Grace parked in the driveway beside Mason's truck. They were on one of the last streets that butted up against the mountain, in a quaint neighborhood that blended in with the trees. Mason's house appeared to be a rustic cabin built with stone and wood, matching the design of most of her neighbors. This far north, there was still plenty of light in the sky, even though it was nearing eight. There was also a chill in the air this evening, making her wish she'd worn a jacket.

"Home sweet home," Mason said as she pushed the door open and flipped on a light inside. "Nothing fancy, I'm afraid."

"Looks cozy," she said as she went inside.

There was no entryway. The front door opened into a large living area. Off to the right was the kitchen with a bar separating the rooms. Beyond the living room was a hallway where she assumed the bedrooms were. The back wall of the kitchen was a breakfast nook with large windows. A small table was shoved against the windows and there were only two chairs there. The kitchen looked immaculate, as if rarely used. And perhaps it wasn't.

"Water okay? Or something stronger?"

"Water is fine." She put her dinner bag on the table next to Mason's. "You live alone?" There had been no cause for her to even contemplate Mason's personal life, but she knew the answer to the question. She did not sense any other presence in the house.

"Are you asking if I'm single or not?"

"Being single and living alone aren't mutually exclusive." She pulled out a chair and sat down. "I assume you live alone. I *don't* assume you are single." She smiled. "See?"

There was a napkin holder on the table and Mason pulled out two, handing one to her. "Are you curious about my status or simply making conversation?"

"Meaning am I nosing into your personal life?" She took out the sandwich and opened the wrapper. The smell made her mouth water.

"I've noticed whenever we have a conversation, you tend to keep it very formal." Mason bit into her sandwich with a groan. "I missed lunch."

"Yes, I know. I was with you." She took a bite too, relishing the taste of the juicy chicken. "And formal?"

"Yeah. Like…formal. Polite. Overly polite."

Grace smiled. "Okay. So are you single or what?"

Mason laughed. "Yeah. See? Not so formal."

"So?"

"A town this size…and at my age, not a lot of options."

Grace met her gaze. "You mean, options for a lesbian?"

Mason smiled too. "See? If you were still being all formal and polite, you wouldn't have asked that question." She took another bite of her sandwich. "What gave me away?"

"Gave you away?" Grace shook her head. "Nothing, really." Then she frowned. "Why? Are you in the closet?"

"No. Since I've been back, that's not a subject that comes up, though."

"You're kinda young to have given up on love." As soon as she said it, she knew she'd invited questions if Mason was inclined. And apparently she was.

"What about you? Got a guy waiting for you back in New Orleans?"

"A guy?"

"Or gal."

Grace nibbled on one of the potato wedges, wondering how she should answer. The truth seemed far too depressing to say out loud. But she was too old to make up stories about having a lover waiting for her back home. Wasn't she?

"New Orleans isn't really home." She wasn't sure if she was reaffirming that to herself or simply making Mason aware of it. "And no, there's no one waiting on me. Guy or gal." She picked up her sandwich again. "I doubt I'll return to New Orleans when I leave here. October or November...I'll probably head to Florida."

"You think it'll take that long to find our killer?"

"I hope not. But I plan to stay anyway. I need someplace quiet to write. I've got my room booked through October."

"Wow. How much is that going to set you back?"

"It's not cheap, although Donna assured me that she's giving me a break on the price."

Mason leaned her elbows on the table. "So...guy or gal?"

Grace pondered the question. "Do you need a label?"

"Either? Both?"

Grace shook her head. "Neither." She held her hand up, stopping Mason's next question. "Why did you move back to Gillette Park?"

Mason sighed, a long sigh that Grace knew meant she wasn't going to ignore the question this time.

"There was this girl." She smiled quickly, then it faded. "We'd been dating for a couple of years. We still had our own places, but it was serious. Or so I thought." She twisted the cap off her water bottle and took a sip. "I...I asked her to marry me." She put the cap back on. "She said no."

"Ouch."

"Yeah. She...she wasn't ready. Hell, I don't even know if I was, really. But it changed things. We had such a good relationship before and...well, it changed. Mostly my fault."

"You broke up?"

"I suppose you could call it that. I was hurt and embarrassed and—"

"Why embarrassed?"

"Why? Because I had a ring and I got down on one knee—the whole thing. I was so certain that she'd say yes, I wasn't prepared for a 'no.' Anyway, my mother...she needed me here." Mason gave her a half-smile. "And yes, it was an excuse and I took it."

"So what? That was how you broke up? You left?"

"Things had become uncomfortable. Again, my fault. I couldn't get past her saying no and I started dissecting everything about our relationship, wondering where we were headed, if anywhere. I think she was relieved when I left."

"Do you talk?"

Mason shook her head. "Not anymore. At first, we did. Then that dwindled to once a week…then a couple times a month." She shrugged. "I've been back over five years. We haven't spoken in the last two, at least. She's in a new relationship, so…"

"Some people don't need—or want—to get married. You shouldn't take the blame for that or think you weren't worthy or whatever else you're placing on yourself."

"I feel like, because she said no, that I was invested in our relationship much more than she was. I found myself questioning everything she did and said, which wasn't fair. Because you're right. It wasn't that she didn't want to marry *me*…she simply didn't want to get married." Mason stretched her legs out. "I don't still harbor regrets, if that's what you're thinking. If I'd stayed—well, if I hadn't asked her to begin with—we'd still be living apart. Our relationship wouldn't have ever progressed past where we were. So, I'm okay with everything."

"So having a broken heart isn't the reason you don't date now?"

Mason smiled. "Back to what I originally said, a town this size, options are limited."

"But not totally dry?" she guessed.

Mason laughed. "Yeah…pretty dry, Grace. Let's see…in the five years I've been back, I've been on maybe three dates, if you'd even call it that. There's a group in town, they meet once a month. Either at someone's house or out at a restaurant. Sort of a meet-and-mingle type thing. I used to go to that and I made a few friends, but…those that were around my age were already partnered up. Most in the group are older." She stood up and folded up her sandwich wrapper. "In the winter, when things are slower, I'll join them. Summers, I usually stay busy."

As she ate the last bite of her sandwich, she wondered if that was an excuse that Mason used. That the summers were busy, because of the murders. She suspected that Mason rarely joined them in the winter either. None of her concern though. She was simply trying to get along with her well enough to work together. She didn't care one way or the other about her personal life.

"Will you take me to the spot where Jason Gorman was found?"

"Sure. You weren't interested in going today, though," Mason reminded her.

"Too many people. I work much better alone, without an audience. I don't expect to find anything there. I'd simply like to compare where he was found with the vision that I had."

"Okay."

"I'd also like to go back to the bridge…alone."

Mason's eyebrows shot up. "Alone?"

"Yes. I think I can find it easily enough. You could wait in the parking lot."

"Why alone?"

"Less distractions for me…less for them."

"Ah, yes…*them*." Mason sat down again. "I don't mind keeping my distance, but staying in the parking lot is too far. If something should happen to you, then…"

Mason left the rest unsaid because she obviously had no idea what could happen to her. The only fear Grace had was that she would disappear into another realm and lose track of time. She'd been doing this long enough that she wasn't actually *afraid* of the other side. Not physically, anyway. Unwarranted fears—like a child might get from watching a horror movie—snuck in sometimes, clouding her judgment, making her question what was real and what wasn't.

"Is it possible for me to get access to the police file? Or the complete file, I should say."

"I thought you had a copy."

"The M.E. or coroner's reports are missing on a lot of them."

"Yeah. Scott should have that too. The FBI put together a comparison a few years ago. Keep in mind that over the last twenty-three years, there have been many different medical examiners involved. Police department is different, sheriff's department is different. Different guys doing the reporting. There's not a pattern, though, Grace. Some of the strangulations were done by wire, some by rope, some by hand. Some died by asphyxiation. Even the knife wounds are different. Different knives, different strike patterns."

"Which all suggests different killers."

Mason nodded. "We know that's a possibility, but not probable. At least according to the FBI profilers it's not probable. If that was the case, you'd have to have serial killers working in sync."

"Yes, for twenty-three years. I get that."

"Copycat killer…that's been tossed about. But out here? Maybe in a large city, but here in Gillette Park? It's not that kind of town. Low crime rate. In fact, other than the murders, there's really no crime at all. Not with the locals. Now, during the summer months, when tourists come around, sure, there'll be some petty stuff. Even then, it's hardly worth mentioning."

"Drugs?"

"Some high schoolers from time to time get into trouble, not much else. The town has grown, brought in new people, new businesses, but the crime rate has stayed the same. The population is older, maybe that's why."

"Older?"

"There's not much opportunity for kids after graduating high school. Most leave for college and don't return. Or if they do, it's when they're already married and have a family and are returning to their roots—and returning to parents and grandparents. You'd be hard-pressed to find twenty-somethings here."

"But the town has grown. Who moves here?"

"Young retirees, mostly. And a lot from the tech industry, those who work from home. Some come to catch the tourists. Got some new businesses in the old downtown area that cater to them."

"And the murders don't scare them away?"

"Well, like I said before, it's more of an Old Town thing."

"Surely some of the victims have been from the new influx of people."

"Sure. Some. Not Jason Gorman, although his parents would fall into the left-and-came-back group. Mr. Gorman has an online business that he manages."

Grace shook her head. "I'm not sure—if I grew up here and knew about the murders—that I'd be able to come back with young kids. That's got to be so hard."

"I'm sure it is. I'm sure guilt will eat at the Gormans too."

"How many victims are there, Mason?"

"Jason Gorman makes fifty-five."

"My god," she murmured.

"You think about a town this size—fifteen thousand people now—a couple of murders a year isn't that unusual. What's unusual is that the murders are random and that they happen to young kids. A town this size, if it's anywhere else, your murders are going to be drug-related or gang-related or they'll occur during an armed robbery or home invasion or some other violent crime. Not random. That's the difference."

So many questions, Grace thought. Her instincts told her there was more than one killer, but she could see how that made no sense whatsoever. The fact that it had been going on for twenty-three years was nearly too much to comprehend. Add in that people seemed to accept it as a way of life and you had a horror movie in the making.

She pushed away from the table. "I should go. Thank you for dinner and the company."

"My pleasure," Mason said with a smile. "What time should I pick you up?"

"Not too terribly early. I want to read through the file again and I'd rather do it in the light of day," she admitted. "About nine?"

Mason walked her outside and they both paused, looking overhead at the myriad of twinkling stars in the clear sky, their brightness obscured somewhat by the rising moon. The chilly air made her shiver.

"Are the nights always cold?"

"Depends on your definition of cold. The elevation here is over eight thousand feet. Even in the heart of summer, the nights are pleasantly cool." Then she smiled. "Coming from New Orleans, one might say cold. I did hear a front was coming in, though. Snow in the higher elevations only. I doubt you'll be subjected to it."

"It's beautiful here, Mason. You have a nice home." She tilted her head. "It suits you."

"Oh?"

"A little rugged, yet nice around the edges." She turned, then called over her shoulder, "See you in the morning."

CHAPTER FIFTEEN

Lucy heard the baby crying and it reminded her—once again—of when she was all alone and very scared when Faith was born. Stacy had been noncommittal on whose baby it was. From the sound, it was close to their own room. That suggested that it might be someone like her. Someone locked in here, against her will. If so, they were quiet. Much like she and Faith were quiet. Sometimes she could hear a woman's voice, trying to hush the baby. Sometimes she could hear Stacy pushing a cart. Probably a cart with a food tray, like she brought them twice a day.

"Momma, I have something to tell you."

Lucy looked at Faith, who was sitting at her normal spot at their tiny table. She moved away from the door—and the sound of the baby—and joined her. The first time Faith had said those words to her, she'd come out with such a tale, Lucy had been shocked speechless. Then, of course, she'd attributed it to their situation. Faith had no friends so of course she would make up some—someone to talk to, to play with. She hadn't been worried, really. She could only entertain Faith so much. They were limited with their books. They were limited with toys. Then one day, while Faith was in the corner, playing with one of her "friends," Lucy saw the car move across the floor. Faith had laughed while Lucy stared—speechless—watching as the car returned to the other side again. Faith had laughed and had told her friend, Susie, to "do it again" and Lucy's mouth had dropped open as the car once again raced across the floor.

She liked it much better when she simply thought Faith had imaginary friends. At first, she thought maybe Faith was like someone Lucy had seen in the movies when she was a kid. They moved things with their mind. Yes, she'd rather think that than to believe one of her "friends" had moved the car. But then other things would happen. Faith would let her know well in advance when Stacy was going to make an appearance. And Faith told her there would be a baby several days before Lucy heard the first cry. Yes, Faith seemed to *know* things. Things that *they* told her. Her friends.

With a patient sigh, she folded her hands together, giving her daughter her full attention. As usual, Faith seemed to read her thoughts and smiled reassuringly at her.

"It's okay, Momma."

Lucy smiled back at her. "What do you need to tell me, honey?"

Faith's expression turned serious. "There is someone in town, Momma."

"In town?"

"Yes."

"Do you know what a town is?"

"Of course. It's where people live. You used to live there."

"Gillette Park?"

"Yes. Someone came to town. Remember, I told you someone was coming to help us."

She met her daughter's gaze. "Help us do what, honey?"

Faith chewed her lower lip, as if thinking. "A boy was killed the other night. Jason. And in a few days, April will be killed."

This wasn't the first time Faith had said something like that. Over the years, she'd announce—seemingly out of the blue—that a little girl or a boy had been killed. Lucy didn't know what to make of it. She knew all about the murders in town, the boys or girls who would go missing. Like her. Only she wasn't killed like the rest of them. The murders were still going on, apparently. The serial killer. That's what Faith was talking about, she was sure of it.

"This lady is going to find us here," Faith continued. "The lady is going to get us out of here."

"How?"

"Susie is going to help her. But Rusty is mad. Rusty wants to kill this lady. Grace. Her name is Grace."

Yes, Susie was her friend, the one she mentioned most often. And yes, she'd heard Faith mention Rusty before. Rusty was mean. Rusty liked the killings. They made Rusty happy.

"Who is this woman?" she heard herself asking.

"She's like me, Momma."

"Like you?"

"Yes. She can see all my friends too."

Lucy closed her eyes for a second, wondering what response Faith was expecting from her. When she opened them, Faith was whispering, her head turned to her right. Lucy stared at the empty spot, feeling the hairs on the back of her neck stand at attention. Who was in the room with them?

"Grace needs help, though. There's a police officer who is going to help her."

"I see."

"Susie says you're going to have to be ready."

Lucy swallowed. "Be ready?" she asked weakly.

"Not yet, Momma. It'll be a little while yet. Things aren't quite ready, she says. Because Rusty—well, Susie hasn't been able to talk to Grace." Then she nodded, as if Susie was reminding her of something. "Oh, right. And the baby and his mommy, they're going to need our help too."

"The mommy is…what did you say her name was? Abby?"

Faith nodded. "She's been here a long time too."

"She has?"

"Not as long as us, though. She named her baby Andrew. That was her daddy's name," Faith said matter-of-factly. "There's another girl here. She's fifteen now. Her mommy was killed after she was born. She lives with Stacy now. She thinks Stacy is her mother, but she's really not."

Lucy knew Faith was being serious, but she wasn't sure if this information was real or if Faith was using her imagination to fill in the blanks. Because—

"It's real, Momma. Not my imagination."

Oh dear lord. Lucy stood up quickly and took several steps away from her daughter.

"I'm sorry, Momma. I don't want to scare you."

Lucy held her hand up. "Stop. Just…stop. That's enough for now." She waved her hand. "Go…read a book or something."

Faith didn't move from the table and Lucy was dismayed to see she had tears in her eyes.

"I'm sorry," Faith mumbled in a childlike voice.

Lucy hurried over to her. "No, honey. I'm sorry." She pulled her into an embrace. "Sometimes, yes, you scare me."

"Susie says...you have to trust me. Susie says you have to do exactly as I say."

At that, Lucy pulled away. "That's what Susie says, huh? You do remember that I'm the mother, right?"

Faith nodded, but she didn't smile. "Susie says you have to do as I say because it's what *she* says. She says she has a plan."

Lucy turned away from her, not wanting to talk about it any longer. The last few weeks, the last month, it seemed that Faith was mentioning Susie and her friends a lot more often. Too often. Sometimes she feared—stuck in here like they were—that Faith was losing her mind. Who wouldn't go crazy in here? She sometimes wanted to give in to the craziness too.

"I'm not losing my mind. Neither are you. We're going to get out of here."

Lucy didn't turn back around to look at her. She couldn't.

CHAPTER SIXTEEN

"You make it through the file without incident?"

"I did. And I'm starving. Can we stop at Dottie's?"

"Sure. We're on your time schedule, not mine," she said as she pulled out of the Aspen Resort parking lot. "Craving a muffin?"

"Something."

"Did you get coffee?"

"Yes. Agent Kemp bought the essentials that first day. I had two cups while I read through the file."

"Learn anything new?"

"Not really. I'm trying to get more familiar with the murders, that's all. I'm sure the FBI has put all of this data into some fancy program, looking for a pattern."

"They have. Several times, I think." She pulled into a parking space in front of Dottie's and cut the engine. "Uncle Alan called me this morning, wanted to know if we had an update. I told him what you had planned today."

"Did you tell him about the bridge? About what I saw?"

"No. I was going to." She smiled a bit apologetically. "It sounded a little crazy in my mind so I didn't say anything."

"If you want me to be the one to tell him the 'crazy' stuff, I will. Not sure how that's going to help them, though."

"Yeah, well—he's invited us over for dinner tonight. Aunt Carol's meatloaf and mashed potatoes."

"Okay. I can't promise I'll have anything to report, but a home-cooked meal sounds good." They got out of the truck, but before they went inside, Grace stopped her. "You're closer to your aunt and uncle than your mother?"

"Does it show?"

"A little. There's a tone of affection in your voice when you speak of them."

Mason shrugged. "When my dad left, my mother...well, she changed. And we clashed over every little thing. And she started drinking a lot. Uncle Alan and Aunt Carol...their house was a refuge. They were happy and stable and I got along with my cousins—still do. I spent more time over there than my own house." She opened the door to Dottie's. "They treat me more like a daughter than a niece."

"It's good that you had someone."

"Oh, Grace. I'm sorry. I didn't—"

"No, don't apologize. My dysfunctional life is a product of my own doing. Nothing for you to apologize for."

Grace led them to the corner booth and Mason followed. "How old were you when you knew...well, that you—"

"That I was different? Very young. Five or six, maybe."

"Jesus, didn't that scare the shit out of you?"

Grace gave her a quick laugh. "I didn't know that it wasn't normal. And, of course at first, my mother just thought that I had imaginary friends."

"Good morning, Mason." Helen looked at Grace. "I'm sorry, what was your name again?"

"Grace. Good morning, Helen."

Helen was already pouring coffee for them. "Your usual?"

"For me, yes."

"What other kind of muffins do you have?" Grace asked.

"Our most popular is banana nut, with or without chocolate."

"Yes, I'll have one of those." Grace looked at her quickly and smiled. "With chocolate."

* * *

They each had two cups of coffee and finished off their muffins. Grace hadn't seemed in a hurry to get started and Mason relaxed as their conversation drifted from personal to generic. Grace seemed genuinely interested in the town and its history and Mason talked freely about growing up there, back when Gillette Park was still a quiet town and not the small city it had become.

Forty-five minutes later, they were back in the truck, heading to the south side of town where Gillette Creek flowed through town and disappeared back into the mountains.

"This is different than the other day," Grace observed.

"We were on the north side then, where the creek flows into town. This is where it flows back out and into the mountains again."

"Is there a trail like the other one?"

"No. The guys parked and hiked along the creek, following the canyon down. He wasn't very far in. A mile."

"So our killer would have had to park in the same spot?"

"No evidence that he did." She turned off of the side road, finding the small parking area. "Here it is. There are no cameras on this exact spot, but there are on the roads leading to it. Nothing on surveillance to indicate anyone had been here that night."

"So how did he get the body here to the creek?"

"Had to have been through the forest."

Grace nodded. "Your guy lost the trail. Right?"

"Yeah." She got out, then pulled up her handheld GPS where she'd already plugged in the coordinates of where they'd found Jason Gorman. "There's no trail, so be careful."

As was the norm for this time of year, the sky was clear, the air still cool. By noon, it would be warm and pleasant, and then by five or six, the coolness would return again. That pattern would hold until mid-June, when the daily clouds would build, bringing afternoon showers which would dump brief, heavy rain then be gone as quickly as they had come. A break from that pattern this week, though. The cold front would hit them tonight. Tomorrow would be much colder.

She loved the summers and fall the best. When she was a kid, she loved winter and the snow, skiing, and sledding. Since she'd been back, though, she did little more than tolerate the winter months. Living in warm and sunny LA ruined her. She didn't miss the traffic, the hordes of people, the crime...but god, she missed sunny days on the beach in January.

"What are you musing about?"

Mason looked over at Grace as she held a branch out of the way for her. "Am I musing?"

"Smiling."

"Yeah, I was thinking how nice it is today. How nice it'll be all summer, really. And then I thought about the dreaded snow and how great it was to be able to go to the beach in January and work on a tan."

"Not a fan of snow, huh?"

"Not really. Things slow to a crawl and unless you're fond of winter sports, cabin fever sets in quickly."

"You look fit, athletic. You don't ski?"

"Do you?"

Grace laughed. "I've seen snow two times in my life and both times were freak snowstorms in the South."

They both ducked down below an overhanging limb near the creek's edge. "I cross-country ski some, mostly as an excuse to get outside. There are a lot of hills around where you can sled and when I was a kid, I loved it."

"I imagine it's very beautiful. Postcard perfect."

"It is. And it makes for a lovely scene at Christmas and the holidays. But once January gets here, the weeks seem to crawl by. Warm days that tease of spring, then a storm will come and dump a foot of snow. It seems endless, until one day…the snow stops coming." She paused to check her GPS. "Two hundred more feet."

They were silent as they walked on and she slowed her pace as they approached. The crime scene tape had been taken down—mostly to prevent the curious from coming out and trampling the area. She could see broken twigs and kicked-over rocks. They were only about twenty feet from the creek's edge.

Grace walked around her and Mason stood back, letting her work. By the expression on Grace's face, she assumed they weren't alone. That thought sent shivers down her spine and she took a step back, moving away from something unseen—unheard. She found herself holding her breath as she saw Grace's lips move, as if silently talking. She moved around in a wide circle, and again, Mason took a step away. *Damn, but this is some crazy shit, isn't it?*

"It's too new…too fresh."

Mason swallowed. Was that a good thing?

Grace came toward her. "I meant those words for you, not him."

"Oh." She relaxed. "So…nothing is here? Right?"

"He's here, yes."

She felt her muscles tense again. "So…?"

"Let's go."

"Okay by me," she mumbled quickly, spinning on her heels. She heard Grace's quiet laughter behind her.

"I thought you didn't believe in this? Besides, he won't hurt you. Even if he wanted to, he couldn't. They're not in our physical realm, Mason."

"Easy for you to say," she murmured, then stopped. "Say I did believe in this. Why is he here? As opposed to where he was killed?"

"This is where his body was. From my experience, though, they move around."

"Great," she said dryly. *Just great.*

"You don't have to be afraid."

Mason held up her hand. "So…like what? Everybody who dies…there's this…this spirit or whatever…hanging around? Like… *everybody?*"

Grace shook her head. "No, Mason. At least, not in the sense that you're talking about."

"Then *who* do you see?"

"Those who want to be seen. Even psychics—or mediums—who promise to call up a deceased loved one can't always fulfill that. It's assumed—by my profession—that those are the ones who don't want to be seen or heard, for whatever reason. Maybe they died peacefully and don't want to come back. Maybe they're in a place that they don't want to leave." She shrugged. "Just guesses, of course. There's no way to be sure."

"So he's here, but he's not talking. Like the girl at the swing?" *God, am I really having this conversation?*

"He's hiding. Like I said, it's new. He doesn't know what to do yet. This site and the one you found, they're too fresh. I think we should concentrate on past years."

They retraced their steps, Mason's mind full of questions she dare not ask. She had to stop herself several times from glancing behind them, fearing that…that *something* would be following them.

The breeze picked up, rustling the trees, and she nearly jumped when a branch brushed her face. She did turn then, looking behind them. There was nothing there, of course. But she stopped, her brows drawn together. She could see the gypsy woman in her mind, her colorful beads—four or five necklaces—all mixed together around her neck. She had bright red lipstick—she remembered that. A memory, though, like last night, was flitting about in her mind, but she couldn't pull it to the surface.

"What is it?"

She looked at Grace, blinking away the elusive memory. She shook her head. "Nothing."

Grace stared at her for a moment, one eyebrow arched enough to disappear into her bangs. Mason wondered if she was trying to read her, to get inside. Then Grace turned away and continued walking.

Mason did too, glancing back behind them once more.

Just in case.

CHAPTER SEVENTEEN

"I'm sure. Stay here."

Mason bit her lower lip. "I'd feel better if I came with you."

At that, she laughed. "Oh, Mason, *really*? You know you're lying. You'd feel better if you stayed here with the doors locked."

Mason smiled a bit sheepishly. "Okay, so, you're right. But, I'm supposed to shadow you. I'm supposed to be with you. I'm your handler, remember?"

"I'll be fine." She paused. "Are you worried about *me* or worried that I'll attempt a séance without your uncle's permission?"

"I'm not *worried* about you. Whatever the hell you're trying to do here," she said, motioning out to the woods, "isn't something I can help with. Like you said, not in our physical realm. Whatever the hell that means."

Ah. So Mason was back to being Mason, she of the nonbeliever sect. She thought Grace was crazy. That hurt a little. After last night, she thought they'd…well, not bonded, exactly. But she thought they'd talked enough that perhaps Mason could get past the "she's crazy" thoughts. Apparently not.

"She's more likely to talk to me if I'm alone."

"Really? You know, when we were kids, we used to be playmates. Me and Susie."

Grace stared at her, wondering at her tone. A bit sarcastic. A bit…
patronizing? She lifted her chin defiantly. "If you want to go that
badly, come on then. Maybe you and Susie can catch up, reminisce
and all that."

"Okay, so now you're making fun of me?"

"Making fun? Wasn't that what you were doing to me?"

"Oh, crap," Mason muttered as she ran a hand through her hair.
"This shit freaks me out. That's all I'm saying…it freaks me out!"

"Oh for god's sake." Grace held her hand up. "Mason, give me
twenty minutes. If I'm not back, then come find me. Okay? Twenty
minutes."

They stared at each other and she could see the indecision in
Mason's eyes. Mason didn't want to go, but she felt like she needed to.
As she warred with herself, Grace turned and headed toward the trail.

"Okay, so yeah, I guess I'll stay here then."

"Thought that would be your answer," she replied without
turning back.

She didn't know why she was angry. Mason was no different
than anyone else. Maybe that was the problem. She wanted her to be
different. She'd hoped—just this once—that she'd met a person who
wasn't "freaked out" by her. Was that too much to ask? Just this once.
Mason was her own age, she was attractive. Just this once, couldn't she
meet someone who liked her? Who didn't judge her? Why couldn't
she meet someone like Angelique? She blew out her breath, pushing
her thoughts aside. She was here working, not looking for Angelique.
And Mason Cooper certainly was *not* Angelique.

It was cold enough that her breath still frosted and she pulled
the hood up over her head. She had on both her hooded sweatshirt
and her jacket this morning. She stepped on the main trail, the wide
hike-and-bike trail that circled the fields. She kept a watch for the
cutoff that would take her to the right, through the trees and onto
the other, less-used trail that would pass out of the park and into
the national forest. She couldn't remember how far the footbridge
was, but she didn't think it was far. When she came to the cutoff, she
glanced back at Mason's truck before she took the trail into the trees.
She had an uneasy feeling all of a sudden, and she almost waved to
Mason, beckoning her to come after all. Almost. But she told herself
she was being silly. There was nothing to fear. Isn't that what she'd
told Mason?

She kept her mind clear, glancing occasionally at her
surroundings—the tall trees, the smaller underbrush, rocks, fallen
limbs…the sound of branches rustling as the stiff breeze filtered

through them. She could hear the creek in the distance, could picture the clear water as it gurgled over and around the boulders that cluttered the stream. When her mind went to Susie Shackle, she forced it back to the trees, the sound of her boots on the trail, the smell of the forest.

She saw the footbridge a short time later, and she stopped for a moment, taking note of how quiet it was suddenly. The strong breeze had disappeared, the leaves of the quaking aspen trees were still. She could no longer hear the creek, even though she was within sight of it now. She could, however, hear her heart beating, hear each breath she took. She moved on, closer to the bridge now. She wasn't alone.

* * *

Mason tapped on the steering wheel, her eyes alternating between the trees where Grace had disappeared and the watch on her wrist. It had been nine minutes. Grace probably wasn't even at the bridge yet. She tapped the steering wheel a little faster, a little harder. Something wasn't right. Something…wasn't right. She didn't know how she knew it, but her intuition was very strong. Maybe it was the look Grace had given her before she'd disappeared into the trees.

She opened the door, still hesitating. Grace asked for twenty minutes. Did she really want to rush off into the forest and come upon Grace and…and Susie Shackle having a conversation?

"Hell no."

She closed the door and resumed her tapping as the seconds crawled by. After another minute, she was practically drumming the steering wheel.

"Oh, screw it," she muttered as she opened the door again and stepped out into the cold.

* * *

Grace's footsteps seemed hollow as she walked out onto the footbridge, stopping in the middle of the creek. She was nervous, which was unusual for her. She was in her element now…this was familiar. With a deep breath, she pushed the hood off her head and moved to the short handrail, resting her thighs against it as she looked into the water. Ten, twenty seconds later, a face appeared. A young girl, blond hair, pigtails. The girl smiled at her.

"You came back."

"Yes."

"Come closer," the girl said with a giggle. *"Come play with me."*

The other day when they were here, Susie didn't speak to her. Grace had studied her picture this morning, had heard her voice in her mind. The voice in her mind was the one she'd heard back in New Orleans, begging her to come. This wasn't it. Something wasn't right, but she didn't know what.

"How old are you, Susie?"

More giggles and Grace would swear they were from more than one child. Susie bobbed in the water now, her face and head above the flowing creek. Her hair was wet and hung limply on her shoulders. The bow in her hair was drenched and faded. She stared at the bow. A faded blue bow.

No. It should be red. It was red the other day, she was certain. According to the file—which she'd read again that morning—Susie had been wearing a red bow the day she disappeared. Before she could take a step away from the railing, a hand shot out of the water and grabbed her wrist. Grace screamed as the arm—six or eight feet in length—recoiled, pulling her along with it. She screamed again, holding on to the railing with her other hand, but she wasn't strong enough to hold herself against the force pulling her.

"Mason! Help! *Mason!*" she screamed.

The little wooden handrail gave way and Grace tumbled into the cold, icy waters of Boulder Creek. The hold on her wrist disappeared, and she clawed at the rocks as the rushing water threatened to drag her under the bridge. It wasn't very deep and she was able to stand, the water just above her thighs. She looked around frantically, trying to gain a foothold. She took one step, then was pushed hard from behind. When she tried to turn, a hand twisted into her hair, forcing her head into the water. She struggled to free herself, her eyes wide under the rushing water, her lungs about to burst.

"Come play! Come play! Come play!"

* * *

Mason ran, sprinting as fast as she could toward the bridge, Grace's scream still echoing in the trees. Grace wasn't on the bridge, however.

"Grace?" she yelled, her eyes darting around almost frantically, looking for her. "*Grace?*"

When she saw the broken railing, she nearly flew across the bridge. "Oh my god." Grace was in the creek, her arms flailing, her head under the water as if…as if someone were holding her down.

"No!" She jumped over the side, into the creek, jerking Grace up in one motion. Grace swung wildly with her arm, her hand connecting squarely with Mason's jaw.

"It's okay, it's me," she said, stopping Grace's next attempt at a swing. "It's me."

Grace's eyes were wide as she took deep breaths. It was only then that Mason felt the cold, felt Grace tremble. She'd only been in the water a few seconds and her legs were already numb. How cold must Grace be?

"Come on."

Grace had a death grip on her arm. "Don't let go," she said through chattering teeth. "Don't let go of me."

"I've got you, I won't let go," she said just as she slipped on a rock and nearly took them both into the creek again. "Sorry."

"It's so cold, Mason."

"I know. Come on."

They stumbled onto the bank of the creek, to a pile of rocks that were bathed in sunshine. The jacket was drenched and the hooded sweatshirt Grace was wearing was soaked and clinging to her. Mason stood and motioned for her to hold her arms up. She pushed the wet jacket off, then took the bottom of the sweatshirt and pulled it up and over her head. She was wearing a long-sleeved shirt beneath it—navy blue—and it, too, was wet.

Mason took her own jacket off—one she'd almost left in the truck—and draped it over Grace's shoulders.

"Are you okay?"

Grace met her gaze and Mason saw that she was still trembling. From cold or fear, she couldn't discern which. Grace pointed into the creek.

"Something….something—" She didn't finish, though. She stared at the water, a frightened look in her eyes. That frightened look nearly made Mason's skin crawl.

She took Grace's hand and pulled. "Let's go. We need to get you warm."

Grace stood up, only to stumble. "My legs are numb. I don't know if I can walk."

"How long were you in the water?"

"I…I don't know." She shook her head. "I don't know."

Mason squeezed her arm, making Grace look at her. "Grace, *why* were you in the water?"

"Someone…something…pulled me in."

Mason looked back at the bridge, seeing the broken handrail. Could Grace have broken that by herself? A gust of wind rifled through the trees, making them sway overhead. A large black and blue bird landed on a stump near the water's edge, its head tilted sideways as it watched them.

"What is it?"

"Steller's jay. Looks like he's watching us."

Grace stared up at the bird too. "Yes, I'm afraid he is."

Was she talking about the bird? Or something else?

Or both?

"Let's get out of here."

CHAPTER EIGHTEEN

Grace sat on Mason's sofa, wrapped in a blanket. She'd already taken a hot shower, but she couldn't seem to get the chill out of her bones. She was wearing a pair of Mason's sweatpants and a sweatshirt. Mason had thrown all her wet clothes into the dryer.

"Here…drink this."

Grace didn't ask what it was. A light brown liquid in a glass tumbler, it burned her throat as she swallowed it, heating her to the core instantly. Whiskey. She coughed once, then handed the glass back to Mason.

"Thank you."

Mason sat down beside her, surprising her by taking her hands and rubbing them between her own.

"You still feel cold. Maybe I should take you to the hospital," Mason said for the third time.

"I do not have hypothermia. I'm coherent. I'm not dizzy, I'm not confused."

Mason let go of her hands but didn't move away from her. "Are you ready to talk about it?"

Grace gave her a weak smile. "I'm pretty sure you won't believe me. Crazy psychic woman, you know."

Mason ignored her statement. "When I saw you…it was like somebody was…was holding you down."

"Yes. They were." She patted Mason's hand lightly. "Thank you for coming to find me. I…I thought I was going to drown. I couldn't hold my breath a second longer."

"I heard you scream, I heard you yell for me." Mason surprised her by taking her hand again. "If I'd waited the full twenty minutes like you said—"

"You would have been too late, I imagine," she finished for her. She untangled their fingers, not wanting to be clingy with someone she barely knew—with someone who thought she was crazy. "This has never happened to me before. Nothing has ever been…been physical with me. Not like this."

"Tell me what happened."

She leaned back against the sofa, wrapping the blanket a little tighter around her. "You won't believe me."

"Tell me anyway. And I don't think you're crazy."

"Yes, you do."

"No, I don't. I don't understand it, that's all. It's easy to say 'crazy' when you can't comprehend something. I don't think you're crazy, Grace."

"I frighten you."

"Yes." Her expression softened a bit. "No. The situation scares me, not you. So tell me what happened."

Grace took a deep breath, feeling very tired all of a sudden. "I had this…this voice in my head of what Susie would sound like. I'd studied her picture, read her part of the file several times. When I got to the bridge, she was there, like I expected. But it was different. Different from the other day. When she spoke, it wasn't like what I was expecting. She didn't really say anything. It was like she was… toying with me. Teasing, but not in a playful way." She rolled her head to the side, meeting Mason's gaze. "It was the bow. It should have been red. It was red the other day. The file said it should have been red." She shook her head. "But it was blue. The bow was blue today."

"What does that mean?"

"It means it wasn't her. It was someone pretending to be her."

Mason grabbed the bridge of her nose, her eyes closing briefly. "Then what."

"A hand grabbed me…an arm came out of the water." She swallowed, knowing this is where she'd lose Mason. This is when

Mason would start thinking the "crazy" word again. "A long arm. Eight...ten feet. It pulled me in. I...I tried to hold onto the railing. That's when I screamed, when I called for you. I could feel the railing start to break, knew it wouldn't hold. Then I don't know—I was under the water, I couldn't get out. Something was holding me down, under the water."

"That's how it was when I saw you. Facedown in the water, something pushing you, holding you down. But when I reached you, there wasn't any resistance."

"No. Because you can't see or hear or feel them." She swallowed again. "But I can." She folded her hands together under the blanket. "I think I'm scared, Mason." She gave a nervous laugh. "I know I told you there was nothing to fear...but, I think, for me...there is."

"I can't even begin to understand this."

Grace looked at her without blinking. "Yes, you can. You don't want to say it out loud, but you do understand what's happening here because you *saw* it happening."

Mason got up and moved away from the sofa. She stood with her back to her, facing the unlit fireplace.

"What do I understand, Grace? That some dead person was holding you under the water? Someone pretending to be ten-year-old Susie Shackle was trying to drown you?"

She leaned back against the cushion and stared at the ceiling. "I see, hear...talk to dead people. On their terms, not mine. They're not evil. They're not really good or bad...they're just there. A spirit, as you call it." She took a deep breath. "Usually. But there's something else this time. Something that *is* evil. Something I'm not seeing. Something that, I think, could be driving the murders."

Mason turned to her, one hand brushing through her dark hair nervously. "And this is where you start freaking me out. Christ, we're talking about ghosts!"

"Stop thinking of them as ghosts."

"Should I think of them as people?"

"If that'll help, yes."

Mason turned away again. "I can't even begin to comprehend this," she said, almost to herself. She turned to face her again. "Tell me what you're saying. About this evil thing. There's something supernatural out here? Is that what you're saying?"

Grace struggled to keep a smile from her face. Supernatural? Just what was Mason's definition of supernatural? Ghosts, obviously. Scary things going bump in the night?

What did she say to that without sounding like she needed to be committed? What could she say that wouldn't make her sound like a damn freak? Because for some reason, she didn't want Mason to think she was a freak. She normally didn't give it much thought any longer—she had a so-called gift and she used it for good, as best she could. The people she met along the way tended to keep their distance and view her with polite curiosity at best. No one wanted to get too close…just in case. Just in case the dead she was talking to decided to talk to *them* instead.

With Mason, she didn't want to feel that indifference. It mattered what Mason thought of her. It mattered because she felt that, if given the chance, she and Mason could become friends. As much as Mason didn't believe everything she said—and still thought she might be crazy—she could feel them becoming close. And that was something that happened to her so rarely, she didn't want to do or say anything that would jeopardize it. Because something told her she and Mason needed to be close, needed to be as one. Something told her they needed to form an unbreakable bond to defeat this…whatever *this* was.

"I can't be sure what it is," she said carefully. "All I know is that whatever's on the other side, it's evil. Maybe it's something that's here, that's been here all along. It might have nothing to do with the murders."

Mason met her gaze, holding it, not shying away for once. Grace knew she was trying to read her, trying to read between the lines.

"That's not what your gut tells you, though, is it?"

Grace let out a long breath. "No. There was a warning issued that first day when you took me out. And today…well, this was more than a warning. I'm not wanted here."

"Because you can get too close."

"Yes. Because I think it has *everything* to do with the murders. And I can get too close."

Mason moved away from the fireplace and sat down beside her again with a weary sigh. "Okay. So, what's the plan?"

Grace smiled at that. "Plan? I don't have a plan, Mason." She sobered. "This hasn't happened to me before. I'm…for the first time since I was a kid, I'm afraid of what I see, what I hear."

"You mean when you first knew you had a gift?"

"Yes. At first, I wasn't able to tell the difference between what was real and what wasn't. I think I was six or seven, maybe, when I couldn't make my mother see this lady I was talking to. The lady literally disappeared into thin air, as they say, right before my eyes. That was the first time I realized these people I saw—talked to—weren't real. It was a few years later, though, that I realized they were, well, dead people. To my young mind, they were ghosts and yes, it scared the crap out of me. I tried to shut it off, but I couldn't."

"Is this when your family, your mother, started worrying about you?"

"Worrying that I was crazy, you mean? Yes. And it's also when I realized that these ghosts, as I called them then, weren't harming me. I didn't have a reason to be afraid." She paused, meeting Mason's gaze. "They became my friends," she said quietly. "I wasn't a freak to them." She looked away from Mason. "And I know how crazy that sounds."

"I'm not judging you, if that's what you're thinking. Frankly, I think I would have gone stark raving mad if it was happening to me."

"Your adult mind says that now. Children are a lot more open-minded." She held her hand up. "The point of this, though, is that in all my years—I'm thirty-four—I've never had something like this happen to me. Sometimes they will be tricksters, but it's playful. Sometimes the tricks are played on other people, for my benefit. Like a joke just between us. Nothing like this. This was…evil. Whatever this is, it had control of me. Physically." She shook her head. "Not physically, in your sense," she explained. "It was through mental manipulation, so that it was *physical* to me. Not to you. You saw me in the water, alone."

"Like you were lying facedown in the water of your own accord. The only reason I knew you were in distress—other than it's early May and the water is still freezing—was that your arms were fighting whatever was holding you down."

"Yes. And because it's not physical to you, you were able to pull me up without any problem. You did not have to fight with this…this *thing* that had me."

"That's to our advantage, isn't it? He can't hurt you then."

"Are you going to protect me around the clock?"

"If I have to."

Grace smiled. "You say that as if you believe there is something out there."

"I believe it because I saw it. Scares the shit out of me, but yeah, I guess I believe it. I don't have a choice."

No, there was no choice, was there? Their eyes met and Grace had a brief glimpse into the future. Mason's dark hair was sprinkled with gray. She was leading them up a trail. There were large trees around them. Huge trees. There was a dog—a golden retriever—

running beside them. The air was cool. The aspen leaves were turning golden. She was—

"Grace?"

She blinked her eyes, reluctantly leaving the peaceful vision behind. Mason had a concerned look on her face.

"You...you kinda went into a trance or something."

"I'm sorry. Yes, I sometimes—" What? Have visions? Go off to another place and time? Was it true? What she saw, was it true? She looked at Mason again, seeing eyes that were as familiar to her as her own. How could that be?

"You're kinda scaring me." Mason gave a shaky laugh. "Not that it's the first time or anything."

Grace smiled at that. She hesitated only a second before taking Mason's hand. All the familiarity she'd seen in her eyes, she felt it tenfold in her touch. It brought such peace to her—peace to her soul—that tears formed in her eyes.

"What is it?"

A softly whispered question; a question she couldn't answer. Not yet. She wiped a tear away from a corner of one eye, letting a smile form. Peace. That's what she felt. Peace.

And peace was something she'd never felt before.

CHAPTER NINETEEN

Mason paced in front of his desk, not sure how to tell him what she'd witnessed today. She was glad they were alone, however. She certainly didn't want to say it in front of others. Brady and Dalton, in particular. Brady would laugh it off and Dalton most likely tell her she'd lost her freaking mind. Or that Grace had.

She finally turned to look at her uncle. "Keep in mind, bringing in a psychic was a joint decision."

He gave her a lopsided grin, one he used to use on her when she was a kid. "You want to recast your vote, Mason? Too late, I guess. She's here now. But Chief Danner first brought up the idea back in January. We can blame him, if you want. Said it had come to him in a dream. Said some little girl with pigtails was standing at his door."

"Really?"

Uncle Alan shrugged. "Makes no difference now. The FBI pushed, Chief Danner pushed. You went along with it. I had to agree with everyone, didn't I? I couldn't see that bringing her in would hurt anything. As long as she's not crazy, like the last one." He held both hands up. "What's on your mind, Mason? Did she learn anything today? Are we making any progress?"

Mason blew out a heavy sigh. She knew how it would sound to him. She knew what he'd think. Hell, she'd thought the same thing when she'd first met Grace, first started to talk to her. But now? She saw things differently. Because she'd had a front row seat. The fact remained, though, that what she witnessed was in no way associated with the murders. At least on the surface.

"Out with it, Mason."

"We went back to the footbridge in the park. Well, she did." She sat down, facing him. "When we were first searching the creek for Jason Gorman, at the footbridge, she saw...she saw Susie Shackle." That statement was met with a blank stare.

"Uh huh."

"She was in the water. If you recall, Susie's body was found lodged under the old planks that used to be the footbridge."

Her uncle arched an eyebrow slightly. "So the psychic saw her floating under the water or something, did she?"

Mason nodded. "She did. She described her perfectly. Pigtails. Red bow in her hair."

"She could have gotten all of that from the file."

Mason shook her head. "You think she fabricated that? Why? For what purpose?"

"To make her seem legit—I don't know."

"She is legit," she said with certainty, surprising herself. "I believe her. I was there. I saw her reaction." She held her hand up. "But that's not what I wanted to tell you. She wanted to go back today. To see if...if Susie would talk to her."

Her uncle folded his hands together, tapping them lightly on his desk in a nervous gesture. "I'll be honest, Mason...I'm in the camp that psychics are mostly quacks, trying to make a buck off of grieving widows desperate to talk to their dead husbands. All of this sounds a bit...crazy."

"I know. I thought that way too. But what do we really know about it?" She pointed at him. "And you're the one who said to keep an open mind."

"So I did. The FBI seems to think she's legit. Kemp thinks she's legit. And maybe she is. But like most in this town, I'm skeptical. So telling me she wanted to go talk to a girl who's been dead since 1997 makes her sound a little loony."

"I know that. But I've been around her. She's...she's not crazy. At least I don't think she is."

"Okay, Mason. I'll try to keep an open mind, like you say. What happened?"

"I took her to the park. She wanted to go to the footbridge alone." She chewed on her lower lip, wondering if she should tell him how she *knew*, she just *knew* not to let her go alone? How something made her go check on Grace earlier than the agreed upon twenty minutes? Should she tell him all that? No.

"I...*she* thought Susie might be more receptive if I wasn't there. So we agreed on twenty minutes. I stayed in the truck, she went on by herself." She swallowed. "I went out, a little quicker than the twenty minutes. I heard her scream, heard her yell for me." She swallowed again. "When I got there, she was in the creek, in the water, facedown, like she was fighting something—someone—who was holding her down, trying to drown her." She looked at him and he simply stared at her. "I pulled her out of the water."

"So she jumped into the creek to go after Susie Shackle?" her uncle asked slowly, carefully, although a bit skeptically.

"The handrail was broken. She said someone—something— pulled her in, held her under the water."

"Held her under the water?" He shook his head disbelievingly. "No way. She faked it."

"What would she have to gain by staging it? No. I believe it. I saw her. She was badly shaken...scared. It wasn't staged."

"Something pulled her into the water?" The incredulous look on his face matched the tone of his question.

She stood up. "You wanted a psychic. You got one. You wanted me to shadow her. I am. You wanted to know what she's been doing. This is it. Yeah, it sounds freakin' crazy! Don't you think I know that?"

He stood up too, and pressed both hands on his desk, leaning against it. "Yes, we brought in a psychic, hoping she would help us with the murders. I don't understand all this...this jumping into the creek after seeing a dead girl." He shook his head. "From twenty-something years ago! How does that help us?"

Mason said nothing. What should she say? That Grace wanted to talk to Susie? That was really all she knew. What was Grace going to ask her? Did Susie know who killed her? God, these questions were making her own head spin.

"It was rather convenient that she had you wait twenty minutes, isn't it? Gave her time to break the railing, hop in the water."

Mason stared at him. "That's not how it happened."

"Because you believe her?"

"Because I didn't wait twenty minutes. Barely ten, then I went after her. Had I waited the full twenty, she'd probably be dead."

"I guess I have to take your word for it. We hoped this psychic would lead us to the killer...hoped she'd have a vison or something."

"She's a medium."

"What the hell does that mean?"

Mason let out her breath slowly. "She...she talks to...to dead people."

"Oh for god's sake! I knew it! Another quack. The FBI assured me—"

"Uncle Alan, she's not a quack. Just because we don't understand all this—or believe it—doesn't make her a quack. I've been with her. I've seen her." She nodded. "I don't mind saying, it freaks me out, but I believe her."

"So what? She's going to do a damn séance like the last one tried? Wants to talk to Susie Shackle? Her mother threatened a lawsuit the last time. Did you know that?"

"No. I was in high school."

He sat down again with a weary sigh. "So...we got two dead boys. If we're lucky, we won't have another until October." He met her gaze. "The last time we had a psychic in town, we had five murders."

"I know. Why do you think that is?"

"Why do *you* think that is?"

"Maybe because there was a psychic in town."

"And our killer found out? Got pissed? What?" He shrugged. "You'd think if he was scared of a psychic, he'd kill less, not more."

She and Grace hadn't talked about this, but from what she gathered, whatever was out there, whatever evil being Grace was talking about, it was more angry than scared. She didn't share this with her uncle, however.

"That lady was a total hack," he continued. "Crazy. She talked crazy stuff. Scarves and beads."

Mason wanted to say she didn't recall anything about the psychic other than the way she dressed—like a gypsy. Truth was, back in high school, she'd been a little afraid of the woman, although she never told anyone that at the time. She laughed along with the others when they were making fun of her. But now, that long-buried memory was trying to surface once again. Fuzzy around the edges still, but she could see it, hear it as it slowly came back to her. She'd forgotten a book in her locker. The halls were empty, quiet. She remembered the sound her shoes made as she hurried down the corridor to retrieve her book. She had stopped short, however. The gypsy woman was there, her hands outstretched, moving along the rows of lockers. The gypsy had turned to look at her, almost as if she'd been expecting her. Dark brown eyes—black?—had captured hers. She had been paralyzed as the woman moved close to her. A hand—surprisingly strong—wrapped around her wrist. She'd felt dizzy, disoriented. She remembered swaying, afraid she'd fall right there at the feet of this gypsy woman. Her words rang crystal clear, as if the woman were standing beside her right this very minute speaking them.

"You are the one. You are the one who will stop the cycle. You will take a journey far away from here. But you will return—older, wiser. And when you do, you'll find your mate."

"My...my mate?"

"Your soulmate, child. She is a seer. She is young, like you now. She has her own journey to complete. She will find you here. Together, you will stop the cycle."

Mason remembered giving a shaky, nervous laugh. "Yeah, right." She remembered thinking what a nutcase the woman was, remembered thinking that she couldn't wait to tell Brady and Dalton. She had turned to walk away, but the gypsy's voice called to her.

"Your book, Mason. Don't forget your book."

As far as she knew, after she'd retrieved her book, thoughts of the woman—and her words—had disappeared into the wind, as if she'd never had an encounter with her at all. Forgotten for all these years? Until now. Why would she remember them now?

She turned away from her uncle, the woman's words still echoing in her mind. A seer? Her soulmate? Had the woman *really* said those words to her way back when she was in high school? She obviously meant Grace but...oh, hell no. No way would she and Grace—hell, she didn't even like Grace. Grace scared her. Grace—with her blond hair and pretty blue eyes—scared her. No way were they freakin' soulmates.

"Are you okay? You're as white as a sheet, Mason."

Mason shook her head, trying to chase away the memory. A crazy gypsy woman, a crazy psychic...no way was she taking her words to heart. "Yeah, I'm okay." She cleared her throat before looking to him. "So? What do you want me to do?"

"You sure you're okay?"

"Fine. Just trying to hold on to my sanity." She blew out a quick breath. "So?"

"I guess keep doing like you're doing. What else is there?"

"She knew where we should look for Jason Gorman," she reminded him—and herself. "I don't think we should discredit her. Her methods may not be what we're used to—"

"Your defense of her is surprising. I thought you'd be more like Dalton, ready to kick her to the curb."

She shrugged. "I guess because I was there. I saw it." She went to the door, then stopped. "There is something else. She's staying at the Aspen Resort. I'm going to move her in with me." The words were out before she even realized she meant to speak them. She frowned slightly, wondering where they'd come from. Move Grace into her house? Was she crazy?

"Why? Is this because of what happened?"

"Yeah. If I hadn't been there, she would be dead."

He studied her. "You really think that? Really?"

"Yes. So does she. I don't understand this any better than you do, but *something* happened. Something got to her. I don't want to go to pick her up one morning and find that something got to her there. I'd just as soon she stay with me." She gave him a half-smile. "I haven't actually said anything to her about it yet. She may say no. But I think it's the best way to make sure she's safe."

"Okay, your call. If she's agreeable, I don't see anything wrong with it. By the way, Chief Danner got a call from the FBI, asked if we wanted them to send another agent in the interim. Said Agent Kemp wouldn't get back here for a few more weeks."

"What did he say?"

"He hasn't called them back yet, but we'll probably decline. I believe when Kemp comes back, he's bringing someone with him. One of their computer guys to run some algorithms or something."

"Yeah, that's worked out so well for us in the past."

"I think this guy worked with Dr. Jennings on a case a couple of years ago. Some kidnapping."

She nodded, remembering the story Scott Kemp had told her. "Well, maybe something will pan out this time."

"Keep me informed, Mason. I don't care how strange or crazy it is, let me know what's going on." He tapped his desk. "We still on for dinner tonight?"

She nodded. "Aunt Carol's meatloaf."

"Good. It'll give me a chance to get to know this psychic a little better. Where is she now?"

"I left her out front. Sandy has been here longer than anyone. I think Grace was questioning her."

"Grace, huh?"

"Yeah, Grace. Stop referring to her as 'the psychic,' okay?"

When she went into the lobby, she found that Grace had scooted her chair closer to Sandy's desk and was listening raptly as Sandy spoke. Mason paused before interrupting them, taking the time to study Grace's profile. Her blond hair was tucked behind one ear, the other side was hanging loose. Her chin was resting in her palm and, yeah, she was attractive. Pretty. The gypsy woman's words were still rattling around in her mind, and she moved then, not wanting them to replay. Sandy stopped talking as soon as she walked out, and Mason wondered what she'd been saying that was so private it couldn't be said in her presence.

"Ready?"

Grace nodded. "He didn't have any questions for me then?"

Mason smiled at that. "None that he wanted to ask out loud."

They walked out together and she sensed Sandy still watching them. "Did you learn anything?"

"Different perspective."

"Different from mine?"

"She's a mother, a grandmother...so yes, different from yours." They stopped beside her truck. "And your uncle?"

"About as I expected. I don't blame him, though. If I hadn't been there, if someone relayed that story to me, I'd be skeptical too," she said in defense of him. "His idea of a psychic, of what he thought you'd do here, was touch a few objects, make a guess as to who or where the killer was, and be on your way."

"Ah. Like I have a crystal ball?"

"Something like that."

"A gypsy? A scarf on my head, beads? Speaking some magic words as I called up images in my magic ball?"

"I see Sandy described our first psychic."

Grace smiled a little. "Some of the older ones dressed that way. It was more for marketing than anything else. And some were actually of that heritage, so..."

"She came across as a...well, as a quack," she said bluntly, hoping she didn't offend Grace by repeating her uncle's words.

"No doubt. Some use a lot of that for show. Some feel the need to be a little over the top, if only to convince people they're for real or—depending on the crowd they're playing to—it may be expected. And some, that's just how they work."

They got inside the truck, but before she started the engine, she turned to Grace. "I want you to check out of the Aspen Resort. Pack your bags, in other words."

Grace's eyes widened. "What in the world for?"

"You staying there is kinda gonna hinder me being with you around the clock."

Grace held a hand up and shook her head. "Oh, Mason, no. You—"

"I've got a spare bedroom. It's not really up for discussion, Grace."

Grace stared at her, a hint of defiance in her eyes. "I don't need a babysitter."

"Something tried to drown you today. Have you forgotten?"

"I haven't forgotten. I think the only reason he was able to get to me was through Susie. I should be safe in my room. It should be safe there."

"Sorry." She started up the engine. "I'm not willing to take a chance. You shouldn't either."

"I don't want to impose, Mason."

"You're not imposing. It makes sense and it'll save time."

Grace stared at her for the longest time before finally nodding. Mason thought she saw relief in her eyes, something Grace had tried to hide. So she was still a little afraid after all. That made two of them, of course.

But the gypsy woman's words were still there, loud and clear.

Your soulmate. Stop the cycle. Together.

She glanced at Grace as she drove. Grace was looking straight ahead. Then Grace turned her head, locking eyes with her. In that brief moment, she saw the past and future colliding and she had to tighten her grip on the wheel. She no longer knew what was real anymore. She didn't feel like she was in control any longer.

If not her, though…then who was in control?

CHAPTER TWENTY

Grace stood in Mason's spare bedroom, her gaze moving slowly around the room—dresser with a mirror, standard-size bed with a navy spread, end table with a lamp—getting a sense that no one had ever slept in there before. She put her clothes bag on the bed, then turned as Mason came in with the other bag. Grace had her laptop case strapped on her shoulder, and she put that on the bed as well.

"I called my uncle. When I was in his office, I forgot to ask him about the file. He's going to email it to me but also print it out. We can get it from him tonight at dinner."

Grace nodded. "That's right. I had forgotten about dinner. Meatloaf, was it?"

"Yeah. I think it'll be good for him to talk with you, see you in a different light other than…you know, as a psychic."

Grace tilted her head, studying her. A word Mason used earlier came to mind, but she didn't think it was a word Mason would use to describe her. No, but her uncle would.

"He calls me a quack right out in the open, huh? Like he called the other psychic?" Mason blushed but said nothing. "Speaking of this other psychic, I'd really like to talk to her. Any chance someone still has her contact information?"

Mason's brows drew together. "Why do you want to talk to her? That was what? Sixteen years ago?"

Grace opened one of her bags. "I'm assuming dinner is casual."

"Oh, sure. Jeans."

"Good, because that's all I have." She pulled out a pair from the bag. "I want to get her thoughts on it, that's all," she said, answering Mason's earlier question. "Find out what she saw. Did she leave a report when she left?"

"I doubt it. Like you said, she was pretty much run out of town."

"Was your uncle the sheriff then?"

"No. And Danner wasn't the police chief either."

Grace nodded. "So if there's no accounting of what she saw, then I'd like to talk to her directly." It wasn't something she'd considered earlier, but for some reason, now, she had an urge to speak to the woman. More than an urge, really. A compulsion to speak to her was more like it. She looked at Mason with raised eyebrows. "Can you please try to find her contact information?"

"Sure," Mason said a bit reluctantly. "I'll try to find something. But sixteen years, Grace. If we do happen to find her, she may not remember us."

"I'm certain she will." She paused, frowning. "Nora."

Mason's brows drew together. "Nora?"

Grace shrugged. "I don't know. That name just popped in my head." She shook it dismissively, then motioned Mason out. "Let me change." She paused again. "Do we need to bring something?"

"For?"

"For dinner. A bottle of wine?"

Mason shook her head with a smile. "No, no. Not that kind of dinner. Very informal. And if my cousin gets wind that it's meatloaf, he'll be there too."

"And your cousin is who?"

"Brady."

"Ah, yes. One of the deputies I met. You're close?"

Mason nodded. "He was a year ahead of me in school. We played together when we were kids. His older sister…well, I was a little too much of a tomboy for her tastes."

"Is she still around?"

"No. She lives in Boise. Three kids."

Grace nodded. Young kids, no doubt.

"She usually only comes around at Christmas."

"I suppose it's safe that time of year." Grace waved her away. "Let me change," she said once more.

* * *

When they went outside, Mason didn't go toward her truck. Instead, she headed out to the small, quiet street.

"It's only a couple of blocks. Do you mind walking? Or is it too cold?"

"Of course not." Grace fell into step beside her. "The wind has died down. How far was this from your house when you were a kid? I know you said you lived close to the school."

"A quick trip on my bike…fifteen, twenty minutes, I guess. Across town." Mason shoved her hands in her pockets as she walked. "After my dad left, my mom quit cooking, so Aunt Carol used to bring meals to the house. She and my mom had a disagreement over it one time and so, after school, I'd ride my bike over here. Have dinner with them, then go home."

"What kind of a disagreement?"

"My mother said I was perfectly capable of opening up a can of Spaghetti-O's or something or popping a frozen dinner in the microwave."

"You were ten?"

"Yeah. At first, I thought I was in junk food heaven," Mason said with a short laugh. "It didn't register that my mother was shirking her duties. It wasn't until later that I found out she was spending most of the money on booze and not food."

"Is that why you resent her?"

"What makes you think I resent her?"

Grace shrugged. "A guess, nothing more. You came back under the guise of caring for her, yet as far as I can tell, you don't see her or speak to her."

Mason was silent for a few steps, then Grace heard her utter a quiet sigh. "She lives in an apartment over on the new side of town. She's a mess. Overweight. Diabetic, high blood pressure, cholesterol. She doesn't take care of herself. At all. She does nothing to combat it other than pop a handful of pills every day. The doctor told her to quit drinking, change her diet, get some exercise…she's done none of that."

"She still works?"

"Part-time now. She used to manage the office—insurance agency. She's been there forever and I imagine that's the only reason he keeps her on. From what I can tell, breakfast is a Bloody Mary and a scrambled egg. Or donuts that she picks up on the way to work. Screwdrivers follow and by dinnertime, vodka tonics are on the menu."

"How often do you see her?"

Another sigh. "Not enough, Grace. Truth is, she ceased being my mother when I was ten. Whatever obligation I feel, it's forced. I go by and see her every Sunday, take her some food. Even then, she's not very civil. It's almost as if she blames me for his leaving."

"That must be tough."

"I think about how things were when he was still around. We were a normal family. I don't recall them ever fighting or yelling at each other. His leaving was a shock to everyone. He left and she never recovered."

"And you're her sole caregiver?"

"Yeah, if you call it that. It's not like she can't take care of herself. She simply chooses not to. Aunt Carol tries. She takes a casserole over sometimes. My mother is not receptive to her, will barely speak to her. All of her family is in Denver. Two sisters, a brother. Her mother is still alive, in good health. They've offered to take her in, but she's resisted. It'll happen eventually. Her part-time job is barely enough to cover her bills, much less her drinking habit. When her money runs out, she'll have to make a change. She won't have a choice then."

"Will she want to move in with you?"

"That's not an option, Grace. She's barely civil to me as it is."

"You're a reminder of him."

"I guess."

"Why does she stay here? Why not go be with her family?"

"My guess? She's holding on to hope that he'll come back someday. She's wasted her whole damn life…waiting on him."

Grace nodded. She had suspected that was the case. "You really don't know where he is?"

"No clue. Don't care. He abandoned us…me. He never sent child support, never got in contact with me again. I don't give him much thought."

Grace wondered if that was the truth or not. It was none of her business, however, and she didn't know why she was questioning her. She was curious, though, about the relationship with the rest of her family.

"Your uncle is your father's brother. I know you're close with them. What about your mother's family? Your grandmother?"

"Not really, no. We used to go to Denver twice a year to see them. When he left, that stopped. They came a few times after that, but my mother wasn't really herself and I'm not sure they knew how to deal with it. I was probably a teenager the last time I saw them. They call me a few times a year to check on her." Mason pointed to a house on the opposite side of the street from where they were walking. "Here it is."

They crossed the street and walked across the lawn, which was bright green from spring grasses. Two large trees, one only slightly smaller than the other, dominated the front of the house. Their branches reached all the way to the ground.

"What are they?"

"Blue spruce."

Their house wasn't quite as rustic looking as Mason's although it fit the theme of the neighborhood and blended in well with the trees and mountains that surrounded them. Mason rang the doorbell to announce their presence, then went inside without waiting for a greeting.

"It's me," Mason called.

"In the kitchen," came an answering female voice.

She followed Mason through a comfortable-looking living room down a short hallway and into a large, airy kitchen. A woman was at the sink, draining a pot of cooked potatoes. Steam rose around her face. She was short and petite and she tossed a friendly smile at them.

"Just in time to mash."

"This is Dr. Grace Jennings," Mason introduced. "Grace...my Aunt Carol."

Carol Cooper set the pot back on the stove, then paused to grab a towel to wipe her hands before offering one of them to Grace.

"Nice to meet you, Dr. Jennings. Glad you could join us for dinner."

"Please...call me Grace. And thanks for the invitation. It'll be nice to eat a home-cooked meal."

"Oh, when Alan said you were staying at the Aspen Resort, I insisted we have you over. Living in that small space for any length of time would drive me crazy. I'm not happy when I'm away from my kitchen for too long."

"When I'm on the road like this, I do miss having a kitchen," she confessed. "I get by with lots of microwaved baked potatoes."

"I saved her from that place," Mason said as she opened a drawer and took out a potato masher. "Moved her in with me. I've got the room and I'm supposed to be tour guide while she's here. Makes it easier."

"I'm sure it does, honey," Carol said with a wink at Mason, which caused her to blush.

Grace smiled as Mason glanced at her and rolled her eyes. The setting was indeed informal, and before too long, Grace found herself helping to set the table and filling glasses with ice and water. She paused in her task once to taste Mason's mashed potatoes, nodding with approval at the buttery flavor.

"You overdid the butter again, didn't you?" Carol accused.

"Of course. It's my only chance to indulge."

"What does that mean?" Grace asked.

"I don't eat dairy," Mason explained. "Well, not as a rule. I know the chocolate chips in Dottie's blueberry muffins have milk. I mean, I don't eat cheese, drink milk, or use butter." She grinned and patted her stomach. "I'm over thirty now. Gotta watch what I eat."

"Oh, please," Grace said. "That muffin you have for breakfast probably has six hundred calories and if I had to guess, twenty-five or thirty grams of fat."

"So you're saying it's not healthy? It's got blueberries. How can it not be healthy?"

"It's nothing but fat and sugar," Carol chimed in. "If you like blueberries so much, put them on top of oatmeal."

"She hates oatmeal," Grace said without thinking. Mason looked at her with slightly raised eyebrows. "I mean…I would assume you hate oatmeal."

Mason smiled quickly. "Nice save."

"What does that mean?" Carol asked.

"It means she says she can't read minds, yet sometimes…she *knows* stuff."

Carol looked between the two of them questioningly. "Oh?"

It was then that Grace realized Carol had no idea what her profession was. How refreshing that had been…if only for a few minutes. Mason must have realized it too and said nothing else to give her secret away.

"Yeah, these FBI types think they know everything," Mason teased. "But you're right. I hate oatmeal. Well, unless it's in cookies."

Grace smiled and nodded her thanks to Mason. "I can't remember the last time I had an oatmeal cookie."

"Aunt Carol happens to make excellent cookies. And as a bonus, she puts chocolate chips in hers."

Carol laughed. "This one and her chocolate chips. When she was a kid, she had me putting chocolate chips in everything," she said affectionately. "It sort of became a tradition with my oatmeal cookies." Carol patted Mason's arm. "Maybe I'll whip up a batch and you can share them with Grace."

The back door in the kitchen opened and Alan Cooper came inside. He looked at her a bit warily and nodded in her direction.

"Dr. Jennings. Mason," he greeted. "Didn't see your truck out front."

"We walked over."

Carol kissed him quickly. "We were about to start without you. Where's Brady?"

"Oh, I didn't invite him."

"Why not? He loves my meatloaf."

"Because I want to talk to Dr. Jennings later and I'd rather do it in private."

Carol sighed. "I wish you'd leave your police business outside of the house, but it is that time of year, isn't it?" Carol looked over at her. "I guess I forgot why you were in town. FBI agents come around often, but you're the first female one that's been here."

Grace simply smiled and nodded, not knowing what to say to that. If Sheriff Cooper hadn't even shared with his wife that the town had hired a psychic, then she doubted anyone in town knew yet. She supposed they were trying to keep it a secret as long as possible, considering how badly it had gone the last time. 2004. Nora... something.

Dinner seemed to be a bit strained, and she could only attribute it to the sheriff being there. Before he'd arrived, there hadn't been any awkwardness, which was unusual for her. The dinner itself was delicious. The meatloaf was divine, something her own mother had made often, and she'd complimented Carol. Carol had explained the three vegetables choices—brussels sprouts, green beans, and corn. Her husband, she said, would eat the entire offering of sprouts himself as no one else would touch them. She and Mason were fond of green beans, and the corn was for Brady, who, as it turns out, hadn't been invited. She did manage to sneak in a couple of the brussels sprouts. She wouldn't say they were her favorite vegetable, but she didn't loathe them as apparently Mason and Carol did.

"How long do you plan to stay in town, Grace?"

Grace hesitated. Was October an acceptable answer? Just how secret were they keeping her stay here?

"I'll be here as long as I'm needed." That seemed to be a safe answer. She would rather they tell Carol the truth, though. She didn't want to have to watch everything she said.

"Hopefully not too long," Sheriff Cooper interjected.

"Oh, Alan, when you say it like that, it's as if she's not welcome here."

"Not what I meant at all. Just hoping it's sooner rather than later. It'd be nice to put this nightmare behind us finally."

Grace nodded appropriately, chancing a quick glance at Mason, who gave her the subtlest of smiles. With the lack of conversation, it allowed her the chance to observe the others freely. She wondered about Mason's father. Did he favor his brother? He must. Mason looked just like her uncle. Did Mason see her father when she looked at him? And what about Alan Cooper himself? All those years ago, had he felt some responsibility for young Mason and her mother after his brother had abandoned them? Questions she had but she doubted she'd find answers to them. For one, it was curiosity only. Certainly, it had no bearing on her business here.

Despite Carol's protest, she and Mason helped clear the table. "Wonderful meal, Carol. Thank you for including me."

"My pleasure. Mason will have to bring you around again."

"I hope she will."

Sheriff Cooper cleared his throat behind them. "If I could steal these two away for a minute…"

"Yes, go, both of you. I can manage the dishes. Oh, and I made some lemon bars earlier today, if anyone wants dessert."

Grace nodded. "Thank you. I would love to try one." She turned to Mason with a smile. "I could get spoiled coming over here."

She laughed. "Why do you think I come by so often?"

They followed her uncle out into the living room where he muted the TV that had been playing to an empty room. Their smiles faded almost simultaneously.

"Have a seat," he said, motioning to the sofa. He sat in a recliner, but he didn't pop the footrest out. "Mason gave me a rundown of what…well, what you encountered today at the creek."

Grace could tell by the tone of his voice that he was—as Mason had said—skeptical. "Yes. She told me."

"So you think it was…" He looked away for a moment and cleared his throat, perhaps to get his thoughts in order. "Susie Shackle?"

"No. It was someone pretending to be Susie. The first day, yes. It was Susie who I saw. Not today."

He stared at her for a moment, then absently scratched the back of his neck, obviously stalling for time, trying to think of a credible response to her statement. "Is this going to be your plan going forward?"

"Plan?"

"Having these...encounters with...with these..."

"Encounters?" She leaned forward, resting her elbows on her knees. "Sheriff Cooper, I'm not an FBI agent, I'm not law enforcement. I'm a psychic. My methods are going to be different than what you're used to. You hired me to use my gifts," she said, glancing quickly at Mason. "I know you don't understand how it works and I don't expect you to. If it makes you feel better, I don't plan to hold a public séance, as you suggested my predecessor was about to do." She gave him a small smile. "I do hope to talk to Susie Shackle, however."

He stared at her blankly, unblinking. He finally nodded. "Well, you're right about that. I don't understand. From what I'm hearing you say, you want me to stay out of your way."

"I'm here to help. Nothing more. You've got to give me some time and space. I don't have a crystal ball and there's no magic involved. As soon as I have anything helpful, you'll be the first to know." Then she glanced at Mason. "Well, second, I guess."

"Okay. But I would like to know what your plans are. Will you be out and about in town, talking to people? Asking questions? Because it hasn't been advertised that you're here."

"Yes, you inferred that when I first arrived here. And from what Carol has said, she doesn't know either."

He gave her an apologetic smile. "I didn't know how to spring it on her, especially since she insisted we have you over for dinner."

"Which I appreciate, as I told her. Keeping my profession a secret from her would not be my choice. It makes me uncomfortable, actually."

"So we should broadcast it that you're in town?"

"Uncle Alan, I don't think that's what she means. But Aunt Carol? There's really no need to lie to her."

"You're right. Truth is, Chief Danner has wanted to bring in a psychic for the last few years. I always balked. And I said he was crazy and the idea was crazy...so for me to now sanction it, well..."

Grace nodded. "Despite what you think, I'm not a quack, Sheriff

Cooper." When he looked sharply at Mason, Grace smiled and shook her head. "No, Mason didn't tell me. She didn't have to."

"We got burned once, Dr. Jennings. The last thing I want is for the good folks in this town to look at the police department and the sheriff's department as a laughingstock. Nobody wants this case solved more than me, which is the only reason I finally went along with Danner's request to bring you in. The FBI had been pushing it for two years, at least." He spread his hands out. "I feel like we're spinning our wheels here. Yes, Mason has told me everything. How you came to her before Jason Gorman went missing, how you knew he'd be along the creek…how his soccer ball would be with him. All great. Fabulous." He leaned closer. "But nothing really helped us. We didn't prevent the abduction or killing, and in time, we would have found his body anyway."

"I understand. But *you* must understand that I don't have a crystal ball. I'm trying to lead you to the killer." Or killers, she added silently. "In order to do that, I have to have some time to establish a relationship with…well, with the likes of Susie Shackle. So you want my plan? I'm having Mason take me to some of the sites where these bodies were found and see who will talk to me. There is something you could do for me, though."

"And what is that?"

"The psychic who was here in 2004. Did she leave a report or anything? Or better yet, do you have her contact information?"

"Seriously? I already told you, she was a—"

"Quack, yes. I would like to speak to her. She was here for two weeks, I believe. I would like to get her thoughts on it. It might be helpful."

Sheriff Cooper was shaking his head. "Okay, no offense, but she was a freak show. Ask Mason. Half the town was afraid of her, the other half laughed at her. She looked like a gypsy, right out of the movies. She was a nutcase, the way she flitted around town."

"Perhaps. But if you could find something for me…"

He sighed. "I'm sure that's all in a file somewhere. Doubt her contact info is still accurate, but I'll find it for you."

"Thank you." She paused. "Do you remember her name?"

He frowned, as if thinking. "Weird last name…like Nightshade or Nightingale or something like that."

Grace stared at him. "Nora Nightsail."

"Yeah! That's it!" He tilted his head. "You know her?"

"No." She glanced at Mason, who was staring at her. No, she didn't know Nora Nightsail, yet somehow, she felt like she did. She also knew that whatever contact information they had on her would still be good.

Mason was the first to move. "Are we done with work now? I could use a nightcap. Or at least a lemon bar."

Alan stood too. "Whiskey or lemon bars...that's a tough choice."

Grace had to agree, although the lemon bars won out with all three of them.

CHAPTER TWENTY-ONE

Mason stood at her kitchen window, holding a cup of coffee in her hands, her gaze on a dark black and blue bird in the spruce tree nearest the house. Its dark crest seemed to be standing at attention. Steller's jay. When she was a kid—back before her father left—her mother had two bird feeders in the backyard. She remembered the jays would chase off the smaller birds, the feeders swinging wildly when they landed on them. Even the chipmunks would scatter when a jay's shrill voice sounded. She loved watching them. After her father left...well, the bird feeders were just one of several things her mother neglected. That first winter, when the snow was deep and the air frosty, she remembered standing at the window, watching hungry birds coming again and again to the empty feeders. She'd then glanced at their dinner table, where many happy meals had once been shared. It, too, was bare—empty. Her mother had gone out, said she was going to see a friend. Told Grace to "find yourself something to eat" and had left her alone. Animal crackers. That was one of the few things she'd found in the pantry. She'd eaten half, then crumbled up the rest and taken them outside, putting them in the bird feeders. Then she'd gone back to her perch by the window, watching as her meager offering was gobbled up within minutes.

After one last look at the jay, she turned away from the window with a sigh, then nearly spilled her coffee as she found Grace there, watching her. Their eyes met, and she could actually feel Grace trying to crawl inside her head, read her thoughts. Instead of fighting it, she relaxed, opening herself, curious as to what Grace could learn. Their gazes were locked together, neither blinking. She saw Grace's blue eyes darken, saw recognition there. Grace let out a breath, then released her hold. Mason finally blinked, then brought the coffee cup to her lips, her hand shaking slightly.

"Good morning," Grace finally said.

"Morning. How did you sleep?"

"Very good, thanks. No dreams." She picked up the cup that Mason had placed beside the coffeepot. "At least I don't think so."

Mason watched as she added a heaping teaspoon of sugar to the coffee, then stirred it slowly. She was wearing a baggy T-shirt, a solid navy-blue color. A sleep shirt, she assumed. She had slipped on jeans, but her feet were bare. Mason found herself staring at those feet... pretty feet, she noted. She didn't know why, but she was surprised to find red polish on her nails.

"Pedicures help me relax."

Mason jerked her head up, embarrassed for having been staring. "Sorry."

Grace leaned against the counter much like she was doing. "I don't like massages—something about strangers touching me, I guess. So a pedicure is the next best thing."

As Grace sipped her coffee, Mason couldn't help but feel like the other woman was assessing her, perhaps weighing whether she should ask questions or let it be. Apparently, Grace decided to let it be.

"I'd like to visit some of the sites from 2004."

"Okay. You've read the file more recently than me. Were they using GPS to mark locations back then?"

"I believe landmarks were still being used at the time. So many feet from such-and-such and grid markers. Coordinates were added to the file later, so yes, we can use GPS."

Mason nodded. "Yeah, the public land around town is broken up into grids. May I ask why that year?"

"There were five killings. Why? The psychic was here. Was that the reason?"

"Do you think it'll be duplicated this year because you're here?"

"You had another year—2012—where there were five murders. No psychic. There must be something else."

"I figured you'd stay up half the night reading the file Uncle Alan gave you."

"I did think about it. But it had been a rather...*eventful* day." She took another sip of her coffee. "And not to badger your uncle, but if you could call him later this morning, see if he found Nora Nightsail's contact info, that would be nice."

Mason nodded. "How did you know her name?"

Grace shrugged. "I've long stopped questioning these things or trying to explain them. Simply saying that the name popped into my head doesn't sound nearly as sexy as saying I'm a mind reader, huh?"

Mason smiled at that. "You keep saying you're not a mind reader. I don't believe you."

Grace smiled too and put her coffee cup down. "Why don't you get a bird feeder?"

Mason shifted uncomfortably. "Don't you already know?"

"I could guess."

"Oh, come on, doc...it's just us here. You don't have to pretend." Grace added coffee to her cup, then stirred in a little more sugar. "I can only hear what you allow me to hear." She looked up and met her gaze. "You opened up to me, so yes, I took liberties. It's not something I like to do. In fact, I make it a point not to. People should be allowed their privacy, especially in their own mind."

What did that mean, exactly? Was she saying she could read her mind at will, if she wanted to? Hell, was she reading it right now?

Grace's smile told her that she was.

But then Grace laughed. "It's written all over your face, Mason. I am *not* reading your mind." She waved a hand. "It doesn't work that way, anyway. It's not like I can stare at you and capture your thoughts. Think about it. How much stuff is going on in your mind? It's a jumbled mess. How could I make sense of it?"

"Then how did you know about the bird feeder?"

"I told you. You opened yourself up to me. You invited me in."

"And what did you learn?"

"I probably know more about you than you know yourself."

And what the hell did that mean? Did she already know what the gypsy lady had told her back in 2004? Back when she was in high school? Had she read that in her mind? She shook that away, not wanting that thought to be foremost in her mind, in case Grace was still poking around there. Then she mentally rolled her eyes, knowing she was being ridiculous. So some weird psychic woman told her a crazy-ass story back in 2004? Didn't make it true. Yeah, she thought Grace Jennings was cute. So? Didn't mean they were freakin' soulmates. Christ, she wished she'd never even remembered the damn thing in the first place.

She swallowed and met Grace's gaze. "Do you believe in soulmates?"

Grace stared at her for a long moment before shaking her head. "No. It's too farfetched, isn't it? Billions of people, what are the chances? It's fanciful enough to make for a good romance book but highly improbable in real life." She shrugged. "Then again, I am a bit cynical when it comes to that sort of thing."

"Cynical?"

Grace gave her a quick smile. "Perhaps I'm wrong." She moved away, taking her coffee with her. "I'm going to shower. Looks like another beautiful day. Hopefully warmer than yesterday."

Mason watched her go, then poured out her cold coffee and refilled her cup. So Grace was cynical about soulmates and about love, if she was hearing her right. She had no family, she had no friends; it stood to reason she had no love life. They were similar in that regard. Before Shauna, there really hadn't been anyone. Certainly after Shauna, after she moved back here, there was no one. Truth was, she never really even thought about dating.

Her gaze was drawn out the kitchen window again. The jay was still there, watching her, his head tilting sideways, as if studying her.

Why didn't she get a bird feeder? Here at the foot of the mountain, there were always birds in the trees. Why didn't she get a feeder? Why didn't she sit outside more than she did? Why didn't she hike the trails? Why didn't she ski more? Why didn't she date? Why was it that—once she moved back to Gillette Park—she'd quit living?

She'd joined a hiking club but she didn't participate. She'd joined a dinner club, but she could count on one hand the number of times she'd attended a gathering. Even Brady and Dalton—she saw them at Bucky's for beer and burgers, they came over to the house for Sunday football, but they didn't talk. They were like familiar strangers, nothing more.

Why? Had she been waiting for someone? Had she known all along that this day would come? Is that why she'd practically memorized the files going back to 1997 and the beginning? Had she been biding her time, unknowingly waiting for someone? For Grace?

She shook that thought away. No. Like Grace, she didn't believe that. Did she? No, of course not. Sixteen years ago a stranger issued a prophetic statement. Didn't make it real. She closed her eyes for a moment. *Did* she believe it?

Outside her window, the bird was still there. He'd moved closer without her even noticing. She got a rather odd feeling as tiny black eyes peered into hers.

What did he see there? For that matter, what was he looking for?

CHAPTER TWENTY-TWO

Grace stood next to Mason, looking out into the forest. Mason said there was a trail, but from here, she couldn't see one. Instead of plunging ahead—like usual—she took the time to observe her surroundings. She'd been in town long enough to get used to the towering conifers that seemed to dot every yard, every corner, every open space. The aspens, with their quaking leaves, were mixed in thick stands, their whitish bark a contrast to the dark of the pines, spruce, and firs. She took a deep breath, enjoying the fragrance of the forest. She listened to the sounds around her—the wind in the branches, the faintest call of birds, the scolding of a squirrel. It was a tranquil setting…calm and quiet. She could close her eyes and feel a serene peacefulness envelop her, settle around and on her, wrapping her up in a protective blanket. She could almost feel the barest of touches as it swirled around her…around them both.

Beyond that peace, though…there was something *else*. She could sense it, yet it was out of reach, out of sight. It was there, nonetheless, beyond the stillness.

"Grace?"

She opened her eyes, staring out at the trees instead of Mason. "Yes, I'm here," she said, answering Mason's unasked question. Mason gave an uneasy laugh beside her.

"I'm not sure what you want me to do."

Grace smiled at that. "I was just getting my bearings, that's all. We're still alone."

"Okay, good. So...?"

"I'll follow you. When we get close, I'll take the lead. Hopefully, I'll be able to find it without that," she said, motioning to the handheld GPS device Mason carried.

With all the technology their phones offered them, this deep in the forest, there was absolutely no signal whatsoever. The old, rather chunky device blinked steadily, leading them toward their target location.

Mason had a lightweight backpack on, a water bottle shoved into each side pouch. Inside was lunch—apples, peanut butter crackers, and two energy bars—and a first-aid kit, along with other essentials she said she usually took with her. Mason hadn't listed all the contents, but Grace assumed it was "emergency" items, should they get lost, like a flashlight, perhaps some matches, maybe even a flare gun. She wondered if Mason would be quite as prepared if their phones weren't useless, something Mason said was the case in most of the forest that surrounded the town, save the area around the park.

"There's a trail out here, but it's much closer if we bushwhack. I doubt our killer followed the trail anyway."

"Yet the body was dumped close to the trail?"

"Yeah. Thirty feet."

"If the killer didn't use the trail, that suggests he's very familiar with the area."

"Most everyone who grew up around here knows the area. There's not a lot of outside entertainment, other than the forest," Mason explained. "When I was a kid, we didn't even have a movie theater. The park was little more than a playground. Our entertainment was riding our bikes out into the forest and playing. By the time I graduated high school, I'd traveled over all these trails, just like my friends had."

"Even during the summer months?"

"Never alone, no. Groups of four or more, usually."

Grace ducked under a branch that Mason held up for her. "When you were with your friends, did you talk about the murders?"

"Yeah. Some."

"Some?" she prompted.

"Not as a group, no. But sometimes, like when Dalton, Brady, and I would be under the bridge, playing, we'd talk about it."

"Like what?"

Mason looked back at her. "Quit beating around the bush, Grace. Ask what you want to ask."

"Okay. I want to know what you talked about. Specifically."

Mason stopped walking and turned to her. "Specifically? Grace, I was a kid. You think I can recall conversations I had back then?"

Grace met her gaze and nodded. "In this case, yes, I do," she challenged her. "I think you remember exactly what you talked about." She saw Mason clench her jaw. "Were you afraid? Did you take extra precautions even if your parents didn't tell you? Did you avoid certain areas?"

"Yeah, I was afraid. We all were. It was something you didn't say out loud, though. At least, not in a group."

"But it was safe with them? They were your closest friends?"

Mason nodded. "Brady was a year ahead of us in school, but we always hung out together, especially during the summer."

Grace studied her for a minute. "You're not as close now." It was a statement, not a question. Mason shrugged, then started walking again.

"I left after high school, they stayed."

"You didn't keep in touch?"

"Some. They both got married—and divorced—by the time I moved back. We get along, but no, we're not close like we were back then."

"Isn't it unusual that the three of you—close friends growing up—all went into law enforcement?"

"I guess. Not so much me and Brady...it runs in the family. Dalton? I think he just followed Brady's lead." Mason stopped and checked the GPS. "Five hundred feet." She motioned to her left. "This way."

Grace nodded and followed, suppressing the questions she still had. Perhaps tonight she'd revisit them. Now, she needed to concentrate. This was the first of five sites she hoped Mason would lead her to today. They were visiting them in order. Juliet Bateman. Age eleven. She went missing on May 9th—a Sunday—and was found four days later. The Batemans had gotten home from the First Presbyterian Church ten minutes before noon. Juliet had changed out of her church clothes and went next door to play with the neighbor while her mother prepared their Sunday meal. She walked out of the front door and was never seen again. Well, not until they found her body, out here in the middle of the forest.

She did wonder if the drop sites were significant in any way. She'd only glanced through the new file that Sheriff Cooper had given her last night.

"Mason, has the FBI run any kind of analytics on these drop sites?"

"Yes. Several times. Completely random. No pattern. No repeat sites."

"Clusters?"

"The results should be in the file Uncle Alan gave you." Mason glanced over her shoulder at her. "I think it was three years ago that they last ran something." Mason stopped then to check her device. "Rumor has it that when Kemp returns, he's bringing a guy with him."

"A guy?"

"Someone to run some algorithms and do your analytics, I guess." She held the device up to show her. "We're close. Forty-eight feet."

Grace touched her arm, pulling her back. "Let me go first." She didn't think she'd need direction—she could feel the energy from here.

She looked at the forest floor, wondering if it would change colors like before. She moved on slowly, feeling a charge in the air. She heard Mason behind her, perhaps ten feet or so. Up ahead, fallen leaves stirred and twirled, as if the tiniest of tornadoes were dancing across the surface. The miniature storm passed and the leaves settled back down again.

"Juliet? Are you here?"

She moved closer, jerking her head up as laughter sounded in the trees above them. She saw the shape of something—a child?—jump from branch to branch, darting in and out of boughs, then it was gone.

"Who are you?"

Grace tilted her head, trying to determine where the voice had come from. "My name is Grace." She took a few steps, stopping where she'd seen the leaves moving. "Juliet?"

"Why are you here?"

"Why are *you* here?"

The image she'd seen in the trees darted behind the trunk of a large pine. She moved to follow it, walking quickly. "Juliet?"

"You know why I'm here. He left me here."

She felt her thudding heartbeat as she moved again quickly, circling the tree. There was nothing there, though. The voice came from up higher now—she'd climbed the tree again.

"Who left you here?"

"Can't tell you."
"Why not?"
"Because he'll hurt her."
She frowned. "Her? Who?"
"Can't tell you."
A burst of air—as if someone had turned on a fan and held it to her face—was so strong she turned away from it. It was gone as quickly as it had come and she knew Juliet had vanished with it. The forest was just the forest again. She turned around slowly, looking for Mason. She didn't realize how far away she'd walked. Mason was leaning against a tree, the GPS device still held in her hand. Her eyes were a bit wider than normal, her face pale. Grace stepped in front of her, meeting her gaze.
"Are you okay?" she asked quietly.
Mason swallowed and nodded. "You…you talked to her?"
"Yes."
Mason looked past her. "And she's gone now?"
"Hiding, probably."
"Did…did she know I was here?"
Grace smiled and patted her arm. "I don't know. I didn't ask her." She walked past Mason, then stopped. "I know you have a lot of questions. If you want to talk tonight, we can. I'll try to explain it in a way that you can understand."
Mason was silent as they retraced their steps. Grace was quiet too, wondering if perhaps she should have pushed more. She didn't sense anyone—anything—else out here except Juliet. She should have pressed, yes, but Juliet was gone so fast.
"Did you see her?"
"In the physical sense? No. Not really. There was a shape is all, up in the trees. Then she came down and hid from me."
"I couldn't really hear what you were saying."
"She didn't stay long. She wouldn't talk. Said he'd hurt her if she did. And not her, meaning Juliet, but *her*, as in someone else."
Mason stopped walking. "What does that mean?"
"I'm not sure. Could be the 'he' that I tangled with yesterday and 'her' could be another spirit. Or she could have meant him, as the killer and her as another person."
Mason ran a hand through her hair. "This is crazy."
"Yes. I know."

* * *

"Deb Meckel, age sixteen. Junior in high school," Mason said as she pulled to a stop at a trailhead near Gillette Creek.

Grace looked at her, wondering at her clipped words. They were the first ones she'd spoken since they'd left the forest.

"How far in?"

"Not far. This trail follows the creek. Her body was found five feet away from the creek bank."

"You were in high school in 2004. Did you know her?"

Mason nodded. "Yeah. Deb was a year behind me. We weren't friends, if that's what you're asking."

"She was in the band. Played the clarinet," Grace said, remembering what she'd read in the file. "How many of the victims did you know, Mason?"

"Back then, Gillette Park was a small town. I knew them all, in some form or fashion. Either they were the brother or sister of someone my age or they were close enough to me that I knew them directly."

"Were any of them *good* friends?"

Mason shook her head. "No. I mostly hung out with Brady and Dalton and a few other guys. Nobody from our group was a victim but, 2004, yeah…Glenn Spiller was one of the guys in our group. His little brother was a victim."

"Gary Spiller. Age ten," she said automatically, remembering him from the file.

"Yeah. Gary."

"How did Glenn take it?"

Mason looked at her sharply. "How the hell do you think he took it?"

Grace held up her hand. "I'm trying to understand the pulse of this town, Mason. You say you didn't talk about it. A friend from your group lost a brother. Did you not even talk about it then?"

"What does that matter? Are you putting me on your couch again, Dr. Jennings?"

Grace blew out a breath. "No. I'm sorry. It doesn't matter." She opened the door and got out. "If you could show me the spot."

Mason slammed her door a little too forcefully. "I don't want you inside my damn head."

"I'm not in your head! Christ, I told you, I—"

"You can't read minds…yeah, yeah. I don't believe you."

"What makes you think I even want to read your damn mind?"

"That's what I want to know! Why?"

Grace held her hands up. "Why are we arguing?"

"Because this shit freaks me out!"

She let out a sigh. "Oh, Mason, I'm sorry. Let me go in alone. You can—"

"No. Not after what happened at the creek. No." Mason, too, blew out a breath. "I'm sorry, Grace. I'm trying. God, I really am."

"I know. You're handling it better than most."

"You…you just take it in stride like it's no big deal and I—"

"Mason, we'll talk about it tonight. You can ask me anything you want. Okay?"

Mason finally gave her a half-smile. "I'm not sure I want answers to these questions I have."

She smiled too. "Probably not."

CHAPTER TWENTY-THREE

After a rather heated discussion—carried out mostly in loud whispers—Mason reluctantly agreed to hang back as Grace continued along the trail to the spot where Deb Meckel was found way back in 2004.

As she'd told Grace, she wasn't friends with Deb but she knew her. Deb had lived in their neighborhood and when they were younger, they'd walked the same path along School Road. Deb was rather homely and shy, as she recalled. Brady had graduated the year before and she and Dalton were seniors. After Deb went missing, Aunt Carol had insisted that she stay at their house for a few days. She remembered talking to Brady that night, just the two of them. Talking about Deb Meckel. Normally, after the first murder, there was a period of rest, where everyone could relax a bit. Usually. The second murder wouldn't happen until late September or, more likely, October. Usually. But 2004 was different. Deb Meckel was the second murder and it was still May, two weeks until school let out. She and Brady had speculated that it would be a bad year. She didn't know what they based it on. At seventeen, had she had a gut feeling?

Grace stopped and Mason estimated she was still ten to twenty feet from the spot, according to the coordinates in the file. She'd already pocketed the GPS. She was staying back, like Grace had asked. Not too far. A hundred feet, maybe. Close enough that a quick sprint could get her there if something happened. Yeah, like something pulling Grace into the creek again.

She shook her head at that thought. Did she really believe some long-armed *thing* had reached out and pulled Grace in? At the time, yeah. She'd seen Grace in the water, seen how scared and shaken she'd been. Yes. Maybe that's what had her reeling. She *believed* it. Yes, she did.

Grace's hands were moving now. Was she talking to someone? To Deb Meckel? Mason felt a wave of embarrassment—shame—wash over her. Would Deb recognize her? Would Deb remember her? Would Deb remember how she sometimes wouldn't speak to her? Would ignore her? Would make fun of "those girls" in the band?

You're being ridiculous, she thought to herself. This wasn't Deb Meckel. It was—well, it *wasn't* Deb Meckel. Anyway, they'd been kids. Deb had been an easy target. She and Dalton had hung with a different crowd—the popular kids. Deb wasn't in their group. Deb played the clarinet. Deb—

Grace moved to the water's edge and Mason automatically took several steps in her direction, waiting...watching. Again, Grace's hands moved. Yes, she was talking. Mason had noticed that, even with her, Grace's hands were animated as she spoke. Mason let her gaze settle on Grace, her blond hair shining in the bright sunshine. She was wearing a long-sleeved T-shirt today, one that was left untucked from her jeans and the sleeves were shoved up to her elbows. It was navy too, something she'd noticed about most of Grace's clothes. Was that a favorite color? The hooded sweatshirt she'd worn that morning had been left in the truck.

She jumped as a loud squawk sounded near her head. She jerked around, finding a jay—a Steller's jay—hopping on the limbs in the tree next to her. He turned, his head cocked as he stared at her. She found herself looking into his dark eyes. He jumped closer to her, his wings outstretched, the deep blue a contrast to the black of his head and crest as a streak of sunlight hit it. He came closer still, so close that she could—if she wished—reach out and touch him. His eyes weren't dull. They were shiny and alive. He opened his mouth but no sound came out. He moved out to the edge of the branch, the weight of him making the tip bend, bringing him eye level to her. She stood there, paralyzed, almost afraid to breathe, afraid she'd scare him and cause him to take flight. He stretched his neck out...so close now, he—

"No!"

Mason found herself pushed roughly away from the bird, which squawked loudly before flying off across the creek. She barely kept her balance and as she righted herself, she saw the frightened look on Grace's face.

"What's going on?"

It was Grace staring at her now, not the bird. "What…what did you see, Mason?"

Mason frowned.

"In the tree," Grace clarified.

"The bird? Just a jay. He was practically tame. I could have touched him if—"

"Mason, it wasn't a bird." Grace took her hand and tugged her back along the trail. "Come on. We should go."

Wasn't a bird? Of course it was a bird. She knew what a jay looked like. But Grace's voice had an urgency to it and the hand that held hers was squeezing tightly.

Wasn't a bird? Then what the hell was it? And why the hell were they holding hands?

CHAPTER TWENTY-FOUR

There was something about chopping an onion that normalized things. Maybe the smell. Maybe the rhythmic slicing and dicing. Maybe it was just the prospect of cooking a meal that made things seem normal. Grace knew Mason would indeed "freak out" when she told her what had been in the tree.

Her plan to visit all five sites had been a bit ambitious. After the third one—a trip to the park to look for Fran Frenzil, age ten—she'd called a halt to their excursions. Fran Frenzil had been rather talkative. She'd also shown herself. Whereas Juliet Bateman had been a dark blurb of a shadow dancing in the trees and Deb Meckel had been nothing more than a voice, little Fran Frenzil—bright red hair flowing past her shoulders, green shorts and a yellow top—had kicked a dirty soccer ball beside her as they walked. Little Fran Frenzil had only one shoe but that didn't seem to deter her.

"He was big. Mean. But the other one is the one who hurt me."

"Hurt you how?"

Fran had looked around them, as if making sure no one was listening. *"Down there,"* *she said in a whisper.*

"How old was he? The one who hurt you?"

Fran had stopped, her shoeless foot resting on top of the ball. She appeared to be thinking…remembering. *"High school."*

"Did you know him?"

She shook her head. "There were others there. In the basement. I could hear them. I heard a baby crying."

"Others? A baby?"

"I shouldn't tell you. He might hurt them. Especially Faith."

"Faith? Someone like you?"

"No. Someone like you."

"The one who hurt you…was he the one who left you here? Or was it the other one? The mean one?"

She kicked the ball and ran after it, saying nothing else. Before Grace could catch up with her, Fran disappeared into the forest.

Grace had called to her, but she didn't answer. On a whim, she'd walked over to the playground, conscious of Mason following at a distance. At the swing set, she called for Missy Higgins. The girl—age nine—had been there, but she wouldn't talk. The swing started swaying, higher and higher, and Grace had watched it, back and forth. But it stopped suddenly, as if someone had jumped off and another had stopped the swing with their hand. She wondered—a bit crazily perhaps—if Missy and Fran played together.

She'd been spent after that. Mentally drained. Too drained to even relay the conversation to Mason. So she'd called an end to their searches, offering to cook dinner for them instead. A quick trip to the grocery store, then back to Mason's house. She'd showered and changed into comfortable clothes—sweatpants and a T-shirt—and now here she was, chopping an onion like things were perfectly normal.

"What is it we're cooking?"

Grace smiled. "Oh? Are *we* cooking?" She paused in her task. "Do you like to cook?"

Mason shrugged. "I know how, if that's what you're asking. Well, I know enough to get by. Cooking for one, though…it's easier to pick up something or pop a dinner into the microwave."

"Yes, I know. I'm guilty of that too. Sometimes. Cooking is a stress release. Sometimes I need it."

"Like tonight?"

She nodded, not bothering to lie. She would tell Mason everything she learned today soon enough. She stilled the knife again. "I would love a glass of wine. Do you have some?"

"I do. Anything in particular?"

"No. Just wine." She paused again. "A nice red."

Mason smiled. "Don't know about nice. Your nice and my nice might be completely different. I've got a couple of blends. There's a merlot that Dalton left here." She opened a cabinet at the end of the kitchen. "There's a sweet red too. Brady's."

Grace wrinkled up her nose and gave a quick shake of her head at that suggestion. "A blend is good."

While the onions sautéed, she sliced the portabella mushrooms into large chunks. She'd already seasoned the chicken breasts. Mason set a glass of wine near her and she paused long enough to take a sip, quickly nodding her approval. She assembled the dish, something she'd learned to make years ago. Simple, yet elegant. Well, fresh basil would have made it better, but there was none to be found at the grocery store. She mixed the onions and mushrooms with the chicken and popped it into the oven. Pasta, which she would season with an Italian dressing, would serve as their base. A vegetable medley—she'd found a bag in the frozen foods section at the store—was heating and would be mixed in with the pasta right before serving. Simple and quick, yet elegant enough for wine. She smiled at that thought as she picked up the wineglass.

"Smells good."

"Thank you."

"Can I help with anything?"

"I've got a handle on it." She leaned her hip against the counter, watching Mason. How quickly their relationship had changed. She wasn't one to make friends, but they were dangerously close to that now. She didn't have the patience to get past people's initial shock and all the ensuing questions. Of course, once those questions were answered, not many actually wanted to be friends with her. When she'd first met Mason, she thought it would be the same. It was different somehow. Now it was different. Oh, Mason had questions. She figured tonight she'd have dozens of them. It was different, though. She felt so at ease with the woman, it was as if she'd known her for years. And Mason was comfortable enough around her to voice her disbelief openly. And, of course, there was the vision she'd had. Perhaps that was the reason she felt something growing between them.

Mason was sitting at the table, slowly rotating a drink glass between her hands. A light-colored drink tonight. Gin and tonic, perhaps? She had a frown on her face, as if contemplating a question. Grace took the opportunity to study her. Her dark hair was still damp from her earlier shower and Mason had it slicked behind both ears. For the first time, she noticed that—even though she wore no earrings—her ears were pierced. Her eyebrows were dark and thick, making her expressions more pronounced. Mason must have felt her staring and she looked up, her rather long eyelashes blinking a couple of times as their gazes held.

"I…I saw a Steller's jay. In the tree. The same kind of bird that was out in the tree this morning. The bird that made me think of my mother's empty bird feeders."

The feeders that she put crumbled animal crackers into, Grace added silently. Only it wasn't the same kind of bird. Grace feared it was the *same* bird. With a sigh, she pushed off the counter and joined Mason at the table.

"The same kind of bird that was watching us at the creek, after you rescued me."

"Yeah. The same. I'd forgotten about that."

"I didn't see a bird today, Mason. It was a…a creature of some sort," she said carefully.

"Part monkey, part…I don't know, exactly. It had the body of a monkey, but the face was…it was something with sharp teeth, like a cat or something." She shook her head. "No, not a cat, exactly. It changed. Just…a scary demon-like face. Human face. Then it changed to look kinda like a baby. It held a knife. When I pushed you out of the way, it was swinging the knife toward you."

Mason's hand was trembling ever so slightly as she took a sip of her drink. "I realize now I was hypnotized by the bird. I couldn't look away from it. I lost track of time. I lost sight of the fact that I was supposed to be watching you. I saw nothing but the bird." Mason looked at her then. "If you hadn't been there, would it have hurt me?"

"I don't know," she said honestly. "What was the bird doing?"

"Nothing, really. He was looking at me, getting closer and closer. He wasn't scared of me—tame. At the end there, I thought he was going to peck me in the head with his beak."

"And maybe that's all that would have happened. I don't know."

"Was everything…okay out there?"

Grace nodded, knowing what Mason was asking. "Yes. No issues. I saw nothing out of the ordinary." Then she laughed quietly at that statement. "Ordinary for me," she clarified.

Mason seemed to relax a little. "What happened at the last site?"

"Fran? She said something that I wasn't expecting. Something that makes me question who we're looking for." She set her wineglass down. "When I asked her if she knew who did this to her, she said no, she didn't know him. But there were two. She described him as big and mean, but he wasn't the one who hurt her. In her words, 'hurt her' meant the sexual assault, not the killing. And the one who hurt her was a boy, high school age."

Mason's mouth opened in disbelief. "High school?"

"That's what she said. She also said there were others, in the basement. She said she could hear them. Now, what that means, I have no clue. She wouldn't elaborate. And when I asked her who had left her there, the big and mean one or the high school boy, she ran away."

Mason rubbed her face with both hands. "Jesus...this is for real, Grace?"

"Real in my world, like is she telling the truth? Or real in your world?"

"Both, I guess."

Grace didn't bother answering that question. She assumed Mason didn't really need an answer. "She said something else, something that Juliet had said too. Fran said she shouldn't talk to me because he might hurt her. Again, the 'her' is referring to a third person. Faith. She said her name was Faith." She leaned closer. "She said, when she heard the others in the basement, there was a baby crying. So when she said he might hurt her, she could be referring to the baby. Of course, Fran was killed in 2004. The baby would be all grown up now."

"Oh, man." Mason stood up, pacing now. "What the hell am I supposed to do with this information? Two guys? High school? A baby? How am I supposed to relay this to my uncle?"

"Mason, sit down."

"I don't know how to process this, Grace."

"Sit down," she said again.

Mason did, and this time when she picked up her drink, her hand was shaking badly. Grace gave her a few moments to collect herself, then decided to change direction with their conversation.

"Why aren't you still close with Brady and Dalton?"

Mason seemed shocked by the change of course. "Why does that matter?"

"It doesn't really." She rested her chin in her palm. "Is it a product of this town or something else?"

"Meaning?"

"I'm not sure. Whatever bond you had as kids, would your being gone a few years erase that? What about Brady and Dalton? Are they still close?"

"I was gone eleven years...more than a few."

"Did they know about your personal life?"

"The guys knew I was gay back in high school. Not an issue." She spread her hands out. "I'm not sure why, Grace. I came back...yeah, and things were different. I mean, we still go grab a beer at Bucky's. And football season, we get together to watch games."

"But?"

"I don't know. It's just different. We don't...talk."

"Ah. Superficial."

"Yeah. Nothing too serious."

"To avoid talking about the murders? To avoid talking about your feelings?"

Mason stared at her, eyebrows raised. "Am I on your couch now?"

"Sorry. It fascinates me is all. The fact that no one talks among yourselves about the killings. I assume when you talk about it now, it's only in the context of law enforcement."

"Right."

"Why is that?"

"What is there to say?"

"I think that all of you are afraid of who the killer might be. You're afraid it's someone you know, someone who walks among you... maybe a friend. So you keep your distance—just in case."

"Oh, come on. I know Dalton is not the killer. I know Brady is not the killer."

"I'm not saying you think they are. I'm talking in general terms. About everyone. The town has a secret and everyone keeps it." She stood and went to the stove, heating the water for the pasta. "Do you go to church?"

"Church?"

Grace added a little more wine to her glass. "We haven't been to the new part of town, but down here on this side, I haven't noticed any churches. I'm sure there are some."

Mason nodded. "There are a couple in Old Town, yeah. And the Baptists built a new church, oh, five or six years ago. They finished it right about the time I moved back. It's over in New Town."

"And you?"

"No. I don't go to church. Not since I was ten." She shook her head. "Well, that's not entirely true. Whenever I was around, Aunt Carol made me go with them. Methodists."

"Your mom stopped going?"

"Yeah. And it suited me fine. You?"

Grace shook her head. "No. Despite being raised in the South, my mother wasn't a churchgoer. And Rich talked a good game, but no, he never made the effort. Besides..." She stopped. Did she want to go there?

"You're not a believer?"

Grace met her gaze. "I don't know, really," she said easily. "I talk to dead people. What does that say? Their spirit—their soul—is caught between here and the afterlife? If you *believe*, is that even possible? If you believe—when you die, your soul leaves your body and you go to heaven, right? You don't get stuck somewhere in between."

"Maybe what you see and hear isn't their soul."

"No? What is it then?"

"Hell, I don't know."

Grace smiled. "Fran was playing with a soccer ball. Missy plays on the swings. What does Susie Shackle do? What does Deb Meckel do?"

"What do you see? What do they look like?"

"They're not all the same. I think it depends how much they want to show of themselves. Juliet was nothing but a dark shape, moving among the tree branches, then down, then back up again. Deb wouldn't show herself at all. Fran looked like a ten-year-old girl, in the flesh. The only thing out of place was that she only had one shoe."

Mason nodded. "Yeah, I think that was in the file. When they found her body, she only had on one shoe."

"They all said a version of the same thing. They didn't want to talk because they were afraid he'd hurt her. If the *he* is a living, breathing human, then that suggests he has a captive. It also causes me to wonder how he would *know* they were talking to me. But if the *he* is like them…another spirit or…or worse, then—"

"What could be worse?"

"Worse, meaning, for the most part, they are harmless. I see them in a different realm, not in our physical world. But there is something else out here. There was something in the creek that *did* reach into my physical realm. It's not something that is gentle—nonthreatening—like them. It's also something that is more powerful than them. At least, I'm assuming."

"So let's say the 'he' is a real person," Mason said, making quotes in the air. "Why a captive? And why would they care? They, meaning the…the ones you've talked to."

"You're probably right. If there was someone missing in town that's now a captive, you would know about it. And why would they care? I don't know. It was the tone of their voice. They were concerned for this girl's safety. Fran said it wasn't someone like her. It was someone like me. Human. Flesh and blood, I assume." She stood up quickly. She'd forgotten about her water and it was already boiling. She turned it down, then added pasta.

"And this is all speculation, Mason. Only one other time have I run into something that I would consider evil." She remained standing, resting a hip against the counter. "I attended a small university in Georgia and studied parapsychology. Some of my classmates talked me into going to a very old cemetery in Atlanta—Oakland Cemetery."

"Oh, god...a *cemetery?*"

Grace smiled. "A bunch of paranormal geeks on a fieldtrip... yeah."

Mason raised her eyebrows. "Friends?"

Grace shook her head. "No, not really. They were likeminded, although it was always a competition. Whereas I might see the spirit in human form—like Fran today—others would see her only as an apparition." She waved her hand in the air. "Anyway, I went with them one night. We slipped in after midnight. It was one of the few times I've been afraid." She crossed her arms, feeling chills as she remembered that night. "I saw...a lot of people. I watched as a man was hung from a tree...a Union soldier. I saw shootings. It was as if everyone rose from their graves to reenact how they were killed. But there was one guy...he was a killer. A murderer. He reenacted his killings. He had a sword and it was...well, lots of blood and gore. I was seeing everything as if it was happening, in full color with sound. He *knew* I could see him. He laughed so hard each time he killed. Then he chased us. It was so real—to me. Not to the others. They saw a shape or an apparition—a ghost-like appearance, like you might see in a movie. I saw him, as if he were in the flesh. I could see the evil in his eyes, could see the sweat on his brow, could smell his foul breath, his rotting teeth. And the sword. He kept swinging the sword as he chased us—the sword that was dripping with blood." She shook herself. "I always wonder if his victims—is that their fate? To reenact their murder night after night?"

"I don't know what to say to that."

"You can say you don't believe me. That's what they all said. They thought a ghost was playing with us, teasing...chasing after us in fun. They couldn't see his face, read his expression—see his murders— hear their screams. I was deathly afraid, they were not. Ignorance is bliss sometimes."

"Why could you see him and not them?"

She smiled a bit ruefully. "Different levels of talent, one of my professors would say."

"So all psychics are not created equal?"

Grace drained the water from the pasta, wondering how to answer that question in a way Mason would understand. "All mediums are psychic." She turned to look at her. "But all psychics are not mediums. Some psychics can read minds at will and others cannot. There are varying degrees of skill. As in all professions." She put the pot down. "Now don't get me wrong. It isn't a matter of needing to practice more. At least, not for most. The skills—gifts—that you have are limited."

"So what makes you think that this other psychic who was here in 2004 would know anything?"

"Because she wanted to talk to Susie Shackle. Why she wanted to do it in a séance setting, I don't know. Perhaps she was hoping to draw them all in at once."

Mason held her hand up. "Okay. You're starting to freak me out again."

Grace laughed lightly. "Then how about we eat? The chicken should be done." She paused. "Thank you for allowing me to have this conversation with you. It's not often I get to talk about my work with someone."

"Because there are no friends?" Mason asked in a gentle tone.

Grace nodded. "Other freaks like me, I know from online forums and such. Not friends, but acquaintances and colleagues. It's more of a safe place for us to ask questions and relay experiences. I'm more of a lurker than a participant anyway."

"Quit calling yourself a freak."

"Why? I am one."

Mason opened the oven and removed the chicken dish for her. "You are not."

"Oh, Mason, you know you thought that about me. Don't lie."

Mason laughed. "Okay, at the risk of you reading my mind, yes, I may have thought something along those lines." She was still smiling as she looked at her. "I don't think you're a freak, Grace. You're... special. I can't imagine the burden you must have lived with...are still living with."

Grace squeezed her arm. "Yes. Thank you for understanding. And for thinking I'm special."

CHAPTER TWENTY-FIVE

Mason sipped her coffee, keeping a watch out the window for the bird. She was almost disappointed when it didn't show. Well, disappointed wasn't the right word. She'd prepared herself for it so it was a bit anticlimactic when the only birds she saw were chickadees.

"Why animal crackers?"

She jumped at the sound of Grace's quiet voice behind her. She turned around, finding her much like yesterday morning...in the same oversized sleep shirt but sweatpants replaced the jeans she'd had on yesterday.

"In the bird feeder? It was the only thing in the pantry that they could eat. A couple of cans of soup, not much else." She sipped from her coffee. "There was always soup."

"You hate soup now."

Mason nodded, not caring if Grace had guessed that or knew it by other means. Other means, probably. Much like she knew of the animal crackers. "If my mom happened to be at home, I wasn't allowed to go over to Aunt Carol's for dinner. I did know how to use a can opener so it was usually soup or some other form of dinner in a can. A treat was a frozen dinner I could put in the microwave."

"Was she abusive to you in other ways? Physically? Verbally?"

"She was…she was critical of me. I wasn't pretty enough, I didn't dress right, my friends were boys and not girls. Things like that. Important things to her. She wasn't concerned about my grades, only what boys I could date." She moved to the coffeepot to pour some into a cup for Grace. "She was worried about me marrying the wrong guy and possibly ending up like her, I think."

"Like her? Meaning she married the wrong guy?"

"He wasn't around anymore, so yeah."

"Did she consider the possibility that *he* married the wrong woman?"

Mason frowned. "He abandoned us, Grace. Left without a word. If he married the wrong woman, he should have had the balls to face it, not disappear as if he could erase that part of his life. And yeah, I am still bitter."

"I know you are. But you were ten. There could have been some underlying tension in their marriage that you weren't aware of." Grace held her hand up. "Not taking sides at all, Mason, just offering an alternative."

Yes, she was bitter, and yes, she had wondered if perhaps her mother had been the sole reason he'd left. They'd seemed happy, normal. She didn't recall any yelling or fighting. After he left, her mother turned into a stranger—a stranger she didn't like or care for. Had she been that stranger to her father all along? Had he finally had enough and left?

"He left me too, Grace. Not just her…he left me too, without a word, without a goodbye." She squared her shoulders, holding on to the hatred she still felt for him. "There are no excuses."

"No, there aren't." Grace stirred sugar into her coffee. "When did you tell her you were gay?"

"Oh, one night during a fight. Dalton and I were going to the prom together. She thought we were dating. She proceeded to list off all of Dalton's shortcomings and was on the verge of forbidding me to go with him." She glanced at Grace. "His main shortcoming was that his parents were divorced too." She shrugged. "So I told her we weren't dating and why." She smiled then. "Apparently Dalton's shortcomings weren't so short after all, compared to my being gay. She said she didn't want to hear another word about it."

"And knowing you, you never mentioned it again."

"Knowing me?"

Grace smiled and sipped her coffee. "You're a little stubborn, a little defiant. I can picture you leaving for college with barely a wave goodbye."

Mason nodded. "That's pretty much how it was. By that time, my mother and I were barely coexisting. There was no love on either side, believe me."

"How did you make it financially?"

"I worked two jobs while I went to school. Got financial aid. And Uncle Alan sent me money now and then. I managed. I was used to eating soup, you know." She shoved away from the counter. "So, what's on the agenda today? Finish up with the 2004 sites?" If Grace wondered at her abrupt change of subject, she didn't show it.

"No. I think I want to jump to 2012. See if we can find out why there were five killed that year."

"Does it matter?"

"If there was something that triggered it, it would be good to know. Especially if my being here causes a repeat of that."

"Oh, I got a text from Uncle Alan. A couple of phone numbers for you to try for the psychic."

"Good. Thank you." She added more coffee to her cup, then, with a brief smile, retreated to the spare bedroom.

Mason blew out a breath, then turned again to the window, her gaze on the trees without really seeing them. What was it about Grace that made her open up? She'd never told anyone much of anything about her childhood, much less the intimate details. Years dating Shauna had never produced any talks like this. She tilted her head thoughtfully. What *had* she and Shauna talked about? Shauna grew up in Los Angeles. Mason had joined her on occasion for family dinners. She had two older brothers who had both moved away. Her parents seemed normal. Other than that, she didn't know much about them. She didn't know what her parents did for a living, didn't know where the brothers had moved off to. And in turn, Shauna didn't know anything other than her parents were divorced and Mason had left home at eighteen. What had they talked about?

Movement out of the corner of her eye brought her attention back to the present and she felt her breath catch as the blue bird—a Steller's jay again—hopped into view. It jumped from limb to limb with ease, getting closer and closer to the window. She watched its movements, only slightly conscious of her heart beating a little faster than normal. Was it just a bird...or was it *the* bird? It flew down to the limb closest to the window and she stared at it, its gaze holding hers for the longest time, neither of them blinking. Its head tilted slightly, as if trying to read her expression. Then, quick as lightning, it lunged at the window, beak open in a furious cry. A flurry of blue and black hit the glass and Mason jumped back, embarrassed for the startled gasp that left her mouth. The bird flew off as quickly as he'd arrived and she watched him sail past the trees and up the side of the mountain, disappearing from sight.

Her hand was trembling as she put the coffee cup down. She'd spilled most of it on her hand, and she was frankly surprised that she hadn't dropped the damn thing. She turned away from the window in a rush and went in search of Grace. She heard the shower running in the spare bathroom, and she hesitated at the door for a second or two, then knocked several times.

"Grace?"

"Yeah?"

She turned the knob, finding it unlocked. She pushed the door open. The mirror was foggy from the steam. Grace was peeking out from behind the shower curtain, her eyebrows raised questioningly.

"I'm sorry...but...well..."

"What's wrong?"

"The bird. It came back. It...it flew at the window." She gave a shaky laugh. "It scared me and I didn't want to be out there alone." She knew how ridiculous that sounded, but she couldn't take the words back now, even if she wanted to.

Grace nodded, her expression serious. "He must feel threatened," she said, almost to herself. Then she looked at her. "I'll be done in a minute, then we can—"

"Oh, yeah, sorry. I didn't mean to barge in on you." She backed up and closed the door, resting her forehead against it. *You're a cop, for god's sake. Scared of a damn bird?*

"Mason?"

She stared at the door, then opened it again. "Yeah?"

"This is the closest someone has come to seeing me naked in years."

She smiled at the shape behind the shower curtain, hearing the teasing tone in Grace's voice. "Well, if it makes you feel better, this is the closest *I've* come to seeing someone naked in years too."

CHAPTER TWENTY-SIX

Despite Mason's teasing tone when she'd left the bathroom, Grace knew she'd been shaken. She hurried through her shower and dressed quickly—jeans and a T-shirt. She stared in the mirror for a second, debating with herself on whether to bother with the barest of makeup that she usually applied. A quick moisturizer was all she took the time for.

Mason was nowhere to be found, however. She placed her shoulder bag and the sweatshirt she'd grabbed on the sofa, then went back down the hallway, hearing movement in Mason's bedroom. She paused at the door.

"You okay?"

"Yeah…come on in."

She found Mason sitting on the bed, lacing up her boots. It was her first time to peek into her bedroom and she glanced around quickly. The top of the dresser was cluttered with folded clothes and she recognized several of the uniform shirts that Mason normally wore. She looked back at her, seeing one of those shirts on her now. Her duty belt was slung over a chair that was against the wall and a jacket was tossed casually across the seat of the chair. She walked fully into the room, going to sit beside Mason on the bed. Mason looked at her and smiled.

"I'm okay, really."

Grace nodded. "Did you see anything other than the bird?"

"No. Steller's jay. Same as before. When it looks at you, though, it's like it has human eyes."

Grace wanted to tell her that it most definitely wasn't human, but she only nodded. "I'm wondering why it's targeted you. Meaning, you and not me."

"Maybe because I'm an easy target," Mason said with an uneasy laugh. "Doesn't take much to scare me."

Grace leaned closer and bumped her shoulder affectionately. "I didn't hear a shrill, girly scream so it must not have scared you too badly."

"Why do you think it did that?"

"Flew at the window? I'm not sure. Maybe like you said, trying to scare you. Warn you. You're the one hauling me around, showing me around." She shrugged. "Guessing, of course. I haven't run into something like this before."

Mason swallowed. "Well, it worked. It did scare me, despite the lack of a girly scream."

"I know. I would like to find out who he is, but...if no one will talk to me, that's going to be difficult."

"Because they're scared too."

"Yes. But what we learned yesterday is that they're not scared for themselves—I mean, they're already dead, what can he do?—but they're scared for someone else." She patted Mason's leg, then stood up. "We should get started. And if you'll pass on the phone numbers, I'll try to call Nora Nightsail."

* * *

She had no luck with either of the phone numbers Sheriff Cooper had passed on to her. The first one was disconnected—maybe an old landline number. The second had voicemail although it was a computer-generated greeting so she had no idea if it was for Nora or not. She didn't want to assume it was, even though she felt certain that she would be in contact with the woman somehow. She left a brief message, without going into too much detail, asking Nora to call her. She'd done a Google search on Nora Nightsail and had found a website that looked promising—psychic readings in person or over the phone—and she'd called that number too. It, too, went to voicemail and she'd left a message there as well.

Now they were heading out into the forest again, this time past the north side of town where Gillette Creek dumped out of the mountains and into the valley, where it would wind its way through town before flowing back into the mountains. She opened her shoulder bag and pulled out the pad to look at the notes she'd jotted down earlier. The first victim was Thomas Houston, age thirteen. He disappeared while at the library. Video surveillance showed him going into the bathroom—alone. He never came out. His body was found four days later. Cause of death was drowning.

"When you returned to Gillette Park, did you have any aspirations of catching this guy?"

"Aspirations? I am a cop, you know."

"Okay, that question didn't come out right. Sure, I know everyone wants to get this guy, but I mean, was that your main goal, come home and end the terror that was upon your hometown?"

Mason glanced at her quickly. "Like a hero? Come riding back on a white horse to save the day?"

"Yeah, something like that. From what I've heard and read, this is really the only crime in town. As a cop, it's got to eat at you. I assume, anyway."

"I'll admit, yeah, I thought when I came back, with my experience in LA, that I'd be able to get a handle on it all. And yeah, maybe catch the guy right away and end the terror, as you said." She put her turn signal on and took a left on a small, unpaved road that was quickly engulfed by trees. "I knew all about the murders, of course. From Brady, from my uncle. So when I got back, I read the file ten, twelve times, memorized a lot of it, visited the sites. Didn't take me long to realize that the only way we were going to catch this guy was if he screwed up or we got damn lucky and stumbled upon him."

"Or he got caught in the act. I find it amazing that after all these years, no one has seen a thing. Almost as if he has help, don't you think?"

"I guess I know what you mean by that. And *that* I can't quite comprehend."

Mason drove them deeper into the forest, finally stopping in a small clearing that had been cut into the woods. It was a primitive parking lot, big enough for five or six cars. A wooden sign was hung on a tree, pointing the way to the Old Ponderosa Trail.

"So named for the stand of pine trees that the creek flows around," Mason explained. "Old growth. It's in a very rocky area and they survived both logging and fires. Twelve or fifteen trees, I think there are. Huge trees. Biggest ones I've ever seen."

Grace's breath caught. Huge trees, like in her vision? Perhaps. But she pushed that thought and her vision aside. She wanted to know more about the young Mason.

"Was this trail here when you were growing up? Did you hike it?"

"The trail was, but it wasn't an official trail. A place where locals went. And yeah, I've been there many times. Once the town started growing and tourists started coming more, they updated the trail system, created these little cutouts for parking. During camping season—which will be starting very soon—these parking spots will be full."

Mason locked the truck, then they started up the trail. The body was found relatively close to the creek, propped against a tree. Like sometimes, items were left with the body, like Jason Gorman's soccer ball. For Thomas Houston, his schoolbooks were left with him.

"When you're not working, do you use your downtime to hike, explore?"

"Not as much as I thought I would. When I moved back, I thought I'd be all over the trails, like I was when I was growing up." Mason shrugged. "It's different though. The town has changed. Brady, Dalton...they've changed. *I've* changed."

"Do you have friends, Mason?" she asked gently.

"Friends? Sure." Another shrug. "I know a lot of people in town. There's a hiking group that I belong to...I just don't get to meet up with them much." Mason stopped walking. "No. That's a lie. I choose not to meet up with them. I go to Bucky's almost every night. And Brady and Dalton come by most nights too. And we try to talk, like old times, but the murders always come up. Always. It's like we can't have a conversation about anything without the murders hanging over us. And we don't *want* to talk about it, so we end up not talking at all. Other people, they don't talk about it. It's there, but they don't talk about it. But for Brady and Dalton, it's like this murder investigation is front and center in their lives, both in their private lives and work. Nothing else matters."

"It's why they're both divorced," Grace said with certainty.

"Yes. And I've fallen into the same trap. It's all I think about, like it's my sole existence."

"You have a copy of the file by your bed." Mason looked at her, startled. "I saw it this morning."

"I only moved it there since you've been in town. Trying to brush up on the facts. But yeah, at first, I'd read the damn thing nightly. Memorized it." She started walking again. "I feel like, if we don't solve this case, I'm going to disappear. I feel like I'm already disappearing, Grace. Like them, there's nothing in my life anymore. Nothing. No joy, no laughter. Nothing interests me. Nothing. That's the real reason I don't meet up with the hiking group. The reason I don't have friends."

"Your uncle doesn't seem to be affected."

"Oh, yeah, he is. He and Aunt Carol put on a show in front of people, but it's there. He's withdrawn from her, hardly talks. In his eyes, he's a failure. We all are. Twenty-something years, fifty-something kids killed…and we've been nothing but inept."

"Serial killers are clever. If they weren't, they would never evolve into serial killers. They'd be caught after one, maybe two. Look at the Green River Killer, for instance. Didn't it take nearly twenty years to catch him? In this case, though, I don't think we're dealing with simply a serial killer." She held her hand up. "And I know you don't want to hear that."

"It's not that I don't believe you, Grace. You know that, right?" She stopped again. "I like being in control and I'm not now. That damn bird…you…everything. I'm not in control of any of it."

Grace raised her eyebrows. "Control of *me*?" She smiled. "I'm the freak, remember? There is no control, Mason. I can't even control it."

"Grace, please stop calling yourself a freak. I told you, I don't think of you that way."

"So you say."

"I don't." A quick smile. "Well, before I met you…yeah. Maybe. And maybe at first too. But to me, you're…normal." Then she tilted her head. "Except when—"

"Except when I'm not." She started walking along the trail again. "I know, Mason. It's hard for you. I know. And if it makes any difference, you've been the absolute *best* about it. Ever."

"Yeah? Ever?"

"Yes." She turned her head to glance at her. "Being around you, I do actually feel somewhat normal. It's nice. It's been so long since, well, since anyone treated me like a friend. Thank you, Mason."

She didn't add that she hardly recognized it. It had been so long since she'd had extended conversations with anyone, so long since she'd been around someone in a relaxed, informal setting like this. Of course, relaxed was a comparative term, wasn't it? They were, after all, hunting a serial killer.

"I guess I haven't had a friend in a while either." Mason checked the GPS device she held, then continued walking. "I thought I would immerse myself in the community when I got back and I found that hard to do. Most of the people I went to high school with have moved. Besides Brady and Dalton, those that stayed, I wasn't really close with them. So I kinda keep to myself."

"Other than Bucky's?"

Mason gave a quick laugh. "Yeah, my second home."

"When this is over with, do you think that will change?"

"I don't know. It's hard to picture this town without that shadow hanging over it." Mason glanced at her. "Like I said, it's almost like there are two towns…the old and the new."

"The killer belongs to the old."

"Yeah. And if you go back to map the disappearances, they all happen in Old Town, whether at the school, the park, the library, wherever. Never on the valley side." Mason checked the GPS again. "We're coming up on the site."

Grace looked around, only now noticing that the trail was hugging the creek, its clear water rushing down toward town in frothy bursts. "Will we see the big trees?"

"No. They're up higher. The trail gets rather steep and rocky." Mason glanced at her. "Why? Do you want to?"

Grace smiled, hoping it didn't look as wistful as it seemed. "It would be something *normal*. Perhaps after this is all over with, you can show me."

Mason smiled at her. "Something normal, huh? Yeah, that would be nice. I enjoy your company."

Grace arched an eyebrow.

"Really," Mason said with another smile. "I like you."

Grace returned her smile. God, when was the last time someone said those words to her? Before she could answer, however, her phone rang. They both frowned at the same time.

"I didn't think we had service out here."

"We don't. The trails on the east side of town are about the only ones that get a signal and that's if you're lucky."

Grace opened her shoulder bag and fished out her phone. "Yes, hello. This is Dr. Jennings."

"Hello," came a pleasant, almost singsong voice. "This is Nora Nightsail. You've left a couple of messages. How can I help you? You said something about Gillette Park?"

"Oh, yes. Thank you for calling me back." She looked at Mason and nodded. "I know it's been a number of years, but I was hoping you might have some recollection of your time here. The town has hired me, much as they hired you."

"So you finally showed up there? I didn't think it would take this many years for everything to fall into place."

Grace frowned. "What do you mean?"

"You are the seer, aren't you?"

Grace chanced a glance at Mason, then looked away quickly. "Yes."

"Yes, you are. And I've been expecting your call for years. Have you found the young woman? Well, not so young now, I suppose. I met her when I was there. She was in high school. She plays a part in this. She was to leave for a few years, then return." A pause. "Have you found her yet? You can't win without her. You must find her."

Grace met Mason's eyes, holding them. She looked inside, seeing questions—curiosity—and beyond that, a quiet confidence. She turned from Mason, walking farther away. "Yes. I found her."

"Good. Good. Then your journey is almost over. It will be a rocky ride. She will be afraid. Afraid of the unknown. You must help her get past it. You need her. She needs you. You'll learn more soon."

"How...how do you know all this?" she asked stupidly. "I mean—"

Nora Nightsail laughed delightfully. "There is someone else you need to talk to. Let me think; her name will come to me."

Grace waited, glancing over her shoulder to find Mason watching her. She gave her a quick smile and turned her back to her once again. Nora Nightsail was a psychic. Despite Alan Cooper's assertion, she was no fraud, of that Grace was certain.

"Patricia Brinkman, yes, that was her name. She's probably in her late eighties by now."

"Who is she?"

"She was the town's librarian for years. She'll know the history. I spoke with her several times." Nora Nightsail paused. "Have you learned about the fire?"

"What fire?"

"Talk to Miss Brinkman. She'll have the history you'll need. The fire is important."

"I'm surprised you still remember this town. It's been a number of years."

"Yes, I didn't realize it had been sixteen years until I went back and looked at my notes. I haven't thought of that little town in years, to be honest. After your call, though, lots of memories came flooding back, like they were supposed to, I guess. I wasn't exactly welcomed with open arms. They were afraid of me, I think. It didn't matter. I knew at the time that I was only a precursor to you."

Grace's head was spinning and she couldn't hold on to a thought long enough to ask the many questions that she had.

"There is something very evil there, Dr. Jennings." This time when she spoke the sing-song tone was gone from her voice. "Very evil. Have you encountered it yet?"

"Yes, I believe so. There have been a couple of incidents."

"There was this boy—killed a few years before I got there. Paul something. I believe he was twelve or thirteen. I spoke with him in the park there by the school. He was very forthcoming, if I recall. One of the few. Most wouldn't talk to me. He told me to find this girl—" She paused, as if thinking. "I'm sorry, the name escapes me. She was one of the first ones killed."

"Susie Shackle?" she guessed.

"Yes! That's it! I tried several times, but she wouldn't come to me. I had planned to go out to the park one night, do a proper séance, but...well, that didn't go over too well. I was asked to leave town. Rather rudely, I might add."

Grace nodded. "Yes, that's what I heard."

"It didn't matter one way or the other. Susie Shackle wouldn't come to me. She was waiting for you all along. She'll come to you when the time is right."

"Why me?"

"I don't know the answer to that. Perhaps Susie will shed light on it when you talk to her."

"She hasn't been receptive to me yet."

"Then it's not time."

Time for what, she wanted to ask, but she didn't. "Is there anything in your notes that might be helpful to me?"

"I don't think so, dear. This is your journey, not mine. Find Patricia Brinkman. She'll shed some light, I'm sure of it. She has something. You'll need to find it."

Find it? Grace blew out a breath. "I see," she said a bit more abruptly than she intended. Apparently, Nora Nightsail didn't feel the need to be cooperative.

"You don't need my help, Dr. Jennings. Things will progress as they're meant to." Grace heard a bell jingling in the background. "I'm sorry, but I must go. A client is here for a reading."

"I understand. Thank you, Ms. Nightsail. I appreciate your taking the time to return my call."

"Call me Nora, please. I..." A long pause. "Wait! Don't hang up. I'm...I'm seeing..." Another long pause. When she spoke, her voice was softer, quiet. "You're in a box. The box is in a...a cave or a cellar. It's dark, damp. There are voices in the background. Crying."

Grace was clutching her phone tightly, her chest tight. "There's a baby crying."

"Yes! A baby! They're trying to hush it." Nora's voice lowered to nearly a whisper. "They don't want him to hear."

Grace closed her eyes. It was her dream.

"Rusty."

Grace frowned. "Rusty?"

She heard Nora Nightsail let out a frustrated breath.

"It's vanished. I'm sorry. You must be careful, Dr. Jennings. Very careful. There are minions, I fear. They can be harder to spot."

"Yes. I believe you're right."

"She will help you, of course. Mason. Yes, that was her name. Mason. You two are linked now. It took this many years for you to find each other. Together, you will break the cycle. But you both must have the same conviction. You must go in as one. Your souls need to be connected. As one. It is the only way to defeat him." That was all. Dead silence followed.

Her hand was shaking as she looked at her phone, seeing the "no service" message at the top where bars would normally be. She held it up to Mason to see.

"No service. I heard her as clearly as if she'd been standing here beside me." She slipped the phone back into her bag. Mason took her own phone out of her pocket, showing it to her. Neither of them had cell service yet her phone rang. Not only that, she'd carried on a conversation with a psychic without there being any static whatsoever.

"What did she say that rattled you?"

Grace brushed at the hair on her forehead. "Do I look rattled?"

"A little, yeah. A lot, actually."

Grace nodded. Yeah, she was rattled. Nora Nightsail knew far too much, didn't she? How much should she tell Mason? She met her gaze. Soulmates? Was that what Nora had been trying to say? No, she couldn't tell Mason that. "She had a vision. At the end, she had a vision. I was in a box. The box was in a cave or a cellar, she said."

"Your dream. It's your dream."

"Yes. My dream. There were others. A baby was crying."

"What does it mean?"

"The dream or the vision?" Grace took a deep breath. "My future, I suppose."

"So this is like a premonition or something?"

"A vision. Visions like that—from a psychic—usually come true. Or some semblance of them."

"Oh, man."

Grace tried to force a smile to her face, hoping she managed. "Yes. Something to look forward to." She motioned up ahead, intentionally dispelling the vision from her mind. "How far?"

Mason stared at her for a long moment, as if to say something. Grace could tell she was warring with herself, and she had half a mind to try to read her, to see what was causing this distressed look. Mason pushed it away though, nodding finally. "Fifty feet or so."

Grace tilted her head. "Are you okay?"

"I'm not sure."

No. She wasn't sure she was either. How did Nora know Mason's name? Mason never indicated that she and the psychic had ever talked. And why would they? Mason would have been in high school at the time. Well, Nora Nightsail *was* a psychic. Why *wouldn't* she know those things? But what of her warning? What of her directive that they had to be linked, they had to be as one? What did all of that mean? She pushed those questions away. She couldn't think about it now. She needed to focus on the here and now.

They walked on along the trail, Grace trying to look for signs, trying to concentrate, trying to get the image of her in a locked box out of her mind. Her dream had been vague, at least what she remembered of it. Waking, coming out of the nightmare, it had been very vivid, but the only thing she remembered now was the feeling of doom. The vision itself—the dream—had faded to black rather quickly.

Up ahead, she saw the forest floor change, a dark film spreading out from a tree along the creek bank. She held out a hand, touching Mason's stomach as she held her back. Mason stopped and Grace could hear her uneven breathing.

"Stay here."

She moved closer, watching as the rocks and twigs turned nearly black. A tree, between the trail and the creek, was at the center and she walked toward it. As she stepped into the circle of black, she felt the temperature change. Not hot, like she was expecting, but cold. She closed her eyes for a moment, trying to clear her mind. She heard the creek, the water making a rhythmic, almost musical sound as it traveled over and around rocks, rolling along unimpeded down the mountain toward the valley.

Before she opened her eyes, she knew she was no longer alone. He sat near the tree, legs crossed, a wet, muddy book—its pages fat and swollen from rain or the creek—lay in his lap. The jeans had dirt stains on the knees. His hair was longer than the picture in the file, a bit shaggy. He smiled at her then and she found herself smiling back.

"*Hiya, Grace.*"

"Hi. How do you know my name?"

He shrugged but didn't answer. "*I don't get many visitors,*" he said, his voice cracking, permanently stuck in puberty. "*Not here anyway. My mom came only once.*"

"Did you talk to her?"

"*No…I tried. All she did was cry.*"

"Where does she go?"

"*To the cemetery. Up on Prospect Hill. I don't like it there.*"

She nodded. "Cemeteries are scary."

He laughed. "*You got that right! We usually stay away.*"

"We?"

He shrugged again. "*Too many mean people there.*" He looked past her. "*Who's your friend?*"

Grace turned, finding Mason staring at her. "Her name is Mason," she said, her eyes never leaving Mason's. Mason visibly swallowed and Grace smiled at her, hoping to ease her mind a bit. She turned back to Thomas. "Who hurt you?" Whatever smile he still sported faded immediately, and he shook his head, his shaggy hair falling into his eyes.

"*Nope. Can't say.*"

"Why not?"

He shook his head again. "*Susie says he'll hurt her.*" He looked around, as if seeing if anyone was watching. "*There's a baby now too. We got to be careful.*"

"Who is *he*? Is he the one who hurt you?"

"*No, no, no. He's like us. Only…only we try to stay away from him.*"

"Then who is her? Who is the baby? Are they like you too?"

He gave her an incredulous look. "*No, silly. Faith is like you. She's nice. I like her.*" He stood up suddenly, the book falling from his lap. "*You should go.*" He bent to pick up the book. "*Susie knows everything. She's real smart.*" He looked past her again to Mason. "*Your friend is scared.*"

"Yes, she is."

"*Scared for you,*" he clarified. "*I heard about what happened in the creek and how she saved you. She's been marked.*"

Grace nodded. "The bird."

He laughed. *"That's such an old trick."* He took a step closer to her. *"You two are stronger together. You should stick like glue. I don't think he can hurt you then."*

"He the bird? Or he…"

He laughed heartily again. *"A hawk or an eagle…now that would scare you! Not a noisy old jay! But he must like it. He always shows himself as a jay."* He looked around again, then took another step closer. *"His name is Rusty. He's…he's really mean. I try to stay away from him."*

Rusty? That's what Nora had said. "How long has he been here? This Rusty?"

"I don't know. I first saw him at the library."

"The library? That's where you…" *What? Went missing? Vanished?*

Thomas nodded. *"I still like the library. I go there at night. It's peaceful there."*

"Why at night? Because there are no people there?"

"Cause he's not there. He only goes there when people are inside. He likes to scare them." Thomas looked up quickly, as if listening. *"You should go now! Hurry!"*

Before she could comment, he disappeared into the wind. The forest floor turned back to its natural color almost instantly. She didn't hang around to watch. Instead, she turned, hurrying back to Mason.

"Let's go."

Mason didn't question her. They retraced their steps in a fast walk, neither talking. In the distance, she heard a bird squawking in the trees. They both turned to look behind them as they walked. As the sound got closer, their fast walk turned into a run. In a matter of seconds, the blue bird was upon them, swooping down and brushing their heads as he flew past.

"Son of a bitch," Mason muttered as she swung at the bird.

"Keep going, Mason!"

"He's pissing me off!" Mason grabbed her arm to stop her. "Stay behind me, Grace."

"Mason—"

Before she even knew what was happening, Mason had her gun out and took aim. Grace instinctively covered her ears as Mason fired. Feathers flew and by all accounts, the bird should have dropped from the sky. Instead, it hopped onto a limb, its head cocked as it watched them.

"That was a direct hit." Mason looked at her. "I'm sure of it. Why isn't he dead?"

Grace's eyes widened as the bird transformed into a catlike creature, only its face was now that of a baby. A baby with teeth. Long, sharp teeth. There was blood oozing from its shoulder and she saw the bullet wound. Mason hadn't missed.

"What do you see?" she whispered.

"The goddamn bird!"

"Okay, good. It's injured."

"I should shoot him again."

Before Mason could do just that, the cat-baby screamed, showing off razor-sharp teeth. Grace jumped and grabbed onto Mason's arm and tugged her along, walking fast. The scream was loud and shrill and she barely resisted covering her ears. Mason, on the other hand, showed no reaction.

"Do you not hear the scream?"

"No. There's nothing."

Mason stopped and looked behind them. Grace turned too. The baby was gone. It was now the bird again. One wing drooped, hanging low against the branch, blood dripping down its feathers. As she watched, one of those bloody feathers dropped, floating lazily downward, getting caught in the breeze. She stood, transfixed as the feather, moving from side to side as if attached to a string, headed slowly toward them. A mere five or six feet away, the feather turned into a knife.

"*Mason!*"

She pushed Mason out of the way and ducked down as the knife flew over her head, slamming into a tree behind them. She scrambled toward Mason.

"Do you see it?" she asked urgently.

"No. See what?"

"A knife. It was a feather. Now it's a knife." She pointed at the tree where the knife was stuck. "There."

Mason got up and went to the tree. Grace's eyes widened as Mason reached out for it, her index finger running along the edge. She gasped as blood spurted from her fingers. Mason, however, showed no reaction.

"It's a feather."

Grace stood up and went to her, taking her hand. The blood was running down her palm, dripping onto the forest floor. Grace looked at her, seeing the questions in Mason's eyes. Her hand was now covered in Mason's blood. She put her finger on the deepest cut, hoping to stem the flow. She squeezed her finger tightly, holding Mason's gaze.

"What do you feel, Mason?"

Mason swallowed. "You holding my hand."

"What else?"

"Um…it feels kinda good."

Grace squeezed tighter. "Does it hurt."

"No. Should it?"

She saw movement and looked back down the trail. The bird had fallen to the ground, its broken wing hanging down as it tried to fly. Grace folded Mason's injured hand inside both of hers.

"Go away!" she yelled.

The bird stared at her for a moment. Then it opened its beak. The sound she heard, though, wasn't that of a jay. It was a baby's cry. No, not a cry. A scream. She squeezed Mason's hand tightly.

"Go away," she said again, this time firmer, with certainty. "Go… away. You can't hurt us."

The bird hopped onto the low limbs of a young spruce, still watching them. Then, without much ceremony, it ducked into the tree and disappeared without looking back at her. She stared at Mason's hand. The blood was receding now, vanishing as if it had never been there. The cuts on her fingers closed, leaving smooth skin behind. With a relieved sigh, she removed her hands from Mason's. There, in the tree where the knife had been, was a lone blue feather, stuck on the bark.

"Okay…so that was really weird."

Mason tilted her head. "You'll explain later, I'm guessing." She started walking. "Not that I mind you holding my hand."

Grace bumped her shoulder with a smile. "Come on. Let's get out of here."

CHAPTER TWENTY-SEVEN

Mason leaned her hip against the kitchen counter, watching as Grace flipped through the file. The remnants of their early dinner—very late lunch, really—was still on the table. Grace reached for the plastic cup that was beside her—watered-down Coke. The ice had long melted, but Grace didn't seem to notice. Mason's fingers tightened around her own glass, a whiskey tumbler that she'd added more than a splash to. She took a sip now, the smooth bourbon relaxing her.

Grace hadn't wanted to talk. There had been fear in her eyes... out there in the forest. The bird with the broken wing apparently wasn't a bird, at least in Grace's eyes. Whatever the hell it was, she'd done more than nick its wing. She'd had her Glock 22 aimed right at it. She'd fired, and, accordingly, the bird should have been reduced to nothing more than a pile of bloody feathers.

That wasn't the case though. Sure, she could have missed. She could have misfired. But she didn't. She was confident in her skills. She didn't miss. The bird wasn't just a bird, apparently. She'd seen the feather, she'd watched as it floated toward them. Then Grace had pushed her down, much like she'd done before out on the trail. Grace had ducked down, had covered her head as the feather sailed by. Then there was nothing, the feather was caught—harmlessly—on the bark of the tree.

Only it wasn't a feather, was it? She'd felt it. It was soft. But Grace's eyes had widened, she'd taken her hand, held it gently, as if afraid she'd hurt her. Mason had been afraid she'd let go of her hand. She looked at her now, her blond hair tucked behind one ear, not the other. Her chin rested in her palm as she read, her brow somewhat furrowed. Mason allowed herself to look shamelessly... the lips slightly parted, the tip of a pink tongue coming out to wet them. From a distance, her skin appeared smooth and unblemished. Up close, Mason had noticed the tiniest of scars on her forehead, a sprinkling of freckles on her nose, and laugh lines at the corners of her eyes when she smiled.

Was she a freak? If she was old, unattractive, would she think Grace was a freak? Admittedly, yeah, she hadn't been looking forward to being the psychic's point of contact. And yeah, she'd had preconceived ideas of what Grace would be like...and what she *wouldn't* be like. Those had proven false. She wasn't like Nora Nightsail and she wasn't odd or peculiar. She was—

What? Normal? Normal compared to who? She took another sip of her drink, her eyes still on Grace. Okay, so she was a little attracted to her. Physically, yes, why wouldn't she be? Blond hair, blue eyes... cute. Something else though, something deeper. The prospect of the unknown? Danger? Did that draw her? Grace was confident, sure of herself. In control. Did that draw her? Or was it like the gypsy woman had said all those years ago? Were they soulmates? Was it destiny that they were here together?

"You're staring."

She blinked several times, chasing away her thoughts. Grace hadn't looked her way. She still seemed absorbed in the file. Damn, was she reading her mind? There was a slight smile on Grace's lips, and she took a deep breath, trying to dispel any thoughts of Grace from her mind.

"I'll take a splash of what you're having, if you don't mind."

Mason moved toward the table and picked up Grace's cup to discard it. She paused, looking at what Grace had been studying. It was a photo of a boy. A school picture. He was dressed up, his hair combed neatly.

"Who is that?"

"Thomas Houston. The boy I spoke with today." Grace turned to look at her then. "His hair was longer, shaggy. Cute kid, huh?"

"Yeah." She took a glass from the cabinet and added a little whiskey to it.

"Does the name 'Rusty' mean anything to you?"

"Rusty?" She set the glass down beside Grace. "No."

"Nora mentioned it. The name came to her, but she didn't elaborate. Then Thomas said it today. Rusty. And he's afraid of him. I think this Rusty is the one who's been chasing us."

"I don't remember the names of all of the kids killed, but I don't think there was a Rusty."

"No, I went through the whole file. There's not."

"What did he say?"

"Thomas was very friendly and talkative. The 'her' who they are all protecting is Faith. I have no idea who she is or how old she is. Thomas said there was a baby now, meaning recently."

"That's the baby that—what was her name? Fran?—talked about?"

"I don't think so, no. Fran said there was a baby there the night she was hurt. Fran was killed in 2004. This has to be another baby."

"This makes no sense."

"It makes sense if our killer has a family and now a baby. Mason, serial killers live two separate lives. They integrate themselves into society just like normal." She turned in her chair. "I think that's what drives the fear in town. That the killer is one of you, that he walks among you, shops, goes out to eat. Normal stuff."

"Grace, it's been twenty-three years. If he walks among us, why the hell can't we find him?"

"Because he doesn't work alone, Mason. And I don't think I'm simply talking about the other thing that is out there. Fran indicated there were two, one big and mean and the one who hurt her, the high school kid. Hurt her, meaning sexually assaulted. At first, I thought she was referring to two separate planes—her physical, back then, and her spiritual now. Maybe she was talking physical all along. Two guys."

"You're making my head spin," she murmured.

"He said I need to talk to Susie. He said Susie was smart. Susie knew everything."

"Susie Shackle? In the creek?" Mason shook her head. "No. Absolutely not."

Grace cocked an eyebrow at her, making it disappear into her bangs. "Absolutely not? Are you like...giving an order?"

"Grace, no, not the creek again."

"Well, I'm not exactly looking forward to taking another dunk, if that's what you're referring to. I need to talk to her, however. Fran said it too. Susie is the one I need to talk to." She seemed to hesitate. "Nora also said that Susie was who I needed to find."

Mason stared at her. "Oh, no. No. You're not talking about a…a séance, are you?"

Grace gave her a rather cute, rather amused smile. "Séance? Like bring out my Ouija board?" She laughed then. "Some psychics do that for show. It makes for great theater. Some swear by it, though. I've never had the need to use one." Again, Grace seemed to hesitate. "Nora said something else. She said there was someone in town I needed to speak with. A librarian. Patricia Brinkman. Do you know her?"

"Patty Brinkman? Sure. She was at the public library forever, it seems. A stickler for rules, always hushing anyone who was talking."

"Is she still alive?"

"I don't know, to be honest. I haven't been to the library since I've been back in town. She was old when I was there. I seriously doubt she's working, if she is still alive." She sat down at the table with her. "I can give my uncle a call. He'd know."

"I'd rather not. I'm thinking we should speak to her in private. Nora didn't specifically say that, but that was the impression I got."

Yes, Nora Nightsail, the gypsy psychic. Grace obviously didn't have any concerns that she wasn't legitimate. She wondered what all Nora had said to her. For some reason, she didn't think Grace had relayed everything yet. She'd been visibly rattled by the call, but maybe it was as she said: Nora's vision matched the dream she'd had.

She glanced at the photo that was still facing them. Thomas Houston. Killed in 2012, along with four others. She looked over at Grace. "I saw a feather."

"I saw a knife." Grace reached out and touched her hand, turning it over. She gently touched a spot on her finger, rubbing back and forth. "You were bleeding pretty bad. There was a deep cut here. Blood was dripping down your hand, onto the leaves, enough to cover my hands as well."

Mason watched her fingers as they touched her, wondering if Grace could feel her rapid pulse. How long had it been since someone touched her like this? "Was it…was it the same…creature? Catlike?"

"Similar, yet different. This time, the face was that of a baby. A baby with long teeth." Grace removed her hand and Mason wrapped her own around her whiskey tumbler. "It was wounded in the shoulder."

"I made a direct hit."

"Maybe there's no such thing as a direct hit. It's obviously more than a bird." Grace stared at her for a moment, taking a deep breath. "You're not going to like what I'm about to suggest."

"Probably not."

"I want to go out tonight."

Mason shook her head. "Oh, hell no. We barely have a handle on this during the day."

"I think we'll be safe. I want to talk to Thomas some more."

"Go back out into the goddamn forest? At night?" Mason shook her head firmly. "No way, Grace. No way."

She smiled at her again, a smile Mason thought was meant to be reassuring. "Not the forest. The library."

Mason frowned. "The library?" She looked at the photo of Thomas Houston again. "Is that where he was last seen?"

"Yes. The file says he went into the restroom and never returned."

"Why would he be in the library? He was out in the forest."

"He said he goes there at night. The 'Rusty' he was referring to, he said he first saw him at the library." Grace held her hand up when she would have spoken. "No, I'm not trying to find Rusty. Not yet. Thomas said Rusty doesn't go there at night. He only goes during the day when there are people there. He likes to scare them."

"Scare them?" Mason drank the last of her drink, aware that her hand was shaking slightly. "Over the years, yeah, there've been some people say that…well, that weird things happen there, that the place is haunted. Books fall off shelves, papers get scattered as if by a strong wind. Speaking of Patty Brinkman, she used to complain of books being rearranged, things like that. I think she blamed it on kids playing pranks on her, though." She stood up. She wanted another drink, but she put the glass down and took a bottle of water from the fridge instead. "The old library burned down. Back way before I was born. They built this new one on the same spot."

"The fire," Grace murmured.

"What?"

"Nora asked if I'd learned about the fire yet. She said Patricia Brinkman would have the history of it. She said the fire was important. So what happened?"

Mason shook her head. "It's not something people talk about. It was a tragedy all the way around. The town was real small back then, and it shook everybody pretty hard, I guess. Five kids were killed in the fire. High school kids. Arson."

Grace looked at her in shock. "And five kids died? If it was arson, then—"

"The kids killed were the ones who started the fire, Grace. From what little I've heard over the years, everyone thought they got their punishment so they didn't see the point of putting their parents through the trauma of a big investigation."

"You're kidding me? Surely insurance adjusters came out, someone to investigate. I mean—"

"I don't know all the details. The fire got blamed on faulty wiring, I think. The building itself was ancient, so it wasn't a stretch to sell that story."

"So who was killed? One of them could be this Rusty." Grace grabbed her arm and squeezed. "This could be it. This could be the link. It must be. Why else would Nora direct me toward Patricia Brinkman?"

"The link to the murders? The murders started in 1997. The fire was in the '80s, before I was born."

Grace was flipping back through the file, going to the beginning. Mason watched as Susie Shackle's photo appeared. Grace's finger was running along the words, rereading. She tapped her finger.

"Here. She was last seen at the library." Grace looked at her. "The *library*. And I'm supposed to talk to Patricia Brinkman. Again, the *library*."

She tapped the page much like Grace had done. "Read more. She left the library. I think she was last seen outside the building, heading home."

"Regardless! It's the library, Mason! Where can we find out about the fire? Newspaper archives or something? Or maybe we should try to find Patricia Brinkman right now."

"My aunt and uncle. My mother. They were all in high school at the time, but they don't talk about it."

"So these were classmates of theirs?"

"I guess so. My aunt and uncle have never mentioned the fire to me. And my mother has only said a few things about it."

"So let's go talk to them."

"Now?"

Grace tilted her head. "Would you rather go out to the library?" Then the teasing expression faded. "Yes, now. But I think we should go out to the library afterward too. Do you have a key?"

Mason gave a quick laugh. "Why would I have a key?"

"Just hoping. Can we break in?"

"There are cameras all over the place. No, we cannot break in."

"Are there cameras inside and out?"

"The library has cameras inside that run during the day. The city has cameras outside that run all the time."

"Gonna be hard to sneak around then."

"Well, just because there are cameras, doesn't mean anyone monitors them. Not unless…well…"

"Unless someone goes missing. Let's hope that's not us."

CHAPTER TWENTY-EIGHT

Aunt Carol was standing over her stove, stirring a pot when they walked in. Even though Mason had announced her presence, she could see the surprise on Aunt Carol's face.

"What brings you around? And if it's dinner, I've got plenty. Brady should be popping over any minute."

"No, no. We already ate something," she said, glancing quickly at Grace, then back at her aunt. "Is Uncle Alan home?"

"Not yet, honey. He's running late, I guess." Aunt Carol turned to Grace. "I'm glad you came by. I made those oatmeal cookies we were talking about."

"Oh, how sweet."

Mason moved closer. "It's actually you we wanted to talk to."

"Me?"

"Looks like you're making your famous spaghetti sauce. Think it can simmer on its own for a bit?"

Aunt Carol stared at her. "You look so serious, Mason. Is everything okay?"

"Yeah, sure. Just..."

"Do you know why I'm here, Carol?"

Carol turned to Grace, nodding. "Alan told me last night that… well, that you weren't exactly an FBI agent."

"Then you know what I do?"

"He said you were a…a psychic." She stumbled over the last word, but Grace smiled warmly at her.

"I promise I'm not crazy. Or a fraud."

"Aunt Carol, Grace wants to ask you about the fire. The library."

Aunt Carol whipped her head around. "The fire? Whatever for?" She put the lid on the pot and wiped her hands on a towel. "I try not to think about that horrible, horrible night." She shook her head. "I certainly don't want to talk about it. No."

"Aunt Carol, Grace thinks the library might be linked to the murders."

Aunt Carol shook her head firmly. "No. That happened back when I was in high school. The murders didn't start until much later."

"Carol, please. If you could give me a little history of it. Please. It's very important."

Aunt Carol closed her eyes for a moment, and Mason could tell she was going back in time. When she opened her eyes, she had a bit of a faraway look there. "I…I knew them. I was friends with Judy, especially. Good friends."

"When was the fire? What year?" Grace asked gently.

"It was in the fall, the aspen leaves had already turned. It was a cool, crisp, windless night…October 5th, 1984. It was a Friday." Aunt Carol sat down heavily in the chair at the breakfast bar. "Alan was a senior. I was a junior." She glanced over at her. "Your mother was a senior too."

Mason nodded. Her father was a grade ahead of Uncle Alan and her mother and would have already graduated.

"Tell us what happened," Grace coaxed.

"That year, oh, there were barely three thousand people in town, if that. Everybody knew everyone's business." She folded her hands together. "It was some kind of a dare. We'd all heard whisperings about it at school. I don't think anyone thought they'd actually go through with it. And the girls—Judy—they were simply tagging along with their boyfriends."

"It was just the five of them?" Mason asked.

"Six. Bruce Shackle got out. He had burns on his arms, but he made it out. No one else did."

Mason and Grace exchanged glances. "Shackle? Any relation to Susie Shackle?"

"Oh, yes. She was his daughter. I don't think he ever got over the fire, then to have his daughter…well, it was too much for him, I think. He hasn't been the same since. Couldn't keep a job. Turned to drinking." Aunt Carol glanced at her quickly, then away. "His wife stays with him though."

Grace leaned forward. "Who was killed, Carol? Was one of them named Rusty?"

Carol's eyes widened. "Mark Meyer, yes. How did you know everyone called him Rusty? Russell was his middle name, I think."

"Just…from research," Grace said vaguely.

Her lips pressed together. "Rusty was a bully. Can't say anyone cried any tears over him."

"Aunt Carol, how did Mr. Shackle get out and no one else did?"

"Bruce never talked about it, and I don't think anyone dared ask him. He and Rusty ran together back then. Most kids were afraid of them. I know I was. After the fire, Bruce changed his ways, straightened up."

"So it was really arson?" Grace asked.

"Oh, yes. They intended on burning it down. They succeeded."

"And no charges were brought against Bruce?"

"Six kids went to the library that night. One came out. All six should have died, to hear most people tell it. What good would it have done to bring Bruce up on charges? He was lucky to get out alive."

"What about the families of the others? Rusty Meyer, for example. Are they still in town?" Grace asked.

"No, no. From what I remember, they moved on up to Montana. I think they had family there. Judy's family moved away too." Aunt Carol looked between them. "Why are you asking about the fire? That's a cloud that hung over the town for years…until another cloud took its place. The fire tragedy has taken a backseat to the murders now. Some in New Town probably don't even know of the fire."

"I'm trying to get a history of Gillette Park, that's all," Grace said a bit evasively. "A new library was built in its place?"

"Yes. Took several years to get it up and running again, but we're proud of it. Still, those of us who were around back then, it's hard to even drive by the place and not think about that night."

"Who was the librarian at the time?" Grace asked casually.

"Oh, Patty Brinkman was. She got the new library up and running too. In fact, they practically had to force her into retirement."

"She's still alive?" Mason asked.

"Yes, but she's not in good health. Frail, I think. Why do you ask?"

"For my benefit," Grace said quickly. "In case I need to speak to her."

"Well, from what I hear, she can no longer manage on her own. Has one of those home health nurses come by. The poor thing never married and she has no family around. She's over ninety, I'm sure."

"Tell her about the library. The part you're leaving out."

"And which part would that be?"

Mason tilted her head. "You know what part."

Aunt Carol waved her hand in the air. "The library is not haunted. Don't be silly."

She wasn't being silly and Aunt Carol knew it.

"I'm a big believer in haunted buildings," Grace offered. "I've seen many."

Aunt Carol gave a nervous laugh. "The Gillette Park library is not haunted, Grace." She stood up quickly and glanced nervously at the back door as if afraid Uncle Alan would come in and hear them. "I should really get back to my sauce." She paused on her way to the stove. "Let me get you some oatmeal cookies before you go."

So, they were being asked to leave in a very polite, "here's some cookies" kind of way. She was about to protest—maybe Grace had more questions—but Grace was motioning her up.

"Thank you for your time, Carol. We'll get out of your way."

Aunt Carol was putting cookies into a plastic bag for them. "You're going to the library, aren't you?"

"We didn't say that."

"You don't have to, Mason. I know you as well as my own children. Besides, Grace is a psychic. Alan told me what she's doing here." She closed the plastic bag and Mason noticed that her hands were shaking. "You really think you can *talk* to them?" Before Grace could answer, she held up her hand. "No. No. I don't want to know. It's too crazy to even think about."

"Was Judy your best friend?" Grace asked gently.

Mason was surprised to see Aunt Carol's lip quiver. "Yes. We were so close. Yet, we had been arguing. I hated Butch Duckworth. He was…no good for her. He was always in trouble. Always. I had begged her to break up with him." She shook her head. "We'd had a terrible argument at school that day." She wiped at a lone tear. "That's what I carry with me. I was so ugly to her, as if I had a right to criticize her boyfriend."

"So you knew what they'd planned?"

"Yes, I knew. That's what our argument was about. I should have told someone. I could have maybe stopped—"

"Aunt Carol, it's not your fault."

"I could have stopped it!"

"Some things are destined," Grace said quietly. "You shouldn't bear the weight of your guilt, Carol. They made choices too."

"So did I!" she said with a hard tap on her chest. "I chose to keep quiet. And they died."

Mason took her hand. "You told Uncle Alan that night, didn't you?"

At that, another tear escaped her eye. "Yes," she said weakly.

"And that's why neither of you ever talk about it. I finally understand."

"Oh, Mason…it was a horrible blow to us. Yes, I told him. Like I said, there had been whisperings, but no one knew for sure and no one knew when. But I knew. And I told Alan that night. He had picked me up and we were doing what most kids did on a Friday night—driving around town to see who was out and who was gathering in the parking lot of Gillette's Burgers. We were there in the parking lot with the others when the flames shot up like the Fourth of July. I don't think either of us could believe that they'd really gone through with it. Everyone hung around, expecting to see Rusty and his crew come driving by, gloating and showing off." She handed the bag of cookies to Grace. "And of course, they never did."

CHAPTER TWENTY-NINE

"So you had no clue, I'm assuming."

They were parked across the street from the public library, a two-story brick building that was on the corner of Miner Street and Axe. What appeared to be an old-fashioned drug store—it advertised fountain drinks—was next door and beyond that was a craft store. She wondered if those buildings were there when the old library burned or if they were new or remodeled.

Mason shook her head to her question. "Not a clue, no. I mean, I knew they were close in age. My mother mentioned the fire from time to time when I was a kid, but no details. Makes sense now why Aunt Carol and Uncle Alan totally avoided the subject."

"That's a lot of guilt to carry around."

"I guess they kept it to themselves all these years. Aunt Carol telling me and you...that's probably the first time she's talked about it." Mason turned to look at her. "You're really going over there? It's awful dark, Grace."

"There's a streetlight."

Mason looked up and down the street. "Still—it's kinda dark."

"I don't anticipate there being a problem. According to Thomas, Rusty doesn't hang around here at night," she reminded her.

"Do you want to know what scares me?"

"I think I already have an idea."

Mason smiled. "What scares me is that when you talk about them, I don't think it's odd any longer that we're discussing them as if they're real people and you talk to them as if they are."

"I often wonder if it's lonely for them. They're stuck in this realm—I'm assuming stuck—with no one to talk to, other than, you know…"

"Others like them? Do you think they get together?"

"I don't know. I'd like to think so, but no, I don't suppose they do. I imagine Fran kicks her soccer ball all alone and Missy swings by herself. And Thomas reads his books." She shrugged. "And they're not all here. Some may not want to show themselves. Some may have gone…" She waved her hand in the air. "Wherever they go and they don't want to come back."

"So you think when someone like you comes around, someone they can 'talk' to," she said, making quotations, "that it's a highlight of their day?"

"It depends on the situation. Sometimes, yes, there are the ones who are overly chatty and more forthcoming. Other times, they are more cautious, more withdrawn. Of course, maybe that's how they were in real life." She opened the door and got out, looking at Mason who was still inside. "They can see things too, Mason. In different realms, different levels. When I talk to them, I sometimes think they know more about me and my mindset than I do myself. It's those times that I wonder who is the so-called psychic and who is the subject."

She closed the door, letting Mason take what she wanted from that statement. She wouldn't admit it out loud to Mason, but there were times when she'd had more friends who were dead than alive. She crossed the street, hearing Mason close her truck door. She turned back to her.

"Stay there. I'll remain within sight."

Mason hesitated, obviously trying to decide if it was safe or not. She nodded finally and leaned back against her truck. Grace turned her attention to the library, glancing along the bricks on the lower level, then higher. She smiled when she saw him, sitting on the ledge of a window on the second floor, swinging his legs back and forth as if he hadn't a care in the world.

"*Hiya, Grace.*"

"You'll fall," she said teasingly.

He laughed. *"Amazing, but I've got great balance."* As if to prove it, he jumped—floated—to the window next to him. He walked without care, doing a little dance at the edge. *"See? Piece of cake!"*

"Is Rusty here?" she asked, getting right to the point.

"Why? You want to tangle with him again?"

Tangle? Didn't she use that word with Mason when she was talking about Rusty? Would Thomas know that? "No. Just making sure we were alone. I wanted to talk to you." Thomas held his hands out, then jumped again, this time landing with a graceful thud beside her.

"No…you really want to talk to Susie." He brushed the hair out of his eyes. *"You found out about the fire, huh?"*

"How do you know?"

He shrugged. *"Lucky guess."* Then he laughed, the giggly laugh of a thirteen-year-old. *"No, not really! Someone followed you."*

"Who?"

He shook his head. *"No, no, no. I can't tell you."*

Grace noticed that he held his schoolbooks under his arm. She motioned to them. "Do they go with you all the time?"

He looked almost embarrassed. *"I like to read."*

"What happened, Thomas? What happened when you went into the restroom?" He stared past her and she noticed that his gaze was on Mason. She turned, seeing Mason still leaning against her truck.

"He was in there," he said quietly. *"I tried to scream, but he clamped his hand over my mouth."* His words were spoken slowly, matter-of-factly, without much emotion, and she simply nodded and waited. *"There was someone in the vent. They pulled me up into the duct in the ceiling."* He shook his head. *"He was very strong. The one who pulled me."*

"Where did they take you?"

His face twisted. *"Susie says I shouldn't talk to you. Not yet."*

"Why?"

"Because he'll hurt her if he finds out. He'll try to hurt all of them."

"The baby?"

He nodded. *"Yeah. And the others. Faith and her mom too."*

"Where did they take you, Thomas? Maybe we can help the baby. Maybe—"

"No! Susie says it's not time!"

"Okay. So who are the others you speak of?"

"No. You should really talk to Susie."

"Will she talk to me?" She looked around them. "Is she here now?"

He shook his head. *"No. She doesn't like it here."*

"Because of the fire?"

Thomas nodded. *"Rusty blames her daddy."*

"Blames him for what?"

"Something went wrong that night. Susie's daddy did something wrong." Thomas came closer to her. *"Rusty was really mad."*

"So mad that he targeted Susie?" she guessed. "Who hurt Susie?"

Thomas shook his head. *"He's mean."* He turned away from her and took a jump, landing with ease on the second-floor window again. *"Something's going to happen tonight."* He pointed toward Mason. *"You need to stay with her. He can't hurt her if you're with her."*

"Hurt her?"

"You'll know if they're coming. Someone will warn you. We can help you." His gaze went to Mason again. *"They're going to try to kill her because she protects you. With her gone, Rusty can get to you. Then there'll be no one to help Faith."*

Grace's breath caught. "Kill her?" He disappeared then, melting into the window, as if crawling inside the library. She turned quickly, glancing at Mason. She was still leaning against her truck. Grace looked back at the window, surprised to see Thomas' face in the glass, looking out at her from inside of the library. He lifted a hand to her and she nodded at him, then turned to go to Mason.

She walked up to her, grabbed her arm, and tugged her toward the door. "Get inside."

"What's going on?"

"Get inside, Mason. Now!"

She hurried around to the passenger's door and hopped in, slamming the door behind her. "Lock the doors."

"What's wrong?"

"Lock the goddamn doors!"

Mason did, then turned to her. "What the hell's going on?"

Grace took a deep breath. "He said someone's going to try to kill you."

"Kill me? Geez...what the hell have I done to piss them off?"

"You need to take this seriously."

Mason started the truck. "Grace, that stuff out there, that's your world. If someone is going to try to kill me, it won't be from your world. It'll be right out here in the open." She pulled out onto the street. "I'm not worried about some guy trying to take me out. I can handle that. I'm more worried about you. What else did he say? You look shook up."

"Of course I'm shook up! Someone's coming after you. They don't just kid about things like that, Mason. Someone is going to try to kill you."

She turned onto the street that would take them home, but she only slowed slightly when she approached her house. "Let's go talk to Uncle Alan. You tell him what you learned."

"No." Grace shook her head. "I can't talk to him about that. He doesn't believe me. He may *say* he doesn't think I'm a quack, but he doesn't really believe that." Grace reached over and touched her arm. "Let's go home, Mason. I'll tell you everything. You can decide what you tell him. If you still think we should meet, then we'll do it tomorrow."

Mason stopped the truck in the middle of the street, halfway between her house and her uncle's. Her fingers tapped on the steering wheel indecisively. "Why do they want to come after me?"

"Because you're protecting me."

"Get to me, get to you."

"I'm the real threat to him, not you. Rusty, I mean. He is who is driving all this. At least, I think so. Thomas said they were going to kill you because you protect me. If you're here, Rusty can't get to me."

Mason let out a breath, then put the truck in reverse, backing down the street until she came to her driveway. They both saw him at the same time. Dressed in dark clothing, the hoodie pulled over his head—he stared at them as they stared back. Time stood still for an instant, then he bolted around the neighbor's shrubs and disappeared. Mason flung her door open, but Grace grabbed her arm before she could get out.

"No, Mason! We have to stay together."

"Grace—"

"No! We can't be separated." She squeezed her arm tightly. "We have to stay together, Mason." She met her gaze, the interior light casting shadows on Mason's face. She looked into her eyes, seeing questions. "Do you understand me? We must stay together. We are only strong together. We both serve a purpose now. He can't get to me if you're there. And the killer can't get to you if I'm there. The wheels are in motion now. We can't stop them. When it's time, Susie will let me know."

Mason stared at her, unblinking. "You're kinda scaring me again."

Grace didn't blink either, and, unconsciously, she felt her fingers tighten on her arm. "Thomas said something would happen tonight. It's a young girl," she heard herself say. "She won't be in her bed in the morning. Her mother will call the police. She's eight. We'll find her under the footbridge. Where Susie Shackle was found. It's a message meant for us."

"Oh, Grace," Mason whispered.

Grace could see the footbridge, could hear the water…the girl was wearing pajamas with Winnie the Pooh characters on them. Like Susie Shackle, she would be strangled. There was something on the footbridge. Dark. A stick? A limb? A snake? Yes, it was moving, slithering away.

"Grace?"

Grace blinked the image away. "Let's go there now."

Mason's eyes widened. "The footbridge? Now?"

"She'll already be there when we get there," she said with certainty.

"But you said—"

"Yes. If we let it play out, then yes, her mother will call the police in the morning. We could go out then and find her. But she's there now. I…I can see her. She's in the water. She's been strangled. She's wearing Winnie the Pooh pajamas."

"Son of a bitch." Mason pulled away with a squeal of her tires. "Maybe we can catch the bastard," she said excitedly. "Maybe—"

"No, Mason. She's already there. He's gone."

"It's nine thirty." She slammed on her brakes at her uncle's house. "I've got to tell him. We can't go out alone."

"Mason—"

"No, Grace. If what you're saying is true, then it's a crime scene. I've got to play it by the book."

"Very well. But I won't be interrogated. I know what I know. I can't tell him *how* I know." When Mason would have gotten out, Grace grabbed her arm. "Stay together."

"Right." She pulled out her phone instead. "Stay together."

CHAPTER THIRTY

Mason didn't even feel the cold water of the creek as she waded in next to the footbridge, the water reaching past her thighs. Brady was beside her and he slipped on the rocks, nearly going under. She grabbed his arm to steady him, almost losing her balance in the process.

Her uncle and Dalton were on shore, holding high-powered flashlights. Grace stood behind them, arms folded protectively around herself.

"Thanks," Brady murmured to her. "I can't see a damn thing."

The little girl was where Grace said she'd be. Her brown hair was matted around her face, and Brady paused, as did she, when they found her.

"Three killings and we're still in goddamn May. Gonna be a hell of a year."

Mason wondered if he knew that he'd glanced at Grace when he spoke, as if it was her fault. Is that what they all thought? A psychic was in town. The last time a psychic was here, five kids were killed.

The girl was lodged between the bank and the crossbeams of the footbridge, much like she imagined Susie Shackle had been all those years ago. It meant something, of course. As Grace had reminded her on the drive out here, they'd never recovered a body in the same spot before.

"Are you sure she's dead?" Dalton asked.

"She's under the water, man…yeah, she's dead."

"Treat it like the crime scene it is," Uncle Alan reminded them.

"Hand me a light." Mason held her hand out for it. "I think she's tied. She would have washed downstream if not."

"Looks like a wire," Brady interjected. "Not a rope."

It took them several minutes to free her; the wire was bound around the girl's wrist and one of the pylons in the water. Mason grabbed her arm when the wire was removed, holding her tight. She could no longer feel her legs or feet and she wondered if they'd be able to get the girl out without help.

"Just a kid," Brady muttered under his breath. "Just a damn kid."

They pulled her against the current, to where Dalton was waiting. Mason handed him the flashlight as she clung to a rock. He took a couple of steps into the creek, reaching for the girl as Uncle Alan held the other light. She and Brady scrambled out too, both struggling to find footing on the slick rocks.

"I can't feel my feet," he said. "You?"

"No." Her teeth were beginning to chatter and as soon as she got out, Grace was there, helping to draw her up.

"Oh my god! I know her," Dalton said.

She and Grace turned to look, following the beam of light they held on her face. The strangulation marks around her neck were prominent. And yes, as Grace had said, she wore Winnie the Pooh pajamas.

"That's April Trombley. Christ, that's my cousin's kid." He looked at them, his mouth opened in shock. "Derrick Trombley. He married my cousin, Jennifer."

Mason nodded. Derrick Trombley used to date Brady's sister way back when. Derrick Trombley used to pick on them and tease them. Derrick Trombley was a dick. Now Derrick Trombley's eight-year-old daughter was dead, victim of the Gillette Park serial killer. Victim number three this year.

"How did you know she was here?" Dalton asked bluntly, facing Grace.

"Dalton…" Mason warned.

"No! I want to know. She hadn't been in the water much more than an hour. How did you know?"

Grace took a step toward him, not shying away. "You know why I was hired, Deputy Wilcox. So don't play stupid and act like you don't know how I *knew*."

"Yeah...used your crystal ball, I guess. Couldn't have used it a little earlier, huh? Maybe stopped this killing before it happened?"

"Dalton, that's enough," Uncle Alan said firmly.

"No! What the hell good is she? I don't know how much you're paying her, but it's too damn much!" He turned away from the body. "Christ! My cousin's kid!" He spun around to face Grace once again. "Why didn't you stop it? You knew what was happening!"

Brady put a hand on his arm, but Dalton jerked it away. Mason walked in front of him, shielding Grace.

"You've lived here your whole life, Dalton. You know how this plays out. Don't try to place blame."

Uncle Alan stepped forward too. "Hike back down to the truck, Dalton. Let's call it in. Get Neal Addick out here again. See if he can find the tracks of where our killer came from."

"What the hell for? We do the same damn thing every time! It doesn't do any good!"

"Deputy Wilcox, do your damn job." Uncle Alan gave him a push toward the bridge. "You know the drill."

Dalton's shoulder's slumped as he stepped onto the bridge, then he turned, pointing his finger at Grace. "You are useless! *Useless!*"

The look on Grace's face—even as the shadows tried to hide it—made Mason want to pull her close and hold her. Crushed was too passive a word to describe it. Grace looked both devastated and shamed.

"Best get her out of here, Mason. Knowing Dalton like we do, when the others get here, he won't be the only one pointing fingers."

Grace didn't need any prompting, and she spun on her heels, heading across the footbridge in the dark. Mason flipped on her small light and followed; the cold she'd pushed away for a few moments hit her full force. Her wet clothes clung to her. She took several shuffling steps, her feet still feeling like blocks of ice.

"Grace, wait up."

"I don't want to talk," Grace said rather brusquely.

"Can you at least slow down? My feet are numb."

At that, Grace stopped and turned around, concern showing on her face. "I'm sorry. Yes, you must be frozen." Grace surprised her by taking her free hand and enveloping it in two warm ones. "God, you're like ice. Come on."

Grace took the flashlight from her and led them down the trail, still clutching her hand. By the time they got to the fork where it hooked up with the manicured hike-and-bike trail, Mason's teeth were chattering and she felt tremors travel along her body, head to toe.

"We need to get you out of these clothes."

Mason tried to smile. "Haven't had that offer in a long time."

Grace squeezed her hand but said nothing. Dalton was standing beside his truck, phone held to his ear. Grace gave him only a cursory glance while she led Mason to the passenger side of her truck. Mason didn't protest as she got inside. It was only slightly warmer.

Grace turned the heat on high and Mason held her hands up to the vent, warming them. They didn't speak and she only had to give Grace directions one time as she meandered them through town. They heard several sirens along the way and she knew others were heading to the park. Yeah, the wheels were in motion. Everyone knew the routine like the backs of their hands.

And the town was about to know about Grace. Even if Dalton didn't broadcast it, people would be curious as to how they'd found April Trombley when her own mother didn't know she was missing from her bed. The old-timers would remember 2004; they would remember the rather peculiar Nora Nightsail who roamed the streets decked out in her scarves and beads. People laughed behind her back, but really, most were afraid. Maybe not so much afraid of her, but rather afraid of what she might be doing. The thought of a séance in the park to call up little Susie Shackle, killed in the spring of '97, probably caused nightmares for some.

As soon as she walked inside the house, she began taking her wet clothes off. Grace preceded her into her bedroom and went immediately into the bathroom.

"You should soak in hot water," Grace said as she began filling the tub. "A hot shower is nice but you should soak."

Mason didn't argue, even though she never took baths. When she peeled her wet jeans off, Grace stood up abruptly.

"You want coffee or hot tea?"

"Whiskey."

Grace nodded and left but didn't close the door. Mason pulled her shirt off and tossed it on top of her wet jeans, then quickly ditched her bra and underwear and stepped into the tub of hot water. She closed her eyes and let out a quiet sigh, the chill finally starting to leave her body. She heard Grace come back, heard the glass being placed on the edge of the tub...could feel Grace hesitate—watching her, perhaps?—

before leaving again. She opened her eyes then, finding the whiskey within reach. She took the glass, taking a large sip and swallowing it slowly. She heard movement in the house, heard water running. She assumed Grace was showering, trying to wash away the events of the day, maybe.

They should talk. No doubt Dalton's words had struck a nerve. Grace needed to know that Dalton didn't really blame her. Or did he? Maybe he did. She and Dalton hadn't really spoken much since Grace had gotten there. He'd made it no secret that he wasn't thrilled with having her in town. So maybe he did blame her. This killing hit close to home. They would be looking for someone to blame. And why not? You put your kid to bed, in your own home—there should be some semblance of security, shouldn't there? You don't want to be woken up during the night by the police telling you your eight-year-old daughter isn't sleeping soundly in her bed after all. No...she'll be forever sleeping under the footbridge at Boulder Creek in her Winnie the Pooh pajamas.

Mason closed her eyes again, thankful it had been dark when they found her. Her features had been obscured, shadowed. Not like Donnie Redman. She could still picture his face, the bright sunshine kissing his cheeks for the very last time.

She opened her eyes then. It was going to end, wasn't it? This was the year it would end. The cycle would end, as the gypsy—Nora Nightsail—had told her back in 2004. She was a part of it. Grace was a part of it. Together, they would end the cycle. Not without a fight, it seemed. How many would die? A premonition—or perhaps a foreboding—told her that they wouldn't all make it through unscathed. Who would bear the brunt? Would it be Grace, locked in a dark box somewhere? Or maybe she would be the one. She was the one who was apparently marked. Maybe both. Maybe neither would make it out alive. That seemed wrong, though, seeing as how—according to Nora Nightsail—they were soulmates, destined to meet here in Gillette Park. Destined to meet. Perhaps destined to die together too.

She stood up then and drained the water, then turned the shower on. She didn't want to think about it anymore.

CHAPTER THIRTY-ONE

Grace sat on the sofa, her attention split between Mason—who was still in the bathroom—and the words Dalton had spoken. She had a tumbler in her hand, but she'd taken little more than a sip of the whiskey she'd poured. To say his words had stung were an understatement. She'd heard them before so they weren't a shock, but for some reason, they hurt more this time. She knew why. Because Mason had heard them too. She was useless. A failure. She should be used to it by now, yet it still hurt. Useless.

She needed to get over it, though, and fast. There wasn't time. It had been many, many years since she'd allowed herself a pity party. She certainly wasn't going to indulge in one now. Not in front of Mason. Mason was the one person in so very long who treated her like a friend—who didn't look at her with disgust or, worse, revulsion. Or the opposite: teasing, making fun. She rolled her eyes. What? Was she going all the way back to grade school in this pity party?

No. Mason reminded her of Angelique, didn't she? Angelique, the goddess from the sea, never once made fun of her, never once looked at her with disgust. No. She said Grace had a gift and that she should embrace it, not run from it. She could have gone to college and studied anything, *been* anything. But she had a gift. Many a lonely night, Angelique's words came back to her.

And many a lonely night, memories of Angelique in a different light came back to her. She'd come of age on the beaches of Hawaii. She'd been a timid and shy—naïve—fifteen-year-old when she'd met Angelique. She'd been a sensual, sexual woman when she'd left the island at seventeen. Angelique had taught her many things—about life and about love. While she'd gotten on with her life—professionally, at least—her love life remained unsettled. No one ever touched her the way Angelique had. Most were afraid to try. Most were afraid of *her*...repulsion rearing its head. So she withdrew and retreated into her own little world until she'd cut herself off from all but the most professional of relationships.

She'd dared, only once, to talk to another psychic about her so-called issues with developing—nurturing—personal relationships. This woman, who'd been much older than Grace at the time, said it took a special person with enough trust to get beyond the layers...to find the heart and soul that lay beneath. "Why do you think so many of us are alone? We can see things, Grace. We can see into souls."

Those words, too, stuck with her. She had a gift. A gift she couldn't refuse and couldn't return. It was a part of her, one of the many layers. So she'd immersed herself in work, teaching, dabbling with local law enforcement, then the FBI. It had been fulfilling. Enough. She'd been able to ignore the loneliness, push it away, pretend it wasn't there. She had to remind herself that a lot of her loneliness was of her choosing. She was attractive enough to garner glances and even some interest. She accepted dates for dinner. It was only when her "gifts" were brought to light that their interest changed. Some ran. Some laughed. Some flat-out thought she was a nutcase. Some looked at her with pity.

Those were the worst. Pity. She let out a heavy sigh and leaned her head back. Yes, those were the absolute worst. She closed her eyes, impatiently wiping a tear away. The fingers of loneliness were circling her heart, squeezing tightly...threatening—like they sometimes did—to choke the very life out of her. Sometimes she could escape its clutches. Sometimes not.

"Grace?"

Her name was spoken quietly, almost as if Mason were afraid to disturb her. She rolled her head to the side and opened her eyes, finding Mason watching her.

"You want to talk?"

She stared at her for a second, then cleared her throat. "Talk? No need. It is what it is, Mason."

Mason sat down beside her and took the glass from her hands. She was surprised that it was empty. She didn't remember drinking it.

"Do you hear those words often?"

"Yes," she said without hesitation. "So I should be used to it, right?"

"What he said…that was uncalled for, Grace, but I can't apologize for him."

"You don't have to apologize for him. He needed someone to lash out at. I'm the obvious target."

"Oh, Grace…I'm so sorry."

The words were barely more than a whisper in the quiet house and they seemed to hang in the air. They were spoken sincerely, from the heart, and they completely broke her. She felt her lower lip tremble as she tried to keep her emotions in check, tried to keep the tears from spilling, tried to hold on to some pretense of strength. It was an epic fail.

"I'm…I'm a freak. I have no friends…and no one…no one loves me," she managed before her tears strangled her.

She didn't protest when Mason moved closer, she didn't fight the arms that gathered her near, and she didn't pull away when she found herself in a tight embrace. She clung to Mason willingly, nearly slumping against her as her tears fell. Embarrassed? Yes, she would be later. But not right now. Right now, she needed Mason's strength, needed her comfort. She needed this human contact that was both familiar and foreign at the same time. Familiar? Yes, something about Mason was familiar, wasn't it? Had Nora spoken the truth? Were they destined to meet? Was all of this *supposed* to happen?

Warm hands rubbed her back, whispered words soothed her, and—to her surprise—soft lips grazed her cheek. As her tears lessened, something else grew. She became aware of each touch, each breath, each subtle brush of Mason's lips. Oh, she just wanted to let go, to sink against Mason, to turn her head slightly to meet those lips. It had been so very long. The kiss would be familiar, she knew. The kiss would take her back to the only time in her life when she'd connected with someone. Angelique wasn't her destiny, though. She knew that back then. Just as she knew now that, yes, Mason *was* her destiny. Only it wasn't time. Not tonight. Something told her it wasn't time yet.

So she pulled away—gently—trying to untangle from Mason. Mason loosened her hold but didn't let her go completely.

"Sleep with me tonight."

Whatever she may have been expecting Mason to say, those words were not it. She stared at her, trying to read her, trying to get inside so she would know what Mason *truly* meant by them, would know what Mason was thinking. Whether she was too spent to read or Mason was keeping things locked up, she didn't know. The words made her mind a jumbled mess, she knew that.

"Please, Grace."

"Why?"

"Because you're not a freak or a failure. You're not unattractive or unlikeable." Mason leaned closer and brushed her lips lightly. "And because, for the first time in a long, long while, you make me want to get close to someone—to you."

"Oh, Mason." She touched Mason's cheek with her fingers, letting them run along her jawline, to her lips. "It'll just complicate things, don't you think?"

"Can they get more complicated, Grace?"

Yes, they could. They probably would. Surely. She made it a point to never have preconceived ideas of how these assignments would play out—they were all different. Never once had she thought an attractive woman would make her an offer such as this, though. Not while she was working, out in the field. She was exposed then. All of her oddities and "gifts" were on full display when she worked. No one would be— *could* be—attracted to that. Usually, it was quite the opposite. Usually, everyone kept her at arm's length. This time was different. Mason must feel it too. Destiny. Was that what Mason was thinking? Did she have any idea how linked they were?

The look on Mason's face was gentle, though, and sincere, and Grace was tempted to lean closer, to kiss her, to see where it might lead. She liked Mason. She liked her a lot. Mason treated her different than most. It would be nice to forget about life for a few hours— maybe the whole night. It would be so easy. Lean closer. Kiss her. Touch her. They could retreat to the bedroom, close out the world for a while. But it wasn't time. Just like Susie hadn't come to her yet because it wasn't time. She and Mason—it wasn't time yet. So she let her hand fall away, landing on Mason's thigh. Before she could say anything, try to explain, Mason stood and pulled her up.

"You're right. We shouldn't complicate things. I would feel better if you would sleep in my room, though. I have a king bed." Mason held her hand up when she would have protested. "There was some guy snooping around the house earlier. Your friend Thomas gave you a warning. I think we should heed it."

Yes, Mason was right on that account. They would be safer together. She had almost forgotten about the guy in the dark hoodie. "All right." When Mason turned to go, Grace stopped her with a light touch on her arm. "Thank you, Mason. I don't feel quite so freakish—or alone—with you."

"You are who you are, Grace. I think you're pretty remarkable, actually." She gave her a hesitant smile. "Should I apologize about earlier? I was being too forward, I guess. We barely know each other. I was—"

"No." Not too forward, no. Did Mason feel what she already knew? That it was their destiny? Saying it like that kinda took all the romance out of it though. "I like you, Mason. A lot."

* * *

It had been a very long time since Grace had shared a bed with someone. She'd feared it would be awkward, but then she really wasn't surprised that it wasn't. This was Mason, a woman she'd known a week, yet it had been a jam-packed week, hadn't it? They'd spent nearly every hour together, quietly getting to know one another. There was nothing awkward about their day-to-day interactions and there wasn't anything now. She simply got in beside Mason, who had already turned the light out. The large king gave them ample room, and she admitted that she did feel better—safer—being in Mason's bed instead of alone in the spare room.

"Thank you."

"You're welcome."

Grace smiled. Did Mason even know what she was thanking her for? Probably. "I don't often get spooked on these types of cases. Actually, not ever, really." She turned to her side, facing Mason. "There was one case, where the victim's blood was found in her home but that was the only sign of foul play. No forced entry, nothing missing except her. Her car was still in the garage. They suspected the husband, but there was no evidence whatsoever. By the time they called me in, it had been four or five weeks since she went missing. As soon as I walked in, I knew she was still there. I mean, not in the physical sense, but she was there. At first, she wouldn't come to me. Took me three visits before she'd show herself."

"The husband did it."

"Oh, yes. But she didn't want him arrested."

"Even after death she still loved him?"

"Quite the opposite. Seems she'd been haunting him, driving him mad." She remembered the crazy little laugh the woman used when they talked. "The poor guy was afraid to stay in the house, but he couldn't leave because he knew the police were watching his every move. Anyway, I thought it was odd what she was doing. It wasn't something I'd seen before. Turns out, she wasn't acting alone. There was another presence in the house, one who refused to come out to me. But this second presence was controlling the woman. They continued to harass the husband until he put a gun to his head."

"And it went down as either guilt or grief?"

"Yes. I mean, I confirmed that he did kill her. He used one of their kitchen knives—which was found with the body. He buried the body about six miles from where they lived. So she was found and everything got tied up nice and neat. But the woman and this other presence essentially committed murder. I remember the sound of laughter...*evil* laughter. I went back in after they took the husband's body. The woman was no longer there. Just this other presence... and he was laughing." She swallowed, remembering how scared she'd been. "The whole time, he never showed himself, never spoke to me. Until that day. He said, 'I can't be stopped' in this deep, raspy voice."

"He killed both of them," Mason guessed.

"Yes. He drove the husband to kill his wife—and by all accounts, they had a very loving relationship—then he used the woman to drive him mad."

"So this...this presence lived in that house?"

"I don't think so. It was a newer house in a subdivision. I think he picked the house at random."

"Okay, so that's a little disturbing. Like he does that sort of thing a lot? Others like him?"

"I don't know. A woman suddenly snaps and drowns her three kids. A teenager kills his parents and younger siblings. A guy drives his car into a crowd of pedestrians. Someone takes an assault rifle and kills his coworkers. Did they all act alone?"

"There always seems to be a reason to explain it."

"Yes, there does. As a society, we need to have a *reason* for these acts, don't we?"

"You're describing pure chaos, Grace."

"How many times have you apprehended a criminal who doesn't know why they did what they did?"

"Yeah, but—"

"So you chalk it up to their not wanting to take responsibility or their wanting to plant some seed of doubt or perhaps they want to go with temporary insanity."

Mason rolled to her side too and they faced each other in the darkness of the bedroom. Grace could barely make out her features but knew she was only a few feet away.

"Why don't more police departments use you or others like you?"

"Because we can't often produce evidence that would hold up in court. And sometimes, if we're involved even a little, the defense will use that as…well, as if it's all for show. Theatrics."

"Tell me about your life."

"My life?"

"Yeah. When you're not doing this. You said you're from New Orleans. Tell me about your life."

Grace curled her legs a bit and bumped knees with Mason. Instead of moving them, she relaxed, enjoying the contact.

"I wouldn't say I'm from New Orleans. I was a visiting assistant professor and taught for a semester. When it ended, I didn't leave, thinking I'd stay put and do more research for my book. New Orleans is a wonderfully old city with so much history."

"And haunted places?"

She smiled, recognizing the teasing tone in Mason's voice. "Oh, yes. It is very active. A psychic's paradise."

"Did you make friends there?"

"Not really, no. I had dinner occasionally with other professors, but I think it was mostly curiosity on their part."

"You don't trust many people, do you?"

"No. People don't usually trust me either." She reached out under the covers, finding Mason's hand. "I do trust you, Mason." She felt Mason's fingers squeeze her own.

"When I was in LA, I had a ton of friends. Then I met Shauna and *she* had a ton of friends. And I moved back here and…and it's like they all disappeared. I don't keep in touch, they don't keep in touch."

"Was Shauna the one you wanted to marry?"

"Yeah. That was a stupid thing to do."

"Stupid because she said no?"

Mason laughed quietly. "I'm glad she said no. At least one of us was thinking clearly."

"Do you regret moving back here? Losing your friends?"

"No. I mean, I liked it there, it became home…for a while. Then it wasn't. It was almost like this place was calling me back. I think I always knew I'd end up here again. In the back of my mind, I knew I'd come back."

"Yet it was different when you got here."

"Yes. My relationship with my mother was different. Brady and Dalton...different. Even Uncle Alan...it's a little, I don't know, different somehow. Now Aunt Carol, no. She's the same. She treats me like one of her family. She always has."

She shifted a little, stretching her legs out. "When are you going to see your mother?"

Mason sighed. "Sunday—tomorrow. Unless I have an excuse not to go."

"Do you need an excuse?"

"No. I don't know why I bother, actually. I usually take her some food." She could see Mason smile in the darkness. "Soup. Canned food."

"Payback?"

Mason laughed. "Yeah. Kinda childish, I know. I don't stay long. The place is usually a mess and I find myself wanting to clean up."

"Can I go with you?"

"Why on earth would you want to do that?"

"Why do you think I dreamed about you? You and you father?" Their hands were still clasped and she felt Mason shrug. "I'd only met you the one time, yet I had a dream about you. There's a reason for everything. And something tells me I should meet your mother."

They were both on their sides, facing each other, only a foot or so apart. They were still holding hands. The room was dark, shadowy. If she wanted, she could invade Mason's privacy but she wouldn't do that. She was content to learn things on Mason's terms. She closed her eyes, enjoying the closeness, the familiarity she felt with this woman. The peace she felt.

"Okay. You can go with me."

"Thank you," she murmured quietly.

"What's the plan then? Tomorrow. For us."

Grace kept her eyes closed. "I don't want to think about it. Patricia Brinkman. That's one plan. But we'll think about it tomorrow."

They were quiet for a long time, their hands still clasped, their feet touching, her eyes still closed. Then Mason's fingers tightened against her own.

"Good night, Grace."

She opened her eyes for a second, then closed them again. "Good night, Mason."

She felt sleep trying to claim her and she didn't try to fight it. She knew she was safe. She also knew she would dream.

But Mason was here. She was safe.

CHAPTER THIRTY-TWO

Mason was a sound sleeper. She didn't toss and turn much more than shifting from her side to her back. When she opened her eyes, she was surprised to find herself nearly tangled with Grace—arms and legs both. She smiled and blew blond hair away from her nose. Her arm was clutched by both of Grace's and one of Grace's legs was between hers. She moved her head slowly, finding Grace still sound asleep, her eyelids fluttering as she dreamed.

What kind of dream was she having? Her hand twitched ever so slightly, her mouth moving as if forming words. As she watched her, Grace's expression changed and she squeezed—painfully tight—against her arm. Mason barely stifled a startled scream when Grace sat up abruptly, her eyes wide.

"It's okay," Mason whispered quietly. "It's me."

Grace blinked several times, her eyes swimming in terror, then—as if flipping a switch—her expression changed and Mason knew whatever dream she'd had was fading faster than Grace could hold on to it. Grace let out a breath, then ran her hand through her hair. Mason could see the hand tremble.

"I was in a box. It was dark. Black dark." Her voice was still husky from sleep, and she closed her eyes for a moment, then opened them.

"A baby was crying." She lay back down. "I couldn't get out of the box." She turned her head to look at her. "You were trying to find me." Under the covers, Grace's hand latched around her arm again. "It's dark, musty. An unfinished basement, a cellar...something like that."

"Is the baby there with you?" she heard herself ask.

"No. It's close, but somewhere else." The grip on her arm relaxed a little. "The box is locked. You'll need a key to get me out."

"So this is something that's going to happen?"

"Yes. I've dreamt it a few times and it matches Nora Nightsail's vision. You'll have to find me. It'll be dark." She closed her eyes again. "A tunnel. There are...large baskets or carts that you push or something."

Mason arched an eyebrow. "Like a mine shaft? They used carts to move the gold out. They were wooden at first, then metal. They ran like...like on a mini-train track."

Grace was nodding. "Yes. Something like that. Are there tunnels here?"

"Yeah. There are old mines all over the place around Gillette Park. They're closed, the entrances boarded up, but that doesn't mean that someone didn't open them up again."

"Are they on public land?"

"A lot of them, yes. There's private land too, especially on the west side."

"Have any of our victims been found on private land?"

"I don't know. Fifty-something sites now, there may have been. The FBI put together an electronic mapping of the sites when they were looking for a pattern. That would be the quickest way to know."

"Not that it matters, really. I doubt our killer would dump a body close to home."

"Maybe the pattern is where they *haven't* dumped."

Grace sat up. "You're right." Then she shook her head. "No. The FBI would have accounted for that. There would be an obvious gap."

"Let's look at it anyway. Maybe it's not a gap to them, but it would be to a local." She got out from under the covers. "How did you sleep?"

"Good, I think. I don't remember waking up."

"Me either." She paused on the way to her bathroom. "Breakfast at Dottie's?"

"Yes. Breakfast to go." At Mason's raised eyebrows, she explained. "We need to go by your mother's. We need to find Patricia Brinkman.

And I'd like to go to the park. Nora mentioned a Paul who she talked to. I'd like to find him. She said he was killed a few years before she got there."

"Okay. Whatever you want."

She wasn't in a hurry to see her mother. It's not like she went *every* Sunday. She feared a trip to the park, though, might have them heading back to the footbridge to try to find Susie Shackle. For some reason, the thought of the footbridge brought a feeling of...what? Fear? Maybe intuition, but she thought they should stay away from the footbridge.

"Mason?"

She looked up, realizing she was still standing in place, lost in thought. She smiled briefly. "Yeah?"

"The footbridge scares me too. And you should make time for your mother."

Their eyes met and Mason nodded. What else had Grace been able to read? She turned away, wondering if Grace knew how adorable she looked first thing in the morning, tousled hair and sleepy eyes. She was smiling as she closed her bathroom door, thoughts of the footbridge fading, replaced with warm and fuzzy thoughts of Grace.

She quietly laughed at her reflection in the mirror. Warm and fuzzy? Yeah. Grace made her feel...warm. Grace made her want to get close, to cuddle, to kiss and touch. She hadn't had those feelings in forever. She wondered how long it had been since Grace had been intimate with someone. Would it feel as brand-new to Grace as it felt to her?

Brand-new, but not. There was a familiarity with Grace, something just under the surface, something that told her they knew each other well.

They were connected somehow...in ways neither of them knew, most likely.

In ways she feared they were about to find out.

CHAPTER THIRTY-THREE

Grace bit into her breakfast—she'd opted for a fried egg and biscuit sandwich—and gave a satisfied moan as she chewed. Like the muffins, the biscuit was huge and she imagined it had taken two eggs to fill it. It was light and fluffy and oozing with butter.

"This is sinful," she said around a mouthful. "Don't let me order this again."

Mason laughed and handed her a napkin. "Butter on your chin."

They were driving toward the park. It was another sunny, blue-sky morning. Puffy clouds would gather by noon, she'd learned, but so far, they hadn't had any rain. It was still cool—it was barely after eight—and she wore a sweatshirt over her long-sleeved T-shirt. When she'd shopped for her trip up here to the mountains, she'd found a sports store that sold clothing, but springtime in New Orleans wasn't the time to shop for cold weather items. She'd ended up buying most of her things online. Long-sleeved T-shirts had been on a sale rack, however, and she'd grabbed six of them.

"You know, I never did tell you everything Thomas said."

"No. And I never told Uncle Alan about the guy we saw running from the house either. It's all related, I'm assuming."

"Yes, I'm sure. And if we're offering up assumptions, I'll guess that Susie Shackle was targeted because of her father. Thomas said Rusty blames him for the fire. Well, I suppose he blames him for what happened during the fire or for whatever went wrong and they didn't make it out. Why he waited that many years, I don't know. And why the killings have continued for so long—who knows?"

"You're saying Rusty is the killer?"

"No, no. Our killer is flesh and blood. Rusty is what drives the killings. How, I don't know. Thomas said I need to talk to Susie. He said Susie knows everything. From what I gather, everyone defers to Susie, even though she was...what? Ten when she was killed?"

"When we were at the creek last night—the footbridge—was anyone around?"

"No," she mumbled around another bite of her biscuit sandwich. "We were alone."

"What's the symbolism of putting the girl—April—in the same spot as Susie Shackle?"

"For our benefit, I guess. To let us know that he knows that we now know who he is." She turned to Mason. "Thomas says he was taken from the library, from the restroom, through the ventilation system."

Mason nodded. "Yes, that was the assumption, I think. That was a few years before I came back."

"He says there were two of them. One was in the restroom, the other in the vent. That stands to reason that one of them may very well have walked in through the front door."

"They still have the surveillance video from that day. It's been looked at a thousand times, though."

"Okay, so this is going to sound crazy, but what if Thomas looked at it."

"Oh, Grace...*sure!* Let me call Uncle Alan right now. Thomas Houston can look at it! *That* won't be a problem," Mason teased sarcastically.

"I said it was crazy," she muttered as she playfully slapped Mason's arm. "I'm confident he could point him out, though."

"Say it's a possibility. How do we get Thomas into the station to look at it? Invite him in?"

Grace tried to stifle her laugh because Mason was being so serious. "It's not a vampire movie, Mason."

Mason laughed good-naturedly. "Sorry. Just guessing at the protocol."

"Thomas can show himself anywhere, if I called to him. He may not choose to, though. But if we could get a copy of the video, take a laptop out to the library tonight…then maybe he'd be willing to look at it."

"So he points the guy out. This is from 2012. Even if we could identify him, what's our probable cause to get a warrant? I don't think Judge Sinclair is going to sign off on it."

"Therein lies the problem with using psychics," she said. "You couldn't get a warrant. But you'd know who you're looking at. You can investigate him without a warrant, can't you?"

"To some extent, yes. We can go interview him, check out his house—at least from the outside—and see if anything looks suspicious." Mason turned into the park and slowed. "If all of that pans out, just the fact that we're looking at him might make him too nervous to kill again."

"Only if Rusty is in agreement. Rusty drives this, remember. Like the story I told you last night, our killer most likely does not have free will. Or he didn't at the beginning. Rusty may have driven him totally mad by now."

Mason slowly shook her head as she drove through the parking lot. "Mark Russell Meyer, died in 1984. And we're looking for him."

"Let's not share that with your uncle just yet, shall we? I don't want him to think I'm totally insane."

There were both a police cruiser and a sheriff's car in the lot, along with three other vehicles. She supposed they were still at the footbridge, looking for evidence now that it was daylight. She recognized one of the trucks as that of Neal Addick, the hunting guide. Mason drove past them and nearer to the soccer fields. Paul Whitman, age twelve, was found in the woods beyond the first field, three days after he'd gone missing in 2002…two years before Nora Nightsail came to town. Paul, like young Jason Gorman, had disappeared here at the fields after a soccer match. Unlike Jason, his body had been found very close to where he'd last been seen. His bike—the one he'd been riding that fateful day—was never recovered.

Other than them and the police presence, the park appeared to be empty. No doubt word had spread about the latest victim. Still, it was a beautiful Sunday morning. Shouldn't *someone* be out at the park?

Mason's phone rang as soon as she'd pulled into a parking spot. She cut the engine before answering.

"Cooper." Her voice was all business, causing Grace to smile at her. Mason was nodding as she listened to the caller. "Tell him it'll be a little while. We just got to the park." A pause. "No, no. Grace wants to check out something else," Mason said, flicking her gaze to her. "Copy that."

Grace raised her eyebrows questioningly.

"Uncle Alan wants you to go to April Trombley's house, go into her room, see if you can find anything. There was no sign of forced entry. Window was open, screen was in place. The mother said the window was closed when April went to bed."

"So they put the screen back on after they got the girl out."

"No prints." They got out and started walking around the fence that circled the field. "How do they lure the kids out?"

"Maybe Rusty plays a part in that. He showed himself to you as a Steller's jay. Thomas says he often uses the jay. Maybe he shows himself to these kids as something that's meaningful to them. Maybe April likes puppies. So she sees a puppy outside her window. She opens it up, takes the screen off. Maybe even climbs out to play with the puppy."

"She was eight years old. Could she take a screen off?"

Grace shrugged. "Why is the park empty?"

Mason looked around, as if just then noticing the absence of cars. "It's Sunday, isn't it? Guess it's a little early. People are at church, maybe."

"Or people are avoiding it?"

"Third killing and it's still May. I remember the vibe in town back in 2004. After the third killing, everyone was on pins and needles. Then the fourth. The park was completely empty. No kids at the library. No one riding bikes around town. It was a long summer. Like everyone was locked behind closed doors, holding their breath, waiting..."

"Including you?"

"I was a senior in high school. My mother didn't care much what I did. Aunt Carol was the one who made sure I stayed close to Brady. She kept tabs on us. She had rules and we followed them. I left town in August, though."

"And drifted away?"

"Yeah, pretty much."

"Did you drift back in too?"

"Meaning what? Did I pop back into town without much fanfare?"

"Did you?"

Mason shrugged. "Uncle Alan knew I was coming—he offered me a job. I stayed with them for a couple of months until I bought my house." She looked at the GPS device, then motioned up ahead. "We're getting close. He wasn't left very far past the fields."

"Wonder what happened to his bike."

"You think the killer took it?"

"There have been odd things. Deb Meckel and her clarinet. Paul's bike was never found. The opposite for Lucy Hines. Her bike was found on the trail along School Road. She was never found, however."

"That's right. She was one of the two who we've never found. What year?"

"Lucy disappeared in May, 2009. The other, Abigail Lawrence—Abby, they called her—disappeared in 2012. She was sixteen. She was one of those who seemed to disappear into thin air. One moment she was there, the next..." Grace held her arm out, pressing it against Mason's stomach, halting her progress. "I see the spot."

As with the other times, the forest floor was discolored where she imagined Paul Whitman had lain. She stood still, watching as it darkened, the leaves turning black as if someone had poured tar over the top, covering them.

"You're Grace, aren't you?"

She looked up, seeing the young boy sitting on a tree limb, almost hidden in the branches.

"How do you know my name?"

"Thomas told me. And Susie said to be on the lookout for you."

She took a step closer. "So Susie knows I'm here?"

He grinned at that. *"Of course. Susie knows everything."*

He glided out of the tree, landing some four feet in front of her. He wore glasses and she noticed the right lens was missing. "What happened to your bike?"

He pounded his fist on his thigh. *"I loved that bike! He took it and hid it in the woods. Then a few months later, he came and got it. Rode it right on out of the park as if he owned the thing."*

"Who is he?"

Paul smiled and shook his head. *"Susie says I can't tell you. It's not time."*

"Time?"

"She's got a plan. She doesn't want anything to happen to Faith." He stepped closer, lowering his voice to almost a whisper. *"Rusty doesn't like Faith."*

"Who is Faith?"

"Faith is like you.

"Like me how?"

"She talks to us. We go visit her. Play with her. She's real smart. Susie has taught her a lot."

"She can see you?"

"Uh huh. But not her momma. Her momma thinks she's crazy."

Grace swallowed. "Who is her mother?"

"Lucy."

Grace's eyes widened. "Lucy?"

"Yeah. You and your friend were just talking about her. And Abby. She's there too, but they don't both know it." Then he shook his head. *"Well, Faith knows, but Lucy doesn't. Abby just had a baby."* He grinned. *"Andrew."*

Grace stared at him, trying to keep her thoughts from spiraling out of control. "Where are they?"

"I can't tell you that! It's not time!"

"Why don't they leave?"

"Leave? They're locked up! They can't leave." He took a few steps away from her. *"Susie says I talk too much."*

Grace looked around excitedly. "Is she here?"

"No, no. Not her."

"It's me!" came a familiar voice from the trees.

She looked up, seeing Thomas now sitting on the branch where Paul had been. "Hi, Thomas."

"Hiya, Grace. Susie told me to keep an eye on you. Susie says we can't let anything happen to you."

He pointed to where Mason stood and Grace followed his gaze. Mason's eyes were fixed on her, and Grace gave her a nod, trying to let her know that everything was okay.

"Mason—I like her," Thomas said before hopping down to the ground beside Paul. *"She's going to protect you."*

"Yes. I think so."

"She's kinda scared, though, huh?"

Grace smiled. "Yes, a little."

Paul laughed. *"More than a little. She doesn't have to be scared of Rusty, though. You do, but not her. She only has to worry about Johnny and—"*

His words were shut off as Thomas clamped a hand across his mouth. *"Paul! No! Susie said not to tell yet!"*

Grace smiled at these two boys—one twelve, the other thirteen— killed a decade apart. Had she been wrong all along? Did they interact? Play together? Have a social club? Did Fran and Missy play together? Did Susie Shackle hold town meetings which they all attended?

"Forget everything he said," Thomas was saying to her. *"Susie says she's gonna talk to you very soon."*

"At the footbridge?"

"No, no. You should stay away from there. Rusty controls the footbridge now. But one night. Very soon."

"How will I know when?"

Thomas shrugged. *"She didn't say."*

She watched as Thomas nearly pulled Paul along with him, hearing only a *"You talk too much"* muttered from Thomas as they went back into the tree.

"You should go see Mason's mother. There's a picture there of her father. Pick it up. You'll know then."

Grace arched an eyebrow. "Know what?"

"Why he left. You'll know everything from the picture."

"Do you know why he left?"

"Yep."

"Tell me."

"No, can't. But you go look at the picture."

Before she could ask more, they faded away, disappearing into the leaves. It was only then that she noted Thomas didn't have his books with him. She let out a breath, then turned to Mason. "They're gone."

Mason came closer to her, eyebrows raised questioningly.

"Paul and Thomas. Paul was very talkative, like Nora said. Thomas came by to make sure he didn't say too much. I don't know why they're being so secretive about it all, but they are." She debated whether to tell Mason everything. Maybe Mason knew who this Johnny was. But even if she did, it would make no difference. They couldn't question him. They had no evidence of anything. Besides…Susie had a plan.

"Let's go see your mother."

"That's it? You talked for quite a while. That's all I get?"

Grace retraced their steps, heading back to the fields. When Mason came up beside her, she decided to share some of what she knew. "Lucy Hines and Abby Lawrence are apparently being held captive. Lucy has a daughter—Faith. I still don't know how old she is. Lucy has been there since '09, right? So Faith could have been born any time after that. Abby has a baby. A boy. Andrew."

"The baby in your dreams?"

"I imagine so." She stopped walking. "Faith is like me, they said. She can see them, talk to them."

Mason swallowed nervously. "Is that a good thing?"

Grace smiled. "Yes. That's a very good thing. Now we just have to wait."

"Wait for what?"

"Wait for Susie Shackle to contact me." She bumped her shoulder. "Let's take a break from all this. Let's go see your mother."

"Can't."

"Can't?"

"I'm supposed to take you over to April Trombley's house first."

Grace sighed. "Oh, yeah. I forgot."

"And what about Patricia Brinkman?"

Grace nodded. "Yes. After your mother though."

CHAPTER THIRTY-FOUR

Lucy noticed that Stacy looked more tired than usual today as she pushed the cart into their room. When Stacy came earlier that day—she hesitated to call it morning or breakfast because sometimes it was breakfast fare and sometimes it was sandwiches and she never really trusted the time on the windup clock Stacy had given her—she'd had puffy bags under her eyes as if she hadn't slept in a while. Now, her feet were dragging as she took the plates from the tray and placed them on the table.

"Are you feeling okay?"

Stacy looked over at her and nodded. "I brought some magazines for Faith."

There were three, it looked like, and Stacy put them on the small table too.

"Whose baby do we hear crying?"

Stacy stared at her for a moment and when their eyes met, Lucy thought perhaps she might actually answer her. But no. Stacy pulled her gaze away and started backing out of the room. The door banged into the cart, but Lucy knew better than to help her. Neither she nor Faith were allowed near the door when Stacy was there. She'd made that mistake years ago and had gone four days without food as punishment. As soon as the door closed, she listened as all three locks were engaged again. Then she nodded at Faith, who had been patiently waiting to take a look at the magazines.

"What kind did you get this time?"

Faith made a face. "A hunting magazine again." Then she smiled. "Backyard gardening. That'll come in handy, Momma."

Lucy laughed and Faith joined in. They sat down to their meal of rice and chili beans. All the while Faith turned the pages of the gardening magazine, staring at the colorful pictures.

"When we get out, can we have flowers, Momma?"

"Sure, honey," she said automatically.

Faith looked up at her. "You don't believe we're getting out, do you?"

"I don't want you to be disappointed, Faith."

"Grace is coming to help us. I know she is. Thomas said he talked to her just today. And the police person's name is Mason. He says she's scared." Faith smiled. "Scared that Grace talks to him and scared of Rusty."

Lucy ate her dinner, not knowing if Faith expected her to answer or not. Lately, she'd been more animated than ever when talking about her special friends.

"There's something I need to tell you, Momma."

Again? Lucy sighed. "What is it?"

"We're going to have to help Mason get the keys."

"The keys?"

"Yes. The ones that Stacy has. All of the keys that we need will be there."

"And how will we do that?"

"Susie says you'll have to find a way. She says you may have to knock Stacy out."

"Knock her out?"

"Yes. Take her keys, then lock her in here."

"Then what? We're out there?" she asked, pointing to the door. "We don't even know what's out there. We don't know *who's* out there, Faith."

Faith blinked at her. "We have to do what Susie says."

"Susie?" Lucy hit the table hard with her fist. "Who is Susie? One of your so-called friends?"

"She *is* my friend. She's my best friend."

"Oh, Faith. Who is Susie? Who is Thomas? Who are all these people you talk to?"

Again, Faith stared at her, blinking several times. Her voice was almost grown-up now. "Don't you know, Momma? Don't you know who they are?"

Did she know? Did she dare say it out loud?

"Yes, Momma."

Lucy put her spoon down and rubbed both her temples. "Who is Susie?" she asked quietly.

"Her name is Susie Shackle. She was killed in 1997. She was the first one the mean man killed. Thomas was killed in 2012. The mean man didn't kill you, though, Momma. Do you know why?"

Lucy's stomach turned over and she feared she would lose the dinner she'd just eaten. Wouldn't that be pretty? Chili beans and rice thrown up all over their tiny table. *Oh, Lucy…why did you throw up? Well, you see, because my daughter talks to dead people.*

"I know why, Momma."

Lucy swallowed down the bile that was threatening. "Why?" she asked hoarsely.

"Because he had two sons and one died. His son did something he wasn't supposed to so the man locked him in the box. He died in there because the man forgot about him. So the man wanted another son. You were supposed to give him a son. Only I was a girl."

"And…and who is Stacy?"

"Stacy is his daughter, but he got mad when she wasn't a boy so he killed her momma."

"Oh, dear Lord," she murmured.

"But now Abby had a son. Abby doesn't know it, but the mean man is going to take Andrew away from her. That's why we've got to do what Susie says. So we can all get out of here before he takes Andrew."

"Faith, this is all so crazy." She waved her hand in the air. "How can you expect me to believe this? How can any *sane* person believe all this?"

Faith hung her head and Lucy could see the frustration on her face. When she looked up, Faith met her gaze.

"Momma, you know I'm telling the truth. We only have a few days left. Then it'll be time. Susie has a plan."

Yes, time to bop Stacy on the head and steal her keys. Time to leave the safe confines of their little prison and go out where the mean man lives. Because Susie Shackle, dead since 1997, has a plan.

"It'll be okay, Momma."

Will it?

Faith stared at her and nodded. "Yes, it will."

CHAPTER THIRTY-FIVE

Mason stood outside her mother's apartment door. She could hear the TV blaring from inside. She glanced over at Grace, wishing she'd found something at the Trombley house, something that would have occupied the rest of the day. The only thing she found was a feather—a blue feather—under the bed. She couldn't exactly tell her uncle that Rusty Meyer—disguised as a Steller's jay—had been in the room, could she? *You remember Rusty Meyer, don't you, Uncle Alan? He died in the fire in 1984.* No, she couldn't tell him that.

She'd also suggested that they go by Patricia Brinkman's house, but Grace had been adamant that they go see her mother. It was getting too late on this cloudy Sunday afternoon to be paying a ninety-something-year-old a visit anyway, she supposed. They would save that for tomorrow.

Truth was, she didn't want Grace to meet her mother. She was embarrassed by her, and she didn't want Grace to judge her or make assumptions about her based on her mother.

Too late for all that too, because here they were, each holding a bag of groceries that they'd picked up on their way over. She normally only brought one bag. Most of the cans of vegetables she brought ended up collecting dust in the panty. Grace had suggested cans of tuna and chicken and a loaf of bread. The apartment complex, while starting to show its age, was neat and tidy. A small enclosed patio was adjacent to the front door and Mason peered over the fence, seeing her mother's large shape in the recliner.

"I don't want to stay long."

Grace nodded but said nothing.

Mason finally knocked on the door. After she did, she looked across the fence again. Her mother was struggling to get out of the chair.

"She's a mess. I'm embarrassed for you to see her."

"Mason, from what you've told me, she ceased being your mother when you were ten. Whatever she's become, that's no reflection on you. And what you've become...that's no thanks to her."

Mason gave her a quick nod as she heard the lock turning.

Her mother opened the door, a scowl on her puffy face. "Didn't think you were going to bother coming by."

"Hello, Mom." Mason motioned with her head. "This is a friend of mine. Grace."

Her mother's gaze landed on Grace, and she was surprised by how long she stared at her. Long enough to be uncomfortable. She glanced at Grace, who didn't seem fazed by it.

"Brought a friend, did you? Thought you needed to show me off?" She took a step back, opening the door wider. "Well, come in."

Her mother maneuvered back down the tiny entryway and into the living room. The usual clutter was there—newspapers and McDonald's wrappers were on the end table. On the coffee table was a laundry basket of clothes that needed to be folded. Not two, but three coffee cups sat beside it. And last night's vodka and tonic glass. Other than that, it wasn't too messy. She'd seen it much worse. As her mother sat down again, she headed to the kitchen. Grace followed, then stopped in her tracks.

"Good grief."

"Yeah. She doesn't take the trash out much." The smell was worse than normal, and she didn't know if that was because of the weeks' worth of dirty dishes strewn across the counter or the weeks' worth of trash. Grace started clearing a spot to put the bags—moving three empty vodka bottles aside—but Mason stopped her. "Don't. Once you start, you'll never stop."

Mason dropped her bag on the floor, motioning for Grace to do the same.

"I haven't had a chance to clean up," her mother called from the other room.

Mason looked at Grace and rolled her eyes. "Right. She's been *very* busy."

Grace smiled at her. "Is this why you're a neat freak?"

"Am I?"

"Your kitchen is immaculate."

Mason laughed quietly. "Maybe because I eat at Bucky's most often. Come on. Let's get it over with."

They went back into the living room where the TV was still blaring. Her mother had the good grace to mute it finally.

"Everything going okay?"

"Compared to what?" Her mother's gaze slid to Grace. "Are you that weird psychic woman that's in town? Heard whisperings about you. Finding that Trombley girl before her own mother even missed her."

"Yes. I am that weird psychic." Grace surprised her by moving in front of her mother. "Do you want a reading?"

"I most certainly do not! Some fools might fall for that crap, but I won't!"

Grace looked around the room as if searching for something. She moved to the entertainment center where a cluster of picture frames were set haphazardly. Mason watched as Grace picked one up. It was the one of her father. He was at Uncle Alan's house in the backyard. There was a cookout. She'd been a baby at the time. He was smiling. He looked happy. She turned her gaze to her mother. Her mother's eyes never left Grace. In fact, she was following her every move.

"You don't favor him."

"No, I don't."

Grace put the frame back, then turned around, facing her mother again. Mason knew with certainty that Grace was trying to read her mother, trying to get inside. For what reason, she didn't know. Several seconds passed and her mother shifted uncomfortably in her chair. Mason finally cleared her throat. Grace smiled. Her mother put the TV's sound back on.

"Yeah, so we're heading out, I guess."

"Fine."

"I'll try to come back next weekend."

"Bring something other than veggies and soup. I'm sick to death of soup."

"Yeah, it gets old, doesn't it?"

Grace stopped beside her chair. "Nice to meet you, Mrs. Cooper." Her mother looked at her, not Grace. "You don't need to bring her back around. Don't want the neighbors to think I'm chummy with a psychic, of all people."

Grace didn't seem upset by her rudeness. She only gave a slight shrug before heading to the door. Mason shook her head. Why did she even bother? When was the last time her mother thanked her for bringing food? Had she ever? No. It was as if her mother expected it just because she had given birth to her. And Mason supposed that's the reason she did it. Because it was expected. She walked out without a goodbye.

They looked at each other across the hood of her truck. The sky was clouding over, the sun hiding. Rain was forecast for early evening. Rain and colder weather. Even now, the breeze hinted at the approaching cold front. Grace felt it too. She crossed her arms as if to keep warm.

"I told you she was a mess."

"Yes, you did. And I told you, whatever she's become—whatever she's made of her life—it is no reflection on you, Mason. So you don't have to apologize for her."

They got inside the truck, and she glanced only once at her mother's door before she pulled away. Why did she keep coming by? She got no joy out of it, no sense of accomplishment, no satisfaction in providing some help to her. She wondered how much money her mother spent on booze. There was no need for her to save some back when she knew Mason would come by with food. Did that make her an enabler?

"You're wondering why you do it?" Grace held a hand up. "And no, I'm not inside your head."

"I should stop."

"Why?"

"Because I'm not helping her. She spends her cash on vodka. I provide the food."

"Not to sound rude or anything, but she must eat way more than only what you bring by."

"She's obese, yes, I know. She eats fast food burgers, frozen pizza—junk. Bloody Mary. That's her breakfast. If she had eggs in the house, she might take the time to scramble a couple. If not, she eats donuts or some other pastry."

"And she's diabetic?"

"She is, among other things. She has pills for all of her ailments so she thinks she's fine." She pounded the steering wheel. "I should stop coming by. It's depressing. I get nothing out of it, and I'm pretty sure she gets nothing out of it. We don't talk. We're not involved in each other's lives. There is just this invisible string that binds us."

"So cut the string."

Mason glanced at her. "I thought you were going to say something like it was admirable of me to keep coming by, regardless of the abuse."

"Abuse when you were a child? Was it abuse or neglect?"

"Verbal abuse. Neglect, certainly."

"Yes. And now the abuse is emotional, isn't it?" Grace reached across the console and rested her fingers on her arm. "People can't make you feel guilty unless you allow it. Whatever game she plays with you emotionally—it takes two to play it, Mason."

"So you're saying I *should* quit going over there?"

"If you're only doing it out of a sense of obligation—because she's your mother and she needs help—then I think you're going about it in the wrong way. You bring her food, but she doesn't need food, Mason. She's not destitute. She chooses to spend her money on things other than food. That's her business. You can't *make* her eat better, you can't *make* her stop drinking. You can't *make* her treat you differently. In other words, *you* can't control her. Don't let *her* control *you*."

"You're right, of course. I don't enjoy coming over here. I spend the days before dreading it. Then after I see her, I spend the next few days being disgusted by it. Because she doesn't change. She won't change. She doesn't listen to her doctor and she certainly doesn't listen to me."

"Then let it go. Make peace with it. You're not responsible for her. She's a grown woman making her own choices. There can only be an intervention if someone allows you to intervene. She, clearly, is not at that point."

Mason glanced at her quickly as she drove them back through town. "What did you learn there?"

"Learn?"

"Come on, Grace. I've been around you enough to recognize the signs."

"Think you know all my tricks, do you?"

Mason smiled at her. "A few. You were trying to read her."

"Your mother has no defenses, no shield."

"You're saying it was easy?"

"You're right about one thing. She is still living in the past. She sees herself as young, thin, pretty. Desirable."

"When I was a kid, she was…well, I wouldn't say thin but certainly not what she is now."

"No, no. Back further than that. High school. The image she has of herself is when she was in high school."

Mason arched an eyebrow. "Why high school?"

"Because it was during those years that she was truly happy."

"What are you saying? She wasn't happy when she was married? Grace, I told you. After he left, her world fell apart. And therefore, so did mine." Grace didn't say anything and Mason glanced at her again. "What is it you're not telling me?"

"It's not my place, Mason."

"Oh, come on! You can't do that."

"I can and I will. End of discussion."

No amount of prodding on her part could get Grace to budge. She finally gave up. By the time they pulled into her driveway, the front was upon them. Huge, cold raindrops pelted them as they ran from the truck to the house. They stood under the covered porch, watching the rain for a moment.

"The temp dropped drastically, didn't it?" Grace leaned closer to her as if to get warm. "Is there a chance of snow?"

"You ask that with a bit of excitement in your voice."

Grace smiled as they walked inside. "Guilty. I told you, I've only seen snow twice. It would be fun."

"Snow in May is not uncommon although I don't think this front will do it. The higher elevations get snow in June some years."

She went into the kitchen and put the bag she carried on the table. Grace had offered to cook again but Mason took her to Adler's Barbeque instead. They got sliced beef sandwiches and potato salad and a tub of sauce that Mason loved so much, by the time she was through adding it, the buns were soaked and soggy.

When she turned around, Grace wasn't behind her. She panicked for a second then found Grace in the living room. Mason paused, watching her. Her lips were moving. She was talking to someone.

God…who was in her house?

CHAPTER THIRTY-SIX

Grace nodded approvingly after taking her first bite of the barbeque sandwich. "Very good. You're right. The sauce is excellent."

"Yeah, but you didn't drown yours like you're supposed to."

Grace smiled as sauce ran past the corner of Mason's mouth and onto her chin. Without thinking, she reached out and wiped it away with her napkin. "If you're not careful, you'll need a bib."

"I could drink this stuff."

"Growing up, we lived all over, as you know. Overseas too. But I have early memories of my mother picking up barbeque—ribs and sausage and pulled pork sandwiches that were piled so high, I couldn't get my hands around it—and it'd be wrapped in what she called butcher's paper. It would be soaked in grease and sauce and we'd sit down to a feast of that with coleslaw and black-eyed peas. We didn't have a lot of money—this was before she married—so it was always a treat when she splurged on a big dinner like that."

"You and your mother were closer back then? Before she married?"

"It was just the two of us, so yes. There was starting to be tension, though. By the time I was six or seven, I was...talking to people," she said with a smile. "You know, people my mother couldn't see. By the time she married, I was nine. Rich—my stepfather—didn't have much patience—or tolerance—for it all."

"That's when you learned to hide it?"

"Yes. As best I could. I was afraid they'd send me to a mental institution."

Mason put her sandwich down and wiped her mouth with her own napkin this time. "Would your mother have really done that?"

"Honestly, I don't know. I didn't want to take the chance. You said once that I was the forgotten one. That's true. I called it invisible, but forgotten might fit better. I disappeared into the shadows of their little family. Hid in the corners and watched from afar."

"Oh, Grace. That's awful. You were just a kid. You didn't—"

"I was a kid. Yet I wasn't. I knew things that kids my age shouldn't know. I learned a lot of dirty, dark secrets that a ten-year-old or twelve-year-old had no business knowing." She put her sandwich down and took a swallow of her water. "I admit, I wasn't a happy child. And I felt left out. But some of that was my own doing. I chose to stay in the shadows. It was easier that way." She smiled slightly. "Out of sight, out of mind. That came in handy when I was a teenager." She picked up her sandwich again, wondering why she was sharing these little bits of her life with Mason. She met her gaze, seeing compassion in Mason's eyes. Again, memories of Angelique came to mind when she looked at Mason.

"When I was fifteen, we moved to Hawaii." She paused to take a bite of her sandwich. Should she share that with Mason? Should she tell her about Angelique? "I saw her on the beach. She'd been surfing with a group of guys. It was getting on to sunset. The colors were vibrant—red and orange—and she rose up out of the sea, her skin bronzed and dripping wet." She smiled at Mason. "I'm pretty sure I fell in love that very moment."

"Tell me."

"She was seventeen. Angelique. It took me weeks to get my nerve up to go talk to her. It was all so sickly romantic when I think about it. I lost my virginity on my sixteenth birthday. She knew all my secrets and she never once made fun of me. She's the one who encouraged me to embrace my gifts, not run from them." She sighed. "And I cried my eyes out when we left the island a year later."

"You were what? Seventeen then? Why didn't you stay?"

"That was never an option. I had one more year of high school. We both knew it was temporary from the start. Maybe that's why it was so intense."

"You never saw her again?"

"No. We said our goodbyes and that was that."

"Did your mother know?"

"No. I was invisible, remember? Point is, I was seventeen when I left and Angelique remains the only person I've ever had a connection with. I'm thirty-four years old and I've only had a handful of lovers." She smiled. "Less than a handful, actually."

"Because?"

"Because they find out who I am, what I do, and they run. Usually one dinner date is enough for most. And I think that those who stuck around for more did it only out of curiosity."

"Oh, come on. You're attractive, you're nice. Who wouldn't want to stick around?"

Grace rested her chin in her palm, her eyes on Mason. Was it only last night that Mason had wanted to sleep with her? She never once thought Mason suggested it for any reason other than she was attracted to her. She never got the sense that she'd taken pity on her or was trying to make up for how Dalton had treated her. She smiled at that thought. Would she offer sex anytime someone spoke to her like that?

"What's with the smile?"

"Can't I smile?" She picked up her sandwich again and took a bite. The bun was getting soggy from the sauce and part of it fell away. She picked it up with her fingers and ate that too.

Mason leaned back in her chair. "So? When are you going to tell me about earlier? Who was in the house?"

Grace was surprised it had taken Mason this long to ask. She took a swallow of her water, wondering what all to tell Mason. She glanced out the cluster of windows by the table, noting that dusk was upon them and the shadows were heavy outside. It had been a long day and an equally long night before that. She felt tired, both mentally and physically. She knew someone would be coming tonight. Thomas had told her so. She should tell Mason that, at least. They were coming just to scare them, he'd said. Nothing more. Even so, she was tired and not really prepared. She thought maybe it would be later, after they'd gone to bed for the night. Not right then, not only an hour after Thomas left. She wasn't prepared, and it startled her enough to make her gasp. It startled Mason too.

Grace nearly dropped her water bottle as Mason jumped up, bumping the table in the process. A flurry of blue feathers danced across the window screens before the bird flew off. But it was the man running in the backyard—man or boy—that had both of their attentions now. When Mason would have gone out the door to chase him, Grace grabbed her arm.

"No! That's what they want, Mason. To separate us. We have to stay together."

"Did you see the damn bird? God, I hate that thing!"

"I saw it. And the guy—it can't be the big, mean man that they all describe. He looked too slight, suggesting a teenager or perhaps a young adult."

Mason went around the table and jerked the curtains closed, shutting out the darkness that had fallen. Grace could tell that her hand was trembling. She held her own up. Yeah, so were hers. Apparently, it had frightened her more than she thought.

"What's going on, Grace? Who were you talking to earlier?"

"It was Thomas. He came to warn me that someone would come tonight—to scare us. I assumed he meant later, like after midnight."

"Why didn't you tell me?" she demanded.

"I was going to. After we ate." She looked at what remained of her sandwich, her appetite having vanished. "I thought we could have a normal dinner with normal conversation." She waved her hand in the air. "Without all of this. For once."

Mason blew out her breath. "I'm sorry." Then she pointed at the window. "The next time I see it, I'm shooting the damn bird." Instead of sitting down, she opened a cabinet and took out the bottle of whiskey. She poured a little in two glasses and slid one across the table to her.

"Thanks."

Mason leaned against the counter, cupping the glass with both her hands. She had yet to take a drink.

"Do you worry you'll end up like your mother?"

Mason looked at her questioningly. "You mean the booze?"

"Yes."

Mason sat down with a sigh. "I used to worry that I might. After I moved back, that is. While I was gone, I didn't give it much thought. I drank at dinner parties and get-togethers. I drank when we went out to clubs. I never kept anything at home though. When I moved back, when I saw how bad it had gotten with her, yeah, I thought about it." She took a sip then. "I have a beer or two at Bucky's. This bottle," she said, motioning to the counter where it sat. "It's for those nights when the wind is howling and the snow is piling up. Or those nights after we've found a body and I can't sleep."

"Stress release?"

"You're going to say that's a terrible time to drink, aren't you?"

Grace touched her glass to Mason's, smiling at the gentle clinking sound they made as they touched. "I don't think there's anything wrong with calming our nerves with a shot of whiskey." She took a sip of her own. "Did your father drink?"

"He used to keep beer in the fridge. On weekends, I'd see him drink one or two. Never wine. Never this," she said, holding up her glass. "My mother used to have wine in the house, but it was rare she opened a bottle."

"Why do you think she turned to alcohol then?"

"I don't know. Maybe it numbed her enough when nothing else did. Food gave her comfort, but it didn't numb her like booze did. Now, she obviously needs both." She put her glass on the table and twirled it around. "When I left, she'd gained weight, but nothing like this. I hardly recognized her when I saw her again."

"Are you saying that once you left, you never came back to visit?"

"No. And we didn't talk on the phone either."

"Wow. I didn't think anyone could top me and my mother's relationship."

"Aunt Carol was more of a mother to me than she was."

"And your uncle was the father figure?"

"Yes." Mason picked up her glass again. "Why are we talking about this?" She met her gaze and held it. "What do you know that you're not telling me?"

Grace knew Mason would get back to that sooner or later. And she supposed with the turn their conversation had taken, she'd been expecting the question. But was it her place? Should she be the one to tell her? Maybe there was a reason. A reason Thomas had told her to look at the picture. Maybe it was time Mason knew the truth. Maybe it had a bearing on this case, a bearing on the outcome. She couldn't imagine why, but Thomas directed her there for a reason.

"Tell me." Mason's directive was quiet, yet firm.

"You already know, Mason."

"Tell me anyway. Grace...I need to hear it. Please?"

Mason whispered the last word, and as their eyes held, she knew that, yes, Mason already suspected the truth. How could she not? She looked nothing like her father. She looked exactly like Alan Cooper—her smile, her eyes. She and Brady favored each other far too closely to be only cousins. Grace slid her hand across the table and took one of Mason's. She squeezed it gently.

"Your father—when he found out you weren't really his daughter, he left."

Mason's expression didn't change much, but her face lost some of its color. She nodded and drank the last of her whiskey in one gulp.

"Does Aunt Carol know?"

"I don't know, Mason. If I had to guess, I would say she does not."

Mason stood up and went to the bottle again. But instead of pouring more, she simply put it back in the cabinet. "That's why my mother never pushed for him to pay child support. She knew if she did, the truth would come out." Her fists clenched. "And that's why Uncle Alan felt obligated to send me money when I left for college."

"Mason, don't—"

"Don't what?" She ran a hand through her hair. "Damn. I'd long thought that might be the case but...but hearing it out loud, knowing for sure." Mason turned her back to her and leaned against the counter. "It's like...nobody wanted me."

Grace went to her and turned her around. "Oh, Mason, don't do this to yourself. That's not true."

"Isn't it? She certainly didn't want me. She made that quite clear after he left. I knew she blamed *me*." Mason tapped her chest. "She always blamed me for his leaving and I didn't know why. I never knew why she was so mad at *me*."

"Mason, you are the only innocent party in this. You are the only one who didn't have a choice."

Mason folded her arms defensively across her chest. "When did you know? When you picked up the photo of him?"

"Yes. And your mother truly loved him. That's why she blamed you for his leaving. That's why she still blames you."

Mason shook her head. "I can't see my mother and Uncle Alan having an affair. I mean, look at her! And Aunt Carol, she's like the nicest, sweetest person you'll ever meet."

"I got the impression that this was a short-lived fling. The circumstances of what caused it, I don't know."

"But you could find out?"

Grace shook her head. "No. I mean, yes, I could. But I'm not going to. If you want to know, you should ask." Grace took her hand and unfolded her arms. "You're not to blame, Mason. I know that you truly know that. You're angry and rightfully so. Whatever transpired between the three of them, you've suffered the most because you're innocent in it all. Since you were ten years old, you've been blamed for something you had no part in."

Mason made a fist and when Grace thought she would pound the countertop she simply opened her hand and placed her palm down softly instead. "I don't know if I'm more hurt or angry. I feel betrayed. And really, my father is innocent in this too. I can't blame him for leaving." She met Grace's eyes and Grace saw a hint of tears there. "I loved him. He was a good dad. That's why I couldn't believe he just left without a word." Her lower lip trembled. "Without telling me goodbye. I know he must have loved me too."

"Oh, honey." Grace put her arms around Mason and pulled her into a tight hug. "I'm so sorry. I shouldn't have told you." Mason nearly went limp in her arms and Grace held her tightly. "I'm sorry. I shouldn't have said anything. It's not my place—"

"I suspected it all along." Mason pulled out of her arms, wiping at her teary eyes. "I look more like Uncle Alan than Brady does. More than Amanda too. She looks exactly like Aunt Carol. Me and Brady…" She took a deep breath and wiped another tear from the corner of her eye. "None of it matters anymore, I guess."

"It does matter, Mason. I think keeping this secret from you has taken its toll on them as well. I'm not saying your aunt needs to know—what purpose would that serve? But you should talk to your mother about it. And your uncle. Get it out in the open."

"I can't do that to him. Like you said earlier, he's been a father figure to me. I don't want to do anything to change that." Mason went to the fridge and took out a bottle of water. "Don't apologize for telling me, Grace. I'm glad I finally know the truth. As far as what I'm going to do now—I don't know." She motioned to the window. "And we've got a damn bird stalking us and some guy was in my backyard. I still haven't told Uncle Alan about the guy from the other night. Probably the same guy."

"Probably, yes."

"How does it work, Grace? Does this guy see the bird? Or does he see what you see?"

"You mean how does Rusty control them? I wouldn't imagine they could see or hear things like I do." She shrugged. "I really don't know how he does it. Like the husband and wife who killed each other. Does he drive them mad? Can he manipulate them once he does? Is it subliminal? Does he show himself to them in ways that they can see, hear him?" She shrugged once more. "I don't know. I can only guess."

Mason tilted her head. "Are you as exhausted as I am?"

"Yes," she said without hesitation. "It's been a long couple of days. I only hope we get through the night without any more visitors."

"First thing tomorrow, I'll need to let Uncle Alan know."

"Yes, I agree. While you're talking to him, I'm going to go through the file again. I want to read up on the two missing girls—Lucy and Abby. And let's don't forget about Patricia Brinkman." She moved closer and touched Mason's arm, squeezing it lightly. "Are you okay?"

Mason nodded wearily and attempted a smile. "I'm okay, Grace. Like I said, it's what I suspected. The only shock is having it confirmed."

Grace tightened her grip for a moment, then released it. She gave her the tiniest of smiles in return. "Let's go to bed, huh?"

CHAPTER THIRTY-SEVEN

Mason wasn't sure how she felt. Numb, maybe. Yes, she'd long suspected that her uncle was really her father. But it wasn't until she'd come back that she did. When she drove away from Gillette Park at eighteen years old, she hadn't really given it much thought. Her father had left when she was ten and she hated him for that. Because of him, her mother had turned into a stranger and Mason had nowhere to turn except to Uncle Alan and Aunt Carol. Once she was in Los Angeles, she found new friends, a new life, and Gillette Park had receded to the back of her mind. When she returned, however, things became clearer. She'd looked at that very photo of her dad that Grace had. There wasn't much resemblance, really. Her father and Uncle Alan didn't look alike at all. Much like Brady and Amanda were opposites— Amanda looking like a carbon copy of Aunt Carol—so were they. It wasn't only that she favored Uncle Alan and looked more like a twin to Brady, however. It was the way Uncle Alan treated her, the way he sometimes looked at her. The way he tried to take care of her. Always. So yeah, she had suspected. Only she didn't have the nerve to ask him…ask him or her mother.

A warm hand found hers under the covers and she smiled in the darkness. Whether by intuition or other means, Grace seemed to know the turmoil in her mind. That simple touch seemed to relax her. She squeezed the fingers, then folded her hand, keeping Grace's fingers entwined.

"I'm okay."

"I know you are. You're strong, Mason."

"Am I?"

"Yes. Stronger than you think."

"I hope you're right." She rolled to her side, facing Grace. "When this is over with, you're still going to hang around until October, right?"

"I am."

"Good."

"Why good?"

"I'd like to get to know you better without all of this hanging over our heads. Take you up to the big trees. Have a picnic. Get to know each other," she added quietly. "Go on a date or something." She felt Grace's fingers tighten against her own.

"I…I haven't slept with anyone in years, Mason. I'm a little scared by the prospect. I sometimes feel like part of a freak show and that's the only reason—"

"Grace, do you not know how attractive you are?"

"I feel like I have this big blemish on me. No matter what I do, it won't go away."

"It's what makes you who you are. It's no blemish. I like you, Grace." She couldn't see Grace's face clearly in the darkness, but she could tell she was smiling.

"I like you too, Mason. You remind me so much of Angelique." Grace brought her hand from under the covers and touched her face lightly. "You're honest, true." Her finger traced her lower lip. "Safe."

Mason closed her eyes, loving the light touch on her skin. "I haven't slept with anyone since I left Los Angeles," she admitted quietly. "I hardly gave it a thought, really. I told you, I drifted away from everything and everybody."

"And you were afraid you'd disappear too," Grace said, her voice quiet, almost a whisper. "It'll be over with this summer, though. Sooner rather than later, I think."

"You feel that? Or know it?"

"I don't know. Both, maybe."

Grace moved her other hand under the covers, touching her. The rain was still spattering the windowpane outside.

"I...I remembered something the other day. It was something that I think I was supposed to forget, and I did. Something Nora said to me back when I was in high school."

"So you did talk to her then?"

"I did. Only I didn't remember it. Then the other day, I had this... this fleeting memory, but it wouldn't quite come to me. Not then. But later, when I was talking to Uncle Alan, yeah, I remembered. I remembered it all. We were alone in the hallway at school—I had forgotten a book in my locker. She knew my name. She said I was the chosen one. She said I would go on a journey but that I'd return to Gillette Park. And when I did, I'd meet my...my mate. A seer." She felt Grace's fingers tighten on her own, but she said nothing. "She said that we would end the cycle. Together."

Grace nodded in the darkness. "Yes. She said something very similar to me on the phone. We need to be as one—mind, body... soul."

"You are the seer."

"Yes, I am."

"Do you believe all that?"

"What? That this is our destiny? Do you?"

"If someone had asked me that a week ago—no. It makes sense, though. Why did I come back here? It was almost like I was compelled to return to Gillette Park. And when I did, it wasn't with the intent to meet someone, date. I came back to...to wait. Now I know I was waiting for you."

"I didn't want to take this assignment. I told you that. In fact, I told the FBI that I wouldn't take it."

"You said you felt like something was attacking you when you read the file."

"Yes. What I didn't tell you was that I heard a voice—a young girl's voice—begging me to come. I know now that what I was feeling was a war between Rusty and Susie. Rusty wanted me to stay away. Susie wanted me to come. And so, now here we are."

"And now here we are." She smiled in the darkness, thinking she was being so calm about it all. Here she was, holding hands under the covers with a woman she'd met seven days ago. A woman who, by all accounts, was her soulmate. God, did she really believe that? A woman she'd labeled a gypsy told her that back in 2004. Did she believe it? Yet here they were, lying in her bed, holding hands.

"Mason?"

"Hmm?"

"Destiny or not, I'm still a little scared."

"You are?"

"My dream…and Nora Nightsail's vision. The box. The darkness. That's where my dream always ends. That's where her vision ended too. There's never anything else."

"What are you saying?"

"I'm saying I'm afraid that's how I will end. Locked in a box. You won't be able to find me. I'm afraid that I'll—"

"No! I'll find you. I wouldn't stop looking, Grace. I *won't* stop looking."

"Why? Why won't you stop?"

Mason drew her brows together. Why? She didn't know why, really, she just knew she wouldn't. "I won't stop looking, Grace. When the time comes—if it comes—I won't stop until I've found you."

She reached her arm out and pulled Grace to her, their bodies flush under the sheets. It felt nice to be this close and she savored the moment. Grace, too, relaxed against her.

"Whatever happens, I'll find you. Because I'm *supposed* to find you. We were supposed to meet up here, weren't we? I don't think we were supposed to meet only to have one of us not make it through this ordeal. So I won't stop looking. Because we have stuff to do. We're going to take a hike to the big trees. We're going to have a picnic." She moved closer, her forehead touching Grace's. "We'll hike to some hot springs. I'll show you what it's like to live up here in the mountains." She felt Grace's arm snake around her, pulling her even closer.

"Yes. The big trees. I think you're right about them."

"What about them?"

"I saw us. In the future. You were getting gray, we were older. You were showing me the big trees," she finished sleepily.

Mason smiled as Grace buried her face against her neck, her breath warm. She closed her eyes, a peaceful feeling settling over her like a blanket. A protective blanket. And in her mind's eye, she pulled that blanket up tight around them, knowing they'd be safe tonight.

But who knew what tomorrow would bring?

CHAPTER THIRTY-EIGHT

Grace was conscious of only two things when her eyes fluttered open at dawn. One, she was still being held protectively in Mason's arms. And two, for the first time since she'd read the file back when she was still in New Orleans, she hadn't woken from a nightmare. There were no gruesome details of murder racing through her mind, no lingering image of her locked in a dark, dark box, her fists pounding desperately on the door. And there were no fading sounds of a baby's cry.

There was only the early morning light peeking in through the curtains. It was still and quiet, the only sound that of Mason's even breathing. She closed her eyes again, enjoying the closeness for a few more moments. It felt so familiar, but it shouldn't, should it? Only once in her life had she felt this closeness, only once had she woken up with a lover—way back when she and Angelique were saying their goodbyes. Not once since then had she spent an entire night with someone.

She and Mason weren't lovers. Not yet. They would be, she knew. Soon. She could feel that, *see* that. Was it simply their destiny? As much as she gave credence to visions and prophesies, it was always pertaining to someone else, not her. It was rare that she had any foreshadowing of her own future. Yet she could see herself clearly, thirty or forty years down the road, walking among the trees, a gray-haired woman beside her—Mason. The salt and pepper in her earlier vision was totally gray now. She allowed herself to look more closely, again enjoying the sense of peace she felt at the vision. They each held hiking sticks as they maneuvered along the trail, pausing to look at the view, pausing to note a bird. There were two dogs walking with them. Golden retrievers again. One was staying close, the other—a puppy—was darting between the trees, beckoning them to hurry and catch up.

"You're smiling."

Grace opened her eyes, finding Mason watching her. She looked into her sleepy eyes, knowing with certainty that they would fall in love—knowing with certainty that forty years from now, they would be walking together along a mountain trail.

"You're going to find me."

"Yes. I'll find you."

She closed her eyes again, resting her face on Mason's breast. "We're going to get a dog," she murmured. "Or two."

"Okay."

CHAPTER THIRTY-NINE

Mason hesitated, wondering if she would look at her uncle the same way now. Grace smiled at her reassuringly and nodded.

"You can do it. He's the same man he was before."

"You're right, though. I need to talk to him about it. After all this is over with. I'll talk to him and my mother. Get it out in the open."

Grace nodded at her again. "Yes. Afterward. It'll all work out, Mason."

"It's just getting to the 'afterward' that's gonna be hard. He's never going to believe you."

"But he'll believe you. Go on. Tell him. I'll be fine out here."

Her uncle was standing behind his desk, looking out the window. He turned when he heard her light knock on the doorjamb.

"Got some news?"

Mason sat down in the chair across from his desk. He looked at her for a long moment, then he, too, sat down. His eyes had a wariness about them and Mason wondered what it was he was bracing himself for.

"A couple of things I wanted to pass on to you. The other night, when we found April Trombley, there was a guy at my house. He was in the front yard, wearing a dark hoodie, dark clothes. We were in my truck. He took off running when we saw him."

Her uncle leaned forward. "Young, old? Short, tall?"

"Medium to slight. Young, I'd say. I didn't go after him. I didn't want to be separated from Grace." At her uncle's raised eyebrows, she shrugged. "Because Thomas Houston said we shouldn't be separated."

His mouth parted slightly. "I see. Thomas Houston." He leaned back again. "He was killed in…"

"In 2012."

Her uncle hit his desk with both hands. "Oh, come on, Mason. You expect me to believe—"

"Anyway, this same guy came to the house again, yesterday evening, right before dark. In the backyard. The guy just kinda looked at us through the kitchen windows, then took off running up the hill behind the house."

"And what do you think that means?"

"Grace is pretty certain—and I tend to agree—that this guy is one of the killers or one of the guys who works with him."

Uncle Alan shook his head quickly. "The FBI insists there is only one killer. Twenty-three years, Mason. They say there's no way there are multiple killers. No way."

"There were two guys involved in Thomas Houston's murder. When he went into the restroom, there was a guy waiting in there for him. The second guy was up in the ventilation ducts."

Her uncle stared at her blankly. "And you know this how?" He held his hand up. "Don't tell me. Thomas Houston told her."

"Yes, he did."

Her uncle got up abruptly, his chair banging back against the wall. "And you *believe* this?" he asked her.

Mason nodded. "Yes, I do."

"Jesus Christ, Mason! Some dead kid is telling her who killed him? How crazy is—"

"She's a psychic! For god's sake, what else were you expecting when you hired her?"

"I wasn't expecting crazy shit like this! What am I supposed to do with this information?"

"You said you wanted me to keep you up to date. I am."

"Oh, Mason. What the hell are we doing here? This is like 2004 all over again. We've got a damn crazy psychic running around town spewing nonsense!"

It was Mason's turn to slam her fist on his desk. "She is *not* crazy!"

He narrowed his eyes at her. "She's talking to dead people, Mason. What the hell do you call it then, if not crazy?"

She stood up too. "Why are you being so goddamned close-minded about this? She's a psychic. That's what psychics do. They goddamn talk to dead people!" She pointed at his chair. "Now sit down and listen to what I have to say. It gets a lot crazier than just Thomas Houston."

She thought his hand was shaking as he steadied it on the desk when he sat down. She took several deep breaths, then sat down too.

"Did Aunt Carol tell you we came asking about the fire?"

He nodded. "Shook her up pretty bad."

She met his gaze. "Just listen to what I'm saying. You don't have to comment. Just listen." She leaned forward, resting her arms on her thighs. "One of the kids killed in the fire, Rusty Meyer, he's the one who is driving the murders." She ignored her uncle's expression as his eyes widened. "Susie Shackle was the first one killed, to get revenge on Bruce Shackle. Grace doesn't know who is doing the killing, but she's certain there's more than one guy. This guy is holding two captives—Lucy Hines and Abby Lawrence. Lucy went missing in 2009. Abby in 2012."

She stood up then, pacing, wondering if she should tell him about the bird. She wouldn't even know where to start. Grace saw it as something completely different. No. She couldn't explain all that to him. He would think she'd lost her damn mind. *If he doesn't already.*

"There's a baby. Grace says it is Abby's baby. A boy. There's also a young girl. Her name is Faith. She's...she's like Grace."

"Like Grace?"

"Like...like a psychic, I guess."

"Oh, Jesus," he whispered.

"Grace says that's a good thing."

"Of course she does."

She turned to face her uncle. "Grace is waiting to talk to Susie Shackle. She says that Susie is the one—"

"Jesus Christ, Mason! A séance? Stop!" He held his hand up to her. "Just stop!"

"I told you to listen. Just listen."

"This is crazy!"

"Yeah. It is crazy. It's also real."

His head shook quickly from side to side. "It can't be real. I can't make myself believe it."

She stared at him, the words out before she could stop them. "You know what can't be real? That your brother, Don Cooper, is my father. Now *that* can't be real. Can it?" He wouldn't hold her gaze, try as she might. She swore she saw his lower lip quiver as he turned away from her. She walked around his desk, next to him. She knew this wasn't the time. Grace had told her it wasn't the time. But…

"I know you're my father," she said quietly. "I know that's why he left. And I know that's why my mother hates me so much. I know all that."

He turned toward her then, and yes, his lip was quivering. "Mason…I don't know what to say."

"You don't have to say anything. I just wanted you to know that I know." She moved away from him. "Does Aunt Carol know?"

He cleared his throat. "No. At least, I don't think so." He spread his hands out. "Mason…it was a one-night fling, a one-night—"

"Mistake. A one-night mistake. And yet here I am, the result of your mistake. Kinda makes *me* the mistake, doesn't it?" She sat back down in the chair, a heavy sigh leaving her. "Where did he go? Did he really disappear?"

Uncle Alan sat down too. "I haven't spoken to him since that day I found him in Boise. We had…we had words, yes. He blamed me and rightfully so." He met her gaze then. "He loved you, Mason. It broke his heart to leave you."

"Yeah. Must not have broken it too badly. He never bothered to contact me since."

"Best I can tell, he made off to the West Coast. I stopped trying to contact him years ago. He wanted nothing to do with me, so I let him be." He folded his hands together on top of his desk. "I'm very sorry, Mason. I don't even know what to say to you."

She stood up then, shaking her head. "I don't know either. I don't know what I *want* you to say. I…I haven't processed it all yet."

"How did you find out?"

"Grace…Grace confirmed it. I…I'd suspected for years, I guess. Deep down, I think I knew all along." She moved away from him, not wanting there to be some awkward hug between them. "As soon as Grace talks to Susie Shackle, I'll let you know." She held her hand up. "I didn't mean to state that so matter-of-factly. I know you don't understand…or believe. But trust me, it's very real. I've seen it up close and personal." She moved toward the door. "I think it'll all be over with very soon."

"Mason?"

She turned to look at him, eyebrows raised.

"I'm sorry, Mason. We didn't think you'd ever find out. That's why we never said anything to you."

"The truth is golden, though, isn't it?" She shrugged. "I don't need an apology, Uncle Alan. Honestly, I'm not sure how I feel about the whole thing yet." She walked toward the door, then paused. "I don't know if I hate you or love you. I just don't know right now."

CHAPTER FORTY

Grace could feel the tension permeating, could sense Mason's withdrawal. She didn't need to read her to know that she'd talked to her uncle about...well, about *that*. So she said nothing. Mason would talk if she wanted to. Grace wasn't going to push her. She glanced out the window instead, watching the passing trees without really seeing them.

"I don't think he believed much of what I said." Mason glanced at her quickly as they drove through town. "You expected that, though."

"Yes. He'll believe it soon enough, I guess. He won't have a choice."

Mason seemed to exhale...and relax. "So, what do you plan to ask Patricia Brinkman?"

"I have no idea. I guess I'll start with the fire."

"You think she may have some inside information or something?"

"Nora seemed to think so." She couldn't help herself as she reached over and touched Mason's arm, squeezing gently. "You okay?"

"Honestly, I'm not sure. And I didn't mean to bring it up. It just kinda came out during a heated exchange."

"A heated exchange because he didn't believe you?"

Mason smiled. "Would you? Anyway, we didn't really talk about it much. He was pretty shocked, I think. I'll talk to him again after all this is over with."

The neighborhood they were driving through was mixed with older, well-kept homes and some newer houses that had been built. Here and there were older, shabby homes, some looking past salvaging. The house Mason parked in front of was one of those homes.

"This is it?"

"Yeah, this is the address that came up for her."

"It looks a bit like it's falling down around her."

The sidewalk was cracked and buckled in spots with weeds growing through. The bottom step was rotted, the board missing on one corner. The old, white paint was chipped and faded, most having fallen off, leaving behind dull, gray siding.

They walked gingerly up the wobbly steps and Mason knocked several times on the old front door. "There's no car around. I guess whoever comes to check on her isn't here yet."

"Then I don't imagine Patty can answer the door, if she's as frail as your aunt says."

Mason knocked again. "Miss Brinkman?" she called. "It's Mason Cooper, with the sheriff's department." She knocked again. "May we come in?" When there was no answer, she shrugged. "I guess we wait."

Grace paused, her head tilted. She wasn't getting a sense of a presence here. The house was empty, she was sure of it.

"I don't think she's here."

"She doesn't drive. She doesn't have any family. Where would she be?"

"Try the door."

"Grace, we can't just break in."

"Try the door, Mason."

With a sigh, Mason turned the knob, finding it unlocked. She pushed the door open. The walls of the entryway were bare, cobwebs hanging where perhaps a framed portrait had once been. The air was stale and as sunlight streaked inside, she could see thick dust floating about.

"Miss Brinkman? Patty?"

Grace wanted to tell Mason that she wasn't here, but she let her call for her. As Mason went into another room—the kitchen?—Grace eyed the rickety stairs. Instead of going up, she went to the back of the house. A sweet, putrid smell filled the air and she wasn't surprised by what she found.

The curtains were drawn, leaving the room in shadows. A thick, fluffy comforter adorned the bed, covering dull sheets, the white having faded to a dingy yellow long ago. A boney, arthritic hand clutched the top sheet, the fingers forever clinched around the dirty linen. The look on Patricia Brinkman's face was anything but peaceful. It was a look of terror.

"Grace?"

She didn't turn as Mason came up behind her. She couldn't pull her eyes away from Patty's face.

"Jesus," Mason whispered.

"Look on the pillow. By her hair."

Mason took a step closer, then stopped abruptly. "Oh my god." She whipped her head around. "He was here."

"Yes."

The blue feather lay next to Patty Brinkman's head, resting on the pillow, the quill tucked in her pale white hair. Yes, Rusty had been there. Had he killed her? No, not likely. Not unless he'd scared her into a heart attack. Something had terrified her though. That was permanently etched on her face.

"I need to...I need to call it in, Grace."

"Yes. Okay. I'm going to look around."

"Don't touch anything. In case—"

"I know."

Mason went out into the hallway and Grace circled the bed, assuming this was where Patty Brinkman spent most, if not all, of her time. There was a TV mounted in a corner and a remote for it sat on her nightstand. There was a glass of water with a straw inside, something you might find in a hospital room. A tray on her dresser was filled with prescription bottles, eight or ten, she guessed at first glance.

What was missing in the room was personal things. No pictures, no trinkets, no keepsakes. It looked more like a guest room, which led her to believe that Patty's natural bedroom was upstairs. She probably couldn't handle the stairs any longer and had moved down here, without all her things.

She looked up to the ceiling, wondering where her room was. Up there, she was certain. She turned away from the bed, absently hearing Mason on the phone as she headed to the stairs. The banister looked unstable so she hugged the wall side of the staircase as she walked up. The steps creaked with her weight and judging by the dust that had settled on the wood, she didn't imagine anyone had been up there in months.

Years, she corrected, as her face tangled with spider webs at the second-floor landing. She brushed them away, then paused, looking both to her left and right. There were three doors. She guessed two bedrooms and a bathroom. She went to her right, but when she reached for the doorknob, she paused. Mason had said not to touch anything. Feeling a bit foolish, she pulled her sleeve down far enough to cover her hand, then turned the knob and pushed the door open. The curtains were pulled closed and it smelled musty...and old. She flipped on the light, glancing around quickly. The bed was neatly made, but there was no other furniture in the room. She went back to the hallway, opening the second door. It was a bathroom, and it, too, looked like it hadn't been used in years.

The third door was indeed Patty Brinkman's bedroom. This room was filled with life. Several nice prints—nature scenes—hung on the walls. The dresser was cluttered with figurines of owls—something she collected, perhaps. An oversized chair with a lamp and a small table was in one corner. Several books were stacked there and reading glasses lay beside them. The curtains were left half-opened, letting in the morning sunshine.

She stood still, quiet, letting her mind go blank as she searched. Searched for what, though, she didn't know. Nora Nightsail said Patricia Brinkman would know the history. She closed her eyes. No. Nora said Patricia Brinkman would *have* the history.

"She'll have the history you need."

She slid her gaze to the nightstand beside the bed. The top was covered in what was once a pristine white doily. She went to it, reaching out to touch the lace around the edges. She wondered if perhaps Patty had made it herself.

A small lamp with a pull string sat on top and she pulled the chain, the light illuminating the nightstand and bed. Instead of opening the top drawer, she pulled out the second one. There was nothing in the drawer except a spiral binder, one like kids used to use in school. It was green. In bold, black letters, handwritten across the top: *The History of Gillette Park.*

Grace noticed her hand was shaking as she reached for the binder. Should she just take it? Would Mason let her remove something from the house? The woman was dead. Was this now a crime scene? She heard a siren in the distance, heard voices outside. She went to the window, seeing Mason out front talking to an older man. A neighbor, perhaps.

She went back and snatched the binder out of its hiding place, pausing to close the drawer and turn off the lamp. She left the bedroom door as she'd found it—ajar. She hurried back down the steps, shoving the binder up under her shirt as she went.

By the time she got back to the front door, several people were now outside. A police car was already there and she heard Mason's voice, a bit louder than a normal conversation. She walked out onto the porch, seeing her talking to an officer. Grace recognized him as one that she'd met that first day, but she didn't recall his name.

"You don't need to know," Mason said, glancing at her as she walked up.

"This is our jurisdiction."

"I don't answer to you, Sheffield. You got a problem with it, talk to Sheriff Cooper." She pointed. "In fact, he's here now."

"You had no business going inside." The man—Officer Sheffield—turned to her. "We're going to need to interview you, ma'am."

Mason laughed. "Come on, man. You know why she's in town. There's not going to be an interview. Besides, Patty Brinkman was old and in poor health. Probably natural causes."

Alan Cooper walked over. "Mason, you two get out of here. I'll handle it."

"Sheriff Cooper, I think—"

"You think what, Sheffield? An old woman died. Like Mason said, we all knew Patty was in poor health. If there's something to be concerned about, it would be why her nurse wasn't here. Maybe you should check on that."

"The neighbor said the nurse comes at nine o'clock," Mason supplied.

"So she's late?"

Mason shrugged.

He nodded at her, then motioned them away. "Go on. I'll let you know what we find out."

Grace felt Mason take her arm, and they walked rather quickly back to Mason's truck while Officer Sheffield was pleading his case for jurisdiction. They didn't speak until they were a block or two away.

"What did you tell your uncle?"

"Nothing, really. Just that you wanted to interview her and when she didn't answer the door, we went inside." Mason reached into her shirt pocket and pulled out a blue feather. "I took this. Didn't know how we'd explain a damn feather being in there."

"And I took this." Grace pulled out the binder from beneath her shirt.

CHAPTER FORTY-ONE

The first thing Mason did when she got home was to go around to all the windows and securely close the blinds and curtains. It was early afternoon and a few clouds were forming, but the sun was still bright. Normally on a day like today, she'd have most of the windows open, letting in the breeze, the smell of late spring, the hint of summer that was right around the corner. But not today. No. Today they were hiding. Windows closed and locked. Doors locked too.

"I'm starving, by the way."

"There's not much here, I'm afraid."

Grace tossed the notebook she'd stolen onto the table. "Pizza. We'll order pizza." She went to the cabinet and took out the bottle of bourbon. "You're okay with pizza, right?"

Mason noticed the nervousness in her voice. "You're as scared as I am, huh?"

Grace nodded as she added whiskey to two glasses. "Yeah, pretty much." She held the bottle up. "Might need to replenish this. I think we might drain this tonight."

She took the blue feather out of her pocket, placing it on top of the notebook. Had the damn bird really been in Patty Brinkman's house? What did it mean?

Grace picked up the feather, holding it by the tip as she twisted it back and forth between her fingers. Mason watched her, seeing the concentration on her face. Then Grace put the feather back down.

"I don't get a sense of anything from it. It's just a feather."

"So maybe it's not—"

"Oh, yes, it is."

"Do you think she was murdered?"

Grace took a rather large swallow of her drink, then looked at her. "I don't think she died naturally, no. Certainly not peacefully. Whether she was murdered in the traditional way, I'm not sure. She had a death grip on the sheets. Maybe she was frightened to death."

"Both the front door and back door were unlocked. The neighbor that I spoke to hadn't seen anyone around. Could have happened last night, though."

"Where was the nurse?"

"Yeah, the neighbor said it was unusual for her not to be there. If she couldn't make it she had a sub come for her, or so he said."

"Patty appeared to be bedridden. Wonder why she was still living there and not at a nursing home or assisted living or something?"

Mason finally picked up her glass, holding it before drinking. "Aunt Carol said she didn't have any family. Maybe there was no one to force her to go."

"Having a home nurse can't be cheap." Grace sat down and moved the binder toward her. "Do you think we should tell your uncle that we have this?"

"Let's read it first. It may be exactly what it says: a history of Gillette Park."

Grace took a deep breath. "Only one way to find out."

* * *

The handwritten accounts of the longtime librarian started with the fire in 1984. There wasn't much prose involved—certainly no elaboration—only the facts. It wasn't until page four that Patty offered some reflection. *"Why wasn't Johnny Herchek with them?"* Mason saw Grace pause over the words.

"Who is Johnny Herchek?"

"Lives back in the woods. Off the grid. Guess you'd call him a doomsday prepper."

"One of the mountain men that Agent Kemp was telling me about?"

"Yeah. There are a few families like that."

"So he has a family?"

"I think so. From what I know, he only comes into town for supplies a handful of times a year."

"Was he ever a suspect?"

Mason shook her head. "No one's ever been a suspect, Grace. But yeah, he was looked at. All of them were looked at." She drew her brows together. "Why?"

Grace didn't answer her. Instead, she flipped through the pages, barely glancing at the words. The rest of the binder was filled with accounts of the murders. Being the librarian, Patty Brinkman must have known most, if not all, of the victims. Grace stopped at 2004, reading slower now. She tapped her finger, drawing Mason's attention.

> Nora Nightsail was a little peculiar but I have no doubt that she knows what she's talking about. She says I must wait, that there will come a woman—years from now—who will need my journal. I'm not sure how my little journal can help stop the killings, but I will do as she says. The police are so inept, I can't imagine the killings will stop anytime soon.

"And here."

> Nora came to see me again today. She asked about the fire. She seems to think it may have triggered something in town, something that started the killings. I told her I didn't think so. The fire was in 1984. Young Susie Shackle was the first one killed in 1997. I'm not sure what to think of that. Her daddy should have been killed in the fire too. I hate to speak ill of the man since he's been through so much, but Bruce Shackle was as mean as the rest of them. Rusty Meyer was nothing but a hoodlum and the ringleader, but Bruce, Butch, and Johnny were thugs that tagged along with him. Of course, Rusty and Butch don't terrorize anyone any longer and Bruce—now a drunkard—is only a shell of himself. And Johnny—from what I hear—went off the deep end after the fire and lives like a hermit back in the forest. How he ever got him a wife to live out there with him, I'll never know.

"If they all ran together, why wasn't this Johnny with them at the library that night?"

Mason assumed Grace wasn't expecting an answer as she continued to flip through the pages. She paused in 2012 and Mason noted she was reading Patty's account of Thomas Houston. Grace had a sad smile on her face, and Mason glanced to the words, smiling too as Patty described him as a smart, studious chatterbox who never learned how to whisper in the library.

Then Grace flipped to the end of the binder, looking through the last few pages. "Oh my god, look at this."

> Strangest thing happened yesterday. A pretty blue Steller's jay came to visit. Sat right on the windowsill outside, watching me. I thought it must have been hungry. It's been years since I kept feeders. Not that I had anything to feed it. I did find some old crackers on the shelf. Stale, they were, but I took them out back and tossed them on the ground. The bird showed no interest in the crackers at all, just watched me from the windowsill. When I came up here to my room, I opened the curtains, and lo and behold, the bird flew up to the second-floor window! He stayed there until dark. When I got up today, he was gone. Maybe he'll come back.

"When was this?"
"Four years ago."
"There's not much after that."
"No. The last entry was two years ago."

> I guess Nora Nightsail was wrong. No woman has come to see me yet and the killings continue. I fear my time here on earth is coming to an end soon. It's all I can do to make it up the stairs to this bedroom. The doctor says my heart is failing me and he has prescribed yet another pill for me to take. I have enough medication here to open up my own drug store! Oh, well. I can't complain about my life. I'll be ninety next week. I've had a good, full life although I do wish I'd married that Michael Cole way back when he asked me.
> Oh, and a Steller's jay came to visit again today. Much like the last time, he hung out on the windowsill. Was it the same bird? A little spooky. He seemed to be staring right through me. Maybe it's a sign. I only hope he's not

a harbinger of bad tidings. Maybe he is. Maybe he's come to take me away from this world. I'm very tired. I suppose I'm ready to go, if he has come for me. My regret is that I wasn't able to give this journal to someone. Who will read it now?

"That's it."

Mason leaned against the counter, watching Grace. "Why do you think Nora Nightsail wanted you to read that? I know we haven't read word for word, but it's not much more than what Patty Brinkman said herself, it's just a journal."

Grace closed up the notebook with a sigh. "When I spoke with Paul, when Thomas came to make sure he didn't say too much, he let slip a name. He said that you wouldn't have to worry about Rusty, that Rusty could only hurt me. He said you would only have to worry about Johnny." Grace slid her empty glass over toward her. "Johnny Herchek is your serial killer."

CHAPTER FORTY-TWO

"I think it'd be best if you came over here."

Mason was on the phone with her uncle. They decided it would be safer—for them—to not leave the house. It was dark. And it was quiet. She'd tried—unsuccessfully—to get Thomas to come to her. She had a nagging feeling about their going out and Mason had agreed. Did Rusty now know how much they knew? Had he known they were going to Patricia Brinkman's house? Is that why they killed her? Because yes, she did think that Patty Brinkman was murdered. But if he knew all of that, why didn't he know about the journal? Maybe he did. Maybe he couldn't find it.

She moved into the kitchen, putting their drink glasses in the sink. Why couldn't he find it? She'd known exactly where it would be. As she'd told Mason, she didn't know *how* she knew, she just knew. And after reading the journal, the bird—*the damn bird*, as Mason would say—had been at Patty's second-floor window, watching. Why wouldn't he have known where she put the journal?

None of it really made sense though. Had the journal really been sitting in that drawer for two years? And if Nora knew of the fire, knew that the journal would help them, why hadn't she asked to see it herself? Well, they'd kinda run her out of town, she reminded herself. Maybe she never got the opportunity to see it.

"Grace?"

She turned, finding Mason watching her. She let out a breath. "Yes, sorry. Just going over things in my mind." She moved closer to her, touching her arm lightly. "He's coming over?"

"He is. Got news on the nurse. She pulled up just when Uncle Alan was leaving. Two of her tires got slashed, probably during the night."

"Oh, how convenient," she said dryly.

"Yeah. She called the police this morning too. Then had to get a wrecker service out to replace the tires. She said she'd tried calling Patty to let her know she'd be late."

"And now she feels terrible—guilty—that Patty died when it was out of her control all along." Grace shook her head. "Everyone's just a bit player in all of this. Me, you. Everyone."

"You sound frustrated."

"I am frustrated," she said a little louder than she intended. "I feel like my hands are tied. How long do I sit around and wait for Susie Shackle? Or do we wait? Is this journal enough for your uncle to pay Johnny Herchek a visit? To get a warrant?"

Mason shrugged. "It depends on how much credence they put into what you say. I mean, they hired a psychic. If you tell them this is who you think the serial killer is, then surely they'll follow up on it. Why else hire you?" A knock on the front door interrupted their conversation. "That'll be him. You ready?"

Grace nodded, wishing Thomas or Susie would come to her, would confirm what she was about to tell Sheriff Cooper. But as before, it was quiet. It was *too* quiet.

Then the quiet disappeared into a spray of gunfire and the squealing of tires.

She jerked her head around, her eyes wide as her breath left her.

"Mason!"

The name was wrenched from her throat as she ran toward the door.

"Mason!"

CHAPTER FORTY-THREE

"Momma, come sit."

Lucy sucked in an audible breath. Faith had been engaged with her "friends" for the last two days, speaking to her only when Lucy asked her a direct question. Even then, Faith had seemed annoyed with the interruption. She'd finally let her be. Faith had spent most of that time in the corner of their room, her back to her, her words whispered or mumbled, too much so for Lucy to make out what she was saying. She was thankful, really. Because Faith scared her. Lately…Faith scared her a lot.

She really didn't want to sit now. She didn't want to hear what Faith was about to tell her. Something was going on, she could tell that. Feel that. Even Stacy had been unusually nervous, her eyes darting about whenever she brought them their meals. When Stacy had come earlier, her face was bruised. Her right eye appeared discolored and there was a split on her lower lip. When Lucy had asked her about it, Stacy had nearly run from their room.

"Momma?"

"Yes, okay, I'm coming." Her feet felt like they were moving through thick mud as she made her way to the tiny table to sit down across from Faith. The table was chipped in one corner and her fingers found the imperfection, worrying over it as Faith stared at her.

"Momma, I know that the mean man comes to get you some nights. I know what he does to you."

Lucy gasped, the sound out before she could stop it. Of all the things she was expecting Faith to say, that was not it. She'd been so careful, so quiet. She'd intentionally blocked it from her mind, hoping Faith would never know. Faith was ten. How many more years did Faith have before he would come take her instead? She endured what she did, hoping it would be enough. She never wanted Faith to have to go through what she'd been subjected to.

"How…how do you know?"

"I wake up sometimes when he comes. I pretend to sleep because I'm scared of him. But Susie told me what he was doing to you."

Lucy hung her head, feeling tears form in her eyes. "Oh, Faith… I'm sorry," she managed.

Faith's tiny hand found its way across the table to hold hers. "Susie says he takes Abby out sometimes too." Faith's voice was quiet, serious. "He and his son are going hunting tonight. Charles is his name. They're going to find a young girl, Momma. They're going to bring her here, like the others. They're going to do to her like they do to you. Tomorrow, when they're through with her, they're going to kill her." The small hand squeezed hers. "When Stacy comes with our first meal tomorrow, that's when you'll have to get her keys."

Lucy raised her head, meeting Faith's gaze. "I can't. I—"

"Yes, you can! You have to! Susie says it's time. Susie says—"

"Stop it!" Lucy jerked her hand away, nearly tipping the chair over as she shoved away from the table. "Stop it!" She wrapped her arms around herself, her back to Faith. "We don't know what's out there, Faith. We don't know *who* is out there. If we make him mad, if we—"

"Grace is coming. She's going to help us." She heard Faith get up and come toward her. "Momma, listen to me. Susie says it's time. This will be our only chance."

Lucy shook her head. "I can't," she whispered. "Faith, I'm scared. I'm scared of you. I'm scared of who you talk to. I'm scared that you believe you're talking to dead people." She drew in a shaky breath. "I'm scared that you expect me to try to escape from here." She looked around their room—their tiny, dingy square room with the exposed toilet and bathtub, the twin bed they shared, the stack of magazines and books that served as Faith's school. She turned to look at the door, knowing there were three deadbolts, each with a different key.

Yes, she'd thought about escaping. In the beginning. Then Faith came along and Lucy didn't dare take a chance. If they killed her, then what would happen to Faith? Who would take care of her? No, she couldn't take a chance.

"You *can* take a chance."

Lucy covered her face with her hands, as if that would keep Faith out of her mind. Her tears were flowing now, seeping from between her fingers. Her daughter talked to dead people. Her daughter could read her mind. Her daughter scared the shit out of her.

She lowered her hands, meeting Faith's gaze with teary eyes. Faith's eyes weren't that of a crazy person. They were the same warm, gentle eyes that she was used to. Hazel eyes that matched those of Barry Shepherd. Trusting eyes. That was one thing she'd seen in Barry. He'd been as scared as she was, all those years ago. But his eyes had helped calm her.

"They killed him. Barry. He would have been my daddy."

Lucy closed her eyes. "Quit reading my mind."

"I can't help it, Momma."

She took a deep breath and wiped at the tears on her face. She finally cleared her throat. "Okay. Tell me what you want me to do."

CHAPTER FORTY-FOUR

"Mason!"

Grace ran through the open doorway, her heart lodged in her throat by fear of what she might find. Mason was kneeling on the porch, her hands bloody as she pressed down against her uncle's chest. Wild, scared eyes met hers.

"He's been shot! Call 911!"

Grace did as she asked, her hands shaking as she fumbled with her phone. Her voice was surprisingly calm when she requested police and an ambulance, but her eyes were glued to Mason and Alan Cooper.

Alan wasn't moving and Grace could see multiple shots to his torso. She knelt down opposite Mason, not knowing what to do.

"The shots were meant for me. He…he stepped in front of me, shielding me." Tears fell down her cheeks. "Goddamn, Grace. They were meant for me."

* * *

Grace stood in the corner of the waiting room, absently listening to the various conversations going on around her. The room was filling, family and law enforcement both. Some friends too, she imagined. Brady Cooper had a look of disbelief on his face as he tried to console his mother. Carol was as white as a sheet, and even from here, Grace could see her hands trembling as they clenched and unclenched around the strap of her purse. Mason was having an animated discussion with Chief Danner, who was shaking his head at whatever Mason was telling him. Grace was about to go over to them when a familiar voice sounded in her ear.

"*Come outside.*"

She turned, but Thomas did not show himself. She glanced over to Mason again, but her back was to her. With a nod, she slipped from the room, the automatic doors closing behind her in a near-silent whoosh. She walked down the brightly lit hallway to the lobby, then out another set of automatic doors. The hospital was larger than she would have expected for a town this size and they even had a trauma unit. She wondered if this was the first gunshot victim they'd had.

"*Over here.*"

Thomas was leaning against a tree next to a bench. So as not to be seen talking to a tree—which would probably indeed get her labeled the crazy psychic woman—she sat down on the bench. The air was cool and a breeze made her wish she'd thought to grab her jacket. But it had been a whirlwind of activity, with the neighbors all coming over, Carol Cooper running down the street from two blocks away and the sound of sirens breaking the stillness of the night. Mason was in shock and had stood by quietly as Grace cleaned her up, washing her hands of Alan's blood. She'd driven them to the hospital in silence. As soon as they parked, Mason had turned to her.

"It was the same car. Dark sedan. The one that Jason Gorman got into."

They'd held hands then, sitting quietly in Mason's truck.

"That should have been me."

"No. Whether we call it destiny or fate, no, it wasn't supposed to be you. They may have intended it to be you, but there are other forces at work now, Mason. To be honest, I don't understand it much more than you do."

And she didn't. Yes, probably, Mason was the intended target. That would leave Grace vulnerable then, wouldn't it? If Mason was out of the way, there was no one else in town who believed her. There would be no one willing to go out to Johnny Herchek's place with her. Because she knew that was the journey she was on. She knew that Thomas was going to tell her that. And she knew that she would most likely get to meet Susie Shackle finally.

"That was a close call. For Mason, I mean," Thomas said.

"Who was it? Was it Johnny?"

"No. His son. Charles."

"Johnny is what? In his fifties now? So his son must be thirty or so?"

"I don't know. He's the younger one. The other one died." Thomas surprised her by sitting down beside her. *"He locked him in a box. He died in there."*

Grace felt her heart tighten in her chest. "The same box he's going to put me into?"

"Yes. Stacy has the key. Stacy has all the keys."

Grace closed her eyes, not knowing who Stacy was. "Why am I going to be put in a box, Thomas?"

"Because he's going to catch you. It's the distraction that's needed. You'll fight him. The box is in the tunnel. While he's there, Faith and Lucy can unlock Abby's room and get her and the baby out. They're supposed to steal the keys from Stacy."

"And Mason?"

"Mason is going to have to rescue Ginny from Charles. Virginia is her real name."

"Who is Ginny?"

"They're out hunting for her tonight. Rusty picks the victims. That's who he picked."

"How does Rusty communicate with Johnny?"

"Johnny's got this talking doll." Thomas wrinkled his nose, his voice dropping to a hoarse whisper. *"A blowup doll. He uses it for…sex."*

Grace shook her head slowly. "And it…it talks?"

"Yeah. And Rusty took over the doll. Johnny's crazy as a bat, to be sure. Charles is scared of him and he does whatever he says. But Charles is about to lose his mind too. Poor Stacy is terrified of both of them. Johnny hits on her a lot. He doesn't like her."

"And Stacy is who?" she asked weakly.

"That's Johnny's daughter. There's another girl there too who thinks she's Stacy's daughter, but she's not. Her momma was killed after she was born. Johnny does…well, bad things to her."

Grace bit her lower lip. "And the one killed? Like you? She was one of the victims from town?" Grace remembered the one. She was seventeen. Her body was found the next spring.

"Yeah. She doesn't come around though. She stays back in the canyon."

Grace closed her eyes for a second, trying to keep her composure. "Okay. And Susie?"

"Susie is going to be with you at the house. Susie is going to show you how to get through the booby traps."

"Booby traps?"

"Oh, yeah. Johnny has his whole place booby-trapped. Got pits dug out, snares, trip wires, shooting nails and arrows. Some little bombs. Even has a couple of shotguns set up. And some spears too." Thomas grinned. *"All kinds of cool stuff."*

"So if someone went in on their own…"

"They'd never make it."

"So if we'd gotten a warrant and the police went out there…?"

"Oh, yeah. That's what couldn't happen. He's got the mine rigged with dynamite. He'd blow the side of the mountain off and kill everybody, including Faith and the others."

"I see. So just Mason and I will go in." She grabbed the bridge of her nose. "Who all are we rescuing?"

"Faith and her momma, Lucy. And Abby and baby Andrew."

"What about Stacy and the other girl?"

"Stacy calls her Rebecca. She's not a little girl anymore. I think she's fifteen or so. But she's slow, you know? And like I said, Johnny is mean to her. But she's never been to school. Never has been out of the house. Of course, neither has Faith. But Faith is real smart. Her momma taught her a lot."

"So we're to get Stacy and Rebecca too?"

"Susie only said Faith and Lucy, and Abby and the baby."

To say her head was spinning was an understatement. She stood up, walking away, trying to collect her thoughts.

"Don't be scared, Grace."

"Easy for you to say." She turned around to face him. "I'm a psychic. I *see* you. I *hear* you. That's all I do. I don't go in to face people like Johnny Herchek. Because he's *real*. I'm not cut out for rescuing—"

"You're stronger than you think, Grace. Susie says you're the one we've been waiting for. Susie says you're going to set us all free."

Her eyes widened. "What the hell does that mean?"

He moved away from her, floating into the night. She stared after him, thinking he'd come back, thinking he'd say more. But he faded from sight and she blew out a breath. Yeah, what the hell did that mean? Set them free? Did that mean that they were *stuck* here?

She moved again to the bench, sitting down and leaning her elbows on her knees. Now what? Did she and Mason head out to Johnny Herchek's place, hoping that little Susie Shackle would show up to guide them through the booby traps? She leaned her head back, looking into the dark sky, the sky littered with stars. What did it all mean?

"Go to Mason."

She jerked her head around. It was Thomas' voice, but he wasn't showing himself. She stood, looking around for him. "Thomas? Please. I have more questions."

"Go to Mason. Take her home. You'll be safe there. Tomorrow. At first light. It'll be time."

"I don't know if I can do this," she said, her voice sounding nervous to her own ears.

"Susie will meet you tomorrow on Old Mine Road. Mason will know the place. Tell her to bring bolt cutters."

Grace felt the barest of touches across her cheek, then it was gone. The walkway outside the hospital was lined with aspen trees. The leaves on the one across from her rustled as if a strong wind had blown them.

"Go now. She won't want to go, but you must make her."

"Am I going to get out of the box?" she heard herself whisper.

There was no answer. She stared at the aspen tree for the longest time, finally letting out a heavy breath. She had to believe she'd get out of the box, didn't she? She'd had a vision. But what if that vision was wrong? She'd dreamed of the box. And in her dreams, she never got out.

Did she believe her vision or her dream?

She spun around and headed back inside. She would do as he said. She would take Mason home. They would get up before dawn. They would go to Old Mine Road—wherever that was—by daybreak. They would wait for Susie Shackle.

Tomorrow, it would end. One way or another.

CHAPTER FORTY-FIVE

"I can't leave, Grace."

Grace squeezed her arm tightly. "You have to." She leaned closer. "It's time. Thomas said—well, it's time. Let's go home. I'll explain."

Mason glanced around them, wondering who was listening to their conversation. She took Grace's hand and led her away from the group. "Grace, he's not out of surgery. I don't even know if he's going to live or die. I can't just leave."

"A girl will be abducted tonight. Virginia. They call her Ginny. They don't plan to kill her until tomorrow. We can stop this one."

"Christ," she murmured. "Chief Danner didn't believe half of what I was telling him. What am I supposed to tell him about this?"

"Nothing. We have to go in alone. Just the two of us. I'll explain later."

Mason stared into her eyes, noting the seriousness there. She also realized she didn't have a choice. She trusted what she saw in those blue eyes. And she remembered Nora Nightsail's words, those spoken to an innocent, wide-eyed teenager all those years ago.

"You are the one. She will find you here. Together, you will stop the cycle."

The cycle of murder.

No, she didn't have a choice, did she? So she nodded, albeit a bit weakly. "Okay." She glanced over at Aunt Carol, who was dabbing at her eyes with a tissue. "How do I explain my absence to them?"

Grace held her gaze and Mason saw a bit of defiance there. "We're going after the man who shot him. Tell them what you want. But we must go."

* * *

It was going on eleven by the time she closed the door and locked it behind her. Crime scene tape was fluttering in the breeze and the bloodstain on the porch—in the glow of the light—was still prominent. Grace had taken her arm and urged her past it, hurrying them up the steps and through the door.

Aunt Carol didn't understand why she'd left. Mason could see that in her eyes. Brady too. She told them she had to check something out…she and Grace. Dalton was there too and both he and Brady had looked at Grace suspiciously. She closed her eyes for a moment. She should be there with them. Waiting. She shouldn't have left. She took in a deep breath, then opened her eyes, finding Grace watching her.

"Is he going to make it?"

Grace met her gaze, unflinching. "I don't know, Mason."

"Why don't you know?"

"I'm sorry. I wish I could tell you something, but…"

"Yeah, you didn't hire on as a fortuneteller, did you?" She opened the cabinet where her whiskey bottle was, but Grace stopped her when she would have poured some.

"Don't."

Mason pulled away from her. "Don't?"

"I know you're angry."

"Angry? I don't even know what the hell's going on! I open my front door to see a car speeding by, a damn automatic weapon hanging out their window. I saw the bastard! And Uncle Alan pushed me away and then…" She pounded her fist on the counter. "Goddamn it! Yes! I'm angry!" She spun around. "I should be at the hospital. I should be there with them."

"Mason, you have a job to do."

"What job?" she demanded. "I don't know what to believe, Grace. I don't know what to think anymore. I don't even know what the hell's going on!" she said again loudly.

"Mason, stop."

"No!"

She brushed past Grace as she strode into the living room. She'd leave. That's what she'd do. Head back to the hospital. That's where she should be. Aunt Carol might need her. Hell, Brady might need her. She picked up her keys only to have Grace beat her to the front door. She leaned against it, blocking her way.

"No, Mason."

"Get out of my way, Grace."

"No," she said with a firm shake of her head.

Mason's anger bubbled over and she grabbed Grace's arms, intending to push her away from the door. Grace held her ground though, the look in her eyes telling Mason she wasn't going to budge.

"Goddamn it, Grace. You're pissing me off!"

"I don't care! You want to take your anger out on me...fine. But you're not leaving. We're staying here."

Mason stared at her; Grace's eyes were issuing a challenge. No, Mason didn't know what was going on. Everything seemed all messed up. Everything. She wasn't in control and she *hated* not being in control.

"Neither of us are in control right now, Mason."

Mason closed her eyes. "Get out of my head, Grace."

She was surprised to feel Grace move closer to her, close enough that their bodies were touching.

"I'm sorry, Mason," she said quietly. "I know you want to be there with them."

Mason opened her eyes, finding Grace only inches away. Her blue eyes were as familiar to her as her own. That was impossible, of course, yet...

She leaned closer—almost as if she were being *pulled* closer—touching Grace's lips. Desire gripped her then, desire mixed with her lingering anger. Her mouth was no longer gentle as she pressed Grace against the door. Hands—desperate hands—clutched at her, and Grace's mouth opened fully to her, a whimpering moan drifting up, around and between them. It was Grace's moan, but it could have been her own. She was engulfed in fire—a sweet, hot, delicious fire that seared her senses and smothered whatever thoughts she tried to cling to.

Her angry kiss softened, eliciting another moan from Grace. Her arms pulled Grace to her, holding her close, their mouths fused as their kiss again turned heated and fiery hot. She seemed to lose all sense of time as she pressed Grace against the door. Her mind was empty—blank. Nothing there at all to crowd out her desire.

She was breathing heavily—so was Grace. She pulled away from the kiss just enough to meet Grace's eyes. Yes, Grace felt it too. They weren't in control. Neither of them. And they both knew it.

"Make love to me."

Mason nodded numbly at Grace's request. No, she wasn't in control. This fire that had been simmering was ignited now. There were no thoughts of the hospital. No thoughts of anyone. Just she and Grace. Grace was the one to flip the light off. Grace was the one to take her hand. Grace was the one to lead them down the hallway and into her bedroom.

Maybe Grace was in control after all.

CHAPTER FORTY-SIX

Grace wasn't entirely sure what possessed her to be so bold. Her body had simply come alive, Mason's fierce, angry kiss turning passionate in a matter of seconds. Her skin seemed electrified with every touch and each kiss sent her spiraling deeper and deeper into oblivion, until her mind was empty of everything except Mason.

She turned her head now, watching Mason sleep. The lamp was still on, yet it must be three or four in the morning by now, she guessed. She dropped her gaze to Mason's lips—her mouth—reliving the anticipation she'd felt as that mouth had moved across her skin, drawing out moans as lips brushed her nipples before a wet tongue bathed them. She'd been lightheaded—dizzy—by the time Mason had kissed across her stomach, her hips, pausing at the hollow of her thigh, nibbling her skin, making her writhe beneath her. When Mason had spread her legs, she'd looked up at her, their eyes holding for a long moment. What was conveyed between them went deeper than words, and Grace had simply nodded, acknowledging the bond they were forming, recognizing the connection of two souls and accepting what it meant. The intensity of their stare made her tremble. It was almost as if Mason had crawled inside her and she into Mason.

Her world spun then as Mason lowered her head, finishing her journey. Grace remembered the sound she'd made when Mason's tongue slid through her wetness, caressing her clit with strong strokes before her mouth settled over her. Her eyes had slammed shut then and everything had faded to black. But only for a few glorious seconds. Bright lights—red and yellow and blue—blinded her as she'd lifted off the bed, her hips bucking uncontrollably as she'd climaxed. She'd felt tears wet her cheeks, and then Mason was whispering words she couldn't hear, couldn't comprehend as she'd traveled back up her body, pausing to wet her nipple before finding her mouth once again. The kiss was so gentle, so sweet, and even as Grace had smiled into it, more tears fell.

Mason didn't question her tears and Grace offered no explanation. What could she say? Should she have told her that she felt whole—complete—for the first time in her life? That seemed silly. Or maybe she should have told her that she felt reborn—new. Brand new. That, too, seemed trivial.

Instead, she'd cupped Mason's face, turning their soft kisses passionate again. She'd rolled them over, she'd found Mason's wetness, and she'd brought her to orgasm quickly with her hand. Then her mouth had replaced her fingers, and she'd felt empowered as Mason trembled beneath her, her loud moans disturbing the quiet as Grace made love to her, bringing her to orgasm once again with her mouth.

They didn't talk. They'd slept some, on and off. And they'd touched. They'd kissed—long, languid kisses and short, quick burning kisses. And they'd bonded—mind, body, and soul. They'd done all that without words.

She rolled to her side, loving the feel of the cool sheets against her nakedness, loving the feel of Mason's skin against hers. Mason didn't stir and Grace continued to watch her, letting her thoughts drift to Angelique. Angelique had been, yes, a goddess from the sea. Young, vibrant, and full of life. And love. By all accounts, she and Angelique should not have been friends, much less lovers. Grace had been timid, shy, and still an awkward teen. Angelique was older, poised, confident. What drew Angelique to her, she wondered? Regardless, she'd set the bar very high for future lovers. So high that no one had come close to meeting it. Was that the point all along? To leave Grace searching for someone, not ever settling for less? The feelings that Angelique stirred in her had long disappeared, but their memory remained. Maybe the feelings hadn't disappeared after all. Maybe they'd been sleeping, slumbering away under cover, waiting. Waiting for someone to awaken them.

Mason had awakened them, hadn't she? Grace smiled then and slid her arm across Mason's stomach, closing her eyes with a contented sigh. She needed to sleep. In a few hours, they would be on the Old Mine Road. In a few hours, Susie Shackle would lead them to Johnny Herchek. She had a feeling that—in a few hours—all hell was going to break loose.

So she needed to sleep.

CHAPTER FORTY-SEVEN

Mason stared at the text that had come during the night. From Brady. Her uncle had taken five shots, two of them to his chest. He'd survived the surgery, Brady had said.

"Now we wait."

Now we wait.

There was no "he's going to be fine" or "doc says the worst is over" or any other crumb of hope they could cling to. No. Just "wait" and see.

She blew out her breath, then moved to the coffeepot. Grace had been still sound asleep when she'd woken up and she'd crawled out of the bed as quietly as she could. She'd come very close to waking her. It wouldn't have taken much, she knew. A kiss or two at her breasts—Grace had very sensitive nipples—would have done it. But no. She'd resisted. That time, at least. During the night, no. She hadn't resisted the pull.

And that's what it was, wasn't it? A pull, a tug...a damn yank. She'd been powerless, yeah. Not that she'd tried to fight it, no. She went willingly because she wanted it. And she didn't regret it. It had been too intimate, too special. She tried to remember the first time she and Shauna had slept together. Fleeting images came to her but nothing concrete, nothing specific. She had no distinct memories of it. It certainly wasn't like last night. Last night felt like it was meant to be, like it was something she'd been waiting for her whole life. Which, of course, was crazy. She took a sip of her coffee. Yeah, crazy. Nora Nightsail—the gypsy—didn't think it was crazy, though. No. She'd all but prophesized it. Hell, she *had* predicted it, hadn't she?

"Mason?"

She turned, finding Grace watching her. Grace, with her tousled hair and sleepy eyes. Tousled hair, yes, because she remembered running her hands through it more than a few times. And sleepy eyes? Had Grace had even a handful of hours' sleep? She looked beautiful, however, in her rumpled T-shirt and baggy sweatpants.

"You look tired."

Grace nodded but didn't move. "I am. Good tired, though." She tilted her head slightly. "Do we need to talk?"

Mason smiled and shook her head. Grace smiled, too, then finally moved closer. Mason held her in her arms as if she'd done it a hundred times before. The kiss they shared was quiet, soft, almost shy. She smiled against Grace's lips at that thought. They'd done too much to be shy. When they pulled apart, Grace still had a smile as she went to the coffeepot.

"I wish we could have a lazy day here." Grace looked at her, again, a shy look in her eyes. "Last night was fantastic, Mason."

Mason nodded. "Yeah, it was. A lazy day would be nice. How about tomorrow?"

Grace laughed lightly. "Confident we're going to wrap this up today, are you?"

Mason saw the steam wafting off the top of Grace's cup as she took a sip. "Last night was meant to be, wasn't it?"

Grace met her gaze, nodding slowly. "Yes, I believe so." She put her cup down. "The quote by Rumi comes to mind: 'What you seek is seeking you.' I didn't know I was searching for someone. Not consciously. Did you?"

Mason shook her head. "Honestly, I didn't give my personal life much thought anymore. Maybe because I didn't want to clutter it with some meaningless affair, when—perhaps subconsciously—I was waiting."

"Yes, I think that describes it perfectly for me too." Grace gave her a quick smile. "I'm not sure if that sounds romantic or if it totally takes the romance out of it altogether."

"It doesn't make it any less special, Grace. Last night, I mean. I felt like we were so thoroughly—perfectly—connected."

Grace nodded. "Yes. I felt that too. We were." She came closer, her hand brushing her cheek lightly, her thumb rubbing across her lower lip. "It was perfect, Mason. Natural. Familiar." Grace looked into her eyes and Mason wondered what she was trying to read there. "You made me feel loved last night. I haven't felt loved in so very many years."

Mason took her hand and kissed it, then pulled her into her arms, holding her tightly for a few seconds. She didn't say anything. She knew Grace didn't need words.

When they pulled apart, Grace picked her cup up again, clearing her throat before speaking. "So? Any news on Alan?"

Mason nodded. "Just a text from Brady. Surgery went okay, I guess. They're just waiting, as he says."

Grace's expression softened. "I'm sorry, Mason. I know you want to be there for him. For Carol." She shook her head though. "We can't go there. I'm sorry. We're to meet Susie on Old Mine Road at daybreak. She's going to lead us to Johnny Herchek's place. Thomas says there are booby traps along the way."

"Booby traps?"

"Dug out pits, snares, shooting arrows, that sort of thing. Explosives."

"Damn. So he's got his place secured like a compound or something?"

"It appears so."

"How will we get past it all?"

"Susie."

Mason bit her lower lip. Yeah. They were going to trust little Susie Shackle, the girl Mason used to hand her discarded bows to, to lead them through a maze of booby traps. The girl who died in 1997. The first victim of the serial killer.

"Christ, Grace."

"I know what you're thinking."

"Yeah, you usually do. But still—"

"I mean, I can *tell* what you're thinking. You have to trust me."

"I need...I need to let Brady know. Chief Danner too. I need—"

"I know. But they can't come with us. Just us. It's just you and me."

"We need backup," she insisted.

"They can't go out there. Thomas says they won't make it. Besides the booby traps, there's dynamite. He's got the mine rigged to blow." Grace held her gaze. "From what Thomas said, the box—my box—is in the mine tunnel."

"Oh, Jesus. Grace—"

"And you'll find me in time. I'm going to be a distraction for him. You'll have to get Faith and her mother out. Lucy. And Abby and her baby. And there's another girl there, but she doesn't know she's being held. She thinks Stacy is her mother and I'm not sure if we should try to rescue them or not. And of course, the girl from last night. Virginia—Ginny. You'll have to deal with the son, though. I think Charles is his name."

Mason shook her head as she took a step away from Grace, holding up her hand. "Okay. Overload."

"I know. I feel the same way. I didn't have a chance to ask questions of Thomas and some that I did ask, he didn't answer."

"So we're just going in on trust? Christ, Grace—"

"We have to."

"No, we don't. We can—"

"Mason, stop. This is what we're supposed to do."

"Supposed to do? Go after a serial killer alone? This isn't some goddamn movie! You're a civilian. You shouldn't be anywhere near this guy." She ran a hand through her hair. "We should call Kemp. We should get the FBI here. A tactical unit. A—"

"Yes, I agree. We'll call him. But legally, is there enough for him to move on Johnny Herchek?"

"The FBI hired you. He'll believe what you say. I mean, wasn't that the purpose of your being here?"

"We can tell him everything we know. Even if he does believe me, there's no time. We can't wait for him to get a warrant. We can't wait for him to get a tactical team up here. A girl was abducted last night. She'll be killed today. This morning. So there's no time for all that."

"Oh, Grace…"

"Thomas says Johnny's got enough dynamite set to blow half the mountain down. If the FBI goes in, if they get past his booby traps, if they corner him, then he'll set it off. Everyone will be killed." Grace took her arm, squeezing tightly. "You and me. We've got to be up there before any backup comes in. It's the only way."

She wanted to believe her. She really did. She wanted to believe what Nora Nightsail had said to her. She wanted to think that she and Grace would go in, would end the cycle, would save the day. She wanted to believe all that. But her grown-up, logical mind was telling her that it would never work. She or Grace or hell, both of them, could end up dead. She was a cop. There were procedures to follow. They should wait on Kemp. They should—

"I know it's not logical. And I know you're a cop. But this is the only way, Mason. You and me."

She let out a defeated breath. She wasn't going to win this argument, was she?

Grace gave her a quick, short smile. "No."

Damn. She nodded. "Okay. You and me."

"Good. And we'll need bolt cutters."

She raised her eyebrows.

Grace shrugged. "Thomas said to bring bolt cutters."

CHAPTER FORTY-EIGHT

Sunrise was still ten or fifteen minutes away, but there was enough light in the sky that she could see into the trees clearly. Mason was driving them along a bumpy, gravel road—Old Mine Road—which led up the mountain.

"Grace, last night—we needed that intimacy, didn't we? For us to succeed today, we needed it."

She turned, watching her as she drove. She could hear the nervousness in her voice. "Do you want to talk about it?"

"I don't know."

"You have doubts?"

"Was last night just you and me? Or did we sleep together because of some damn prophesy?"

"Ah. Were we fulfilling Nora Nightsail's vision?"

"Yeah. That."

"I don't know that we can separate the two, Mason. We have this attraction between us, but I don't think it's forced just because Nora said it was so. The timing of it—well, like you said, we needed that intimacy last night."

"We didn't talk."

"No, we didn't. I don't guess we needed to."

Mason had a firm grip on the steering wheel. "I'll find you in the box, Grace. I'll get you out." She glanced at her then. "Because I don't care what Nora's vision is or what your dream is. I felt closer to you last night than I've ever felt to anyone. And I want to feel that again. And again."

Grace smiled at the sincerity of her words. "I think you will, Mason. I'm still scared, but I believe—in my heart—that you'll find me. Because we're supposed to fall in love."

Mason looked at her then, a smile on her lips now. "We're supposed to fall in love, huh?"

Grace met her gaze. "Yes. We're going to fall in love."

* * *

"From what I know about the Herchek place, they use the road past the school to get to it. Creek Road. It follows the creek for a bit, then it climbs up. Their land is on the next ridge. There are a lot of old mines back there. Not too many people use this road."

Truth was, she didn't know how much property Herchek owned or which old mines were on it. She hoped Agent Kemp could find out. She'd been shocked—when they'd called him—that he was already in Denver. They'd rattled off everything they knew in quick succession to mostly silence on his end. But he hadn't questioned any of it. "I told you it'd be one of those crazy mountain men." He said he would take a helicopter to Gillette Park—give him a couple of hours. But no, they didn't have a couple of hours. She'd then called Dalton and told him where she was going. He told her Johnny Herchek was one of those "crazy-ass doomsday preppers" and that she was insane to go out there alone. He'd actually offered to come along, but Grace had shaken her head firmly—no. So he'd agreed to wait for Kemp. She ended the call with a warning of explosives planted along the road and he'd said that if Johnny Herchek had explosives, he'd have already blown himself up.

"Thomas said there was a back entrance to their property from here. That's why we needed bolt cutters."

"And someone is going to…you know, show us the way?"

Grace nodded. "Or so he said."

Mason glanced at her quickly. "You know how to use a gun, right?"

"I'm not comfortable with guns, no, but I do know how to shoot."

"Shooting range or—"

"Yes." She gave her a quick smile. "It's been a few years, I'll admit. And I don't even own a handgun anymore."

"Well, I hope—"

"Mason!"

Mason jumped at Grace's near scream of her name.

"Stop...stop the truck!" Her voice was shaky and Mason saw her hands trembling.

"What the hell is wrong?"

Grace put a hand to her chest. "You hit...you hit a girl." Grace held her hand up. "I saw a girl, you obviously did not. I assume it's Susie."

She opened her door and got out before Mason could comment. So had she plowed over Susie Shackle? Mason gripped the steering wheel with both hands and stared straight ahead. It was really going to happen, wasn't it? Was she strong enough to put her faith in Grace and a dead girl?

She closed her eyes and let her head drop to her chest. She should have let Dalton come along. Brady. Someone else. Not just her. Not just her and Grace. Hell, they—

"Mason?"

She jerked her head up, her eyes finding Grace's. The look there told her not to panic. Grace seemed to be much more confident than she was. She nodded, then looked beyond Grace as if she could see Susie, the young girl that Mason used to play with.

"I'll...I'll guide us from here." Grace closed the door. "A few hundred yards yet."

Mason cleared her throat before driving on. "Are we—are we alone?"

"No."

Oh, man.

"Susie says you probably don't remember, but the red bow that she was wearing that day was one you'd given her."

Mason could see the whites of her knuckles as her hands tightened involuntarily on the wheel. "No, I don't." She coughed nervously. "I gave her a handful of bows, I guess." She literally let out a scream when a hand touched her arm.

Grace laughed quietly. "Relax."

"Oh, yeah. Relax," she murmured with a little more sarcasm than she'd intended.

"Slow down. The forest road is coming up."

To their left was an obscure cutout and if you didn't know it was there, you'd most likely miss it. Mason turned, noting how grown up the trees were. It didn't appear that it got much use. After another fifty yards or so, Grace tapped her arm.

"To the right."

An entrance was barely discernable as the spruce trees had grown almost entirely across the opening. Beyond the branches, she saw the chain.

"Susie says it's a back entrance," Grace explained.

Mason stopped where the thick, heavy chain crossed the road. She sat quietly in the truck before getting out. "There's not like…a bomb or something. Right?"

Grace patted her arm. "Susie will let us know where the explosives are."

Mason turned to her, meeting her gaze. "I'm putting all my trust in you, you know."

Grace nodded. "It goes both ways, Mason. I'll be the one in the box."

* * *

They parked where Susie had said, under a canopy of old spruce trees. The sun was up now, the early morning upon them. She heard birds in the trees and she looked up, expecting to see blue feathers among the branches, but there were none.

"Nuthatches," Mason supplied. She turned to her then. "Ask Susie if she knows what happened to Patty Brinkman."

Grace was surprised that Mason was taking an active role in this, accepting that Susie Shackle was there with them. Grace turned to Susie, knowing Susie could hear Mason. The young girl looked much like the photo in the police file—pigtails and red bow. She was wearing faded jeans and a red and blue blouse.

"Rusty and Johnny visited her that night. Rusty had been going by there nightly for weeks."

"Did they kill her?"

"In a sense. Drove her completely mad. I think she died of fright."

"She says that Rusty visited her every night for weeks. Drove her mad. Says that both Johnny and Rusty went there that night." She turned back to Susie. "Why didn't they find the journal?"

Susie laughed. *"Rusty can't talk to Johnny except when he's in that stupid doll. And Johnny's lost most of his mind. It's Charles who Rusty controls now."*

"Charles is the one who tried to shoot Mason?"

"Yes. We couldn't let that happen. But that man should be okay. She shouldn't worry."

Grace glanced at Mason, knowing she was hearing only one side of the conversation. "She says that Alan should be okay and that you shouldn't worry." To Susie, she asked, "How does Rusty communicate with Charles?"

"*Through the speakers.*" Susie motioned her along. "*We must hurry. When Charles wakes up, he'll want to get rid of Ginny.*"

Grace was about to ask what she meant by speakers—what speakers?—when Mason's cell rang. She was surprised they had service, but she supposed they were still close enough to town. Mason snatched it up, her voice brisk, businesslike as she answered. Grace watched her, noting her expression. The girl—Ginny—had been reported missing.

"Follow protocol, Brady. You know what to do. I'm not able to help." Mason met Grace's eyes. "No. Because we're following up on something. And keep Danner in the loop too." A pause. "Yeah, me and Grace." She nodded. "I know. Dalton warned me." Another pause. "I'll call you. I promise." She pocketed her phone. "I guess you know what that was about."

"Why Brady and not the police?"

"They live outside the city limits. It was the same as April Trombley. Girl went to bed. Wasn't in her room this morning. So, let's go get her, shall we?"

Grace nodded, loving Mason's confidence. "Yeah. Let's go." She started walking, then turned, waiting for Susie. Susie smiled at her, then motioned her along. "What speakers?" she asked after a while.

"Huh?" Mason glanced at her with raised eyebrows.

Grace shook her head. "No. I was asking Susie. Susie said that Rusty communicates with Charles through the speakers."

"Oh."

Susie came up beside her. "*The stereo in his room. The speakers. He thinks it's the Devil talking to him.*" Susie laughed. "*He's so stupid.*"

Susie had been ten when she died, yet she appeared—sounded—much older. Grace was about to ask her when Susie turned to glance at her.

"*I've always been older than my years. My momma used to say I was an old lady in a child's body.*"

Grace wasn't used to being on the receiving end of mind reading and she smiled almost apologetically.

"You were the revenge. Because of the fire. And your father."

"*Yes. My daddy lit the gasoline too soon. The others were still inside. He tried to help them, but...*"

"Who is Faith?" she asked, changing the subject.

Susie smiled at the mention of Faith. *"She's my best friend. She's like you. She can see me and talk to me. When Stacy brings them their meal this morning, Lucy is supposed to get her keys."* Susie's expression changed. *"She's the one I'm worried about. Faith says Lucy is scared."*

"The keys?"

"Stacy has a key ring. It has keys to everything. All the doors. The rooms. The padlocks to the mine." She paused. *"And to the box."*

Grace nodded. Yes, the box. Her box.

"There's a trail up here. This is where you'll need to be careful. I'll point out all the traps and stuff."

"Mason, the trail starts here." She met Mason's gaze. "And the booby traps. They start now too. I'll go first."

"Grace, I should go first. I'm—"

"Mason, Susie is actually going first. Not me."

Mason looked at her a bit sheepishly. "Oh…yeah. Good idea."

CHAPTER FORTY-NINE

Lucy stared at the windup clock, listening to the tick, tick, tick it made as the seconds sped by. Earlier, unable to sleep, she'd been listening and time seemed to be crawling by, making each breath she took shaky with nervousness. Faith, on the other hand, had slept soundly, the prospect of what lay in store for them today apparently not affecting her in the least.

"It'll be okay, Momma."

Lucy pulled her eyes from the clock to Faith, seeing a quiet confidence there, a confidence that belied her young age. She moved to the table, knowing they had at least an hour before Stacy would show up with their meal. Even if she was early or late, they would still know. Faith said that Thomas would alert her when Stacy was coming with the cart.

Yes, Thomas. One of Faith's *friends*. She sighed. Could she do this? She'd slept fitfully, awake more than asleep. Was she alert enough to do this? Was she really going to tussle with Stacy, hit her in the head with the leg they'd managed to break off from one of the rickety chairs that matched the equally rickety table? Their table. Their chairs.

More than ten years she'd been here. Locked in this tiny room. Ten years. It was her home. Hers and Faith's. If they got out, then what? Were her parents still around? What if they'd died? What if they'd moved? Then what would she and Faith do? How would they live? How would they eat?

"Momma, it'll be okay."

"How do you know? If we do happen to make it out of here— which I highly doubt—then what will we do? Where will we go? And if they catch us, if we don't make it out, he'll be so mad, Faith. He'll hurt us." She stood up quickly. "He'll hurt *you*. He may be so mad that he kills us! Is that what you want?" she demanded, her voice louder than she intended.

"I want to get out of here, Momma. This will be our only chance. Today." Faith, seeming so grown up and mature all of a sudden, took her hand and squeezed it tightly. "My name is Faith. You named me that for a reason, didn't you?" Their eyes held. "Today, Momma, you must have faith."

"I'm so scared," she whispered, tears threatening. "What if—"

"What if we're stuck in here forever?"

Lucy swallowed back her tears. Yes. What if they were? Faith would eventually suffer the same fate she did. They'd come get her at night. They'd take her to the tiny room, not much bigger than a closet. They'd tie her to the dirty bed. They'd—

No! Lucy balled her fists. No. She'd fight him herself. She wouldn't allow it. But he would have no more use for her then, not if he had Faith. He would kill her. Then Faith would be all alone. Stuck in here. Forever.

She took a deep breath, finding courage where she thought there was none. She met Faith's eyes again, holding them. She nodded finally.

"Okay. Let's get out of here."

CHAPTER FIFTY

Mason could hear Grace's labored breathing as she walked ahead of her. She'd been in the mountains for over a week, but she doubted she was acclimated enough to the altitude for a hike such as this. They were no longer on the crude road which didn't look like it had been used in a while. She would have thought that would have been safer. Surely there were no booby traps there and she'd said as much, but Grace—and Susie Shackle—had led them into the trees without replying to her comment.

"You okay?"

Grace turned around and offered a quick smile. "My lungs are about to explode." Then Grace stopped. "Susie says we're close."

"Close to the house?"

Grace bent over and rested her hands on her thighs. "My god, I'm out of shape."

"Well, we'll spend the rest of the summer working on that. Deal?"

Grace met her gaze then, her eyes gentling. "Deal." She straightened up again. "Close to where the booby traps start. Susie says we must be very careful from now on. She says we couldn't stay on the road. They've got it rigged with explosives. This way is safer."

Explosives on the road? It stood to reason that they had explosives on the main road up to the house too. Mason looked around, wondering if she'd be able to spot a trap. Trip wires would be the easiest to hide. And the most deadly if they were rigged with sharp flying objects. Grace said—according to Thomas—there were arrows and knives and such to be on the lookout for.

"Mason...here."

Mason looked where Grace pointed. Sure enough, a trip wire stretched across the trail. She watched as Grace stepped over it.

"I wonder how often these are triggered. Deer or anything could trip them."

"Susie says Johnny and his son are very paranoid and they check them almost daily. And yes, there have been some unfortunate encounters with wildlife." Grace looked back at her. "Unfortunate for the wildlife, I mean."

After another hundred yards or so, Grace stopped abruptly. She then took a step backward. Mason did the same. She spotted the snare before Grace could point it out.

"How do we get around it?" There didn't seem to be an easy climb on either side. The snare was between two large boulders, too large to scale.

"Susie says to trip it."

Mason nodded. She looked around, wondering how she could reach the trigger without getting caught in the net herself.

"Go back down. There should be a long tree limb on the ground." Grace pointed. "On the left down there." Grace smiled at her unasked question. "Yes, it helps to have a navigator."

Mason found the limb, but it was very heavy. She wasn't sure she could suspend it over the net to trip the wire.

"She says to throw it at the wire if you can't reach it."

Grace stood back as Mason went to the edge of the snare. The limb was about a foot too short. She crouched down low, then flung it with enough force to hit the wire. The snare was lifted up on all four corners, taking her limb with it as it was suspended above them, swinging back and forth five or six feet above ground.

"Wow. That's quite a pulley system they've got rigged up here." She nodded confidently. "We got this. Lead on."

* * *

For all the confidence Lucy had exuded earlier, her heart was hammering in her chest. Faith said that Stacy was on her way. Faith sat at the table, idly flipping through a magazine but Lucy could see that her hand was trembling. Yes, she was scared too. Lucy stood behind the door, her hand gripping the wooden chair leg tightly. One swing. She would have one swing. Hard as she could. When Stacy fell, Faith would snatch the keys from her belt. They had already torn the bed sheets. They would tie her hands and feet. They would cover her mouth so she couldn't call out. They had it all planned. But she was shaking so badly, fear making the blood pound in her ears, that she could hardly hear the squeaky wheels of the food cart, could barely make out the jingling of the keys as Stacy stood on the other side of the door.

Oh, she didn't want to do this. She didn't want to hurt Stacy. Stacy had been kind to them. Stacy brought them food. Brought books and magazines for Faith. Stacy—

"Momma, look at me."

Lucy turned to Faith, meeting her gaze.

"I love you, Momma. We're getting out of here now. Right now."

Lucy swallowed down her fear. "Yes. I love you too."

She took a deep breath as the door was pushed open and the squeaky cart preceded Stacy into the room. They'd stuffed pillows under the worn, faded bedspread. Fluffed them up to look like someone was there. They had a plan.

"Momma is not feeling well," Faith said when Stacy came in.

Stacy's gaze went to the bed—as they'd anticipated. She took a step toward it, letting the door close behind her. Lucy swung the leg as hard as she could, nearly crying out at the sound it made when she hit Stacy on the side of her head. Dazed, Stacy turned, her eyes wide in shock.

"No! You can't—"

Lucy hit her again and blood oozed from her forehead as she fell to the ground. She stood there, frozen in place as Faith fumbled with the keys, trying to unhook the clasp that was attached to Stacy's jeans.

"Momma! The sheets!"

Lucy moved then, dropping the chair leg and grabbing the strips of cloth they'd torn last night. She pulled Stacy's arms behind her back. Stacy offered no resistance and Lucy feared she was dead.

"Oh my god! Did I kill her? Did I—"

"Momma, tie her! We've got to go!"

While Lucy tied her feet, Faith wrapped a strip around Stacy's mouth. Lucy still wasn't sure if Stacy was alive or not. Faith held the ends up and Lucy took them, tying a knot behind her head. Then Faith took her hand and urged her up.

They stood at the door, looking at each other. Faith was the one to open it. It hit her then that Faith had not ever stepped foot outside these four walls. Lucy, on the nights that he came to claim her, had only gone so far as the small room, two doors down.

"We have to find Abby. Thomas is going to lead us."

Lucy simply nodded. Her part in their escape was over with. Now, she would follow Faith. And whichever one of Faith's friends that was helping them. She glanced back as the door closed behind them, seeing Stacy's limp body on the floor.

CHAPTER FIFTY-ONE

Grace heard the bird even before Susie could warn her. She jerked her head around, but Mason had heard it too. She pulled her gun from her holster.

"No! She must not shoot! They'll hear!"

"Mason, no!"

"The damn bird—"

"No! We're trying to sneak up, remember? You can't shoot at it."

The words had barely left her mouth when the bird flew out of the trees, buzzing their heads. Mason swung futilely as it squawked by them. The jay landed ahead of them, scolding from his perch, his black eyes staring them down.

"Don't look at him. Walk on."

Grace took Mason's hand, pulling her along with them. As they walked near the branch, Grace flicked her gaze to the bird. It was no longer a Steller's jay. It was a baby. The same one she'd seen before— long, sharp fangs, blood dripping from them. The mouth opened and closed as if snapping at her.

"Grace! He can't hurt you. Ignore him!"

Grace squeezed Mason's hand hard as they passed under the tree. Drops of blood fell from the baby's mouth, landing on her arm. Mason jerked away as the baby—no, now a bird again—landed on her head, its claws trying to dig into her scalp. Without thinking, Grace picked up a stick, taking a backhanded swing at the bird. She knocked it away and it fluttered to the ground as if stunned. Mason picked up a large rock, intending to throw it at the bird, but the jay flew away, darting into the thick branches of a spruce tree and disappearing from sight.

"Are you okay?"

Mason touched her head, then looked at her fingers. There was blood on each of them. "I so want to shoot that bastard."

"Let's go! He'll try to warn them."

"We have to go. Hurry!"

They'd made it past five booby traps so far. Susie said there was only one more. They hadn't had any problems maneuvering around them and they'd only had to trip the one with the snare.

"This last one has a mesh net across the trail. It has knives. She'll have to be very careful."

Grace looked at Mason. "Got knives coming up. Mesh net."

"Can we get around it?

"No."

"No," Grace relayed. She stopped when Susie held her hand up.

"Here." Susie went to the side, pointing out the knives that were nearly camouflaged in the trees. Each seemed to be embedded in a board.

"I see it." Mason walked around her, inspecting the mesh.

"How do they fire?"

"I have no idea." Mason walked toward the tree.

"Be careful."

"She says to be careful."

"Ah. Bungee cords. A lot of them." She turned back to the mesh. "I think I can throw something into the mesh—like we did the snare—and get it to trigger. Then we can go around it." She raised her eyebrows. "Unless someone else has another idea."

Grace looked at Susie. "What do you think?"

"I think it's the only way. But you should stay back. Just in case."

Grace turned to Mason. "Yes. But from as far back as you can."

The rock Mason selected wasn't very big, and she stood near Grace, tossing a hard, underhanded throw at the mesh. The rock slipped through without even touching the net.

"Couldn't have done that if I'd tried," Mason mumbled as she selected another rock, this one bigger.

The toss this time hit the mesh in the middle and with a whoosh, twin upright boards came sailing, both with six knives embedded in them. She took an involuntary step backward even though they were well away from the danger.

Mason went to inspect the knives, shaking her head as she did. "Wonder how many deer have gotten caught in this thing. Dried blood on the blades."

"Can we get through?"

Mason walked around the knives to the mesh, holding it up high enough for them to crawl under. "Come on."

"The house is just beyond the trees. Paul is there. He's watching Charles. Thomas is with Faith."

"And where is Johnny?"

"Charles is with the girl. Ginny. Johnny sits outside. On guard. With his shotgun."

Grace swallowed. "I'm the distraction."

"Yes."

"What is it?" Mason asked.

Grace took a deep breath, meeting her gaze. "Showtime."

*   *   *

Lucy took the keys from Faith's fumbling fingers, trying to guess which one might open the door.

"Momma, he says this one." Faith pointed to a key with a red, plastic cap. There were perhaps twelve or fifteen keys. Most were coded with different colored caps.

Faith put it in the deadbolt and turned, hearing the click as the lock disengaged. She wondered why there was only one lock here whereas their room had three. When she pushed the door open, she saw wide eyes staring at her. The young woman picked her baby up protectively, holding him tightly.

"Who are you?"

"Abby?"

The woman nodded. "Who are you?"

"Lucy. Lucy Hines."

At that, the woman's mouth dropped open. "Lucy? I…I remember you from school. But you…you were—"

"Yes. I was fourteen. I've been here since. Like you. Locked up."

"Momma, we must go."

"We're getting out of here. Come with us."

Abby shook her head. "No. No...I can't. The baby. Stacy will come soon. And...and the man—"

"My name is Faith. Stacy won't be coming. And there are two people from town coming to help us escape. You have to come with us."

"She's my daughter," Lucy explained.

They all seemed to jump at once when a shotgun blast broke the silence. Lucy looked at Faith, not knowing what to do. Should they run back to their room? Should they—

"Grace is here."

Faith closed the door and Lucy was amazed at her calmness as she locked the deadbolt with the key. She held a finger to her lips, indicating for them to be quiet. Abby had moved away from them, huddled in the corner with her baby. A baby who was beginning to fuss.

CHAPTER FIFTY-TWO

"This was a damn stupid idea."

Mason crouched down low behind the tree, her heart still lodged in her throat from the shotgun blast. The man—Johnny Herchek— hadn't issued a verbal warning as Grace approached. No. He'd swung the shotgun her way and fired his warning over her head. Grace had ducked to the ground, making her easy pickings for Johnny, who had been sitting in a chair on the front porch, the shotgun resting across his lap. He looked filthy, his shirt hanging open, revealing an equally dirty undershirt. She didn't know if he was drunk or half out of his mind. Bushy hair stuck out from under a faded blue cap and a full beard covered his face. Drunk, she guessed, judging by the bottle that had fallen from his lap. Clear bottle. No labels. Amber liquid. Moonshine whiskey, no doubt.

Despite that, she stayed put. It was the plan. Grace had made her promise. Grace and Susie had made her promise. So she clung tightly to the branch, watching as Johnny jerked Grace to her feet, waving the gun in her face. She could hear their voices but not make out their words. Grace was offering an explanation for her presence. They had argued over what to tell him. It was Susie's suggestion that they tell him the truth—that Grace knew he was holding hostages there. Mason and Grace had both nixed that idea. Something tamer, less threatening. She was afraid Johnny would get spooked and shoot Grace right there where she stood.

So, Grace got lost. She was traveling alone and she got lost. Johnny wouldn't be threatened by that. But he would want to hold her. Susie said he'd take her into the tunnel. And most likely into the box. And while he was doing that, Mason would make a run for the house. Her job was to find Charles, disable him, rescue Ginny and the others. And then, find Grace before crazy Johnny Herchek blew the whole mountain down with his dynamite.

"It'll never work."

For one thing, how would Grace have managed to get to his house without tripping one of his booby traps? But so far, it seemed to be working. Johnny was dragging a struggling Grace with him, into the house. He was yelling for Charles to "Come see what I found" and it was all Mason could do not to pull her weapon and run him down before they disappeared inside.

Nonetheless, disappear they did. She waited, scanning the windows that were facing her. She saw no movement. She took a deep breath, then bolted from behind the tree, running as fast as she could toward the same door that he'd taken Grace through.

*　*　*

"Charles! Goddamn it! Wake up! Got me a trespasser!"

Grace tried to pull away and Johnny slapped her with the back of his hand. Her ears were ringing from the blow.

"It's okay, Grace. Charles is passed out. He won't hear him."

Grace continued to struggle as Johnny pulled her through the house. Everything seemed a blur—the dingy white walls, the clutter, the smell of cigarettes. What wasn't a blur was the bird that hit the window. Blue feathers beat against the glass. Johnny didn't seem to notice.

"Goddamn trespasser, that's what I got here," he mumbled. Then he stopped and jerked her up hard. "What the hell you doing snooping around here, girl?"

"I told you—"

"Car broke down? Got lost? Just so happened to stumble upon my place?" When he smiled, Grace saw his mouthful of dirty, stained teeth and smelled his foul breath. "I got booby traps set up. Ain't no way you got past them."

"I guess I did. I'm here, aren't I?" She tried to pull away from him. "If you could please just call someone. A wrecker service or something. I'll get out of your hair. I'll leave right now. I'll—"

"Leave?" He gave her a humorless laugh. "Why would I let you leave?"

"I don't mean no harm, mister. I got lost. I shouldn't have come up here."

"That's right. That was a mistake on your part." He turned away from her. "Charles! Wake your ass up!"

"I—"

"Shut up! I got you now!" He pulled her up close. "I'd like to have a little fun with you, but you're a little old for my taste. Charles might want to play with you though. Maybe you could teach him a thing or two."

"Please. I don't—"

"I know just where to put you." He laughed. "Ain't nobody gonna find you in there."

"Susie…I'm scared."

"I'm right here with you."

He took her out a back door that was only forty or fifty feet from the side of the rocky face of the mountain. She could see the black, gaping hole that was the mouth of a tunnel. She jumped as the Steller's jay flew at her, clipping her head.

"Goddamn bird!" he bellowed. He swung his shotgun up, firing off a round, and Grace stared in disbelief as blue feathers filled the air and the bird dropped to the ground, his wings moving helplessly. But then it wasn't a bird anymore. It was the baby. A bloody, wounded baby, screaming its lungs out in pain. He doesn't know it's Rusty, she thought. No. Susie had said that Rusty only communicated with him through the doll.

"Goddamn bird," he muttered again. "Flying around here all the time. I fixed him, all right." He yanked on her arm, his meaty fingers wrapped tightly around her wrist. "Come on."

"Where are you taking me?" She dug her heels in as he dragged her along.

"I'm taking you to hell." He nearly bellowed with laughter. "Tell my son hello when you get there." He laughed again. "Yeah, tell him his old man is sorry he forgot about him in the box." Another hearty laugh. "No, I'm lying! He was a no-good bastard."

They were standing at the entrance to the tunnel. Inside, it appeared to be as black as night. She turned around as the baby's screams stopped. It was the bird again. Apparently, even spraying him with shotgun pellets wasn't enough to kill him. There was blood on the feathers, but he flapped them, his dark, beady eyes meeting hers for a second. His mouth opened but no sound came out. Instead, he flew off toward the house, landing on the corner of the roof, watching as Johnny pulled her inside the tunnel. He didn't turn on a light and she wondered how he could see anything. She stopped struggling, fearing the darkness more than him at that moment. She felt them turn to the left. The air was dank, cool…and still. He bumped into something and muttered a quick "Goddamn it," then continued on. Again, they turned, this time to the right. She felt like they were in a maze as he maneuvered them deeper into the mountain.

She gave a startled gasp as a strong, calloused hand clamped around her neck, shoving her against the wall.

"I'll snap your neck like a twig if you move." Then he chuckled. "Might be a quicker end for you, though."

She heard the screech of rusty hinges and knew he was opening a door. *"Susie? Are you here?"*

"I'm here. But I can't go inside with you."

"Why not?"

"The box belongs to Nathan. He won't let anyone inside."

The obvious question—who was Nathan?—never got asked as she was shoved inside the box, hard enough to fall to the ground. Then the squeaky hinges told her the door was closing, and she heard the unmistakable sound of a padlock being snapped into place.

It was darker than dark. Yes, if that was such a thing. She'd never really feared the dark before. But she did now. Because she wasn't alone.

"What's your name?"

She swallowed. "Gra…Grace."

"I'm Nathan."

CHAPTER FIFTY-THREE

Mason felt sweat bead on her forehead as she leaned against the wall, listening. Grace had told her that Charles would be in his room at the back of the house. The others would be down in the basement. The girl—Ginny—was tied to Charles' bed. God, they should have just raided the place. She should have taken Johnny out when she had the chance. Of course, her logical mind, the part that remembered she was still a cop, asked her on what grounds could she have shot Johnny Herchek?

"Should have waited for Kemp," she murmured to herself. Should have brought Dalton along. Or Brady. *Christ!*

She crept along the hallway, eyeing the doors. Last door, Susie had told Grace. She had her service weapon out, gripped tightly in her right hand as she reached out to turn the knob with her left. She jumped back, startled, when she heard the shotgun blast.

Grace!

She took a step back. Grace had told her "no matter what" she was not to change the plan. Take care of Charles. Get the girls out, no matter what. She closed her eyes for a second, putting images of Grace from her mind. She took a deep breath, focusing again on the door. She turned the knob, then pushed the door open slowly, the rank smell of the closed-up room making her wrinkle her nose. An overflowing ashtray was the first thing she saw. That, and an empty bottle of booze. A young girl with frightened eyes looked at her and gasped. Mason put a finger to her lips to indicate she stay quiet. A man lay sprawled out on the bed, his snoring the only thing to indicate that he was still alive. One hand hung limply off the side, the other was up by his pillow. His legs were bent at an odd angle as if he'd simply fallen into bed and passed out.

She went to the girl first. Her hands were tied to the headboard and she was naked. Mason saw bloodstains on the bed and she pushed that from her mind. If she dwelt on it too much, she might just shoot Charles where he lay. She again held a finger to her lips and the girl nodded. She reached out to untie the rope, keeping her eyes on Charles as she did so. When the girl was free, Mason held her hand up, telling her to stay.

"Don't move," she mouthed.

She quietly took the handcuffs from her belt and crept around the bed toward Charles. As she approached, a floorboard creaked under her weight and she stopped, barely breathing as his snoring ceased. His eyelids fluttered but didn't open. She glanced again at the girl, who seemed to be holding her breath as well. Her lips were trembling and tears began falling from her eyes, but she didn't make a sound. Mason nodded at her, then turned her attention back to Charles.

She thought her best option was to cuff the wrist nearest the headboard and secure it to one of the wooden slats. That would still leave him one hand free, but she would have to chance it. She swallowed and her throat was dry as she reached out, the cuff only inches from his wrist.

A loud thump on the window made her jump and she turned, finding a bird—the goddamn blue Steller's jay—clinging to the screen. He let out a raucous cry, then pounded with his beak against the glass.

The young girl let out a scream, and Mason jerked her head back around, startled to find Charles with his eyes opened.

"What the hell?"

She snapped the handcuff around his wrist, then was tossed against the wall as he stood. Her only saving grace was his wobbly legs, and she kicked him hard on one knee, buckling him. He cried out in pain as she jerked his arm up, finally securing the cuff around one of the slats in the headboard. She jumped back as he kicked at her, his arm flailing around him as she stood just out of reach.

"You're under arrest." Then she grinned. "Hang tight. Be right back." She held her hand out to the girl. "Come on!"

Charles jerked hard against the bedframe, and she wondered how much it would take for him to break it. Didn't matter. Short of shooting him, she wouldn't be able to get close enough to tie his other arm.

"Let me loose, you bitch!" He lay on the bed, kicking at the headboard. "Daddy! Daddy! Help me! Some bitch is in the house! Daddy!"

The bird continued to thrash against the window, and she only barely resisted taking a shot at the damn thing. She hurried from the room, pulling Ginny with her. She closed the door on Charles' string of profanity as he alternately railed at her and called for his father.

The girl was crying loudly now and Mason pulled her into a quick, tight hug. "I'm going to get you out of here, Ginny, but there are some others we need to rescue first. I need you to help me, okay?"

The girl was standing there naked and bruised and her tears still fell, but she nodded bravely.

Back in the main house, they hurried through the living room— which was cluttered and filthy—and into the kitchen. She stopped up short. It was surprisingly clean, even with the evidence that breakfast had just been cooked. Interior wall, Susie had told Grace. There were two doors and she jerked one opened, only to find a pantry. She went to the other, shocked that it was locked.

Two, three kicks against the door told her she wasn't going to be able to break it—it was a solid chunk of wood. Shooting the lock off probably wasn't the best choice, but there was nothing left for her to do. She felt like she'd already been in the house an eternity.

"I'm going to have to shoot the lock. Stay back."

She took a few steps away, then took aim at the lock, firing twice, splintering the wood along the doorjamb. This time when she kicked, the door burst open, revealing steps heading down into a basement. The light was on and she took the steps as fast as she could, landing in the middle of a large room. Ginny was close to her, holding on to her duty belt. Four doors—all closed—greeted them.

She went to the first one. It was locked. Yeah. They'd all be locked. Keys. She needed the keys.

"Faith?" She went to each door, pounding loudly. "Faith? Susie sent me. I need the keys." *Come on. Come on.* "Faith! Where are you?"

She heard a baby crying, and she turned, trying to determine which door it was coming from. She went to it, knocking again.

"Who's in there? I'm with the sheriff's department. Faith?"

She heard the deadbolt turn, and she stepped back, waiting as the door slowly opened. A young girl looked back at her.

"Are you Mason?"

She didn't bother asking how she knew her name. "Yeah, I'm Mason. Are you Faith?"

The girl nodded and opened the door a bit wider. Mason went inside, finding two women, one holding a baby protectively. Both of them looked at her suspiciously. And why not? They'd been imprisoned here for a decade or more.

"I'm Mason Cooper with the sheriff's department," she said calmly. "I'm getting you out of here. You have keys?"

"I have them."

"You're Lucy?"

The woman nodded.

"Okay. This is Ginny."

Faith nodded. "Ginny. Yes. They brought you here last night."

The woman with the baby—Abby—shook her head firmly. "No. I can't go. He'll hurt Andrew. He'll—"

It was Faith, the ten-year-old, who spoke up. "He'll hurt Andrew if you stay. He'll take him from you. He'll raise him as his son. You must come with us, Abby."

She heard glass breaking upstairs. She assumed Charles had thrown something at the window. "Find something for Ginny to wear. We've got to hurry!"

CHAPTER FIFTY-FOUR

Grace felt a hand brush her cheek and she closed her eyes, trying to focus inward. She'd never been more afraid in her life, but she knew she shouldn't be afraid of Nathan. Yet she was. She needed to get her composure back. She needed to be in control, not him. She opened her eyes, seeing nothing but blackness.

"How long have you been in here?" Her voice sounded odd—nervous—to her own ears and she wondered if he could tell.

"A long time. He forgot about me."

Forgot about him? Locked him up in here and forgot about him? "Why don't you leave?"

"Rusty won't let me. He won't let anyone cross over."

She remembered something Thomas had said. That it wasn't just Faith and Lucy she was saving. She would be setting them all free. That must be what he meant.

"You don't let anyone come in here, do you?"

"No. It's my box. I guess I'll have to share it with you now, though."

She shook her head. "I'm going to get out."

He laughed. *"But you'll come back. Rusty will make you come back in here, I'd guess."*

"No. I mean, I'm going to get out, in my present form."

Another laugh. *"I don't think so. He's not coming back for you."*

No. But Mason was. She closed her eyes again. Wasn't she? She leaned against the door, then slid down to the floor. Her foot bumped something and she imagined it was Nathan's body. She jerked her foot back, pulling her knees up to her chest and circling them with her arms.

"You want to play a game or something?"

"No."

* * *

"We must hurry! Susie says the man is coming!"

Mason paused at the bottom of the stairs. "Susie is here? Why isn't she with Grace? Ask her if Grace is okay."

"Susie says Grace is in the box. Susie says you must hurry. The man is coming back."

Faith was literally pushing her up the stairs. Mason turned back to look. The others stood at the bottom of the basement steps—Lucy, now holding Ginny's hand, and Abby and her fussing baby. They all had identical looks in their eyes—fright. Faith was the opposite. She exuded confidence.

Loud voices drifted down the stairs and she knew Johnny was trying to get Charles free from the cuffs. She turned to glance at Lucy.

"When we get to the top, I'm going after Johnny. You take the others outside. To the front, not the back." She looked at Faith. "Susie will help you."

"Yes. Susie says yes."

She nearly jogged up to the top of the stairs, hearing the others creeping up behind her. The baby was crying loudly now, and she could hear Abby trying unsuccessfully to hush it.

When she pushed the door opened, she wasn't surprised to see the Steller's jay flying in the kitchen, squawking loudly as he flew from window to window. She could see blood on his feathers and he appeared to favor one wing. The frying pan that had been on the stovetop suddenly sailed through the air, and Mason's eyes widened as it slammed against the window, barely missing the bird. The bird flew toward the stove, shrieking, fighting with an unseen force.

What the hell? Was it Susie? Someone else? Thomas maybe?

Then the outer door flung open and Johnny Herchek stood there, shotgun in hand. Mason didn't know if he was more startled to find her there or the bird. She got her answer when he raised his shotgun, blasting off a round toward the bird.

"Goddamn bird! I'm sick of that bird!"

"Run!" she yelled at the others as she fired, knocking Johnny back out through the door. "Go on! Run!"

She crept toward the back door, her Glock held at the ready. Johnny sat up, firing his shotgun at her. She dove to the floor, hearing the spraying of pellets as they embedded in the wall behind her. She fired again, but Johnny was running away from her. She could see blood on his shirt and knew she'd hit him, yet he showed little sign of it. She stood, only to dive back down as the bird—the goddamn bird—attacked. She swung wildly, knocking it off her head. It came at her again and she grabbed it, flinging it against the wall. She took aim, firing twice. The bird blew up, feathers mixed with blood splattering the wall in dozens of pieces. She didn't take the time to savor her victory.

She ran out back, after Johnny. From inside, she could hear Charles yelling for somebody to "get these goddamn cuffs off me." She stopped at the mouth of the tunnel—it was as dark as midnight inside. Grace was in there. Somewhere. Johnny was in there, surely. With a shotgun.

She took one tentative step inside, then heard a rumble. She glanced behind her, feeling the earth shake beneath her feet. The rumble turned into an explosion. Then another, this one a little closer. Then another. Then another.

"Shit! He's setting off the charges."

She ran blindly into the tunnel, holding her hands out in front of her. She had to find Grace. She had to find her before he blew the whole mountain down...and before the mine tunnel collapsed.

She felt for the wall, then pressed against it, listening. She heard nothing from inside. She blindly reached for her flashlight, unsnapping the leather sheath on her belt and pulling it out. She clicked it on, looking around. The mouth of the tunnel was wide, then it narrowed as it cut deeper into the rocks. Beyond the main entrance, the tunnel split, one veering to the left, the other going slightly to the right. Should she try to find Grace? Or should she look for Johnny and stop him before he blew them all sky-high?

Grace. She had to find Grace. She paused at the split, listening. She heard nothing from either direction. The main tunnel was straight ahead. The one to the left appeared to be a newer tunnel, although she assumed both were dug during the mining heydays more than a century ago.

Another blast from outside caused loose rock to fall from the ceiling and she felt her apprehension grow. If she chose the wrong tunnel...

CHAPTER FIFTY-FIVE

Lucy—like Faith and Abby—was shielding her eyes from the sun. The bright, glorious, wonderful sun. The explosion was enough to shake the ground where they stood, but it wasn't enough to shake the pure joy and elation she felt at being outside. They were hiding in the trees, a hundred feet or so from the house. Andrew, the baby, was crying loudly now, and she assumed he hadn't been fed yet this morning. Abby was rocking him in her arms, trying to calm him. Faith was beside the young girl, holding her hand.

"Should we keep going?"

Faith turned to her then and Lucy noted the smile on her face. "The sun, Momma. It's the sun."

Faith had tears in her eyes and Lucy felt her own run down her face. They embraced tightly, both crying freely now. They were actually out of the house, out of their little prison. Then Faith pulled away from her, wiping at her tears.

"We need to stay close. In case Grace or Mason needs help."

"But—"

"We're free, Momma. Susie says we just have to wait until Grace gets out of the box."

"Who is Susie?" Abby asked.

Lucy gave a half-smile. "Don't ask." She went to Ginny then. The girl couldn't be more than twelve, thirteen maybe. When she reached out a hand toward her, the girl flinched. "I won't hurt you," she said softly. "My name is Lucy. That's Faith. And Abby. And the baby is Andrew."

"Where…where are we?"

"I don't really know," Lucy answered honestly. "But we're out of the house." She took a deep breath of the fresh, pine-scented air. "And we're safe."

Another explosion shook the ground. Safe? Were they really?

* * *

"Did you feel that?"

"It's dynamite. He's got a lot of it."

She stood up, her hands on the door. "He's going to blow the side of the mountain off," she murmured, remembering Susie's words. *God, then I really will be trapped in here with Nathan,* she thought. She slammed her fist against the door. It was only then that she realized it was a metal door. Not wooden. She hit it again.

No! It's not supposed to be like this. Mason is supposed to find her. They're going to get a dog. They're going to fall in love. They're going to—

She spun around. "Nathan?"

"Uh huh."

"You've got to help me."

"Help you how?"

"Go outside. You've got to—"

"I don't like to leave the box. Rusty's out there. He's mean. I like to stay in here. All by myself. No one bothers me in here."

"Please, Nathan. Help me. Go out. There's somebody trying to find me. A woman. Mason. I don't know how, but you've got to show her the way."

"But Rusty—"

"Rusty is injured. Rusty is not going to hurt you. In fact, if we get out of here, then maybe you—and all the others—can leave. Rusty can't stop you." She leaned against the door. "Please?" Fear had crawled up her body, choking her. "Please?" she whispered. There was a long pause before he answered.

"Okay. But if Rusty's out there, I'm coming right back."

"Thank you." She squeezed her eyes shut. "Thank you."

She slid back down the door, feeling another rumble shake the box. How much time did she have? She leaned her head back against the door heavily. This was a stupid plan, wasn't it? So she'd had a dream? So Nora Nightsail had had a vision? So what if Susie Shackle said she needed to distract him? Couldn't they have come up with a better plan? She'd practically offered herself up on a silver platter. And he'd done like they said he would; he'd put her in the box. She'd distracted him, though, hopefully long enough for Mason to get the others out.

Yes, he'd put her in the box. This box. *Her* box. The same box where he'd put his son, Nathan. And forgot about him. How awful must that have been. How many days, weeks, had he been able to survive in this dark, dark box? No, dark couldn't describe it. It was darker than dark, blacker than black.

And she wanted the hell out of it.

Now.

CHAPTER FIFTY-SIX

Mason shined her light along the tunnel floor, then nearly lost her balance as the earth shook from another blast. How close were the blasts now? Almost to the house? Could they hear them in town? Surely. Would Dalton and Brady know where they were coming from? Was Scott Kemp back in town already? Maybe so. Maybe they were already on their way up here. If they didn't get here damn soon, it would be too late.

The Glock felt heavy in her hands, and her palms were damp with perspiration. From nervousness, she knew. It was cool and damp in the mineshaft. She paused, shining her light up ahead at what looked like an endless tunnel. She thought she heard something. Yes. There it was again. Laughter.

What the hell?

She followed the sound, her footsteps crunching on rocks as she walked. Yes, definitely laughter. She could see the glow of a light now.

"Come on, you son a bitch! *Blow!*"

It was Johnny. She moved quickly, finding him in a small cave-like room, perhaps the beginning of a shaft that had been abandoned long ago. He was huddled over a table which was cluttered with what she assumed was bombmaking materials and sticks of dynamite. Blood stained his shirt and one arm hung limply by his side. In his other hand, he held a device about the size of a cell phone. With his thumb, he was punching frantically at it.

"Blow!"

She stepped fully into the room. "Where is she?"

He spun around, surprise showing on his face. He dropped the device and reached for his shotgun. She fired, hitting him in his good shoulder. Even then he held tight to the shotgun.

"Where is she?"

A sickly sweet laugh bubbled out of his mouth and she knew then, with certainty, that he'd lost whatever sanity he'd been holding onto.

"Bombs! Bombs are going off! I knew it would work! I told him it would work! Bombs!"

"Where the fuck is she?" she yelled.

Another laugh. "I put her in hell. With Nathan. Same place you're going."

When the shotgun lifted, she fired three rounds into his chest, dropping him where he stood.

"Goddamn," she muttered. She spun around. "Grace! *Grace!*"

Back in the shaft, she ran on, feeling that she was indeed running into the bowels of hell. "*Grace!*"

But no. She'd taken the wrong tunnel. This one ended. Old, weathered boards blocked her path, nailed up long ago to seal the tunnel. She turned around, sprinting back down the tunnel, her light flashing haphazardly as she ran. When she came to the fork, she glanced toward the mine's entrance. A shape stood there and she killed her light.

"Daddy? Daddy, are you in here?"

Charles. Shit.

"Daddy, where are you? They're all gone! I don't know what to do. The bombs are going off!" He stepped into the mineshaft, but she doubted he had a light. He would have already had it on if he did.

"Daddy!" he yelled.

Yell all you want, but Daddy ain't gonna hear you. She moved slowly along the wall, slipping into the other tunnel. She used her hands to feel her way until she was far enough inside to put her light on again. She hurried now, nearly running, but she came to another split.

"Oh, Jesus…are you kidding me?"

She stepped back and scanned the ground, searching for footprints or some other evidence of which one to take. No footprints. Nothing but rocks and rubble. Then her eyes widened as the rocks moved. One at first, then another…then more. She followed them with her eyes as they turned into the right tunnel. She didn't question it. No, not after everything she'd seen, she didn't question it. She didn't wonder if she was seeing things. She simply followed the moving rocks, not caring who—or what—it was that was helping her

* * *

Grace never knew she was claustrophobic until that very moment. The darkness had practically swallowed her, wrapping around her so tightly she felt like she could no longer breathe. She was trembling as she huddled against the door, her knees held snuggly to her chest. She took shallow breaths, wondering if one of the blasts had closed the tunnel and sealed her in here…with no air. The walls of the box were closing in—she could almost feel them moving toward her. Feel them, yes, but not see. There was nothing to see. No matter how hard she squinted, how hard she peered out in front of her, there was absolutely *nothing* to see. She was in a black hole and it was sucking the very life from her. *That*, she could see.

She closed her eyes against the blackness, hoping to shut it out. She rocked slowly, seeing sunshine, trees. Yes, and blue sky, puffy white clouds. A breeze. A cool breeze. Mason took her hand and squeezed it. Grace looked into her eyes, seeing love there. Grace moved closer, smiling as they kissed. A dog wiggled between them, wanting attention. Mason laughed and ruffled the dog's fur, then she leaned closer for another kiss. "I love you."

Grace opened her eyes, feeling calm now. Yes, Mason would find her. She would take her out of this box. Because they were going to fall in love.

"*Hiya, Grace.*"

She jumped. "Thomas?"

"*Man, it's dark in here.*"

She smiled. "No shit." Then her smiled faded. "Where's Mason?"

"*She's close. You should pound on the door. I think she'll hear you now.*"

She stood up immediately and slammed her fists against the door.

"Mason! In here! *Mason!*" She pounded again, both fists hitting the door in unison. "*Mason!*"

CHAPTER FIFTY-SEVEN

The blasts were getting closer, and Mason could hear pieces of rock falling from the sides and roof of the tunnel. Whatever Johnny had done, it had apparently set off a chain reaction. What did he have? Twenty or thirty charges set? More? She came to yet another fork in the tunnel. Like before, she waited. Waited for the rocks to move. And they did. She sprinted to the right, running fast. She would find Grace. She knew it. Only she had no clue as to how they'd find their way back out of here. It was like a damn maze.

"Mason!"

Her heart jumped into her throat at the faint sound of Grace's muffled voice. "Grace! Where are you?" She ran down the tunnel. "Grace!"

"Mason! In here!"

She ran on, her flashlight bouncing around in the black-dark tunnel. "Grace!"

"Here, Mason! In here!"

The tunnel kept going, but to the right was another cutout, much like the one where she'd found Johnny. She flashed her light around, seeing the padlock. A giant padlock. She ran to the door, touching it.

"Grace?"

"Oh god! Mason!"

"I'm here now. Are you okay?"

"Get me the hell out of here!"

She fumbled with the keys, her hands shaking. "There's like a dozen keys here." She tried one. It didn't fit. She tried another. "Damn."

"It's got a blue cap."

"What?"

"Thomas says it's a blue cap."

She paused. "Thomas is here?"

"Jesus, Mason! Blue cap!"

She tucked the flashlight under her armpit, searching through the keys for a blue cap. There were two. The first one—of course—didn't work. The second one turned easily and the lock disengaged with a satisfied click. She dropped the padlock on the ground and jerked open the door. Grace flung herself into her arms, hard enough to knock her backward, and they tumbled to the ground.

"Oh my god! You found me!"

Mason laughed with joy as she pulled Grace to her, unmindful of the rocks cutting into her back. "Were you worried?"

"Yeah, I was." Grace sat up. "Come on. Nathan says we need to hurry."

"Who the hell is Nathan?"

Grace stood and pulled her up. "I'll explain later. Let's go."

"Yeah, well that's the problem. I don't really know how to get us out of here."

Grace squeezed her hand. "Follow me."

Mason didn't argue. She ran beside Grace, her light shining the way in the dark tunnel. At each fork, Grace continued on without hesitation. Mason was nearly dizzy by the time they wound their way out of the earth. But Grace stopped up short, and Mason nearly ran her over.

"Thomas says Charles is in the tunnel," Grace whispered.

Mason moved Grace behind her, creeping along the wall now. She could make out the faint light at the entrance of the tunnel. She killed her own light, letting her eyes adjust before moving slowly again.

He was sitting on the tunnel floor, his back to the wall. A shotgun was resting on his lap. There was a hulk of a shape beside him and she assumed he'd found Johnny and had dragged his body out. His body and his shotgun. She hadn't heard or felt an explosion in a while and she assumed she'd stopped Johnny before he'd had a chance to detonate them all.

That optimism was short-lived, however. When she got closer, she saw that Charles was holding the same device that Johnny had. She mentally kicked herself for not grabbing it when she'd had the chance. She turned slowly, putting her mouth on Grace's ear.

"He's got the detonator."

She felt Grace nod at her whispered words. She unsnapped her holster, slowly—and quietly—pulling her Glock out.

"I know you're in there," he yelled. "You've got to come out sooner or later." His voice sounded hoarse, perhaps from crying. "Come on, you bitch!" He leaned his head back against the wall. "You *killed* him. You'll pay now, oh, yes you will."

She felt Grace squeeze her hand and she turned to her. This time Grace leaned closer.

"Thomas says he's totally out of his mind."

"Obviously."

"What are we going to do?"

Before she could answer, he yelled at them again. "Come on! I got an itchy trigger finger!" He held up the detonator, waving it back and forth. "There's no other way out."

Grace tugged on her arm. "Nathan says there's a supply room. Where they keep weapons."

She raised her eyebrows. "And who is Nathan?"

"Charles' brother. They have assault rifles in there."

She nodded. "Okay. Lead the way."

They retraced their steps and at the first fork in the tunnel, they went to the left. It wasn't another tunnel after all but a large cavern-like room, bigger than the one she'd found Johnny in. She flashed her light around, landing on several wooden crates. Piled high against the side wall were boxes and boxes of ammunition. She went to one of the longer crates on the floor and lifted the lid. Inside were three rifles, assembled and ready. Black, sleek. She handed her light to Grace, then picked one up, holding it firmly in her hands. AR-15. She hadn't held one of these since she'd left LA. She stepped back, eyeing the crates. Four boxes. Three rifles to a box. *Damn.*

She grabbed one of the magazines—thirty rounds. She slammed it into place, then took another one, just in case. She nodded at Grace.

"Let's go. Stay behind me."

CHAPTER FIFTY-EIGHT

Grace was trying to stay calm. She hadn't relayed to Mason what both Thomas and Nathan had told her. The mine was rigged to blow—as was the house—and all it would take was one push on the detonator and the tunnel would collapse around them. "*And he's totally batshit crazy*," Nathan had said. That went without saying, but still...

Mason held her hand out against Grace's stomach, stopping her movement. "Stay here."

Grace leaned against the tunnel wall, trying to see around the curve. She could just make out the faint glow of light from the entrance.

"*Thomas? Nathan? Are you here?*"

"*Yes,*" they said in unison.

"*I think one of you should go with Mason.*"

"*I'll go,*" Nathan volunteered.

"*Sure, now that he's out of the box, he thinks he can do whatever,*" Thomas mumbled.

Grace smiled at that, then sobered. They weren't out of the mine yet. They still weren't safe.

"Charles! What are you doing, Charles?"

"Show yourself." He stood up and she heard a bottle clank on the rocks. "I'm about to blow this whole damn mountain down. That's what my daddy said to do."

"He's gone now, Charles. You don't have to kill anymore."

He laughed. "I never killed nobody. Had me some fun with some of those girls, but I never killed one. That was his deal."

"All right. Then I'm sure the judge will be lenient on you. Now put the shotgun down."

He laughed again. "Shotgun? You don't need to worry about this here shotgun. Because I've got the trigger. Daddy said if anything ever happened to him, I was to blow everything up. He already set off the explosives along the road. Ain't nobody gonna get up here now. The road's ruined. It's just you and me."

Grace saw Mason move along the wall and she did too. She could make out Charles now. He was standing near the entrance, the shotgun in one hand and the detonator in the other. Something dangled from one wrist and she assumed it was Mason's handcuffs. Her eyebrows shot up as Charles whipped his head around, swinging at nothing.

Thomas laughed. *"Nathan is flicking his ears."*

"Stop it!"

"What is it, Charles?"

"Nothing. You come on out now." He ducked his head. "I said stop it!"

Mason took another few steps closer, her rifle held in the firing position. "Charles? You okay, man?"

"Something's...something is in here." He swung around, firing his shotgun toward the entrance. "Stop it!"

Grace jumped at the sound of the gun, then saw Mason run toward him. He swung back around and Mason fired four or five times, sending him careening against the wall. His shotgun went off again from the impact and she saw Mason drop to the ground.

"Mason!"

"I'm okay. Come on."

Grace ran to her, pausing to glance only briefly at Johnny's body, then that of his son. She didn't have time to contemplate anything. An explosion outside—the house blew into a thousand pieces—sent them both scrambling out of the tunnel.

"Run! Run!"

Grace grabbed Mason's hand. "Run!"

Pieces of the house's roof were falling around them as they bolted along the side of the mountain between the house and the mineshaft.

"This way!"

Grace tugged on Mason's hand. "This way. Thomas says this way." The words barely left her mouth before a blast spewed rock and debris out of the tunnel entrance. They both were knocked to the ground. Mason got to her feet first, pulling her up and urging her on.

"Grace! Come on."

Grace looked above them, seeing rocks—boulders as big as cars—begin to fall from the mountain, sliding down toward them. She felt like she was in a Hollywood action movie as they bobbed and weaved into the trees, shielding their heads and running as fast as they could. Everything seemed to blur—the trees, the rocks, the sounds. Her heart pounded in her ears and her lungs felt like they were about to explode. Finally, Mason slowed, glancing behind them. She stopped altogether, bending over at the waist to catch her breath. Grace did the same, taking in gulps of air. She sunk to her knees, unable to stand.

"Thought...we were...goners," Mason said between breaths.

Grace nodded, still unable to speak.

"Do you think the others are safe?"

Grace smiled and pointed at her chest. "No air," she managed. "No speak."

Mason laughed, then knelt down beside her. "You ran pretty fast."

"Amazing how...being scared to death...will turn you into an... Olympic sprinter." She put her hand on Mason's arm and squeezed it tightly. "Thank you. For rescuing me."

"I had help."

"Yes. Nathan." She looked around, wondering if he'd show himself. For that matter, where was Thomas? "He was in the box with me. Johnny's son. He locked him in there. Left him to die."

"Damn."

"I was scared, Mason."

"I know. I was too."

"But you got them out?"

"Yes. I told them to go out the front, into the trees. Faith was—well, Susie was talking to her."

"I'm sure Susie led them far enough away." She leaned toward her, wrapping her arms around Mason's neck and holding her tight, relaxing for the first time in what felt like hours. "I'm so ready to go home."

Mason pulled back slightly. "Home? New Orleans?"

Grace shook her head. "No, not New Orleans." She pulled Mason closer and kissed her, a slow kiss that made her smile. No. Definitely not New Orleans. "Come on. Let's find the others."

CHAPTER FIFTY-NINE

Lucy watched as Abby and Ginny stared at Faith, eyes wide. Faith paid them no mind as she continued talking in low tones. To them, it appeared that Faith was talking to the trees. Only moments earlier, Faith had told them—with urgency—that Susie said to "run" and Lucy hadn't paused to question it. She'd grabbed Abby's hand and Faith had taken Ginny's and they'd dashed down farther into the trees. When the house exploded, they'd been a safe distance away, but the blast was powerful enough to make the earth sway under their feet. She'd held on to a tree branch to keep her balance. Faith and Ginny had ducked down behind the base of a large tree, and Abby had stood there, indecisive, shielding her baby from flying debris. Lucy had grabbed her, pulling her into the tree branches for protection. It had all been over in a matter of seconds. The baby had been screaming loudly after all that and Abby had finally gotten him to quiet.

"Do you breastfeed?"

"Yes, but—"

"Feed the little fella. I think we're safe now. Faith will let us know if not."

Abby flicked her glance to Faith. "Is she okay? I mean—"

Lucy nodded. "Yes. She—she sees things before they happen."

"Like…like a psychic?"

"Yes. Something like that." How could she possibly explain? She still wasn't sure she believed it herself. She moved over to where Faith was, and she was shocked to see tears in her eyes.

"What's wrong?"

Faith seemed embarrassed as she wiped at a tear. "Susie is leaving. All my friends are leaving now."

"Leaving?"

"They're not stuck here anymore. Rusty doesn't have a hold on them now."

"I see," she said, although she clearly did not.

"We need to go back up. Grace and Mason are looking for us." Faith motioned down the trail. "Susie says we can't go that way. There are booby traps set up."

"Okay." Lucy glanced at Ginny, who was standing there with her arms crossed, huddled into the robe Abby had given her. It dawned on her then that everything in the house was gone. All their meager possessions and clothes—three outfits each—were smoldering now in the remnants of the explosion. That thought brought a surge of guilt. Stacy had been in the house. Stacy—who was the closest thing they had to a friend—was dead. Stacy had been knocked out and tied up. By her. She had, in a sense, killed her.

"Momma, no. Stacy was not our friend."

Lucy met her gaze. "We should have gotten her out."

Faith shook her head slowly. "We didn't set off the bombs, Momma."

"What about the other girl? You said there was—"

Faith squeezed her hand. "Momma, we're out. We're safe now."

"So she's dead too?"

"Not from the bomb, no. He killed her. He killed Stacy too."

"He?"

But Faith looked past her and a smile formed. Lucy followed her gaze, seeing the sheriff's deputy—Mason Cooper—walking toward them. A woman was beside her.

"It's Grace." Faith waved at them.

* * *

Grace squeezed Mason's hand, then motioned for her to go to the others. The young girl looked at her expectantly.

"You must be Faith."

"And you must be Grace."

Grace smiled and nodded. "Are you okay?"

"Yes." Then she looked up and squinted. "It's my first time to be outside. I'd only seen pictures. I didn't know it would be this...this bright."

Grace looked around them. "Where's Susie?"

Faith's expression changed. "She left. They all did. Susie said they were free now."

"Yes. I would have liked to have said goodbye. Especially to Thomas."

"Thomas gave me a message for you. I don't understand it, but maybe you will. He said you should buy Mason a birdfeeder for her backyard and that all the jays will be friendly this time." Faith raised her eyebrows in a rather adult fashion. "What does that mean?"

"Rusty showed himself to me and Mason as a Steller's jay. A very mean Steller's jay."

Faith nodded then. "The blue bird in the kitchen. It was a Steller's jay. Mason shot it. But it wasn't only you that he showed himself to. My momma saw a Steller's jay too. When she went into the woods. There was a cat. But when she got inside, there was only the bird. And the mean man."

"You mean when she was taken?"

"Yes."

"What happened to Rusty?"

"Susie said he lost his power when Mason killed the bird."

"So he's still around?"

Faith shrugged. "I don't know. But Thomas said to tell you something else. He said when you get your puppy, you should name him Tommy." Faith smiled. "He laughed when he said it, but I think he was serious."

Grace laughed quietly. She wished she'd had a chance to see him, to thank him. Then a gust of wind hit them, fierce enough to cause her to take a steadying step back. The leaves of the aspen shook in the breeze, and she looked into the tree, getting just a glimpse of someone.

"See ya, Grace."

She smiled affectionately. "Goodbye, Thomas."

Faith was waving as the image faded and the breeze stilled.

Faith's smile disappeared when their eyes met. "They were my friends. I'm going to miss them."

"You'll make new friends. You'll get to go to school. I'm sure—"

Faith shook her head fiercely. "They'll all think I'm crazy." She looked to where the others stood. "They already do."

Grace nodded. "Yes. I know. You'll have to learn to hide it. And when you need to talk to someone about it, you can talk to me."

Her eyes widened. "You're going to stay? Susie said you came into town just to help us."

"I did, yes. But I've grown to love it here." She looked to where Mason was standing, watching her. "It feels like home."

Faith took her hand and led her back to the others. "Good. Then we'll be friends."

CHAPTER SIXTY

"About got yourself blown up, huh?"

Mason laughed as Scott Kemp pulled her into a hug. "Yeah, I did. Took you long enough."

"Yeah, but I brought the cavalry. He blew the hell out of the road. There were a couple of spots I wasn't sure we were going to make it through."

"What? Was Dalton showing off in his Jeep?"

"Let's just say I'm glad I wasn't riding with him." Kemp walked toward the house. "How many casualties?"

"Johnny and Charles Herchek for sure. Stacy Herchek, the daughter, was in the house. According to the young girl held captive— Faith—there was another female in the house. That hasn't been confirmed."

"And you're sure Johnny and Charles are dead?"

"Besides the fact that I shot them, they're buried in the mineshaft. And I imagine that's where they'll stay. Half the mountain collapsed on them."

"You're damn lucky you got out in time."

She wanted to tell him luck had nothing to do with it, but she knew she'd never be able to explain how they'd had help. It was all pretty much a blur anyway. She looked around for Grace, finding her talking to a man in a suit, another agent that Kemp had brought with him. Dalton was there too, interviewing Lucy. Faith and Ginny were sitting on the back of Dalton's Jeep. Other deputies—ten or more—shifted through the rubble of the house. Chief Danner had made it up, too. She walked over to where he stood.

"You got the bastard, Mason?"

She nodded. "Yeah. It's over. Finally."

"Johnny Herchek. The man came to town so rarely most probably never gave him a thought. He was a troublemaker when he was younger, I know that. Hung with the wrong crowd."

"Were you in town when the fire happened?"

He shook his head. "I'd already left for college. Heard about it, of course. Wasn't surprised to learn who all was involved. Shocked, really, that Johnny wasn't right there with them." Chief Danner raised his eyebrows. "What caused him to start killing, you think?"

Did she tell him that the ghost of Rusty Meyer drove him mad? Did she tell him that it was revenge? That Susie Shackle was the first because of who her father was? Did she tell him all that?

"Some people are just evil. Evil and insanity don't mix."

"Think he was crazy?"

"The man I encountered here today? Yeah, he'd lost his mind."

"Still can't figure out how he was meticulous enough to evade us all these years." He motioned to the other side of the house where a large shed was still standing. "They found the car. Did you hear?"

"Yeah."

"Well, you did a damn good job, Mason. Your uncle will be very proud of you."

"How's he doing? Have you heard?"

"Yeah, I went by there this morning. He's still drugged up, but your Aunt Carol seemed a little more confident than she'd been last night."

"Everybody was in shock last night."

He scratched the back of his neck. "You left the hospital in a hurry."

She nodded. "I knew we'd be coming up here."

"So the psychic, she was legit?"

"Yes."

"I suppose she'll be heading out of town, along with Kemp."

"I think she'd planned to stay through October," she said as nonchalantly as she could. "She's writing a book."

"About our town?"

"No. At least I don't think so." Grace was heading their way now. "Why don't you ask her?"

Grace raised her eyebrows. "Ask me what?"

"Mason says you'll be staying through October, says you're writing a book."

Grace met her gaze and smiled. "Yes, I'm going to stay for a while."

"Gonna write about the town? The murders?"

Grace shrugged. "I don't know that I'll write a book for sure. I just want to take a break and relax. Maybe do some hiking." Grace smiled at her. "Normal things."

Mason returned her smile. "How are the others?"

"Lucy and Faith are going to be fine. Abby is in shock, I think. Ginny is traumatized, of course. Has anyone called her parents?"

Chief Danner nodded. "I spoke with them myself. I also called Lucy Hines' folks. They were shocked speechless. Thought I was playing a bad joke on them or something."

"What about Abby's parents?"

"No, they don't live here anymore. Moved a couple of years after she went missing. But we'll find them." He held his hand out to Grace. "Thank you for ending this nightmare, Dr. Jennings."

"I had help, Chief Danner. I'm just thankful it's over with."

When he walked away, Mason leaned closer, letting their shoulders touch. "You ready to get out of here?"

"I'm ready for a shower. And lunch. And a bed." She grinned. "In that order."

"I'm ready to get out of this uniform."

Grace smiled and bumped her shoulder. "I can help you with that."

CHAPTER SIXTY-ONE

Mason stretched under the covers, but she didn't open her eyes. Grace was gone, she knew that much. Grace had tried to sneak out of bed at dawn, but Mason woke. Grace had smiled and kissed her, telling her to go back to sleep. And she had. Soundly.

She rolled to her side now, pulling Grace's pillow to her. She opened her eyes then, seeing sunlight peeking in through the blinds. She was too comfortable to want to turn and look at the clock. She guessed it was after eight by now. It didn't matter, really. She wasn't taking her shift today. She was taking some time off. A few days. Time to wrap her head around everything that had happened.

When they'd gotten off the mountain, they'd gone by the hospital. Aunt Carol had been asleep in the chair beside Uncle Alan's bed. They talked for a bit, enough to learn that he'd been awake off and on. Brady had been by and had told him the news, she said. They'd then gone by Bucky's and picked up some burgers. Grace got her shower. They'd eaten. And they'd fallen into bed.

They didn't talk. They'd cuddled, they'd touched...and they slept. It had still been daylight when they'd turned off the light and at midnight, she'd woken to a warm mouth nibbling at her breast.

She smiled now, thinking about their lovemaking. It had been different from the first time, yet the same. Different in that it was slower, unhurried. The same in that it was intense, passionate. Different because they were relaxed. The same because they were falling in love.

She didn't remember much about her time in bed with Shauna. At first, she'd intentionally pushed it away, not wanting any reminders. Really, not wanting to be reminded that she'd been rejected. As time went by though, those memories began to fade and she didn't try to hold on to them. She didn't remember it being like this, though. She didn't remember it *feeling* like this.

She rolled onto her back when she heard the door open. Grace was standing there, smiling at her.

"You're awake. Good."

"Good?"

"Breakfast is ready." She went to the window and opened the blinds.

"So you've been cooking?"

"Among other things."

Mason glanced at the clock. It was a quarter of nine. "I didn't realize I'd slept so long. What time did you get up?"

Grace came over and sat on the side of the bed beside her. "It was after six. I had some shopping to do. I hope you don't mind, but I used your truck."

"Of course not." She scooted over to give Grace more room. "You have clothes on."

Grace smiled and kissed her, a slow kiss that made Mason wish she weren't dressed.

"I was afraid I'd get arrested if I went shopping in the buff. And did you know that the hardware store opens at seven?"

"I did. But what in the world did you need at the hardware store?"

"I got you a present. Two, actually. And the guys there were very nice and friendly to me."

"Asked a hundred questions, huh?"

She laughed. "Yes. They wanted to know all the details. I told them the FBI had forbidden me to discuss it and they left me alone after that." Grace pointed out the window. "There. Can you see it?"

Mason leaned up a little on the bed, her eyes widening at the sight. "A bird feeder?"

"Two of them. And we already have customers."

Mason flinched as a blue Steller's jay flew past the window and landed heavily on the feeder, making it sway.

"It's okay," Grace said gently. "We've had several. They seem to all be friendly. Well, not so much to the smaller birds. They've chased them off."

"What prompted that?"

"Thomas. He said I needed to get one for you. I think partly, it's to get us past our history with jays. And also because of your childhood." Grace met her eyes. "You have two memories of the feeders. One was during happier times and the feeders were kept full. The other—well, you know. Animal crackers."

"So this is supposed to chase away that second memory?"

"Not chase it away, no. Put you in control."

"Ah. I can keep the feeders full now."

"Yes. You're in control. Not your mother."

Mason leaned back against the pillow, but she kept her gaze on the feeders. The Steller's jay moved on and a nuthatch took its place. Soon, a little mountain chickadee landed, stole a sunflower seed, and took off again.

"I haven't given my mother a thought in days," she admitted. "Not that there's been downtime this week. But I think you're right. I've been letting her control me. And I think I'm done." She pulled her gaze from the feeders and landed on Grace. "I want to talk to her about Uncle Alan and my father. I do want to get some kind of closure on that."

"Yes, you should. And we should go by the hospital after breakfast. I made a casserole. We'll take what's left for Carol. I'm sure she's sick of cafeteria food by now."

"I can't believe they shot him."

"It was supposed to be you."

"Who pushed him?"

Grace met her eyes. "Thomas. He had to protect you."

"If Uncle Alan had died, I'd—"

"But he didn't. We're all safe, Mason. And it's over. It's finally over."

CHAPTER SIXTY-TWO

Mason held her plate up, smiling as Aunt Carol put a large piece of lasagna on it. Brady put a piece of garlic bread beside it.

"First meal back home, Dad, and you choose lasagna?"

"Your mother makes a mean lasagna."

"Could have had meatloaf."

Uncle Alan pointed his fork at Brady. "That's your favorite meal, not mine."

"It was very good meatloaf, though," Grace chimed in.

Brady frowned. "When did you have her meatloaf?"

"Oh. That's right. You weren't invited." Grace laughed. "More for us."

"Really, Mom? You had meatloaf and didn't invite me?"

"Your father had some police business to discuss with Grace. He's the one who didn't invite you."

Brady shook his head. "Still can't believe it's over with. I think people in town are afraid to believe it."

"That was nice of the Hines' to take in Abby and her baby, wasn't it?" Aunt Carol mused. "I heard Cheryl Hines nearly fainted dead away when they saw Lucy and young Faith. Can you imagine? Going all these years thinking your daughter is dead, only to get her back and a granddaughter too!"

"Where are Abby's parents?" Grace asked.

"Oh, you didn't hear? They had moved to Salt Lake City. They were both killed in a car accident less than a year ago. They've tracked down their kids. They had three other children, all younger than Abby."

"Two are in college. The other is married and just had a baby," Brady said. "I spoke to her myself. She's going to make the trip up here in the next couple of weeks. Abby is going to go back with her."

Aunt Carol nodded. "I'm sure they were elated to hear the news."

"I should go by and see Faith again," Grace said as she took a bite of the lasagna. "See how she's adjusting." She looked up and smiled. "Oh, this is delicious, Carol."

"Glad you like it. I'll send leftovers home with you." She paused. "You're still staying with Mason, I assume?"

Mason noticed a slight blush cross Grace's face. "She is."

"Still worried for her safety?" she asked innocently.

At that, Brady laughed. "Yeah, right."

Grace surprised her by speaking up. "Let's just clear the air, shall we. Save you all the speculating that's going on." Then she smiled. "Mason?"

"Oh, sure. Throw it in my lap."

"If you think it's a big secret that the two of you are an item, save your breath," Brady said. "I've known you my whole life, Mason. If there's one person I can read, it's you."

Aunt Carol nodded. "Yes, I was just teasing. It's obvious the two of you are, well, more than friends." She smiled at them. "I think it's sweet. Mason was always so private about her personal life. I think you're good for her, Grace."

"Me too," Uncle Alan added. "I like Grace."

"You called me a quack," Grace reminded him.

"So I did. Apparently, I was wrong." He gave her a genuine smile. "I'm glad you're staying, Grace. I look forward to getting to know you better."

"Thank you. I appreciate you all welcoming me into your family." Grace glanced at Mason and gave her a sweet smile. "You don't know my history, but I've never really had a home before. Gillette Park, Mason, you all—this feels like home finally."

"Oh, honey, of course you're welcome here," Aunt Carol said as she reached over and squeezed Grace's hand. "Mason has always been a part of our family and now you are as well."

"Thank you, Carol. That's sweet of you."

Mason looked over and met her uncle's gaze. He nodded at her.

"Yes. You've always been a part of our family, Mason. We've always loved you like our own daughter. Happy to have Grace here too."

Mason knew he was sincere. So was Aunt Carol. Because, yes, they'd always treated her as a daughter. She held his gaze a second longer, seeing the love he had for her. She nodded back at him.

"I love you too."

CHAPTER SIXTY-THREE

"You're going too fast! It's all uphill!"

Grace collapsed near a boulder and leaned against it, trying to catch her breath. The puppy immediately jumped in her lap, his little pink tongue tickling her neck. She laughed and pushed him away. "Enough kisses."

Mason sat down beside her and the puppy—Tommy—immediately moved to her lap, his whole backside wiggling as his tail wagged. "We should have gotten two puppies."

"Two? We can barely handle one of them!"

"Yeah, but two, they could entertain each other." Mason picked up a stick and tossed it. Tommy lunged after it.

She leaned closer, resting her shoulder against Mason's as they watched Tommy bring the stick back to them. Mason tossed it again.

"You happy?"

Grace smiled at her. "Very. You?"

"Yes. More than, well, more than I thought possible."

Grace nodded, knowing exactly what she meant. Like Grace, Mason had gone through life not expecting to find love, not expecting to find this contentment and peace in her life.

"You're not bored?" Mason asked now.

"Of course not. It's been a wonderful summer."

"How is Faith? Did you go see her this morning?"

"I did." Tommy plopped down at their feet and alternated between chewing the stick and Mason's boot. "She feels lonely. Which, to you, probably sounds strange, seeing as how it was only Faith and Lucy all those years. But Susie, Thomas, Paul—they were her friends. So she feels lonely now." She took the stick and playfully wrestled with Tommy for it. "I've talked Lucy into homeschooling her."

"Really? I thought you said she needed to be around kids."

"She does. But she's behind, school-wise. Lucy did a great job with her, considering how limited their materials were. Lucy was at the top of her class in school, probably would have graduated as valedictorian."

"And you're going to help?" Mason guessed.

"Yes, although I'm used to teaching college-age students."

"I'm sure it'll be good for Faith, having you around. I mean, you can relate to...well, to—"

Grace laughed. "I don't think Faith wants to be called a psychic." Her smile faded a little. "I don't think I do either. I have a gift, yes. And I've put it to good use. But I'm happy up here, with you." She squeezed her hand. "I think the next time the FBI calls, I'll turn them down."

"Ready for a normal life?"

"I am. I just don't know what I'm going to do. I have a lot of time invested in research so I may write that book I'd envisioned. Or I could teach here at the high school."

"I think you should write about the murders."

Grace raised her eyebrows, surprised by Mason's words. "Really? I thought the town would just as soon forget all about it."

"While it was happening, yes, I think they wanted to push it away and pretend there wasn't a serial killer out there. But now that it's over, I think a history of the Gillette Park Killer would be a good healing mechanism. And it would be a way to keep alive the memories of those killed."

"Don't you think it would be hard for the families?"

"I don't know. Some still live in town. Why don't you talk to them? See how they would feel about it."

She nodded. "I may do that." She leaned closer, kissing Mason on the lips. "I like you a lot, you know."

"I like you a lot too."

Grace smiled into her eyes, seeing love there, a love they hadn't spoken of. Not yet. Over the last few months, their relationship had grown stronger. They'd fallen into an easy, simple routine and their lives had meshed effortlessly. On Mason's days off—like today—they hiked the mountains, bringing lunch in their backpacks to enjoy on the trail. They had a standing dinner date with Carol and Alan once a week.

Mason's relationship with her mother remained a work in progress. After Mason had confronted her about her father, her mother had refused to speak to her for weeks. Mason had taken it all in stride and hadn't been riddled with guilt. When her mother had called, saying she was ready to talk, Mason had invited her over to dinner. It was a strained affair and Grace had retreated to the bedroom to give them some privacy. It was a turning point, though.

Mason nudged her shoulder. "Ready?"

Tommy sat on his haunches, his tail wagging in the dirt as he watched them. Mason stood, then offered a hand to her. Grace adjusted her backpack, then followed as Mason and Tommy led the way up the trail. They were going to the big trees today—a favorite place for lunch. The hike up was strenuous, but the view was spectacular. They'd sit on a bed of pine needles, nestled among the giant trees, looking out over the canyon that had been carved by Gillette Creek. She didn't tell Mason, but each and every time they hiked this trail, she kept a watch out for Thomas, hoping he'd show himself to her again. He never did. She supposed he, like Susie and the others, had no reason to return. She wondered if she'd always think of him when they were on this trail.

Mason and Tommy were getting farther ahead of her and she paused, watching them. Mason had a hiking stick and was carefully picking her way over the rocks. Tommy, his golden fur shining in the sun, would turn back to look at her, silently urging her on. As she stared, things changed. Mason was older now, her hair speckled with gray. Tommy was laboring beside her and a puppy was running ahead of them. The older version of Mason turned, smiling at her, beckoning her to join them. She blinked that vision away, coming back to the here and now. Mason—the real Mason—turned then, looking back at her.

"Coming?"

She nodded and took a few steps, then stopped. "Mason?"

Mason looked at her again, eyebrows raised.

"I love you."

Mason stared at her for a second or two, then dropped her hiking stick and came back down the trail toward her. They stood there, a couple of feet apart, looking at each other. Then Mason smiled and nodded.

"When we made love last night, I wanted to tell you." Mason took a step closer. "I felt like my heart was going to burst, but I was afraid to say the words."

"Don't be afraid."

Mason looked into her eyes, a slow smile forming. "I love you, Grace."

They embraced tightly, both feeling relieved at having said the words finally. They pulled back enough to kiss—a slow, sweet kiss that gave her goosebumps. Then Tommy wiggled between them, demanding attention, and they pulled apart with a laugh.

They held hands as they walked back up the trail. Mason bent over to retrieve her hiking stick, then they continued on without another word.

Grace took a deep breath, smiling contently. Yes, content. Happy. Blessedly so.

She'd found her love. And she'd found her home.

Finally.

Bella Books, Inc.

Women. Books. Even Better Together.

P.O. Box 10543
Tallahassee, FL 32302

Phone: 800-729-4992
www.bellabooks.com